THE PROPHET AND THE WARRIOR

A FICTIONAL HISTORY OF MOSES AND JOSHUA

BY

RICHARD H. GRABMEIER

DORRANCE
PUBLISHING CO
EST. 1920
PITTSBURGH, PENNSYLVANIA 15238

The contents of this work, including, but not limited to, the accuracy of events, people, and places depicted; opinions expressed; permission to use previously published materials included; and any advice given or actions advocated are solely the responsibility of the author, who assumes all liability for said work and indemnifies the publisher against any claims stemming from publication of the work.

Dorrance Publishing Co
585 Alpha Drive
Suite 103
Pittsburgh, PA 15238
Visit our website at *www.dorrancebookstore.com*

ISBN: 978-1-6453-0390-9
eISBN: 978-1-6453-0414-2

PREFACE

I was raised in one of those old-style Lutheran families where every child went to Sunday school and took religious instruction before becoming a communing member of the congregation. My confirmation pastor was a D.D. (Doctor of Divinity), the upper echelon of his field of expertise. I respected the man immensely (especially since we shared first names) even to the point of going fishing with him on occasion. And he, for his part of the relationship, attempted to steer me toward a life in the religious profession—at which he failed. Still, I continued as a relatively conscientious church member for most of my adult life, serving in various congregation offices and raising my children in the church.

As I matured past middle age I began to develop a greater curiosity about things spiritual and I began studying portions of scripture that held the greatest significance for me. I was surprised and disappointed by the fragmentary nature of the instruction I had received during my early religious life. It became evident to me that many clerics, like politicians, avoid subjects that they may have difficulty explaining to the questioner's satisfaction. Sermons and bible studies were usually based on safe subjects and were limited to specific comfortable texts. Anything not fully explainable had to be taken on faith. Any text that might have a negative impact on official doctrine or might be perceived as a chink in the armor of faith was given only momentary attention.

The whole thing became more and more discouraging, especially in the face of changes to theologies that were quite important when I was sixteen but were considered erroneous, obsolete doctrines before I reached sixty years. The more I questioned the religious framework I had built my spiritual life on, the shakier it became.

Then, from somewhere, a distinct spiritual feeling developed within me, a sense or conviction that there was something more than I had in terms of spirituality. It was an awakening to the realization that life need not be lived by following a hard path of truisms laid down by theological scholars. I became convinced that it is right and enlightening to search for a better way, to study the past honestly and to learn valuable lessons from it.

With that realization I began reading Biblical texts anew, studying them as sketches of the lives of people who lived and died during times that were turbulent and dangerous. I came to the realization that ethnic rivalry and warfare has been lived and relived again and again in the small piece of geography that was the world of the Biblical era. And with that realization I finally understood that the heroes of Judaic, Christian and Islamic religions were simply ordinary humans much like leaders of today. They were prophets, priests, politicians and warriors. They had families, friends, allies and enemies. They made love and fought, they killed and were killed, they were strong and they sickened and died—but none were gods.

The Bible abounds in stories of adventure, romance, political intrigue, familial conflicts and stark terror that are fascinating when read with attention to what is implied as well as what is literal. The books of *Exodus*, *Numbers* and *Joshua* are filled with material of this nature. Frequently only a short sentence or a casual reference are all that suggest a much greater story. A good example of this is found in *Numbers 12:1 (KJV)*, "And Miriam and Aaron spake against Moses because of the Ethiopian woman whom he had married." Nothing more is said of the love factor in Moses' life, though it could have been an extremely interesting story considering his earlier marriage to Zipporah of Midian.

The writers of the histories of Moses and Joshua were interested in presenting these figures as representatives of God and they did not dwell on their human sides, except to reinforce their characters as righteous, though sometimes erring, servants of The Lord. For that reason the parts of their lives that would show them as humans with all of the problems and flaws of human beings were given less attention. The writings dealing with Moses, Aaron, Miriam and Joshua tell us little of their personal lives and of their personalities except for occasional glimpses that slip between the lines of pious ethnic accounts of their exploits.

The story of the departure of the Israelites from Egypt and the subsequent devestation by Israel of many of the nations in and near Canaan is a tale of darkness and terror as much as it is about the freeing of a subjugated nation. The books of Moses justify horrific acts of cruelty, destruction, rape, murder and genocide against the people of Israel as well as other nations, as being ordered by God. And while the people subjected to the atrocities described in *Exodus, Numbers* and *Joshua* would doubtlessly have committed similar acts against Israel if the tables were turned, one must ponder whether the accounts of the happenings described were actual history or whether much of it is ethnic legend. And, if it was history, just how accurate was it, given that it is recorded by only one nationality? After all, the histories of wars are largely written from the perspective of the victors, which causes a loss of credibility in certain texts.

It was with this in mind that I was inspired to write *The Prophet and the Warrior*. I wanted to provide an alternative view of the holy four that would expose their human natures as viewed by an impartial observer. The stories within this fictional history picture issues and warfare from the views of multiple adversaries of the Israelites as well as the Israelites themselves. I endeavored to picture the wanderings of these people and some of their failures, triumphs and conquests as we would now, not from the view of religious history but as an objective, though fictional, human study.

The sources of reference for the novel are *The Bible - King James Version* and *The Oxford Companion to the Bible*. The book is not intended to be a detailed scholarly history, but rather a work of fiction, inspired by Biblical accounts, that seeks to provoke thought within the reader's mind.

Richard H. Grabmeier

EPIGRAPH

"Yes, Mister Meyer, it is one of the peculiarities of human nature that we will distrust the word of family member or close associate. Yet, we will blindly cling to an imperfect record put down by men we cannot name, men who were far less educated than we. And we passionately call it 'The Word of God.'"

Dr. Norman Ayleon in
The Scrolls of Elizaphan

TABLE OF CONTENTS

THE PROPHET AND THE WARRIOR

CHAPTER 1

Pharaoh's guard rode in pursuit of Moses for the space of four days.[1] From the king's palace at Rameses they raced swiftly across the fertile lands of Goshen. Their mounts were fresh and the tracks left by the fugitive's mare were sharply distinct, so that they expected to overtake him before the sun had ended its course across the sky. But as darkness descended and the land cooled for the night they halted their pursuit beside a well and hobbled their mounts for water and grazing.

"Princess Khena's foundling rides swiftly, Captain," one of the guards said as he threw some dried sheep dung on their fire. "But then, he stole one of Pharaoh's strongest mares."

The Egyptians commonly referred to Moses as "the foundling" or "the stutterer," never quite granting him full acceptance as equal to themselves.

The Captain took a pull from his water skin before answering. "It matters not, he will slow down soon enough. He is not hardened to ride as we are, his soreness will defeat him."

"I wonder that he did not choose a fast stallion as his mount, or perhaps a tail, strong gelding," another guard pondered.

"A stallion might throw any but the best horseman and flee from him if given the chance and a gelding lacks the spirit of the mare, Areli," the captain returned. "No, Moses chose well—but we will overtake him tomorrow."

On the next day the guard moved more slowly past the bitter lakes into the wilds of Sinai. But as the sun crept low on the harsh land that evening they had not come on Moses. Nor had they been more successful on the third day. On the morning of the fourth day, his tracks had long been lost to sight. For the guard now it was of greater need to find water for their horses and themselves. Their waterskins slapped dry against the horses' shoulders, where desert dust had caked thick on sweat lather that was now dried in the relentless sun. The captain stopped his plodding horse and sat gazing across the untracked wilderness.

"We pursue a dead man," he said. "Surely no man can cross this dry land alone, not knowing where to find water. In a day his horse will die and soon after that the madness of thirst will claim him. There is no need to join with him in the place of the dead. Let us go."

Quietly the Egyptians turned their horses about and rode toward known sheep wells, distant a half-day's ride. And so the soldiers returned to face the displeasure of their king and the coarse derision of the Israelites who exulted at their failure to seize Moses.

For two days Moses rode during the hours of light, stopping only to rest his horse and trickle a little water from his waterskin into the beast's mouth. He took but a swallow or two for himself. There had been no well or sign of life since he entered the Sinai and it was vital that the horse stay alive, for without her he would face two hundred miles of arid wilderness on foot. He would have preferred to travel in the coolness of night, but he was a stranger to the land and he needed his sight in the treacherous terrain.

Once, from a rocky hillcrest, he had seen a group of riders in the distance and hurried his horse's pace. But now, he could not hurry his mount, for she had not grazed or drunk her fill in too long, but must carry her rider on the strength of a few handfuls of barley and a squirt or two of water.

Silently, Moses cursed his hot-headedness. The laborer the Egyptian taskmaster had beaten was likely recovered from the blows he had received and at home, eating meat with bread right now, that and cucumbers and perhaps a piece of melon. He, Moses, had only a little dry bread and was running for his life, while the Egyptian he had clubbed was rotting away beneath the sand or perhaps providing a meal for jackals. He had paid dearly for his harsh act and would pay yet more dearly, he thought, as he surveyed the barren land before him.

Moses had literally been blessed with life. Because of the determination of his mother and sister he had survived where other Israelite boy babies had been drowned in the Nile by a paranoid Pharaoh. Moreover, he had grown up in the very house of the king. He had been rescued by one of the Pharaoh's daughters from an floating basket set among the iris plants that flowered at the edge of the Nile.

It had been a calculated risk by his mother, Jochebed [2], for he was three months old and difficult to hide from the Egyptian guards who policed the Israelite quarters. And so, she had placed the basket near the place where the daughters of Pharaoh bathed daily, knowing that he would be discovered by servant girls gathering iris blooms for the royal house. Hovering near the place was the baby's sister, Miriam, watching to see what might ensue.

"My Lady!" a servant girl exclaimed. "There is a basket floating among the iris plants!"

"Perhaps it is a piece of trash thrown into the river Adna," the princess returned, "lift it out and give it to the groundsmen."

"It is not trash, My Lady, there is a baby in the basket!" Adna had waded in among the water plants and was returning with a considerable burden.

"By the gods of my fathers, it is indeed a young child! Bring it here, Adna."

"The babe stirs, My Lady. I think we will hear the sound of its voice now."

"Yes, and it has a lusty voice. Lift the child's cover, Adna, and see what we have."

"It is a boy, My Lady, and a sturdy lad indeed."

The princess touched a finger to her lips and a look of concern clouded her face.

"He is a Hebrew boy hidden from Pharaoh's guard, else he would long have died."

"Oh, My Lady! He lives against the order of The Great One—to save him put his mother in peril of her life. For is not Pharaoh a god among us? Is he not Horus in an earthly body? ...Shall I deliver him to the king's guards?"

The princess bent to pick up the vigorously crying child and held him close to comfort him. The baby instantly quieted and began exploring her bare breasts—she smiled.

"I think not, Adna. I think we will look for a wet-nurse for him. He is hungry."

"But My Lady, will not The Great One know? ...Does he not know all and see all?"

The princess gave Adna an enigmatic smile. "I think my father does not even know all of his grandchildren, for he has greater concerns. When it is time, I will tell him I have adopted an orphaned Egyptian child—he will not ask further. But you know nothing of this, Adna. Do you understand?"

"Yes, My Lady, my lips are silent. But what of the babe? Who will feed him?"

"Adna, do you see that Hebrew girl further along the river? She has an interest in what we do. Bring her to me."

Adna ran to the girl and brought her forward. She was perhaps four or five and she was very skinny. She looked at the princess with frightened brown eyes.

"What is your name, girl?"

"I am called Miriam[3]."

"Do you know of this baby, Miriam?"

The girl looked at the princess fearfully but said nothing.

"It is as I thought...Miriam, we need a woman who can nurse this child, perhaps even his mother. Would you know of such a person? Tell me and no harm will come to her."

The girl smiled timidly and bobbed her head.

"Good, go and tell the woman what I have said. Tell her she shall nurse the child until he can walk, then she will give him to me."

The girl ran away swiftly and the princess turned to her servant.

"I think I will call him Moses," she smiled, "for I have saved him from the water."[4]

When the child had matured enough to spend his days with her, the princess brought him to her quarters and she called him Moses. He grew swiftly and was of a sturdier build than other boys of his age. And he was set apart by the color of his hair which had a reddish tint, unlike the typical black of the Egyptian children. But there was a thing that bothered the princess. Moses was slow to speak and when he finally did it was slowly and haltingly with lapses of stuttering. This and his different appearance drew scornful teasing from the children of the palace.

Yet as time passed, Moses became a favorite of the Pharaoh despite his difference. For Moses was of an honest and forthright nature unlike many of the young people of the court—it was a thing Pharaoh valued greatly.

In those days Moses had wanted for nothing and had labored for nothing. He was being taught and groomed to be a member of the ruling class of Egypt. Yet, he had been nurtured by his mother who prayed to a god other than the gods of the Egyptians and had tried to teach him to do the same.

And so, he knew who he really was though he didn't pray to his mother's god or any other. His unique situation caused him to draw back from the other young people of the court because of the uneasiness it caused him. Then too, it angered him to see his people laboring as slaves for the Egyptians. It angered him, but he could do or say nothing, lest he be cut off from the good life he enjoyed. So he said nothing and bore an emptiness within his spirit. For though the noble Egyptians respected the special bond between Moses and the king, they did not accept him as one of their own, but secretly laughed at him for his halting speech and his uncertain lineage.

His own people looked at him with scorn in their eyes. For they knew who he was and resented that he did not bear their burdens with them. As the days passed, the sense of aloneness rose in Moses' throat until he thought it would choke the life from him.

On that fateful day, he had ridden to a building site in the barren land of the tombs as was the duty of his station. At an isolated work area he had come on a taskmaster beating a Hebrew. In a fit of rage Moses rode the Egyptian down and crushed his head with his mace. Instantly, Moses knew he had made a terrible mistake. But there was no help for it, so he had a pair of the laborers bury the body far out in the sands.

That night there were whisperings within the court, that one of Pharaoh's taskmasters had disappeared from his duty post. No one knew when or where he had gone. Some thought he had ventured beyond some rocks to relieve himself and had fallen prey to a wandering beast. Others thought he had stolen gold from the builders' treasury and fled to another land. Some thought he had fallen drunk and would yet return. None thought that the Israelites had killed him.

For they said, "The Israelites are like sheep, dull of wit and lacking courage. Would the sheep kill the lion?"

Moses listened with deep concern but he kept silent until the following day. In the morning, as was his office, he rode again to supervise the building site. But now he saw two Israelites fighting with each other, with one very much the superior. Moses rode his horse nearly onto them and held his mace at the ready over the one that prevailed.

"Why do you strike your brother?" he demanded.

The man looked up at him with a knowing leer and said, "Have you become our lord since yesterday? Would you use your mace on me as you did on the Egyptian?"

Moses stared at the man as one who has been hard struck and had no words to return. On that very eve, he took a little food and water and a heavy cloak and he mounted a strong horse and rode into the wilderness.[5] For he knew that the tale of his deed must soon reach Pharaoh and if the Egyptians laid hands on him he would surely be put to death. Too late he realized that the harsh taskmaster had not been the cause of his action, but only the spark in tinder that caused the fire to flare up. He was fleeing, not because he had killed a man but because he could no longer live with himself as neither Egyptian nor Hebrew.

On the third day of his flight Moses chanced on a place where there was a little wispy grass. He got down from the horse which was nickering and stamping about excitedly. There, from a cleft in the limestone flowed a tiny trickle of water. It dribbled into a small natural basin then flowed out to nourish a fringe of grass that clung to the inhospitable soil. Horse and rider drank side by side and when Moses had satisfied his thirst he scooped water with his hands and dashed it against his face. Then, as the horse began eagerly grazing on the grass about the water, Moses prostrated himself and did a thing that was alien to him. He gave fervent thanks to the god of his fathers.

For three more days Moses journeyed and for the first time in all his years he knew the undeniable ache of hunger. His bread was long gone and he chewed on the handful of barley that remained in his horse's store in a futile attempt to appease his hunger. He had found enough water to keep the waterskin filled, but found little to eat, except for a few pistachio nuts from a scraggly bush beside a well. He rode hungry and he slept hungry, dreaming fitfully of pursuing Egyptians. Thankfully, there was enough grass for the horse now, but his own belly groaned as a herd of antelope dashed out of a wadi just beyond the reach of his bow. His heart sank as they disappeared into the vastness of the wilderness and he prayed then in his fear and desperation. He prayed fervently to the god of his fathers for deliverance.

By the morning of the fourth day, he was so famished that he thought he would die. He ate the last few nuts he had picked, though they scarcely stopped the groaning of his stomach. But then, when he thought himself so lost that he would perish alone in the wilds he came on a wide trail of many sheep and goats and dung not many days old. His heart began pounding as though it would break through his ribs and he followed the trail until it came to a well, with watering troughs. Moses dismounted and splashed water across his grimy face as his horse drank. There were people near, that was sure, but were they friendly or would they rob and kill him? Worse yet, they might take his horse and leave him afoot in the wilderness to die of starvation.

As he was sitting there despondently considering his situation, he heard sounds. They were barely audible, but the noises seemed to be plaintive quavering bleats and yes, there were voices, unmistakably feminine voices! He led his horse back behind a clump of bushes and waited.

Jethro, priest of the Midianites, was a chief and a man of wealth and influence. His flocks and cattle were many, but he had no sons to watch over them. Though if it were made known, his seven daughters were as sons to him. At this time of day they herded their father's sheep and goats to the well for water. in the way of women they talked and laughed among themselves as they drew water and poured it in the troughs. Moses watched and smiled, forgetting for the moment the emptiness of his stomach.

But what is this? Another herd comes and with it shepherds, scruffy favored men and ill tempered. They shout loudly at the women to drive their flocks away from the well.

"Daughters of the priest, get your flock away! Our sheep are long away from water and thirst greatly!"

"Wait your turn, shepherds of Joktan, we have drawn water and our flock will drink of it!" one of the women shouted in return.

A large, coarse fellow stepped forward, shaking a staff in his hand, as he roared at the women.

"Nay, you will drive your flock away until our sheep have quenched their thirst! If water yet remains in the well, it is yours!"

"We are not afraid of you, you dung of the desert! We will water our flock and you will not drive us away!" the same woman shouted, waving her own staff in the air.

The coarse one rushed toward her furiously, rage twisting his weathered features.

"Midianite harlot! I will teach you to be afraid of me! I will instruct you with my staff...and mayhap I will take my pleasure with you afterward!"

The women that had been silent took their sister forcefully by her arms and ran. They were swift of foot and left the ruffian shepherd behind, cursing them vilely.

Moses mounted his horse and rode through the sheep and past the frightened women.

His mace was in his hand and his face was contorted with fury.

"Will you teach me too, you desert carrion? Would you take your pleasure with me, sheep dung?"

He spoke freely, as though his anger had loosened the cords that tied his tongue and now he kicked the mare into a gallop and rode the man down, circling him with his mace swinging in vicious circles.

"Will you fight and die, sheep dung? Or will you leave these women be?"

The shepherd was turning as the horse and rider circled him, making an uncertain defense with his heavy staff. The other shepherds had seen the mace and the Egyptian clothing of the challenger and were discreetly retreating. Where there was a single Egyptian, there would likely be an armed troop and they had no taste for fighting Egyptian soldiers. The lone shepherd looked after his departing comrades. With a wild cry of terror, he cast his staff to the ground and fled.

Moses watched as the Joktan shepherds hurriedly drove their flocks to a safe distance. Then a musical burst of giggles broke his concentration and he turned to face the woman who had so boldly confronted the shepherds. Her companions huddled together in a group, smiling and chattering. But she came forward to him calmly, with a dignity that befitted a princess.

"I am Zipporah, daughter of Jethro, Priest of Midian," she said, speaking in a dialect that he understood, yet spoke clumsily.

She looked at him with eyes that were like pieces of dark amber, alive with the fire of her spirit. Her face was comely, softly angular with a firm mouth and jaw. She was darkly tanned as the laborers at the Egyptian temple had been and white teeth accented her full lips.

Moses felt a rush of blood to his face and his sun-burned features darkened hotly. It annoyed him that he should react like a small boy to the presence of a shepherd girl. But then, he remembered, he was a fugitive fleeing from Egyptian justice. He was less than a shepherd, less than she, if it were possible for a noble of Pharaoh's court to be less than a woman. The thought made him speak more haltingly than usual and humbly, something he would not have done less than a week before.

"I am Moses, a Hebrew," he said.

"You do not look like a Hebrew. Are they not bond servants in Egypt? And are you not dressed as an Egyptian?' She stated the questions in the manner of someone of authority.

Moses would have regarded the questions as insolence a week ago, but now he smiled and spoke slowly, haltingly, that he might not trip in his speech.

"You are right, though I cannot freely state the reasons for my absence from Egypt. But it pleases me to help you."

"I am sorry, I ask questions that are not of my concern. My sisters and I thank you for being so courageous in our time of peril. But the sheep still thirst. We must draw water for them."

"Then I will draw water for Areli also, for though she has drunk a little she still thirsts from our long ride."

Moses dismounted and walked to the well with its hard clay water troughs. With its leather cord, he lowered a large jar into the well and drew it up. He poured the water for the mare, then lowered the jar again. He did this again and again until Zipporah's sheep no longer drank.

The women were gathered around him now, smiling shyly at him and venturing words of thanks. Zipporah seemed the eldest, indeed she was past a score of years. The youngest was still a girl, just becoming a woman. Moses could not have accounted the comeliness of the six, for his eyes returned as of themselves to Zipporah. She stood before him, not smiling now, but unlike women of the Egyptian court she looked directly into his eyes as though searching his inner being. She spoke again and her tone had become gentle, with the softness of the evening breeze whispering through the reeds of the river Nile.

"Again we thank you, Warrior of the Hebrews. I had sorely tested the patience of those scurvy rascals. I know not what ill doings would have befallen us if you had not driven them off. Is there something I can do to repay our benefactor?"

Moses looked at her and felt the cords drawing tight beneath his tongue. His mind was consumed by her beauty, so that he forgot about the emptiness of his stomach and his lack of a bed. With great effort he spoke.

"What I have done, any man would do for women such as you and your sisters. I would that I might tarry a while with you, but I dare not, for I flee the Egyptians."

"Then go, Great Warrior. And may the God of Abraham go with you "

She turned about and motioned to her sisters to gather the sheep. As they moved away, Moses wanted to call to her and ask to go with them. Instead he stood by his horse and inwardly cursed his backwardness.

The bleating of sheep awakened Jethro from the sleep he and his wife sometimes took during the hot hours of the day. He threw back the tent flap and emerged into the still, burning sunlight. His flock was filing through the gateway of the pen of unmortared rock that kept the animals secure from roaming hyenas during the night. The younger girls were going to fetch the vessels in which to milk the she goats, while Zipporah approached the tent.

"How is it you return so early, Daughter?"

Jethro spoke tersely, his eyes were still heavy with sleep and it made him irritable.

"We return early because we did not have to wait at the well while those Joktan ruffians watered their flocks, Father." She wore a smile that Jethro thought he had not seen on his daughter's face before.

"How is that, my daughter? You always complain that they get to the well first and make you wait."

"Today we made haste to get there first. But when we made to water our flock, the shepherds came. They called out to us to drive our flock away from the well."

"And did you, Zipporah? Do you bring the flock in, thirsting for water?"

Zipporah flashed a look of annoyance at her father.

"I am my father's daughter and far too stubborn to give way to such churlish men. I fear I spoke rudely to them and moved them to anger. It was a foolish thing to do, I know. But they were as filthy dogs in their speech to us. The big one, who has often been a trial to us, made to beat me with his staff. He said he would make sport with me after he had taught me fear."

Jethro was fully awake now and the tide of anger was swiftly rising in him. He looked closely at his daughters and his anger subsided when he saw they were unmarked.

"How is it then, my daughter, that you escaped untouched and also watered the flock? For I see that the beasts are content and lie down to chew their cud."

"We ran swiftly from the angry shepherd and left him cursing at us. And when we were running, a man came upon a swift horse, swinging a war club. He drove the shepherd before him as the lion drives the jackal. When the ruffian fled, the man returned and drew water for us."

"And who was this man and from where did he come that he should be riding alone in the wilderness? I know of few, save the warriors of Joktan that have horses."

"He was dressed as an Egyptian, but he said he was a Hebrew. He said he could not give his reason for leaving Egypt and I did not press him further. After he helped us I bade him tell me how I might repay him. He answered that he needed no payment, saying that any man would do for us as he had done. He said that he could not tarry, because he fled the Egyptians."

"And you did not bid this man, 'Come to the safety of our tents, for my father's people will protect you'? What manner of man would I be, if I did not return hospitality for his brave service to my daughters? And he a Hebrew...a descendant of Abraham, the same as we. Go, Zipporah, and take your sisters with you. If this man is not yet too far distant, require him to come eat and rest with us."

Moses had not gone far, but had retreated from the well just far enough to let the shepherds of Joktan water their flocks. Hunger had descended on him with its gnawing grip once again and he feared to travel further, lest the shepherds gather their kinsmen to take revenge on him. He sat on a boulder and let his hobbled horse graze on the sparse grass while he pondered the course he should take. He knew that if he were not to die a slow death by starvation, he must make an end to his arrogance and seek out Zipporah's family. Yet, he had a fierce pride and it suited him poorly to ask for charity. Dejectedly he buried his face in his arms and tried to forget the complaining of his belly.

A small thing struck the soil beside him and he raised his head to see what it was. Then something stung him between the shoulder blades and fell to the boulder beside him. A pebble! A small round stone! He leaped to his feet to the accompaniment of tittering female sounds. When he turned, Zipporah and her sisters stood a little way off. The youngest held a small sling and they all were laughing at him.

He laughed then, despite the stinging spot on his back and the greater stinging of his pride.

"Daughters of Jethro, do you return my goodness to you, by pelting me with stones? Have you returned to me to make my difficulty greater yet?"

Zipporah walked close to him. "No, Great Warrior, we come to bid you eat, drink and tarry with us. The pebble was but Ribai's way of stirring you from your reverie. My father and his daughters pray that you will honor us with your presence. Even now, a fat lamb is roasting and our mother prepares cakes and honey. My father opens a new jar of wine to honor you. Will you come and stay the night with us?'

Moses' relief was so great he could have wept—instead he smiled broadly.

"I take great joy in accepting the invitation of the Priest of Midian and his daughters. For in truth, I have eaten little in these last days and my body grows weak with hunger."

"Then come, Moses, and let us make you strong again. Though in truth we would not have guessed your weakness, when you drove off the shepherds of Joktan."

Jethro, chief of his people and priest before them, was indeed opening a new jar of wine. He did so in anticipation of the coming of this stranger and he sampled the wine heartily. His wife had driven him from the rough courtyard where the spit and oven were, because of his constant interference as she and a servant girl prepared food. He was in high humor, excited with the anticipation of a male visitor who was unknown to him. Not that Jethro didn't love his wife and daughters, he did that and fervently. But he sometimes longed for a man as a companion. He visited with the other men of his tribe, it is true. But there was always a certain aloofness in their presence, a certain deference to his position as chief and priest. A stranger would not be so and he would bear news of the country to the west. Did Zipporah not say he was dressed as an Egyptian—yet he was a Hebrew, one of the Children of Israel? Jethro marveled at that, for he knew the Hebrews to be little more than slaves in Egypt. This would be an interesting visit. Jethro savored the wine in his mouth, then refilled his cup and left the tent to await the coming of the stranger.

Zipporah talked with Moses as she led him to the tents of Jethro's people. Her manner was not as the women of the Egyptian court, teasing, trivial and superficial by nature. Rather she spoke to him as would a man, of flocks and weather, of the dangers from the peoples of the east. But she did not ask of him what trouble caused him to flee from Egypt. She knew that in time her father would ask and the secret would be disclosed to them. So they walked close together, but she a half-step behind Moses as she had been taught by her mother, to show deference to a man. Yet, Moses sensed her strong will and he knew her defiance of the Joktan shepherds was a sign of her spirit. If this were born in her from her father, then Jethro the Midianite would be a man to respect. He would soon know, for they approached the great black tent that was the home of the Midianite.

"Hail, Honored Jethro, chief of the tribes of Midian." Moses raised his hand palm outward as a sign of peace and to show he held no weapon.

Jethro returned the gesture. "Hail, Moses of the Israelites, brave warrior, I bid you welcome." He grasped Moses lightly by the shoulders and kissed his cheek.

"Come, enter my home and take food with us."

They entered the tent of Jethro, a large structure of woven goat's hair. A rich rug covered most of the dirt floor, unlike the plain palm mats of poorer households. They sat down and one of Jethro's daughters brought them cups of wine. It was sharp and strong and as Moses drank of it his aching stomach threatened to reject this further insult. In a few minutes the feeling of sickness passed and in its place a feeling of wellbeing settled over him. Then the women brought food, roasted lamb, wheat cakes with honey, dates, raisins and olives and even a fresh melon such as he had eaten in Egypt. When they had served, the women of the household sat down also, a little away from the men.

Jethro, in high good humor, introduced his family to Moses.

"My wife Abinoam, my eldest daughter Zipporah, Vashti, Tirzah, Maai, Ithra, Eshton and Ribai."

"In truth I know the eldest and the youngest already," Moses said, "Zipporah by her strong speech and Ribai by the stinging between my shoulders. But I beg forgiveness if I fail in putting the other names with their proper faces."

Jethro laughed. "By my beard, that is easily forgiven. For I, their father, must ponder that for fear of error. What think you of my brood, are they not well favored?"

Moses smiled and directed his eyes to Zipporah. "They are indeed well favored, both of face and spirit. It surprises me that they are yet without husbands."

Jethro sighed. "It is our custom that the eldest must marry first. I fear that Zipporah is headstrong and difficult to suit."

Zipporah's face flushed and her eyes flashed angrily.

"Out here in the plains there are few men worthy of marriage. They are poor shepherds and drivers of asses and camels. Would you have your daughter wed such a one, Father?"

Jethro sighed. "Zipporah is right, of course. There are few worthy men and those that might be are close kin. But let us talk of other matters. Do you travel far?"

"In truth, I know not where I wander or where I shall come to rest. I fled Egypt in the dark of night and was pursued into Paran. I think Pharaoh's guards have returned to Egypt, but I am a man with neither place to rest my head, nor friends to welcome me."

"Then is it so ill a thing that causes you to flee, that your return be forbidden?"

Moses glanced at Jethro uncertainly, then seeing sincerity in the older man's eyes, he spoke.

"It is a thing for which my death would be the only payment—for I slew an Egyptian.... He was beating a worker, a man of my people and in the heat of my anger I struck him that he died. But he was an Egyptian and there are those who suspect that I am not and for that, in the eyes of Pharaoh, I must die."

All were looking at Moses, but he was most aware of Zipporah who looked at him with admiration. She spoke in even, soothing tones.

"It is an evil thing to be punished for, but not in the doing. For to protect those who cannot protect themselves is a good and noble thing. Would you not have used your war club to protect us? And would not the people of Joktan kill you for it?"

"Yes, they would kill me and may yet if the chance comes to them."

"Zipporah speaks the truth," Abinoam said. "My husband would do as you have done, for he is a man of kindly spirit who detests brutality against those who cannot defend themselves. You bear no blame except for the rashness of your act. And that because of the hot blood of your youth. It is perhaps the will of the gods that brought you here at a time when my daughters were in danger."

Jethro stroked his beard thoughtfully. "And perhaps it is the will of the gods that you tarry here with us. Tell me, Moses, would you stay a while with us? Stay and rest and consider what you will do. You have spoken truthfully, not hiding your trouble. Such a man I trust and it would suit me well to have you abide a while."

"It would suit me well to stay, for both horse and rider are weary. Yet,

I have but a few pieces of silver with which to pay you for my needs. Might there be a way to earn my food and sleeping place?"

"If you would not look with contempt on tending the flocks, there is need for a man who is strong of arm and stout of spirit. The people of the east ever threaten and oppress our spirits." Jethro sighed and nodded at Zipporah. "And it would be a good thing if she might attend to a woman's tasks, for she will one day have a dwelling and family of her own."

"Then let it be so. Your will shall be my will and my arm shall be your arm."

"It shall be. Come, Zipporah, and fill our cups that we may drink to our guest and bid Moses welcome to the land of Midian!"

With the passage of time Moses became as one with the family of The Priest of Midian. Fear of the Egyptians now was past and the work of the grazing lands put new purpose in his life. His muscles became hard like those of a lion and his spirit was as free as the wind of the desert. Astride his horse, Areli, bronzed by the sun and swathed in the loose garments of the harsh land, he was to all a warrior of Midian.

Moses grew in favor with Jethro, his benefactor chief and with Zipporah. The fondness with which she gazed at the Hebrew was not lost by her father and mother, nor did it meet with their disapproval. They talked quietly about it in the privacy of their sleeping tent and resolved to arrange a union of the two.

Since the arrival of Moses, Zipporah was freed from the leadership of the shepherds. She now spent daylight hours with her mother practicing the arts needed by a woman to make a home in a nomadic life. As mother and daughter became closer, their talk turned to marriage and the raising of families. And so it was inevitable that Moses should become the focus of their conversation.

"Mother, of late I have thought much on Moses," Zipporah said one day, as she skimmed the cheese curds from soured goats milk.

"And what are your thoughts, my daughter?"

"He is a fine man, strong of body and spirit—I have known none like him."

"And that is all? Many men of Midian are strong—you walk with him in the twilight—does he not touch you gently as a man touches a woman?"

"He does, he holds me in his arms and caresses me."

"And does he speak of love, Zipporah?"

"Yes, he speaks things of love and desire. He speaks of taking me as his wife."

"And you wish to go to him?"

"Yes, Mother, but how can it be? He has nothing with which to pay Father for my hand, nor has he tent or goods with which to make a home."

"Shall I speak of it to your father? Something may be done, an arrangement made. Your father looks on the Hebrew with favor and it would please him if Moses would stay with us. I think it is because Moses is like the son I could not give him."

"My mother, it would please me greatly if you would make intercession with Father for me. There is no man like Moses in all of Midian."

"Then I will speak with my husband on this matter—but do not tell Moses of it."

That very night Abinoam spoke of her daughter's revelation. Jethro was pleased and showed little concern over the Hebrew's lack of wealth.

"A true man without wealth is still a man of substance," he said. "But an ass is still an ass, were its packs filled with gold. If Moses feelings are as those of Zipporah. we will make an arrangement that pleases all and the Hebrew shall be as a son of Midian."

So it was, that in the morning the priest of Midian arose when the sun was still low behind the eastern hills. He took bread with cheese and a skin of water and followed the path of the sheep and goats into their distant pastures. As the sun rose higher he came upon the flocks and Moses on a hillock where he stood watch over them. Moses turned to Jethro, as he approached. Surprise crossed his face then settled into concern.

"Do you bring evil tidings, My Lord, that you follow our path so early in the day?"

"I do not, Moses. But rather I come on matters of our common concern. I came early because my thoughts would not let me sleep. And what better place to talk freely than in the pastureland where none but the sheep and the gods may hear?"

"You speak wisely, Jethro. But what are these matters of our common concern that so disturb your sleep?"

"Abinoam is distressed. She fears that you will leave us and grieve the heart of Zipporah. It seems my daughter has a fondness for you, that is something more than sisterly love."

"If that is true, Father of Zipporah, it cannot be greater than the feeling I bear for her. From when I first saw her at the well, my eyes have looked on no other and my thoughts fly to her like a pigeon to its cote. But I have neither gold with which to pay you for her hand, nor tent and bed in which to take her to wife." Moses forehead furrowed with frustration. "If I had but a-tenth part of that which I had in Egypt, I would make a worthy match for her."

Jethro placed his hand consolingly on Moses' shoulder.

"It is needless to fret so, Moses. For, you have a horse, a fine young mare of strength and speed, which if bred to a proper stallion could be the beginning of a line that is far better than the horses of Joktan. I would consider her equal to tent and bed, pot and pottage. Would you trade thus?"

"In truth, it is no easy thing for me to part with Areli, for she carried me through the wilderness where I would have died, but for her. And I would give her over to no lesser man than you. But to you I will give her, Jethro, and consider my part of the bargain as the better. But yet that leaves my pay to you for your daughter's hand. Strong and filled with wisdom and love is she and worth many horses or camels. Her balance in gold I would give you for her hand, if indeed I had it. But I have nothing except a few Egyptian pieces of silver. I will grow old and she barren before I have enough with which to pay you."

Jethro pulled Moses down to sit on a boulder beside him.

"Moses, my son, do not throw stones in the pathway where none lie. Did not Laban give his daughters to Jacob to wife, though he had little?

And do I not have need for a man who is strong of arm and spirit as companion, overseer and warrior?"

Moses looked at Jethro suspiciously. "But Jacob paid twice in years for the love of his heart. Laban dealt with him dishonestly in placing Leah in his bed instead of Rachel."

"It is true that Laban was deceitful, yet he obeyed the custom of his people in giving Leah, the elder first. And so, Jacob must serve a second term to gain the love of his heart, Rachel." Jethro looked deep into the eyes of Moses. "But I speak only of the means of giving Zipporah, who is my eldest daughter, as your wife. If you promise to abide with us for twelve years and give me grandsons, you shall have Zipporah to wife within this year, and you shall gain flocks and cattle as your own. As a priest of Midian, so I swear."

"Then so shall it be, for I will happily take Zipporah to wife and serve you faithfully both as shepherd and as warrior for her hand."

"It is good—on the second new moon next, we shall have the betrothal feast. I will send a messenger to the tribes of Midian, that all shall be in attendance. For it is a great thing when the daughter of a priest plights her troth."

CHAPTER 2

In the course of time Moses and Zipporah were wed and set their tent within the compound of Jethro the priest of Midian. In the third year after Moses first saw Zipporah at the well, she gave birth to a son and fulfilled the agreement between Moses and Jethro. Moses named his son Gershom, which means "expelled," to ever remind himself that in his flight from Egypt he had found happiness in a simple nomadic life.

In the second year thereafter, his wife again gave Moses a son and they named him Eliezer, which is to say, "the help of God." Moses was content and he grew in wealth and importance among the people of the tribes of Midian. For as he bestowed grandsons on Jethro, so Jethro increased his flocks. In turn the boys were raised in the teachings of Jethro's people. For, being far from his family and raised as an Egyptian, Moses did not closely follow the teachings of the Hebrew patriarchs. So it was then, that his sons would cleave to their mother's people and be forever as sons of the Midianites.

As the boys grew and approached their first decade, a change began in Moses. He became restless and sometimes short of temper with those near him. Indeed, he was at times filled with a darkness of mood that had no cause and knew no reason. At such times he would leave the closeness of family and friends and wander about in the mountain wastelands, alone except for the sheep he tended. Always, he would return when the time of ill temper left him. But he would remain remote, seemingly occupied by some issue foreign to Zipporah and her sons.

Beyond this aloofness were problems that touched on the daily lives of Zipporah and her family. Moses no longer went with her to the altar of her gods, the altar of Jethro, the priest of Midian. She was forced to bring her sons to worship without her husband and this grieved her. For in her mind, the eyes of others of her tribe fixed on her with scorn and her vexation with Moses grew. And so, when at last her patience and gentle chiding had been exhausted, she returned to the manner with which she had taunted the shepherds of Joktan. In frustration and rebellion she confronted Moses and spoke to him angrily.

"My husband, great warrior, what ill temper imprisons your spirit, that you withdraw from us, your family? You do not join us at my father's worship of the gods, nor speak to us in kindly fashion at the evening meat. You are neither husband to your wife, nor father to your sons!"

Moses looked up from a piece of limestone he was carving to the shape of a ram's head. The hard flint with which he shaped it became idle and his face became as one who suffers some inner pain.

"Mother of my sons, I am here beside you as husband and father. My spirit is withdrawn because I long for a greater worship than I find at your father's altar."

"How then will you find greater worship if you do not visit the altar of the gods? How will you be husband if you bed not your wife? And, how will you be father if you know not your sons?"

"You speak truth, my wife. Yet there is a weakness in me that abides and turns the fire of my spirit to cold ashes. What I would do, I cannot. Yet what I cannot do I must, lest my wife's love forsake me and my sons despise me. But how can a lion hunt when his teeth have fallen from his jaws? ...So I am."

"Are you then ill, my husband? Does this weakness that abides with you spring from some unknown ague? Do you seek the cure in your wanderings?"

"Yes, perhaps I seek the cure in my wanderings. For I seek the god of Abraham, Isaac and Jacob. I have long left my people and my heart is sore within me, that I may see my people again. I pray to my god from the mountains and in the valleys, that he may hear me."

"And does your god hear you? Does he speak to you from within the mountains? Does his voice echo to you in the valleys?"

Moses looked down at the unfinished ram's head and began scraping with the flint.

"My people's god does not answer at the command of man. When he wills it that I shall return to my mother and father, to my brother and sister, then will he speak to me."

"And when he speaks to you, Moses, what of me and your sons?"

"I think my wife and my sons shall see the land of the great river with me."

His talk with Zipporah seemed to kindle a new confidence, a gentle hopefulness in Moses. He began talking to his wife and sons about his boyhood in the king's court. And about the lot of his people as laborers beneath the Egyptian yoke. He spoke of the True God of the patriarchs, the god of the Hebrews, rightfully also the god of the Midianites, since their tree also sprang from Abraham. This brought questions.

"Father," Eliezer asked, "if we are also descended from Abraham, why are we not in Egypt with the Hebrews or they here with us?"

Moses looked at the boy thoughtfully. It would be hard to explain that Midian, the sire of the boy's people, had been exiled to the East, in favor of a more legitimate son of Abraham, Isaac.

"Because Abraham sent Midian to live in the East."

"Why? Didn't he like him?"

"I think he probably liked him just fine. It was because Isaac was his heir, because he was born of Abraham's first wife."

"What does heir mean?"

"If you are someone's heir, you receive his goods and title when he dies."

"Isaac got all of Abraham's things and Midian had to go away?"

"Yes, but I think Abraham gave Midian something before he had to go. Abraham knew he was going to die. I think he was afraid that all of his sons wouldn't get along, so he sent them to different places."

"Father, am I your heir?"

"No, Gershom is because he's the eldest."

"When you die, will I have to go away?"

"No, Eliezer, you will live near your brother just as you do now. You will have flocks of sheep and goats the same as he, because I give you lambs and kids. I want you to be a man of property when you are older and wish to choose a wife so that you will not have to bond yourself as I did to your grandfather."

"Is that how we got our flocks? Did Abraham give Midian lambs and kids?"

"I don't know son, perhaps he did."

The lad's questions had stirred thoughts in Moses that had not entered his mind before. The shabby treatment that Abraham had given his sons, by the concubine Keturah, was doubtless the reason few of the Midianites had love or respect for the Children of Israel. It was understandable that their views of religion and life were different than that of the Israelites, since their forbears had been sent into exile by their own father, a father who claimed kinship with an almighty god. Moses wondered what his reception by Jethro would have been like if he had not come as an Egyptian who had defended the daughters of Jethro.

As time passed, Moses became more preoccupied, almost obsessed, with his desire to find The True God. His searches in the mountains and the plains of his adopted country became longer and more frequent. Zipporah worried about her husband, because he had once again become like a stranger to her and his sons. In her frustration she spoke to her father about it.

Jethro stroked his beard and spoke to his daughter with fatherly compassion.

"Moses is not of us, Zipporah. Though he has been a good and faithful son-in-law to me, he longs for his people. When he came, I thought he might forget his people, because he was driven out from them. But it is not so. Now he seeks his god and perhaps his god will speak to him. If it is so, Moses will leave Midian and go to his ancient people."

"And what of me and Gershom and Eliezer, Father? Must we leave the free land of our ancestors to follow him to a land of bondage?"

"His wife must go where he goes if Moses wills it and his sons with her—it is our law. Gershom nears manhood and he is ever more a Midianite like his grandfather. Eliezer is gentle, as a poet and favors his mother in his heart. I do not know if they would ever be Israelites, or if the Israelites would accept them."

"Then, what should I do, Father?"

"You must wait, my daughter. Time will bring the answer."

It was so. Time did bring the answer, nor was it long in coming. Moses took his flock and departed high into the hills to a place where rains had caused new grass to grow fresh and green. He was gone perhaps the passing of a moon when he returned. His face was flushed with excitement and his eyes burned with an inner fire that Zipporah had never seen.

Zipporah embraced him, then stood away from him that she might study his face

"What manner of tidings do you bring, my husband? Is there no longer grass that you return with the flock so soon? And your expression, you come as a victor from battle. No, you look more like a bridegroom who has taken a new bride!"

"No, my wife, I come as a man who has heard the voice of glory—I have spoken with God!"

"You have spoken with your god? Have you then seen him, this god of yours? Does he abide in some secret place?"

"No, my wife. I did not see his face, but on a mountain where I followed my flock, I saw a bush that burned, yet remained whole.[8] When I went to see what caused such a wonder, God spoke to me from within the fire."

"Your god spoke to you from a bush that burned, yet did not turn to ashes? Was it perhaps the heat of the sun in its shimmering waves that you saw? That and the moaning of the wind in the high mountain?'

"No, Zipporah, do not look at me as one who has been taxed by the heat of the sun. I saw what I saw—a sign of The True God! I heard his voice call to me and I hid my face from him because I feared for my life. Then he spoke to me and gave me his command."

Zipporah tried to avoid the incredulous look that impressed her thoughts upon her features, but failed.

"Your god commanded you? ...And what manner of command did he give you from the midst of the fire?"

"That I must return to Egypt, ...to lead my people forth from the bondage of Pharaoh."

"You, a poor shepherd of Midian, will free your people from the armed thousands of Pharaoh, King of Egypt?!"

"That is what The Almighty God has commanded...I must speak for the Children of Israel, the chosen people of God, that Pharaoh might free my people."

"You who are slow of tongue and painful of speech will speak to Pharaoh? ...The great king will laugh at you in contempt while you are still speaking."

"So I said, but it did not deter God from his purpose. He commanded that Aaron, my brother who is glib of tongue but weak of purpose, should speak to Pharaoh as I bid him."

"You will go then, Moses? ...You will go to the land you fled on pain of death?"

"I will go. Those who sought to take my life are dead and I must obey the Lord's command. I will meet Aaron, my brother, in the wilderness of Paran."

"And what of your family and flocks and what of your promise to my father?"

"You and my sons shall come, as I have promised you. I will ask your father that I might go with his blessing. We shall leave him our flock and our great tent and all that is not needed to eat and sleep on the way. We will take donkeys to carry our provisions and for you and Eliezer to ride, because the younger boy is not yet of size and strength to walk the journey. Gershom and I will walk as we walk with the flocks, for we would fret at riding upon the donkeys."

Zipporah knew it was without purpose to reason with Moses, for he had a fire like that of madness in his eye. She knew that as Jethro had admonished her, she must go with her husband—it was their law. And yet she felt an uneasiness, for this was not the man who had protected her from the shepherds of Joktan. This was a different Moses, a man who set her on a knife's edge with her love for him on one side and uneasiness on the other. For herself, she could abide his strangeness and even madness if it came to that. But, the way he sometimes looked at his sons filled her heart with a deep sense of foreboding.

Jethro offered Moses a cup of wine and sat down beside him beneath the awning at the front of his great tent.

"Is it as I feared then, Moses, you will return to your people?"

"It is so, Jethro. I come to ask your permission and blessing. For I have not yet fulfilled our contract. But I will leave you flock and tent, pot and pottage and pray that it is enough."

Jethro motioned Moses to silence. "I declare that our agreement is fulfilled. For you have increased my flocks greatly. You have been a welcome companion to me and have sired two fine grandsons by Zipporah. Yet it grieves me greatly to see you go and my daughter and grandsons with you."

"And I am grieved to leave. I had thought to live out my life in these plains and mountains. For it is a good life, that makes a man strong and his spirit free. Where I go there is the taskmaster's lash and death for disobedience."

"Then why do you go, my son? I do not understand why you throw a wholesome piece of meat into the fire and take up one that crawls with maggots."

"My father, The Almighty God has spoken to me and he has given me his command. I must go back to Egypt and lead my people out of bondage and back to freedom."

Jethro gazed into Moses' eyes a long time, as though he would search his very soul. "Yes, your wife told me of it.... I think she fears you walk at the edge of madness."

"Yes, she is a good wife—she fears for me because she doesn't understand. Do you think me mad too, Jethro?"

"I see no madness in your eyes, nor do I hear it on your tongue. But I do not know this god of whom you speak. For I have neither heard nor seen him and I would hear you tell me who he is."

Moses turned to face Jethro—his eyes were bright like glowing coals.

"He is the God of Abraham, who was your forbear and mine. When he speaks, the very beasts of the field listen as though it were the roar of the fiery mountain. Where he lays down his hand the waters are stilled and the winds fall silent. He makes the sun to shine and the earth to give of its fullness. He is The Almighty God and he wills that his people should labor under the Egyptian yoke no more."

"Then go, Moses, and free your people. Be it that your god has such strength that he can defy the hosts of Pharaoh and your people are made free. Then I, Jethro, Priest of Midian, shall surely bow down before him."

The family of Moses walked the rocky paths among the hills and scantily grassed plains of the land of Midian, until they came to the edge of the forbidding wilderness of Paran. There, at a little inn beside the camel road that stretched across the harsh land, they stopped to spend the night.[9]

As the night air descended, Moses walked yet a little way into the cover of the wilderness, to worship his god in the coolness of the evening. Having eaten, Zipporah and her younger son, Eliezer, sat in a small room of mud brick and thatch and talked as she sewed a tear in his coat. Gershom, a youth now, wandered among the merchants and camel drivers resting about the inn. Some of their talk he understood and he listened closely to the coarse stories and jokes they told. Others at the inn were such as he had never seen before and their clothing and language was foreign to him. And so he tarried among the campfires and was absent at the return of his father.

Zipporah looked up from her sewing, as her husband entered into the circle of light cast dimly by a small oil lamp. His face was distorted with a look of fear and fury that she had never seen before. This was not the look of jubilation he had worn when he returned from the mountain. It was terror and madness such as one might see in the faces of warriors in the midst of deadly battle. She spoke to him, hoping to restore calmness to his features.

"My husband, why do you look at us so? Have you again spoken to your god? Has he dealt with you evilly, that your face reflects so fearfully the thoughts of your mind?"[9]

Moses was silent for some moments, but his eyes were riveted on Eliezer. When he spoke it was as one in a trance, yet his hands shook as with the ague.

"The Lord God Almighty has spoken to me—I have sinned."

"How have you sinned so evilly, Moses, that you should tremble so? For I have not known fear in my husband these many years. Yet I think that it is fear that moves you so."

"I have sinned against the Lord, for I have not done that which he has required of me."

"How have you so disobeyed your god, Moses? You are a good man who has led a good and simple life—you have done no wrong!"

"I have not circumcised the sons I have sired, as the Lord has ordered—it is a desperate sin which has only one forgiveness."

Moses' appearance changed from one of terror and uncertainty to one of resigned acceptance. Zipporah looked at Moses' face and read her husband's mind. Her own face was now the one contorting with fear.

"What is this one forgiveness, for such a trivial sin!"

By way of answer, Moses withdrew a bronze knife from his belt.

"He must die, to appease the wrath of the Lord."

Zipporah screamed then, a piercing scream of fear and anguish. She threw herself in front of her son.

"Will nothing else satisfy this god of yours? Will it not be enough if he is circumcised?"

Moses stood as though dumb, his knife still in his hand, confused by this new possibility. Zipporah knew she must act before her husband. She took up her sewing flint. Within an instant she had raised Eliezer's shirt and grasped the foreskin of his penis. With a deft movement she slashed away the offending skin and threw it at her husband's feet.

"You have become a bloody brute, Moses! You would kill your own son, who has done no evil, for a god that only you have spoken to! Neither I nor your sons can live with you any longer because we fear you. We will return to Midian tomorrow!"

By now a crowd had formed because of the screaming of Zipporah. Among them was Gershom, who looked at his father with fear and the beginnings of a darker emotion. Moses turned away and walked out into the night. He did not return, but went far into the wilderness and prayed for guidance from his god.

The following morning, Zipporah made porridge for her sons to break their fast, for they would travel long before they stopped again to rest. She did not see Moses, nor did she wish to. For she feared that he might insist that she go with him and she could not refuse his bidding under the law. As it was she invited danger, for it was not permitted that a woman should leave her husband, unless he had ordered her to go. So it was with a sense of relief that she turned her donkey onto the road back to Midian and did not see Moses.

The sleeping man stirred, as first light caused night shadows to creep away before it. Moses pulled his cloak a little tighter about him in answer to the chill of early morning. Consciousness returned achingly as his abused body sought relief from the stony bed on which it reclined. He opened his eyes to a scorpion seeking the warmth and protection of his cloak, its tail curled tightly upright, ready to strike quarry or adversary. Moses sat up with a start and shook the offensive creature from him. He looked about.

This place had seemed different last night—in the moonlight it had looked like a sanctuary. He had fallen on his face before his god and he had prayed for guidance and forgiveness because of his weakness. At last a dark weariness of body and spirit overtook him and he plunged into a fitful sleep, oppressed by horrors of the mind until they finally dispersed with the coming of wakefulness.

Moses slowly stood up and stretched the soreness from his muscles. He remembered dimly what had brought him here, a disagreement of some sort with Zipporah. Oh, yes, it was about the circumcision of the boys. God wanted him to destroy them because of it and he had failed. Or rather, Zipporah had found a better way. She had been angry, more angry than he had ever seen her. And now she was going back to Midian. Moses wondered if he should go with her, or at least try to stop her. No, God had given him a task to perform and there would be no way of denying The Almighty God. It would be better for his wife and sons to return to Midian. They would be much more secure there with Jethro's tribe, than with him in Egypt.

With empty stomach and empty heart, he turned his back on the sun and walked further into the wilderness. For the first day he walked he saw no one. He found a bee's nest and gathered honey into a wild gourd he had found by the way. Further on there were some pistachio bushes that still had nuts on the high inner branches where the antelopes had difficulty reaching them. He followed the tracks of the antelopes until they led him to a tiny, miry water hole. The water was muddy, but not bitter and Moses filled another gourd with it. Thus he walked through the vast arid land and met no one.

He walked with the moon and the stars by night keeping his direction by certain of the brighter stars and when the heat of the day fell hard upon him, he slept in the shade of a rock or beneath an acacia tree until the sun fell towards Egypt. Then he would rise again and follow it. So he travelled for four days, crossing with his feet and staff where long ago he had ridden the brave horse, Areli. On the fifth day he crept wearily, where before he had strode with bold steps. His belly rumbled with hunger and his tongue was dry within his mouth. His honey gourd lay cast beside the track a day's journey back and the last morsel he had eaten were the grubs of a dung beetle he found among some antelope castings. Water had he none since the falling of the sun on the third day. So it was that heat and thirst overcame him so greatly, that when he found an acacia tree, he lay down beneath it to await his ancestors. And he slept.

It was then that his god appeared to him—or perhaps he dreamed—but it mattered little since the message roared through his ears so that he trembled.

"You shall deliver your people from the hand of Pharaoh and your brother Aaron shall be your instrument! He shall meet you in the wilderness and do your bidding!"

Moses drew together his remaining strength and turned toward the voice. A figure bent over him, but he could not tell whether it was man, spirit or god, so dimmed were his senses.

"Drink, traveler. Drink and renew yourself. But slowly, lest you convulse at the shock of it."

Moses felt the spigot of a water skin press between his parched lips and a sweet coolness flowed across his swollen tongue. He drank and felt life return to him. Slowly the mists that obscured his vision receded. Before him knelt a man dressed in coarse clothing like that of slaves. He was filthy and stank of dried blood. Behind him stood several forlorn-looking donkeys, each carrying packs that smelled more evilly than the man.

The man smiled broadly. "I am Ishmael, freeman and hunter. I return to Goshen and from thence to the house of the buyer of hides. Where go you, traveler, that you venture so ill prepared into the wilderness?'

Moses viewed the man's blood spattered visage and tried to control his revulsion. His tongue was thick within his mouth, so that he spoke even more haltingly than was his manner. "I go on the Lord's business, ...to Egypt."

"And who is your lord? Might I know him?"

"He is the Lord Most High, ...God Almighty."

"You blaspheme—or you are an angel. I think an angel would not be found in such a plight as this."

"I am not an angel, nor do I blaspheme...God has commanded me to deliver his people from the hands of Pharaoh."

Ishmael the hunter laughed so heartily that tears of mirth issued from his eyes.

"I think you have suffered greatly from the heat of the sun, my friend. We will sup together, then on the morrow you can return to Goshen with me."

Moses gazed at Ishmael and the hunter was sobered by the burning in his eyes.

"I will eat food with you, Ishmael, but I cannot return to Goshen with you. Is there a place in the hills near Goshen where I might rest and another might find me?"

"There is a cave near the road where you might rest in comfort. It is yet a day's travel, near the Sea of Reeds."

"Then I would go there with you, if you would also find a man for me in Goshen."

Ishmael was reluctant. He had many animal hides and a thirst for the wine they would buy.

"I will take you to the cave. But I have little time to search out a man. Know you where he is? Have you seen him of late?"

"He is my brother, Aaron, son of Amram. He dwells yet among the Israelites unless misfortune has befallen him. I do not know, for I have been gone from him nigh unto twenty years. Yet the Lord says he will come to me and I will not doubt it."

"You may not doubt it, traveler. But what of me—must I believe in him whom I have found lying all but dead in the midst of the wilderness? Must I search for your brother who has been unknown to you for twenty years? Do you take me to be as mad as you?"

And here Ishmael stopped his vituperation, for he saw something in the eyes of Moses that forbade making sport of him. Instead he became meek and spoke further with deference.

"Forgive my tongue, traveler, it sometimes speaks ere I have fully thought. I will seek among the merchants in the marketplaces. I will find your brother and send him to the cave where you are resting."

And so, the hunter returned to the markets of the Israelites. And he spoke of Aaron of Amram. To his surprise there were many who knew him and one went for him, that he might have discourse with Ishmael the hunter.

Aaron had disbelieved Ishmael at first and thought him drunk, as was his weakness, when he spoke of the return of Moses. But when he had questioned the man more closely, he found that the traveler of whom he spoke had returned from the distant land of Midian. That caused him to believe that his younger brother returned and he hurried to go to him. Before the day had passed, Aaron had sought out two mules of strength and speed. In the morning he left on the trade route to Joktan, beside which there was a cave in a hillside overlooking the Red Sea.

CHAPTER 3

From the entrance of the cave, Moses could see the dusty band of the caravan road to Joktan to his right. Far to his left the Red Sea extended to the horizon like a great burnished mirror. It had been a day since the hunter left with his stinking cargo. Moses was glad to part company with the man, not just because he stank, but because he kept up a constant flow of meaningless conversation. His mindless babbling kept Moses from thinking and that he needed desperately to do.

The Lord had directed him to lead the people out of bondage in Egypt. Now he must be a statesmen, a leader of men—he of the stumbling tongue must persuade the people to follow him! Moreover, he must persuade them that he was appointed by God! To do this he must become a magician, like the magicians of Pharaoh, but more skilled. There were signs he must show to convince the people to leave Egypt and also the signs that would convince Pharaoh to let them go. He dozed and dreamed of confronting the mighty Pharaoh, ordering him in the name of the Lord to free the Israelites. He knew that the king of the Egyptians would refuse. Then with a wave of his staff, Moses would order such calamities as Pharaoh had never seen, terrible signs that would bend Pharaoh's will as a branch in the wind. Thus he would show the world the power of his god, Yahweh!

So Moses sat and dreamed. Yet it was not idle dreaming, but planning as he awaited the coming of Aaron. For he must convince his brother first, his elder brother with the commanding presence and the glib tongue of an orator. For Aaron had been so when he was yet a stripling, would not his talent be greater now? He needed Aaron to speak the words that the Lord commanded. Would Aaron do as Moses bid? For Aaron was the elder and not likely to submit himself to the will of the younger. Aaron was quick of tongue, but it was he, Moses, that possessed subtlety—he had learned that art in the court of the Egyptians. Yes, Aaron would do his bidding and with fervor.

On his arrival Aaron fell on his younger brother with cries and tears, like an old woman at the wedding of a favorite daughter.[15] He was as Moses had imagined, handsome and straight in his bearing and much given to effusive speech. Moses clapped him on his shoulders and gave him a heartfelt embrace. Then he held Aaron at arm's length and looked at his sable beard, straight nose and high forehead studded below with strange green-gray eyes. Yes, this was a man who could speak to kings and be heard!

That evening for the first time since he ventured into the wilderness Moses ate bread, bread with goat cheese and a slab of roasted beef rather than the tainted antelope meat the hunter had given him. When Moses was filled with meat and cheese, Aaron went to a coarse, haifa-grass, chilling bag that he had soaked with water and hung in the cave. He returned with a melon and cut it with the knife he carried beneath his cloak. Moses savored the tangy sweetness of the orange flesh in his mouth and it brought back memories of his childhood in the court of Pharaoh. His life had been easy then, easy and filled with good things. But it seemed like a dream now, it lacked the reality of his recent life. His life in the rigorous world of the Midianites was reality, life filled with toil and wandering. He wondered whether the course he was now set on was reality, or another dream.

Moses put down a piece of melon rind and wiped the sweet, sticky juice from his beard with a remnant of cloth Aaron had laid before him.

"How does it go with the people, my brother?"

"They survive, as they have always survived," Aaron answered. "They labor for Egyptians and in return they are fed."

"Like a beast of burden. Like a donkey or a camel."

"Indeed. We Israelites are beasts of burden. We have been so for many generations, so long that the people know no other course. Our lot is hard and grows harder as our numbers increase and the Egyptians view us with trepidation. For the Egyptians fear our numbers and so they make the common laborers work on Pharaoh's temples in the desert where they can cause no trouble. The laborers moan to each other and there are grumblings, but there have always been grumblings. When a grumbler is not discreet in his complaints against Pharaoh the Egyptian guard comes for him and he is never seen again."

"And so others cease their grumbling for fear that they will be the next to enter the maw of the Pharaoh's prison? And if the people were offered another course, would they leave their toiling?" Moses regarded Aaron intently.

Aaron shrugged. "The people are difficult to rouse, they are apathetic because those that live now have known no other life. But you, Moses, you have known a different life, first with the Egyptians, then in the land of Midian. What cause would awaken the people?"

"There is but one cause...the cause for which brave men die...freedom! Freedom and a land in which to live as God intended."

Aaron smiled. "Freedom is unknown to the people, shall they hunger for something they have never tasted?"

"All men hunger for freedom, Aaron. Even a lowly donkey gazes beyond his fence and longs to be free."

"That is true, but when he gains his freedom the lion stalks him. Besides, if the people were free where would they go? And as for God, if the God of Abraham still remains I think he has forgotten us. Why else has he left his people in bondage these many years?"

"Yahweh, The Almighty God, lives and he has not forgotten his people!" Moses glared at his brother with eyes like fire.

"He will lead his people forth from bondage to the Egyptians! He will give them a land of their own where once they dwelled and they will become a mighty people!"

Aaron was surprised by the feeling with which Moses spoke. He answered calmly, almost hesitantly.

"You speak of a land where the people once dwelled. Is it the land of Canaan then, that the people shall go to?"

"It is the same."

"But that land is occupied by many tribes now and it is far from Egypt. If they were allowed to go from Egypt, how would they cross the wilderness?"

"They will go as I have come. The strong, the weak, men, women, children and old ones shall walk until the weak fall. Then the strong shall carry the weak. They will walk until their sandals fall from their feet, then they will make new ones and walk again. They will cross the wilderness."

Aaron looked at Moses doubtfully. "It is a harsh land with little water and little food. How shall such a number be fed and their thirst sated? And many have flocks—what of them?"

"They shall take wheat with which to make bread and drive their flocks from watering place to watering place. And when there is neither forage for the flocks, nor water for their thirst, the Lord will provide."

Aaron was not convinced. "If the people did make it across the wilderness, would they not die of starvation or be forced into bondage to another king? There are many peoples in Canaan and they are rich and powerful. We are nothing but tradesmen and slaves with few weapons and little knowledge of the sword. We would be as dogs barking at lions."

"Do not be of faint heart, Aaron." Moses wagged a finger at his brother. "We have that which neither Pharaoh nor all the peoples of Canaan have."

Aaron sat dumbly, waiting for Moses to explain.

"We have The Almighty God to lead us and protect us! Where Yahweh leads, we must follow."

"Will The Almighty then stand before Pharaoh and demand the people's release? Will he then walk before them and lead them through the wilderness?"

Moses snapped at Aaron angrily. "The Almighty stands before no man, neither king nor slave. But he has appointed those who will lead his people from Egypt to the promised land."

"Have you then spoken to the Lord? If the Lord has appointed leaders to the people, do you know their names?"

Moses grasped his brother's arm and stared into his eyes with great passion.

"The Lord came to me in the mountains of Midian. He spoke to me from the midst of a fire, wherein a bush burned but yet stood whole.[8] And his mighty voice spoke the names of those who will lead. Those he appointed are Moses and Aaron, sons of Amram."

"Is my brother mad! Would he who was driven out from Egypt as a murderer come back to lead the people out also? Would the Lord choose a renegade sheepherder who can scarcely speak, to go before Pharaoh and demand the release of his people?"

"So said I, Aaron, but the Lord was angry with me and appointed you to speak for me!![16] And he gave me signs that I might show to the elders that they might believe in us. Also, having lived with them, I know well the Egyptians and their perverse ways. I have also twice crossed the wilderness and I know the places where there is water. You, my brother, have an uncommon goodliness of appearance and you speak Egyptian like one of the king's own ministers. I will counsel you, but you will speak before Pharaoh!"

In the space of days, Aaron had been convinced of Moses' appointed role as the leader of his people. It was then easy for him to accept his own role as spokesman. Despite inward misgivings, it was a part that pleased him since he had always sought the center of attention in his dealings with the people. The two then carefully laid plans for a meeting with the elders of the Israelites whom they must win over to their mission.

The elders of the people sat in a semi-circle in a clay-brick storehouse that served as a governmental building for the Israelites.[10] Their quick response to the request by Aaron for an assembly was more a matter of curiosity than courtesy. Yet, they were duty bound to represent the tribes in all matters concerning them, even those of little consequence. Gossip had it that Moses, a Hebrew who had grown to manhood in the royal house of Egypt, had returned after a forced exile of nearly twenty years. The fact that he fled because he had murdered an Egyptian did nothing to abate their curiosity. If anything, he had become a folk hero among the Israelites and the marketplace was rife with rumors concerning his return.

So it was that when Moses entered the assembly, followed closely by Aaron, the social murmuring among the elders was instantly stilled. Close scrutiny was dedicated to Moses, for Aaron was well known and respected but the righteousness of the elders was somewhat offended by Moses. For it was commonly known that Moses, a murderer, lived in the land of Midian with a priest of a foreign religion. Worse still, he had married the priest's daughter and sired sons by her. Now he returned without his family and asked for, almost demanded, an assembly of the elders.

So the elders sat, stiff necked, their eyes drawn close with reprobation. They watched and waited with words of censure already formed at the backs of their tongues. The stranger who entered walked with the tightly confident gait of a soldier, that some would later say was arrogance. His red tinged, brown beard was full, yet trim and his eyes glared forth from beneath his thick eyebrows like glittering black stones. He bowed to the elders, not deeply, but enough to make his greeting respectful. Then Aaron stepped forward and spoke.

"Hail, Elders of the People. 'I have heard the cries of my people and I will deliver them from their travail.' So speaks the Lord, the God of Abraham, Isaac and Jacob."

There was an instantaneous murmuring among the elders, whose faces darkened like thunderclouds in the first assault of the rains at the audacity of Aaron's opening speech. Aaron raised his hand with an imperious gesture and stilled them.

"The Lord has sent an emissary to you, to lead you out of bondage to the land promised to our forefathers—it is he, Moses."

Again the murmuring began, more loudly now, but Aaron raised his staff high then cast it down and it appeared as a venomous snake. The elders drew back in horror and their murmuring abated. This sign and others Aaron did before the assembly and for fear of the Lord they believed in Moses. And when Aaron declared that the Lord's promise of a rich homeland for the Israelites was about to be fulfilled, the elders could not contain their pleasure, but praised God for sending them such a leader. Thus Moses became their spokesman to Pharaoh, that he should lead them out of Egypt.

Moses and Aaron then petitioned Pharaoh's minister that they should be given audience with the king. The minister, a gaunt and aging man of great wisdom, expressed the request privately to Pharaoh. Pharaoh was annoyed.

"These bond servants and slaves want audience with me, the king who holds their very lives in the balance? Why should I lower myself to meet with this rabble?"

"There is no reason at all that The Great Pharaoh should lower himself to speak to them...except as an expedient to keep them content."

"What do you mean by that, Minister? I have no need to keep a rabble of slaves content...do I?"

"The Great One has no need to do so, it is merely a matter of practicality, Your Greatness," the minister smiled. "If the rabble are content, they will continue to work efficiently. To refuse them may cause discipline problems."

"Hmph, striking off a few heads will make an end of discipline problems quickly enough."

"That is true, Your Greatness. But it does have a cost in terms of our building projects, since those who are most outspoken are invariably the most skilled workers, those with inventive abilities—then there is the matter of their numbers."

"I know about their numbers, Minister. They multiply like rats in a granary. Everything we've tried to keep them in check has failed. Several decades ago we tried killing some boy babies—that didn't work. They just bred more and smuggled the boys out of the city."

"Yes, Your Greatness, and it left us with a shortage of young, strong laborers that we are still feeling the effects of. Perhaps you should try eliminating the old and infirm, that would reduce the number of mouths to feed."

"And I'd have an uprising on my hands! Those Hebrews are close to their families. If we touched their revered elders there'd be blood in the streets and much of it might be Egyptian."

"That is quite true. What should I do about the audience, Your Greatness? Shall I tell them Your Greatness does not confer with slaves?"

"No...I am becoming curious about the purposes of these emissaries of the bonded. Let them have a few moments—what are the names of these creatures?"

"Moses and Aaron, sons of Amram, Your Greatness. They claim to speak for their god as well as their people—Yahweh they called him."

"Yahweh? I always have trouble with their dialect, but I know the meaning of that word."

"Yes, Your Greatness, it means something like 'I Am That I Am.'"[17]

"That doesn't make any sense at all—but then I've never understood the Hebrews, they have a great fondness for silly riddles. Tell them I'll speak to them, I'm curious about this Yahweh and whatever scheme they have devised."

The news of the coming audience with Pharaoh found its way to the streets and the effects were counterproductive. When Moses and Aaron went to their audience with Pharaoh, the Hebrews did not work, but idled in the streets—Pharaoh was not amused.

"Why do you seek audience with me, Hebrew beggars?"

Moses stood impassively except for a slight bow of his head, though Aaron made a great show of obeisance before speaking.

"I speak for my brother, who is the chosen prophet of our god, Your Greatness. We come to make a fervent request for our people, that they should be allowed to walk into the wilderness three days' journey and make a festival of sacrifice to our god."

Pharaoh gave Moses a stony look.

"And who is this god? Is he a new god, brought with you from the wilderness, that you Hebrews must suddenly go to make a festival to him? And why do you desire to go deep into the wilderness? Can you not make sacrifice to this god here?

Moses made a sign to Aaron and he drew himself up and spoke.

"The Lord God Almighty commands us that we shall make sacrifice to him in the wilderness. This we must do on pain of his great displeasure. For he has the power to destroy us or grant us good."

"I do not know the god of whom you speak, nor do I know of his power.[11] But I know that you, Moses and Aaron, have stirred your people to unrest, so that they mill about idly when they should be working. They are of great numbers, so that it is a burden to feed them. Therefore, tell them to return to their work if they would eat and you shall do the same. Know you both that if your god has the power to destroy you, your Pharaoh also has that power!"

It was then that the will of Pharaoh was set against the will of Moses and many contests of power would soon begin. When Moses and Aaron were gone, the king beckoned his minister to him. He smiled grimly and spoke with malice in his voice.

"A new leader rises among the Hebrews—we shall see how long his people's respect will last. Order that the taskmasters shall no longer supply straw to the clay pits. Let them tell the Hebrew leaders to go out in the fields and pull the wheat stubble that remains after the harvest and knead it into the clay. But they still must make as many bricks as before. If they do not, beat their work leaders. We will see then if they still desire to make a festival to their god."

In the days that followed, the people labored beyond the setting of the sun. For they must scratch the fields for stubbles of straw by the light of day and make bricks by the light of torches at night. But as Pharaoh had envisioned, the tally of bricks fell short and the work leaders were beaten. Then there was an uproar among the Hebrews and the leaders prostrated their bruised bodies before Pharaoh and begged that Pharaoh should relent and give them straw to knead into the brick clay as before.

But Pharaoh sneered, "You have idled yourselves and made a great pretense that you would go into the wilderness to worship your god. But it is known by your king that you have a desire to flee from Egypt and the labors to which you are bonded. Go back to work and pray to your great god that you might not be beaten for lack of bricks."

The Hebrew leaders left Pharaoh with heads hanging, for they knew no way to fulfill the demands of the king. And when they came upon Moses and Aaron in the street they cursed them and would have beaten them, were it not for the presence of the King's guard.

Yet they said, "It is because of you, Moses, that we bear bruises put on us by the taskmasters of the king! You made of yourself a leader appointed by God. You spoke to lead us out of Egypt. But instead you brought the anger of Pharaoh down upon us!"

Moses and Aaron did not give reply, but they walked away quietly and were much shamed. Then Moses and Aaron counseled together that they might decide on a course to take. And Moses prayed to The Lord, that he might be guided, that he might lead the people in the pathway set for him.

When in the space of days he had received the guidance he sought, Moses took Aaron and requested audience with Pharaoh again—and the king laughed, but gave assent. Then Aaron did magical signs before the king, that he might believe on the Lord and leave the people go.[18] Yet also the magicians of the court did magical signs and Pharaoh smiled at the contest—but he refused Moses his wish.

Thus Moses was pressed to do greater wonders than those performed by the court magicians. Now, by order of his god he prophesied a plague on the great river whereby the water would become blood—and it came to pass[12]. But Pharaoh's old wise men spoke of times in the past when the water had become red and it burned to the touch, so that the fish and everything in the river died—and Pharaoh looked on Moses with contempt.

Then Moses prophesied plagues of frogs and noxious insects. And the frogs came up from the foul water of the river and died, so that the land stank and crawled with flies and maggots. The stench and the crawling masses pervaded even the palace of the king, so that everyone in his household was sickened by it and they complained loudly. Then the king called Moses and Aaron and spoke privately to them that they might entreat their god to remove the plagues.

"I will entreat the Lord if you will let the people go into the wilderness to worship," said Moses.

"If you rid the land of these accursed flies and stench your people may have time to make a festival of offerings to your god," Pharaoh said. "But you must stay close so that you can return to your labors quickly."

Now Aaron spoke with great earnestness, with the calm, calculating skill of a diplomat.

"My Great King, when we make offerings to our god we must also condemn the gods of your people and speak strongly against them. For so we must do on fear of condemnation by our god. Will that not cause the Egyptians to hate us and seek to kill us? For your people are the masters of the Children of Israel and it would go hard with us to raise the hatred of the Egyptians. Would it not be better that we take our people away from your people, into the wilderness where these denouncements cannot be heard?"

Pharaoh gave Moses and Aaron a long, calculating look and sighed heavily.

"If it is the only thing that will rid us of this accursed stench and crawling vermin, so be it. Yet I caution you, do not go far but just beyond the sight of my people, lest I send the swords of death among you."

"We have then your promise to let us go and worship?" Aaron asked.

"So I have said—now leave me."

That evening a cool breeze swept in from the sea and with it came seagulls and scavenging birds of every sort in vast numbers. The birds feasted on the rotting frogs and on the maggots which infested them. Then the wind freshened strongly and drove the flying insects into the desert wasteland to perish.

In the morning Pharaoh stood on his balcony in the cool, sweet breeze from the sea. The stench was gone from the air and wheeling gulls were searching out the last of the frogs

"They were not plagues from the Hebrew God at all," Pharaoh laughed. "It was a natural chain of happenings. I have been played as a fool by Moses, but he shall not laugh at me! For today the slaves shall not sing and dance, but they shall return to their labors! So Pharaoh sent word to the taskmasters that the Hebrews must work. And the people were sore at heart for Moses and Aaron had given the elders word that the people should go forth into the wilderness to make a festival to the Lord.

Now Moses and Aaron stood as fools before the people. For they had promised a festival and it was taken away. They were greatly disheartened and counseled together, seeking a remedy to the falseness of Pharaoh's word. Aaron rested his hand on Moses shoulder and looked at his brother with concern. For he knew that his brother's spirit was made low by his failure. He knew also that his brother had a gift, given only to prophets and fools. Aaron fully believed that Moses had been touched by the hand of God and that Moses somehow knew that his people would surely be freed from the yoke of Pharaoh.

"The king is a man of great stubbornness," Aaron said. "Though he fears us because of our numbers he fears more that the people will leave Egypt, never to return."

"Truly spoken, Brother, even now the people build the temple of Rameses and the king's highway at Pithom. Without the labors of the people Pharaoh would be hard pressed to continue his lavish projects. He seeks to keep them here and he does not favor that we speak for the people."

"Then why does he not send guards to cast us into his prison or perhaps take our heads as enemies of the state? It would be easily done and would make a quick end to the danger of insurrection."

Moses shook his head and gave Aaron a knowing smile.

"No, it would lead him closer to a rebellion, Aaron. For to kill us would martyr us in the eyes of the people and would bring forth others to lead. Those that would come forth then would be the hot-spirited young men who thirst for Egyptian blood. Pharaoh is a shrewd man, as well as stubborn. He seeks to make us objects of ridicule in the eyes of our people. Thus he will direct the frustration of the common men away from himself and to us."

"What then can we do, if the king gives us his word, yet refuses his promise to the people after we have spoken to the people?"

"Let us pray to The Almighty. Perhaps the Lord will see fit to give us another lever to pry up the settled will of Pharaoh. Night is upon us and if worry does not too greatly impede sleep God may provide guidance within our slumbers."

In the morning Miriam, sister of Moses and Aaron, brought them bread and cheese and sat with them to break their fast. She set before Moses a bowl of olive oil so that he could dip his bread, for it was dry. The night before she had listened to her brothers as they counseled and now she could hold her curiosity no longer.

"Did the Lord speak to you during the night, Moses? Did he give you answer to your prayers for guidance?"

Moses nodded and dipped a piece of bread in the olive oil.

"God's voice came to me in a dream. He said to look to the forces of nature for an admonishment to Pharaoh. His voice told me that the plague which has passed has sown the seeds of yet another and that the Children of Israel shall be spared it as they were spared the frogs and the flies. I was told that the very skies would cast down torment on the Egyptians and that I must prophesy these things to the king and his people."

"We were spared the frogs and the flies because the Egyptians force us to live on the edges of the desert away from the river," Miriam said. "The frogs were sickened by the foul water of the river and they died before they reached us. And so the flies swarmed about their rotting bodies and stayed away from us. But what is meant by 'the seeds of yet another plague'?"

Aaron stared at Miriam thoughtfully. "Do you remember when we were children, how something killed many of the carp in the river, Miriam? They washed up on the riverbank and then too there were great swarms of flies about them."

"Yes, I remember that people shunned the river for many days."

"And after the flies much sickness came both among people and animals," Aaron said. "Do you think that the sickness is seeded by the flies?"

Moses was watching his siblings closely and an answer came from their words.

"It is so—that is what the Lord speaks of! That is the warning I shall give the king! But what of the torment from the skies?"

"Perhaps a sandstorm?" Miriam speculated.

"I think not, the Egyptians do not fear sandstorms. They loathe their coming but they accept them as a natural part of life," Aaron said. "No, it would be something terrifying to them, something they do not often see."

Moses looked at Aaron thoughtfully. "During my years with Jethro I spoke often with people of caravans from the north. One man, a donkey driver, spoke of seeing great storms where fire was driven from heaven to earth and the rains came as water poured from a jar. He said that sometimes the water came in hard balls like lumps of dried clay. But it was white in color and cold that it made his hand numb to hold it. It is called hail."

"That would be a wonder indeed," Aaron said. "I have heard that at the tops of some very high mountains there is water that is hard and cold, it is called ice and it flows again when it is warmed. But I have never seen it come from the sky."

Moses continued. "There was another thing that the donkey driver said. He said that these storms only happened when the air was hot and heavy, as it is sometimes near evening. He said the heavens would become heavy with swirling, dark clouds. Then it became suddenly cool and with the coolness came a roaring of winds and loud crashing that opened the heavens so that fire came forth. And the fire was so great that it lit the earth with a terrible brilliance. The waters fell from the heavens, both flowing and ice and that which was ice hurt greatly all that was beneath it."

"These are indeed the plagues that the Lord shall loose on Egypt!" Aaron said. "Shall we then warn Pharaoh?"

"We shall warn him of the pestilence to the Egyptian cattle, for that already comes. The flies were heavy on them because they grazed on the good land near the river. Thus the seeds of sickness were planted on them. But the cattle of the people must graze in the dry land where the flies were not. Thus they will not sicken. Yet Pharaoh knows not of these things and so he will come to fear the Lord. But I think he will be angered and he will set his head against the Lord and he will still keep our people in the land."

So Moses and Aaron went and sought audience with Pharaoh that they might warn him of the plague of the animals. And he scoffed at them with contempt and would have sent them to their labors.

But Aaron puffed himself up and said, "If our Lord, The God Almighty, has not the power to do these things, where then are your magicians and counselors, Mighty Pharaoh? Why do they not minister to you on this day? Is it not that the scourge of sickness is on them? Let then the people go to make a festival onto Yahweh, that your people may not suffer this."

And Pharaoh kept his peace for his magicians were already sick with the fever wherefrom they had burning blisters and boils and sickness of the bowels. And Pharaoh knew in his heart that yet another plague had begun. Yet he was angered that Moses should pronounce judgement on him—and he sent them away.

The evil came as Moses prophesied and the cattle and sheep and beasts of burden sickened and died in great numbers, so that the Egyptians could not bury them but piled them in great heaps and burned them with fire. And when there was not enough fuel to burn them they cast the bloated carcasses into the river and they floated to the sea. Pharaoh watched grimly and listened to the ill tidings of his couriers. Within his heart he cursed Moses.

Then came an oppressive heat from the sea. The air was as though a wetted cloth was put over the nostrils and the sweat of those who labored remained on their bodies. Now the first gray clouds gathered on the horizon, rising high over the sea, casting its darkness toward the land of Egypt.

Moses rose early that dark morning and beckoned Aaron.

"It is come—let us go and make a prediction of the coming storm to Pharaoh. He has not yet found his peace from the plague of the cattle and he may leave the people depart, rather than suffer further loss."

When at last they gained audience with the king he looked at them as noxious creatures. For he did not know the cause of the sickness through the land, but blamed it on a curse by Moses. He listened to Moses and did not harm him only because he feared another curse by him. But gladly he would have killed Moses and cast his body in the river to follow the dead cattle to the sea.

Now Aaron stood before the king and spoke:

"Great Pharaoh, know you that our lord, The God Almighty, creator of the world, has spoken to you. In his goodness he has forewarned you of the plagues he would release upon your lands and upon your people. Yet, you would not relent and let the Children of Israel go to make offerings unto Him that made them."

Pharaoh stared at Aaron woodenly, but did not turn an eye upon Moses, his tormentor. Those of his counselors that had sufficiently recovered from their blisters and boils to be in attendance glanced at each other nervously.

Aaron continued. "Know you now, that the Lord will cast upon you such terrible trials that all the Egyptians will cry out in terror and grief if you do not bend your knee to God! You are proud and speak with the tongue of a serpent. You have promised and withheld that which you promised. For that you will suffer if you do not release the people as you gave your word!"

He paused and the eyes of the king turned from Aaron and locked on those of Moses. His countenance was fearsome with the anger that boiled within him.

"Moses! Know you that I will not bend my knee to the god of the Hebrews! Nor will I ever free your people from their labors! There are not terrors great enough to overcome Pharaoh with fear!"

Moses gave a slight nod of his head to the questioning glance of Aaron. Aaron spoke further to the king.

"We know of the pride with which a great king such as you must comport himself, Your Greatness." Aaron spoke soothingly. "Yet in spite of this our Lord would not have it that the penitent suffer further with the unyielding. Send out word hastily, Great Pharaoh, that your people should bring their cattle and families and all that they can gather from the fields under their roofs.[19] For there will be a storm such as none living has witnessed. The wind shall come forth and rend the heavens so that fire shall issue forth and strike to the death that which it touches. And the rains shall come as though the sea were loosed upon the land and it shall have great shards of frozen rain that will destroy all beneath it, both the cattle of the pastures and the fruits of the fields."

Then Moses raised his staff and pointed it toward the sea, where there struck downward the first fire of the storm—then Moses and Aaron departed.

CHAPTER 4

When they had gone, Pharaoh rose and with his councilors went to the great veranda that faced toward the distant sea. Far off the blackening clouds over the sea wheeled in turmoil and streaks of fire coursed downward from the heavens. The crashing of thunder and the flashing in the sky grew in intensity.

Then Pharaoh sent runners to warn the people along the river, that not all should be lost.[19] As the king watched, the storm gained land and the winds lashed out with such fury that all in its path sought refuge where they could, were it ditch or wall of brick. And when the fire and the wind were nearly past, came the rain. It fell so heavily that the ditches filled and the water rose up on the fields and in the streets until it entered over the thresholds of houses and climbed upon the legs of the dwellers.

Then also came the hail, a thing little known by the people. It fell as stones cast from slings and large stones to the girth of figs and even larger. The hail followed the river and it fell until it lay deep on the ground, utterly destroying all that was not beneath a roof. The Hebrews watched from their dwellings in the hills and beside the desert. And they gave thanks that they did not live in the good land by the river as did the Egyptians.

As the first sheets of rain drew near to the veranda, the king and his advisers retreated into the palace. But bludgeoning gusts of wind drove rain and hail through the open latticework of the windows and sent the icy pellets rolling across the floor to their feet. When the storm did not abate and some fist-sized chunks of ice splintered the shutter nearest Pharaoh, he spoke quietly to his sergeant at arms.

"Get me the accursed Hebrew—get Moses."

Moses and Aaron had rested themselves on a marble bench under a portico at the south entrance of the palace. There had been little purpose in attempting to return to the home of Aaron, for they would have been overtaken by the storm. The rains had built up swiftly in a city engineered to a climate that seldom saw rain. And now the streets were awash with water and floating ice. The two men sat silent in awe of the storm, for it was such as neither man had seen in his lifetime.

Moses started with the touch of a hand on his shoulder. He turned to look into the face of the captain of the king's guard.

"Pharaoh bids you enter his presence, Hebrew. Hurry now, for it is a matter of urgency!" He turned abruptly and began striding rapidly down hall of the palace. Moses and Aaron followed, their walking staffs making thumping sounds on the tile floor. Behind them two more guards marched impassively, javelins and shields at the ready.

Aaron glanced nervously at Moses. "Many have entered upon such a procession as this and have not returned. Has the king's fright with this fearsome storm turned to wrath against us? Does he now seek to take our lives in payment for the destruction unleashed against him?"

"Be calm, Aaron. The Almighty protects us, for he has made the storm that even now makes ruin of Egypt. Pharaoh knows that he wrestles with the Lord—he will ask us to stay the Lord's hand. He will not have us executed, or even imprisoned, for he fears that such a thing would bring the sword of our god down upon his own neck."

As they entered The Hall of Petitions the king stood near a window, watching the sheets of water pour down upon the land. Nearby, a lone donkey that had been struck dead by a large hailstone floated in the rising water. The king turned at the sound of Moses' staff upon the floor. His face was that of a monarch who suffers the death of his nation. His features were drawn in tight lines and the color of his face was lost in a mask of grayness. He regarded the two Hebrews stolidly and his imperious manner was gone. In its place was the mien of a beaten man, sorrowful and fearful of a power greater than he.

The king spoke. "Hebrew...it is enough. The land lies in ruin, the palms beside my palace are stripped of all green and spread their branches nakedly in protest to this storm. The waters rise in the streets so that a dead donkey floats beside my garden. And yet the storm rages so fiercely that even the oldest of my counselors have no memory of the like. I will surrender myself and my people to your god, for he is all powerful and righteous. I will bend my knee to him and bow my head before him if you will intercede for me. If your lord will stop the forces that he has brought forth against Egypt, his people shall go and make sacrifice to him and I will not detain them any longer."

Moses made a sign that Aaron should not answer. He spoke to Pharaoh himself in a voice of authority.

"I will intercede for Pharaoh with my lord when I am returned to my people, that the innocent of Egypt will suffer no more.... But I know the perverse ways of Pharaoh—for you are ever contrary to your word! The storm will abate upon my sign but you will remain as unbelieving as before!" Moses turned upon his heel and left Pharaoh.

Now Pharaoh gritted his teeth with anger toward Moses. For he had spoken humbly to the Hebrew, a spokesman of a people of slaves and had been rebuked like a child. He watched the Hebrew depart his presence without due leave and he desired to have him cast into the dungeon where the torturers might have sport with him—but he dared not. For Pharaoh was of a superstitious people who governed their lives and labors by many gods and signs and mysticism. He believed now in the strength of this god of the Hebrew and he feared him.

Yet the insolence of Moses rancored him so that his spirit was set in anger against Moses. Therefore when the storm diminished and Pharaoh could again see the sun over the land his fear lessened. And when the water drained from the fields, now barren of standing crops and produce for the markets, Pharaoh's wrath returned to him.

"It is passed," the king said. "It was a storm such as we have never seen, but yet it was a storm and nothing more. My fear of the fire from the sky and the frozen rain that caused such destruction caused me to speak foolishly to the Hebrews. That man, Moses, chastised me...his king...as though I were an errant child. He used my concern for my people as a lever against me to secure the release of his people from their lawful bondage. He must not succeed in that!"

Again, the king gave order that the Children of Israel should not enter the wilderness to make a festival to their god, but that they should remain and till the fields, that new crops might be planted. And he made the people toil in the fields for exceeding long hours, so that a great amount of wheat was planted, that the people of Egypt might have bread and stores to sell. From his high tower Pharaoh smiled as he looked out over the greening land.

Yet Pharaoh had not won, for when the wheat was risen and about to show kernels, Moses again had a vision in answer to the prayers he made to the Lord. And there was an omen that gave credence to his vision. A light breeze was blowing from the desert to the west—it was too early in the season for such a wind and it did not bode good. Moses and Aaron went then and sought audience with Pharaoh.

Pharaoh had no wish to see the Hebrew again, for his ego was still smarting from the words of rebuke Moses had said to him at the time of the storm. Still, he had a strong curiosity about the powers of prophesy the Hebrew had. Pharaoh remembered that Moses had always been right in the past and it was far better to know what this god of the Hebrews was about than to be ignorant of it. Reluctantly he granted audience. He would listen to what this Moses had to say, but he would not lower himself to communicate with him.

Moses and Aaron immediately sensed a difference on entering Pharaoh's court. The king sat regally on his chair of office but gave no recognition of the Hebrews. The king's advisers hovered about him nervously, but only his minister came forward.

"Speak, Hebrews. For what purpose have you sought audience with Pharaoh?"

Aaron took a step forward. "We come to give the king urgent prophesy from our Lord, the god of the Hebrews."

"And what is this urgent prophesy, that you would encumber Great Pharaoh with it?"

"Yahweh is greatly displeased that Pharaoh still refuses to leave the people go into the wilderness to worship him and make sacrifice. The Lord has stricken Egypt with terrible plagues and fearsome storms and yet Pharaoh refuses to believe and bow down before him."

The minister replied with feigned contempt. "The king bows not to the god of slaves. He worships unto Amon, Osiris and Ra. Why would he then worship to a god without a name? For 'Yahweh' is but a state of being and not a proper name for a god."

"Our God is so called because before the world was, he is.[20] And what he is cannot be made of stone or gold, but is that wherewith all was made. Bow down then, Pharaoh, and let the people go to their worship. For if you refuse the Lord shall send further disasters to the land and the first will be tomorrow. A plague of locusts such as will blot out the sun and darken the sky shall come out of the wilderness. They will devour the new wheat and all that was left after the storm that was sent. They will lay waste to the blooming trees of fruits and nuts and leave neither plant nor tree untouched among your people. There shall be much crying because of hunger in the land."

Yet Pharaoh was unmoved, but scorned Moses and Aaron with signs and scowls. Then Moses turned about and left the king because he was angered at his obstinacy and contempt for the Lord.

But Pharaoh's minister and his advisers were troubled and they counseled among themselves, then laid their fears before the king.

"Each time the Hebrew has come unto Pharaoh he has made a dire prediction. And each time, what he predicted has happened. We can ill afford a calamity such as he prophesies now. Would it not be prudent to let these men go a little way into the desert to make the offerings their god requires? For surely the cost would be less than the calamity this Moses threatens."

Pharaoh saw that his advisers counseled him with wisdom. Already the granaries were emptying of wheat because the first crops of grain and produce had fallen to the storm.

"Very well, bring back the insolent beggars. I will make an agreement with them."

When Moses and Aaron were returned before the king he sought to placate them.

"I have reconsidered your request. Because of the goodness of my heart, I have decided to let you go to make this festival to your god. It is right for each man to serve his god and so keep a morality in his people. But tell me, Moses...who will go? Is it not the men who are of age that serve your lord?"

Aaron replied, "Among our people, all must worship the Lord, our God, Yahweh. Therefore, men and women, young and old will go. And because they must be cared for and no one will stay behind, we must take our flocks and herds with us."

Pharaoh grew angry, that his face was terrible to look upon and he made as though he would strike Moses with his scepter.

"Do you think me such a fool, Hebrew, that I do not know that your intent is to desert your labors? Be careful that you do not overstep my good faith, for I am still your king and you are subject to my judgement. Take your men and leave all the rest behind. Thus serve your god with sacrifice and worship and be thankful for my providence. Now get you out from before my face, for my spirit tires of you!"

Then the king's guard roughly pushed Moses and Aaron and drove them out of Pharaoh's presence. It was the late hours of the day and the breezes freshened from the west.

In the morning the winds blew strong from the west, out of the desert and the wilderness beyond. In the early hours the first few specks appeared in the low sky, which quickly multiplied in number until the sky was darkened with them. The locusts descended as the grains of a sandstorm, so that the earth and everything that stood upon the earth was covered with them. As the voracious blanket advanced it stripped the delta of the Nile of everything that grew. The locusts chewed to the roots of the wheat and every green plant. They ate every leaf and tender twig of the shrubs and trees and even the young bark of them.

Then Pharaoh regretted his arrogance in dealing with the Hebrews and sent a messenger hurrying to Moses, that he would return to his presence. For the king feared that all of Egypt would be laid waste and hunger would reign more strongly than he. For Pharaoh thought that if his empire were made weak in the eyes of the Hebrews they might seek to overthrow him. Indeed, the Children of Israel were a sturdy and troublesome people and their numbers were great.

So it was that when Moses and Aaron entered his presence the king wore a countenance of contrition.

"I grew angry and spoke unjustly to you, Moses. I acted with contempt toward you and your people and toward your mighty god, whom I now know as the mightiest of the mighty and the Lord and master of the world."

"You bow before Yahweh, the true god of all, the god of slaves?"

"The god of slaves, but also the god of kings—I bow before him and pay homage to him."

"And what do you desire in exchange for this sudden, unshakeable faith in our god, Mighty Pharaoh?"

"Because of my obstinacy, I sinned against Yahweh and he has struck Egypt with the power of his mighty hand. Because of me my people will suffer the lingering death of starvation if the locusts are not quickly driven from the land. I beg of you that you will intercede with your god just this time."

"And you will honor him and let us go?"

"I will bend my neck before his presence and cast my scepter to the ground before him. Your people shall seek the high places of the wilderness that they may build an altar to worship him."

Moses and Aaron looked at the king and saw that he was contrite. So they left his presence and the winds that had blown gently from the west strengthened until it roared with great fury. The ravaging locusts were driven before the wind, so that they fell like rain upon the Red Sea and drowned.

Again the king watched the forces of nature turn themselves before his eyes. And when he saw how quickly the locusts were driven from his land, he saw that it was but a strengthening of the wind and not the hand of a mighty god that caused it.

"It is no more than an ill tide upon the sea," he said. "For it came in fiercely, but now it has turned and it is gone. Where it plunged upon the land there is devastation, but where it did not go all is well."

"But yet, Pharaoh gave his word, O Great One," said the aged minister. "Indeed, you promised your faith to their god. Would it be wise to spurn a promise so devoutly made?"

"Moses came to me like a nagging old woman, making mystery of something he already knew. I don't know how he knew of the locusts, perhaps from his days in the wilderness from where he came. But he knew and he used the coming plague to gain my promise to free his people. Thus he dealt with me in bad faith and so I deal with him. The scoundrel is fortunate that I do not pluck out his eyes and let him wander sightless to preach his doleful prophesies."

As though in answer to Pharaoh's threat of sightlessness for Moses a veil now blotted out the sun. The darkness was like that of night and the people of the land looked about with great fear.

Pharaoh pondered the darkness and gathered his advisors about him, but they did not know of what cause the darkness was. They trembled in fear and spoke in hushed voices lest the god of the Hebrews hear and be offended. For they had done mystical incantations and read signs cast with pebbles in the sand and the greatest of them had succumbed to a deep trance wherein he praised Yahweh, god of the Hebrews. But their knowledge was not made greater concerning the darkness. Then Pharaoh's advisors admonished him to send the Hebrews on their pilgrimage before Yahweh should destroy all of Egypt.

So once again the king sent his guards to bring Moses and Aaron before him.

"I have thought of all that has happened," Pharaoh said. "And I know that every calamity that has befallen us has been in the natural course of the earth's forces. The river stank and killed the fish, but that has happened in the past. That the frogs should come out from the banks of the river and die is a natural consequence of the river's foulness. That the flies should gather on the dead frogs is not a mystery and also that sickness follows the flies is known. I can explain these happenings further, but there is no need, for all of them would have occurred and removed without your god.

"Yet neither I nor my wise men can explain the cause of this darkness. They fear that indeed the world shall pass away, or that your god, Yahweh, will strike the Egyptians dead. I am tired to my heart with your constant crying out to me that I should let you go to worship. Therefore, because you did not seek me out with tales of coming torment, prophesying evil against my people, but come at my bidding, I will deal honestly with you.

"When the darkness lifts, you may take all of your people into the wilderness to worship. My servants who are not Hebrews will care for your cattle and all of your animals so that you can travel quickly, unencumbered by them."

Moses looked sourly at Pharaoh and touched Aaron, that he should speak.

"Oh, Great One, we pleasure in your generosity to our people. Yet there is a problem with your kind offer."

Pharaoh stared at Aaron in disbelief and a frown creased his forehead.

"My offer is most generous from a king to his slaves. What problem could exist that you would trouble me with it?"

Aaron sighed and looked imploringly at Moses, then continued in a hesitant, but determined manner.

"It is about the sacrifices, Oh, Great One. We require animals for sacrifice, therefore must take them along with us."

"Then select a few animals and take them with you, but do not trouble me further with it!"

Moses stepped forward with a grim countenance and spoke as one with authority.

"We will take all of our livestock, because we will not know which we must sacrifice until we reach the place of our worship and sign is given to the priests."

"You are a fool, Moses, for you make pretenses that mock your king! I called you here to deal charitably with you and your people. Yet you deal with me as though you were the king and I were your bondservant. I have had enough of your quibbling and crying out for goodness for your people for you will give nothing in return.[21] Get out of my presence, you miserable ingrate, and do not return! For when next you see my face you will die!!"

Aaron took Moses' arm and made to leave with him. But Moses turned to Pharaoh and spoke clearly.

"You have spoken well, Pharaoh. For I will not see your face again, even though you shall wish it!"

Aaron pulled on Moses' arm earnestly, that they should leave Pharaoh's presence while yet they might. For the sky had begun to lighten.

It was yet a little while before Moses made further divination. For because of the anger of Pharaoh he kept to the house of Aaron and he prayed by day and by night that God should instruct him regarding the exodus of the people. He ate and drank but little and no strong drink passed his lips. Neither did he make casual conversation within the household of Aaron. Rather, when he was not praying he sat beneath the fig tree in the garden that Miriam tended with Elisheba[22], the wife of Aaron. And he was silent. So it was that the women of the household spoke to Moses, for they feared that his spirit was ill because he spoke only to the Lord.

"Come, brother, have a little beer, for you are distressed and it eases the mind." Miriam offered Moses a cup of the light fermented drink the poorer Egyptians favored.

"I cannot take strong drink when I am communing with the Lord, Miriam. For it is disrespectful to speak to the Lord when the spirit is light."

"Surely a cup will not distract you from your prayers. Has the Lord spoken to you of late, my brother?"

"He speaks to me, yet I fear that I do not rightly understand his words. For he speaks within my heart, in dreams and visions and I must think with care upon what it is he says to me, lest I do wrong in his sight."

"You will do the Lord's bidding, Moses. I have known it from the day the daughter of the old Pharaoh took your ark from among the reeds and you were not slain. I knew then that God had a special purpose for you."

"And he has a special purpose for you, My Sister. For you, who watched over me in the reeds of the river, and for my elder brother, who came to me in the wilderness, the Lord has need. And now you may begin to fulfill the role the Lord has given you to play, for we will soon leave Egypt.[23] Go to your relatives and friends and tell them to ask for whatever they might need from the Egyptian women. We will have need for gold and jewels to use in trade when we leave this land. But ask also for that which you have need for in your household, be it blankets or pots, wheat or spices."

Then Elisheba spoke. "It might be difficult for us to ask that the Egyptian women give to us of their goods, Moses. For they know we seek to leave the land and that there is little chance they shall get anything in return."

"Not so, Elisheba, for the common people of Egypt are in fear of us and of our god. They care not for the temples and pyramids that their rulers build. They wish only that no more plagues be visited on them and that we shall depart and leave them in peace."

"Then you perceive that it is only the vanity of Pharaoh that keeps us here?" Miriam asked.

"He and the nobles of the land, who live in luxury because of the labors of our people. Yet the common people, who bear us no ill, shall pay the price exacted because of the vanity and greed of Pharaoh."

CHAPTER 5

Miriam and Elisheba looked at Moses with concern because he became as one suddenly turned old when he spoke of the coming affliction of the Egyptian people.

Miriam asked, "What is it that so troubles you, My Brother? Your face is desolate like one who faces death."

He raised weary eyes to her, eyes that held an inward pain, an uncertainty and a regretful submission of the spirit.

"And death I face, not my own or of my family, but of the Egyptians—great numbers will die. I take no pleasure at their deaths and yet it must come, because it is ordained by The Almighty God."

"What do you mean?" Elisheba asked. "Which of the Egyptian people shall die...surely not those whom we ask for goods...not those who were kind and brought bread and cooked lentils when I was ill?'

"There are none of the Egyptians that shall escape the judgement, neither King nor poor farmer, tradesman or priest. Yet not all will die, but the first born of every household, both of man and of beast will die."[24]

Miriam stared at Moses with horror wrenching the muscles of her face.

"No, Moses! That is too grievous a judgement to put upon good people for the sins of their leaders. Can you not beg of God that he might let the kindly folk escape it.?"

"I cannot dissuade the Lord from his judgements, nor would I.... For did not I and only I, survive a like judgement decreed by the Pharaoh of our father's youth? Who then among the Egyptians stepped forward to protest the killing of the newborn boy children? Did one step forward and bid cease to Pharaoh's guard as they cast babes into the river? But yet, I do not glory in the coming slaughter...for such death should not seek out the laughing young. I think...were it by my will...I would destroy the old of hardened heart and selfish mind."

"Then how will this terrible judgement come...if indeed it must?" Elisheba whispered.

Moses sighed deeply. "Seek out my brother Aaron and I will then tell you all. For there are preparations the Children of Israel must make to ward off this scourge. Aaron shall be my voice in telling the people what they must do. Go quickly."

It was then that the young soldier Joshua was first enlisted into the cause of Moses. For it was not possible for Aaron to warn all of the people in time. But Joshua was known as one of the Pharaoh's appointed guards within Israel. He was of upright nature, brave and despite his appointment by Pharaoh's minister, a staunchly religious Israelite. So Aaron went to Joshua and charged him to assist Moses.

"You must gather your brothers-in-arms and instruct them with what I have related to you. Then they must go swiftly to all of the houses of Israel to warn the people of what comes."

"That we will do," Joshua said. "And after it comes?"

"Then your brothers must gather the people together as they flee Egypt. For there will be such a chaos as we have never seen—and you must be a captain to bring order over it."

The scourge of God came, according to the prediction of Moses, to chastise Pharaoh and his people. There was not a mother that did not watch a child grow still within her arms, nor even a herdsmen that did not carry forth the dead of his cattle as well as his kindred. And the path of the angel of death sped irrevocably the length and breadth of the valley of the Nile.

Pharaoh stood before the bed on which lay the body of his eldest child, a daughter who was not yet at womanhood. She was fair, with black hair and skin of golden hue and of the smoothness of carved ivory. And she was greatly favored in the heart of Pharaoh.

"I would, my daughter, that I could bring back your breath of life. Too late, I recant the obstinacy of my heart. For this is yet another of the plagues and trials brought forth upon me by the Hebrew God. Had I set the accursed Hebrews free to follow their Lord, you would still laugh and walk beside me in the gardens.... Indeed, all the temples to the gods and brave monuments to the glory of Egypt would I give up to renew the brightness that your smile bestowed on me!"

Pharaoh's shoulders sagged with his grief and his head hung with despair. But then, anger came to him with a rush that overpowered his sorrow. With a clenched fist he struck his chest and shouted with the anger of a man that must fix upon the cause of his wretchedness and destroy it.

"No!! ...I will not speak as a beaten slave—I speak now as Pharaoh, King of Egypt, a fond father bereft of his daughter's love! I shall visit judgement on the Hebrews and they shall cry twice over to atone for the cries we hear tonight! No more shall Moses, prince of evil, pronounce his deadly visitations on my people! For I have promised that when next he looks upon my face he shall die! And look upon my face he will, quickly as my guards can thrust him into my presence—and he shall die!"

The first wife of Pharaoh, mother of his stricken child, had been weeping quietly from the depths of her soul. Now she looked up at Pharaoh from where she knelt beside the death bed of her daughter—anger burned in her eyes.

"What careless nonsense do you speak, my husband? ...You will turn death into still more death until the tombs are filled and the mighty river floats with bodies! Do you not know by now that the power Moses holds within his staff belittles that of your scepter? How often he came to your court and prophesied dire warnings that you should let the Hebrews go! And always you dismissed his warnings with contempt. But Moses spoke truly and much suffering came upon us. And now your daughter lies quiet and cold while you shout your threats like a donkey braying at a lion.... Would you have the god of Moses take too the sons I have given you?"

The king looked at his wife, astounded by the vehemence she directed at him. For Pharaoh was never chided by his own and it set hard against his ego. Yet, the terrible grief in her eyes reflected that in his own heart and he knew she did not err in her words. He walked to the window where he could see torches darting from door to door and he heard the cries of woeful grief float up on the cool night air. He turned to his wife and she saw in on her husband's face a forlorn expression she had never seen before. Pharaoh, King of Egypt, was beaten.

"You speak truly, My Queen...I must let the Hebrews go, for they are like a festering boil to Egypt. Nevermore shall we know contentment until they are gone from our midst. But seeing that they desire so greatly to leave—they shall do so now! This very night I will purge Egypt of the rebellious slaves. They shall go however they can, every one of them, young or old, well or sick, with whatever they can take with them. I will spew them out of my goodness into the harsh barrenness of the wilderness! And they shall not turn back for I will send soldiers to prevent them. They shall not return to my goodness though they eat scorpions because of the emptiness of their bellies and drink of the bitter waters to slake their thirst!!"

Moses, Aaron and their kin were gathered in the house of Aaron. In the distance, at the first of the more affluent Egyptian homes, the cries of grief and fear had begun.

"The death of the firstborn begins," Aaron said quietly. "The valley of the Nile will ring with those cries before night is spent."

"And in this plague comes the release of our people," Moses mused. "Perhaps it is to seek the promised land, or perhaps it is to eternal peace. It is in the hand of God."

"And Pharaoh," Aaron added. "For the king will be greatly angered if the angel of death descends on one of his. His firstborn is a girl, greatly beauteous and nearing womanhood. It is told by some that the king would make her queen upon his death, for she is a great favorite with him, even beyond his sons. Might not the angel take her over the first son?"

"That I do not know, though it might carry the greater pain for the king if the girl is taken. But, the course that Pharaoh takes will be counseled by fear of the Lord," Moses returned. "He may indeed show anger and contempt and send his guards to slaughter among the people. If that is his decision, a death for a death will not suffice to appease his anger."

Miriam looked at her brothers fearfully.

"Do you think that the king will take vengeance against us? Upon whom will his fury fall, upon young or old...or all?"

"Your brother Moses and I doubtless will be the first to taste of Pharaoh's swords," Aaron said. "But don't despair too soon. I think that he will not risk an insurrection of the Hebrews and the retribution of our god. His people too may rise against him. They are wary of all gods and now fear Yahweh above all others."

"Then what other course will he most likely take, Aaron? Will he set us free to follow the Lord's bidding without shedding blood?"

"That he will and that is why Moses directed that we ready ourselves and put that which we need in bag and bundle. For when Pharaoh frees us it will not be to peacefully stroll along the road in the light of day. He will expel us from the land as one spits out a spoiled fruit. And the time draws near—the cries from the houses of the Egyptians grow louder and close. For death will not stop with the nobles but will come also to the poor—our neighbors and friends."

A cry came then, a shriek of anguish that pierced the night as though it had come on within the room. The heads of all turned toward the door which was barred against the terror beyond. The shriek subsided and a woman's voice cried from beyond the weathered boards.

"Aaron! ...Friend of my husband...let us in, that Moses may intercede with The Almighty God for the life of my child! He lies within my arms, deathly still and I fear that life is flying from him!"

"It is Ruhamah, the woman who cared for me when I was ill," Elishebah said. "I will let her in."

Moses rose and stood before her, barring her way. He looked down on her with his piercing eyes and shook his head.

"She cannot enter though once she was one of us. For she married of the Egyptians and forsook her god. By the decree of the Lord, she cannot enter into our house."

"But she is a friend to me and her child dies. Surely you can show mercy and pray to the Lord on her behalf," Elisheba implored Moses.

"I cannot revoke the judgement of God, Elisheba." Moses turned to the door and spoke.

"Go away, Ruhamah, for the Lord has spoken that the firstborn of the Egyptians shall die. Go and bury your child for he is sacrificed by God!"

The crying outside the door stopped and the silence became heavy among those in the house, so that the wailing of the Egyptians was the only sound. Elisheba's eyes burned with such fury at Moses that the others in the room looked away from her. It was then that there came a banging on the door so strenuous that the bar shook within its slot. And a man's voice was heard, rough and filled with authority.

"Aaron, son of Amram, open to us! We are the couriers of the king and we have a decree for Moses which he must receive and obey within this hour!"[25]

Aaron opened the door and with Moses, stepped out into the street. Before them stood the captain of Pharaoh's guard and a rank of soldiers. The captain held a piece of papyrus, a royal order, which he gave to Moses as he angrily spoke.

"Be it known by you, Moses, son of Amram, that your people are forever banished from the nation of Egypt! Therefore, you and all of your people shall on this hour gather yourselves up and leave the land. Any man who remains behind will fall upon the displeasure of Pharaoh and any man who seeks to return shall fall upon the swords of the king's guard.

"And you, Moses and Aaron, be glad for the king's great mercy that he has not struck your heads from your shoulders and stood them on lances in the marketplace. For he grieves the death of his firstborn, who was a great favorite to him. Now hasten and depart, for the king may yet regret his goodness to you—and I myself will gladly seek retribution for his daughter...and my son!"

The word spread quickly among the Children of Israel and soon the pathways were filled with a throng of people and their possessions. It was a great muddle of shouting men, bewildered children crying in the night and the bellowing and bleating complaints of all manner of livestock.

The family of Aaron left their home and entered into the melee. Elisheba paused at the threshold of her house and sadly looked back into the barren room. Then she wiped insistent tears from her eyes and turned about. Her friend Ruhamah stood in the door of her home across the narrow lane clutching to her breast a small, still bundle. Her eyes fixed on Elisheba and they were filled with pain and bitter accusation. Elisheba's heart went out to her friend so sorely that she would have spoken. But their worlds had parted forever and their friendship had died with Ruhamah's child.

Thus began the exodus from Egypt. A people who had known no other homeland for all the generations that lived and long before were suddenly thrust from it. They walked away from beds and full bellies and all the simple comforts that even slaves in Egypt enjoyed, into a land of scarcity and hardship.

But it must be known that not all were slaves. For many were men in favor with the Egyptians, who dressed handsomely and ate of the richness of the land. Some owned flocks and herds or farmed in Goshen beside the fingers of the Nile. Others were tradesmen or skilled carvers of stone or makers of golden ornaments for the wealthy Egyptians. These Hebrews were not joyful to leave their homes and grumbled at being uprooted by the prophet from Midian. Yet, they were cast out by the anger of Pharaoh to walk with slaves and poor men in a road made slippery with the dung of cattle. Now, at Joshua's firm direction, they gathered grudgingly behind Moses and Aaron and their sister, the prophetess Miriam. For though they would stay, they could not for fear of death—thus the people were joined by a common fate. And behind them rumbled the chariots of Pharaoh.

Moses led the people away from the travelled caravan route that ran along the shore of the Great Sea, because he knew the strength of the Philistines that lived in that country. Most of the Children of Israel were not trained or equipped for battle and to enter into the land of the Philistines would have meant battle and sure destruction. Instead he led them toward the Sea of Reeds and the Desert of Shur on a way which he had travelled when he fled Egypt. And as they trudged in the heat of the Egyptian sun the chariots pressed them so that the people feared for their lives[26]. But when the people were weary so that the little ones and the old people could walk no more, Moses stopped them and set camp near the Sea of Reeds.

That evening Moses and Aaron counseled together. With them was Joshua who had been of the king's own guard and now spoke the words of Moses to the tribes as they marched.

"What make you of the chariots of Pharaoh?" Aaron asked. "They follow close upon us, yet they do not close as if to strike."

"It would not be unlike Pharaoh to wait until we are swallowed by the wilderness, then sack our people and leave them dead upon the sands of Shur," Joshua said. "That is what the people fear. The Egyptians hover over us like an eagle over a lamb."

"There is another thing," Aaron said. "Pharaoh has had time for his anger to cool and relent his rashness in driving us from the land. By now the Egyptians have found that they must do for themselves what we have done before. Their muscles are soft from long disuse and they will groan to Pharaoh that he should return us to our labors."

Joshua looked up sharply for he smelled the brewing of a fight.

"If that is true the chariots will soon descend upon us to take us captive again. Send me, Lord Moses, that I may choose among the people for strong, brave men that know how to hold a sword or spear!"

Moses smiled at the courageous spirit of young Joshua. "And when you have chosen, what will you use for weapons to slay the mighty Egyptians with?"

"We have a few swords and axes and we will sharpen the tent poles to impale them as they ride upon us."

"Spoken as a soldier who trusts in the Lord, Joshua. But I think I know a better way. Listen that you may lead the people in the morning."

Pharaoh sat upon his judgement seat encircled by the nobles of the land.[27] They annoyed him because his soul longed for his daughter and these longed only for release from their newfound burdens. They reminded him greatly of a gaggle of geese with their incessant cackling over this and that. Most greatly excited was his chief architect who now stood before him and complained in a manner that was perilously close to sedition.

"It is impossible, Your Greatness, for me to continue on the temple without the Hebrews. We should not have let them go, for all my masons are of their people, they have a head for stone."

The king fixed him in a dismal stare. "Indeed, I sometimes think they have heads of stone for they cannot be deterred when once their minds are set. Can you not conscript others from among those who are idle or imprisoned to take their places?"

"It is impossible to make beautiful statues and great buildings without skilled men, Your Greatness! What caused us to let them go with all they own? It was madness to throw away the talent and strength they possess!" Too late the architect knew he had overstepped his station.

"Have you then lost a daughter in the first bloom of womanhood—that you can make such careless judgement of our purpose?"

"My humble apology, Your Greatness. I am celibate and forgot the sorrow of my king, for I have neither daughter nor son."

"I see the cause of your callous speech. But have a care lest you yourself carve the statues of which you speak, fettered by chains upon your ankles."

"I also have lost a daughter, My King, and my heart goes out to you as one grieving father to another." So spoke the overseer of the king's fields and vineyards. "Yet, in my grief I must still see to your fields if Egypt is to eat. There is much need to tend them carefully for they have been twice destroyed and hunger lurks nearby. Your vines must be carefully pruned and nurtured and none are more deft at that than the Hebrew women. We must turn the soil that it may be refreshed by air after the unseasonal flood. And behold, those oxen that remain after the plagues stand idle for lack of drivers."

Others called on the king in turn with problems caused by their lack of Hebrew labor. It became painfully clear to Pharaoh that a great portion of Egypt's wellbeing depended on the people of Israel—a people now joined together behind a wild-eyed rebel.

"What then would you have me do, Councilors? ...For when last you spoke you begged me to send the Hebrews from our land lest we all die by the hand of their god!"

Pharaoh's chief priest, he that served the temple of Amon, stepped forward and bowed deeply to his king.

"We were in fear of Yahweh, the Hebrew god, Great One. Yet we have come to understand that the cause of these deaths was not the Hebrew god but the deep displeasure of Amon, because we bent our wills before the Hebrew god. Amon claimed the sacrifice of our firstborn to chide us for the neglect of his various temples. That is why only Egyptians died—to return our oblations to his altar. Thus he proves his power, that we will know that Amon is our greatest god.

"Therefore, we should send word to the captains of the companies of chariots that escort the Hebrews from the land. Bid them encircle the rebels and turn them back. Kill those who raise arms against us and of certainty kill Moses and Aaron, for it is they that spawned the discontent that plagued us!"

Pharaoh regarded the priest suspiciously.

"Where was Amon when the plagues so distressed the land? I saw no evidence of him then, nor did we see succor by his hand, ...And yet, there is a thread of reason in what you say. It may go hard for Egypt if we must depend upon the labors of our own selfish, spoiled people. Very well, it will be done! Send word to the Captains of my chariots to subdue the Hebrews....[27] And make fresh offerings to honor Amon. But I say to you, Priest, that you stand on treacherous ground. For if we suffer yet another siege of evil by the god, Yahweh, it will go hard with you.

Before the first light of morning Joshua raised the Hebrew camp from its slumbers and pointed the people toward the Sea of Reeds. No food did they eat nor did they milk the goats and cows, but they walked toward the waters with haste. Near the shore Joshua and his young men divided the people according to age and strength and put strong, young women and stripling boys with the infirm and the small children. Then he sent them into the shallow waters that they might cross through while the floor of the sea was still firm. Next he sent in such carts as they had and the pack donkeys with strong men to help those that struggled with their burdens. Behind the people and the beasts of burden, sheep and goats entered the water driven by the herdsmen and followed by armed men. And at the last came fatted cattle, cows and great, angry bulls, then a few camels with packs or riders. They surged into the sea in a frenzied torrent, so that the waters splashed high, enveloping the animals in a sea of fountains.

From a high place on the far shore, Moses, Aaron and Joshua watched as the first ranks of people wearily plodded onto dry land. While above the distant shore a haze of dust arose and drifted toward the sea.

"They come," Moses said, "the chariots of Pharaoh come for us."

"Shall I go and gather the armed men and form a line to fight them as they gain this shore?" Joshua's hand was tightly gripped on the hilt of the Egyptian sword he had carried in the service of Pharaoh.

Moses smiled. "I think not, Joshua. Stand at peace and watch the mighty Egyptians."

"But when they gain this shore they will trample us like beetles beneath their carts of war. We must make ready to fight them in the water."

"Be not so ready to mix their blood and yours in the muddy water," Aaron said. "Watch now, the first chariots thunder bravely down the far shore to follow our path into the sea."

The Hebrews who had gained dry land were looking back at the coming chariots and were screaming with terror. Those still in the water increased their efforts to gain dry land. Many of the weak floundered in the shallow water until they were hoisted bodily by strong, young hands and thrust on to the shore.

"See now, how swiftly they come," Moses laughed. "Are they yet as fearsome as you thought, Joshua?"

The first chariots had plunged perhaps twenty times their length into the slimy mire left by the churning hooves of the Hebrew cattle. The wheels of chariots had sunk into the ooze and the horses lost their footing and fell, floundering in the mud. Behind them other ranks at full gallop piled into the mud. Futilely the charioteers cursed and shouted while spearmen sought to right the frantic horses. From the far bank a shout arose and grew louder until the Egyptians stood quiet and listened in dismay to the cheering of the Children of Israel. Then Moses raised his staff and pointed it toward the wilderness. The people walked forward bravely, singing praises to God and Moses, for they were free from the yoke of Pharaoh.

It took but a short while beneath the unforgiving sun of the desert for reality to settle firmly into the minds of the Israelites. As the first day passed they lost sight of the sea and thrust further into the forsaken wilds. They were a generation of people that had only known a land watered by a huge, benevolent river. Now they walked into a trackless, arid wilderness that was a forbidding, hostile place.

To Moses, the wilderness was only an obstacle to be overcome. It was one which had a purpose in the plan of his god, which had been revealed to him. So he led them, not the shortest way across the wilderness, but along the sands toward Sinai. The people travelled with good humor the first day and through the cool of night. They made do with short rests and raised a few tents for shade on the second day so that they might sleep in the unendurable heat of high sun. But by nightfall the cattle were so thirsty that they lowed for water and the herdsmen came to Moses.

"Moses, son of Amram, we have followed you from Egypt because you have passed through the wilderness before," the leader said. "Yet we have found no water except a bitter pool and our cattle thirst close to death. Have you lost your way? There are others among us that say this is not the way to Canaan and we shall die in the desert."

Moses spoke to them with authority, looking each man in the eye so that they turned their gaze away.

"The way we go is chosen by the Lord for his purpose and we will not die in the desert. Go now and drive the cattle in the cool of the night. In the morning we will come to an oasis where there is much good water and forage for the cattle. We will camp there until we are rested and the cattle are fat."[28]

The leader smiled broadly. "Blessed are you, Moses, for you are chosen of God."

Moses regarded the man solemnly. "Remember what you have said. Go and tell the elders that we march by night."

"Will we indeed find water tomorrow?" Aaron asked, as the herdsmen left.

"Have faith, Brother," Moses said, "it will be as I said. The hunter who saved me in the wilderness told me of a great oasis but a few hours walk from here. I have not told the people earlier because fear of death will increase their trust in God and in us."

"I see your purpose in doing that," Joshua said. "They will see the oasis as a miraculous intervention, in which we were guided to water by the hand of the Lord. It will strengthen your leadership for the trying times ahead."

Moses nodded. "But do not take it lightly, Joshua, for everything that has happened was by the Lord's hand. My rescue by the hunter was the work of the Lord and so was the hunter's knowledge of the oasis to which we march. We are but tools with which he works his purpose."

So it was that the people arrived at Elim where there was much sweet water. The flocks and herds grazed on good grass and the people ate of fresh dates from the palms about the water. Also, they dried much of the sweet fruit to sustain them in their travel. Then the people looked on Moses with great favor as their leader appointed by the God of Abraham, Isaac and Jacob. He was a great hero to them and among the thousands of their throng no man spoke evil of him.

When the time of rest at Elim had ended Moses led the people further yet from Canaan. During this time there was meager forage for their animals and still less water. When they came to the place called Rephidim, Moses ordered that an encampment be made. But the place was dry and there was not water for man, much less for the cattle which made a tumult because of their thirst.[29] The leaders of the tribes confronted Moses because of it. They were led by Ethan, a great blustery man, who gave Moses a look bordering on contempt.

"Have you lost your senses, Moses, that you have brought us so far into the desert that there is no water? We pitch our tents, but we must eat dry bread which we can scarcely swallow because we have little to drink and no water with which to cook a proper repast. And look at the animals, they bleat and bellow so that they deafen us."

"Ethan is right," said his brother Barnabas, "we followed you from Egypt, because we believed you knew the way to Canaan. But we should go into the sun at its rising and it is ever on our left shoulder. Do we follow a fool to our deaths in the desert?"

"We go where the Lord has commanded," Moses said. "Do you question the word of your god, who brought you out of Egypt without a sword or spear being lifted against you?"

"We question you," Ethan growled. "It is you that says the Lord has directed such and such, but I have not heard his voice, ...only yours. If the Lord is with us he will find us water. But if we follow a fool our bodies will feed the vultures and hyenas here in the wilderness!"

There was a grim muttering among the leaders who shuffled their feet and cast uneasy glances at Moses. Aaron stood beside his brother and watched nervously as Moses reached for his staff. Then Ethan stepped away from Moses, fearful that the anger in the prophet's eyes spoke of coming violence against him. But instead, Moses spoke calmly to the assembly.

"Let such men as desire water follow me. But stay twenty paces behind for Aaron and I walk in the footsteps of the Lord." Moses turned and walked toward the nearby rocky hills.

"Do you know where water flows, my brother?" Aaron whispered. "It would be well that you do, because I think Ethan looks to take the leadership for himself, with Barnabas as his priest."

Moses smiled grimly. "Ethan is like a ram's horn, he makes much noise but can do nothing by himself. There is water, for there are trees and shrubs growing in a thicket at the foot of the mountain and there are none elsewhere. I saw them from a distance, that is why I encamped."

"But what if the water is deep where only the roots of the trees can reach it?"

"Look at the rocks, Aaron. What do you see?"

"They are streaked, as rocks are where water has long run across them."

"Yes, the streaks come from the clefts where that great slab stands. Beckon to the elders—tell them to come and behold God's blessings."

The leaders advanced slowly. Their eyes were now on Moses with the same attention they had given magicians in the market squares in Egypt. Moses motioned to Ethan and Barnabas to approach.

"Come, you who would doubt the Lord. Tip this piece of stone from its seat and see the Lord's bounty."

The two men grasped the edges of the stone and heaved with all their might. Slowly the slab moved, then tipped forward from the rock face. Behind it was a damp deposit of silt.

Ethan turned to Moses with a sneer. "Is this the blessing you promise, a wall of dried mud?"

"No, Ethan, as always you look but you do not see—behold God's blessing!"

Moses thrust his staff against the caked silt and when he withdrew it, a stream of water trickled from the place he had struck.[30] Then Moses pointed his staff to the sky and spoke with a voice like thunder.

"Know you, Israel, that the Lord has placed a cistern within this rock that his people might drink and believe! Let he who would trust in The Almighty fall on his face before him and let him who would not believe prepare for the Lord's judgement!"

CHAPTER 6

The Children of Israel made their encampment beside the water that Moses had provided. Soon it became known to the people of Amalek, greatest among the tribes of the Edomites, that the Israelites encamped about the Cistern of Horeb. And the Amalekites were angered for the Israelites had many cattle that ate the scant forage and drank the water that sustained the flocks of all the Edomites. Therefore they called upon all the tribes of Edom to join them in a council.

"Our kindred of the lineage of Jacob, the Israelites, are come out of bondage in Egypt and one known as Moses leads them," spoke Sahed, prince of Amalek. "They have descended on us like a plague of locusts. Their cattle strip the land bare and they drain the waters of Horeb."

"This I have seen with my own eyes," a chieftain said. "They are great in number, perhaps thousands with all manner of outcasts joining them day by day. They will leave nothing for our people when they have gone."

"They are more a curse than kin," another said. "Did not their grandsire, Jacob, steal the inheritance that was rightly that of our grandsire Esau? Did they not take the good land of Canaan, while we were caused to drift like the sands in the wilderness? Did they not go crying to Pharaoh in Egypt during the drouth of Jacob's time? And were they not bonded to Pharaoh by their own cause?"

Another chief who had been silent spoke. "What you say is true. They come on us at Rephidim, which is far removed from their ancient land of Canaan. For what cause do they provoke us? Their travel should be by way of the Philistines which is closer to Canaan."

"It is their fear of the Philistines, for they are not skilled in warfare," the prince said. "They descend on us, because they think us weak and scattered. But in that they err. For though they may have greater numbers than we, our men are mounted on swift horses and are sure with bow and spear. We will drive them out, though many of our women will mourn for lost warriors when it is done."

"Truly spoken!" shouted the first chieftain. "They stole from us in the days of Jacob and now they will steal the scraps that Jacob left to Esau. I say we warn them to break camp and leave. If they do not heed us, it shall be war!"

Then the chieftains of all the Edomites pledged their warriors to Amalek, to rid their land of the Israelite scourge[31]. Thereupon three horsemen, exceedingly swift and fierce in battle, rode for the camp of the Israelites to give them warning of the coming of Amalek.

Joshua stood on a high place with the appointed sentry when first the fine trail of dust rose against the desert haze. He shielded his eyes against the sun and watched as the column of dust grew broader until it revealed three horsemen. As they came nearer Joshua could make out the distinct dress of desert nomads. They rode as if they were part of their mounts, flowing as one body in an easy rhythmic canter. They were fully armed, with bows and quivers of arrows strapped to their backs and a bullhide shield hanging over them. They would have swords or daggers too, thought Joshua, and he noted that each carried a light lance with horsehair streamers flying from it.

"Blow the ram's horn to summon the people," Joshua said. "These come not to pass the time of day in simple gossip."

At the sound of the horn, men emerged from tents, with swords, daggers and such weapons as they might possess in hand. Some carried axes with which they hewed wood, others carried crudely made spears, tipped with heads of flint. A few who were hunters, or had been archers in the king's service, carried bows crafted of wood and horn. All these answered now to the insistent reverberations of the ram's horn. They came to the high rock from which Moses and the sentry watched the approaching horsemen and formed in groups around their tribal chieftains.

The horsemen pulled up their mounts just beyond the range of arrows that might be launched at them and loudly hailed the mass of men gathered below the rock.

"Israelites! We are couriers of Prince Sahed of Amalek, chief among the tribes of Edom! Send forth those who speak for your nation for we would speak to you regarding matters of great concern!"

Moses looked out across the people and saw that Ethan and Barnabas conspirer with their kinsmen. He beckoned to Joshua, who stood below with the men he had gathered to him.

"Go quickly with two others, Joshua, and speak for me lest Ethan usurp the Lord's place before the people."

Joshua looked up at his leader and placed his hand on the hilt of the Egyptian sword he always carried.

"Rest easy, Ethan will not take the Lord's place or yours either. My companions and I will see to it."

"Perhaps one day the need for your blade will come to pass, Joshua, but not on this day. Go now and parley with the Edomites."

The men that Joshua chose to go into the field were strong of arm, swordsmen and archers both, men who had stood in the ranks of Pharaoh's own. For though the Edomites were distant kin he did not trust them and the riders before him carried horn bows. As he neared the couriers he saw in them a sullenness of expression that spoke of trouble.

"Hail, men of Amalek," Joshua said. "I am Joshua and I speak for our leader, the prophet Moses. Alight from your horses and let us discuss these matters of great concern."

The center horseman looked down at Joshua but made no move other than to spit in Joshua's direction.

"If your leader is indeed a prophet he already knows the matters that bring us and there is no need for us to dismount nor to discuss this thing. I am Elika of the tribe of Sahed who is prince over the peoples of Edom, whose land this is. I bring word from the council of the chiefs of Edom.

"The people of Israel trespass upon our lands without our leave. You use the land excessively because of your great numbers, so that where you have passed there is no forage for our herds and little water. Your hunters kill all the creatures of the land so we can eat nothing but the flesh of our livestock. And in this our peoples are greatly provoked. Therefore, it is the judgement of our prince and the council of chiefs that the people of Israel shall leave this land with all haste. And that in failing this within the space of three days the armies of Amalek shall descend upon you and drive you from our land!"

Elika turned his horse half about. "Sahed has spoken!"

The three riders sped away in a veil of dust leaving Joshua to mutter his protestations to his comrades.

"We will not leave the land." Moses spoke gravely. "For we must go before the Lord at Sinai. Can the men stand against the onslaught of the Edomites, Joshua?"

"We have but three days to ready ourselves and that is precious little time to turn a rabble into an army.... Yet, I have these men of valor gathered about me, My Lord. Speak to the people that they should submit themselves to the leadership of my men who are skilled in battle. Then with the help of the Lord, we may make an army of these shepherds and farmers that will drive off the Edomites."

"So I will say to the people, Joshua. And I will pray to the Lord that you will be blessed by him."

Joshua gathered about him all the men of Israel who were fit of limb and strong of spirit. He divided them according to their skill with weapons and set one of his men of valor at the head of each skill. Then he divided each skill into smaller companies and set his best men as captains of each company. Thus he had companies of archers and spear men, axe men and those with swords. And he mixed the warriors with those who had known only peace that they might learn a little of the art of battle.

Aaron also led among the people. He gathered about him the old and the young and set them upon certain tasks. They took the tent poles and set on them points of flint. He set the basket makers to making arrows of the canes which they used for great baskets. Also they slaughtered great bulls and old cattle and dried pieces of hide on frames made of desert scrubs so that the warriors might have shields against the arrows of the Edomites. Of the legbones and the jawbones of the cattle they made war clubs fixed with points of flint. In three arduous days the Israelites were more an army than a mere rabble of slaves And Joshua led them.

On the third day the sentries on the high places saw riders crossing the plains from the near hills. They brought this news to Joshua.

"They are the spies of Sahed," he said. "Tomorrow the prince will come with many horse warriors and behind them will be the foot soldiers and the pack animals. Sahed himself will lead until they reach the high bluffs to the east. He will command his army from there."

Aaron nodded in assent. "And will you command your warriors from this high place, Joshua? It is a fitting spot for you can see both hill and plain and tell your captains from which the Edomites come."

Joshua shook his head. "There is no need to see the hills because Sahed's horsemen must come by the plain and it is not of great width. I must lead the warriors myself for most are new to war and may otherwise flee in the heat of battle. For it is a hard thing to see the fearsome horsemen of the desert ride upon you with spears and swords. And it is harder still to stand and fight when those about you breathe their last amid pools of blood."

"You speak truly—I will join you in the fight," Aaron said. "For though I have no skill with weapons, my presence may instill courage in the faint of heart."

"No, Aaron, you are as a priest to the people. You do greater good with Moses on this high place. For the warriors will take it as a token that God is with them when Moses raises his arms in blessing. Take with you Hur, for he is reverenced by the people and attend Moses when the coming battle rages."

"Will you bring forth the warriors at dawn?"

"No, we will enter into our places beneath the veil of darkness when the spies of Amalek cannot see where our warriors lie. In the first light the sons of Esau will ride against us with the sun low at their backs. For if we are so blinded by the sun they will have a great advantage."

Aaron gave Joshua a worried glance. "It could go ill with us if our warriors must face swiftly charging horsemen so blinded."

"Yes, Aaron, it could. But it need not be so if we engage them with cunning."

At dawn, Moses stood on the high place and beside him Aaron and Hur. To the northeast stretched a narrow plain lying between two ranges of rocky hills. In the dim light Moses could barely distinguish a long line of human shapes stretched across the field before him. Here and there a figure walked among them adjusting the forms. He smiled and remembered the duck decoys made of reeds that net men placed on the Nile. His gaze switched to the overlooking bluffs. In the crevices of the hills shadowy figures of bowmen crouched, plain to his sight but obscured to the eyes of the Amalekites. From the heights where he stood he could barely discern the muted outlines of prone bodies far to the front of the decoys. Blanketed and covered with sand and bits of brush in the night, lancemen awaited the coming of Amalek.

To the center of the long line of prone warriors there stood one figure shielded by a solitary boulder. In his hand was a sword of iron, on his body, armor of heavy leather—Joshua awaited Amalek. He raised his sword high in tribute to the prophet.

Sahed sat astride a white stallion at the forefront of the chieftains. Far across the plain early sun was casting shadows along the rocky outcrops of the hills. Lacking a high place to view the Israelites he was forced to depend on scouts, one of which was riding swiftly toward him. The horse slid to a stop but a few paces from Sahed and the scout touched a fisted hand to his chest in deference to his prince.

"Hail, Prince Sahed."

"Hail, Eglon. What tidings do you bring?"

"The Israelites have formed a line of battle between the hills. They intend to meet us lance to lance. Their leader stands high upon the rocks."

"And bowmen...have they bowmen...and are they on the field?"

"I saw none, but they may stand well behind the lancemen and advance to meet our charge."

Sahed surveyed the plain thoughtfully. "It matters little as long as they are to our front. Near spent arrows bounce from bullhide shields upon man and horse. The archers will avail them little, but tell your horsemen to beware of the lancers. A long lance with its butt thrust in the earth will skewer either horse or rider like a fat Iamb made up for the fire."

Eglon snorted. "I have no fear of the Israelites for they have long been servants and slaves to the Egyptians. They will not stand before us, nor will their lances prick our skins before ours are firmly set between their ribs."

"Have not contempt for your adversary until he is fallen," Sahed said. "It breeds carelessness and that is the mother of defeat. The sun rises at our backs. It is time to meet our foe."

With that, Sahed raised high his lance with streamers of colored horse hair and his cavalry moved forward and behind them bowmen and foot soldiers.

Moses watched the narrow band of horsemen assemble just beyond the reach of arrows. To their front a white horse reared high then traversed the line of cavalry at full gallop before racing to a vantage point on a hill overlooking the narrow plain.

"They come," he said.

Then Moses climbed to the very brow of the high place and raised his arms in blessing as Aaron sounded a warning blast upon the ram's horn. Below, the lance men and archers grew tense in their hiding places.

In a few moments a gentle vibration crept across the plain and became steadily greater until the ground beneath Joshua's feet trembled and the air was filled with a sound like distant thunder. Beside him the youth, Anani, stood with a ram's horn clutched tightly in his hands. His eyes were wide with fear, the whites showing in stark contrast to his sun-browned skin.

"Be ready, lad!" Joshua snapped. "When I say, sound the horn and take your axe and shield. Stay by my side and you shall live. But if you flee you shall die today."

The horsemen of Amalek came on, not knowing the still distant figures were only brush filled blankets with basket lids for shields. In the lead rode Eglon and his sons Bela and Sered. They were the first to hear the trumpet of Joshua, the first to see the earth rise up before them, the first in that day's battle to feel the bite of an Israelite lance.

Eglon felt the impact on his shield a heartbeat before the lance entered his left shoulder and he was flung to the ground. Then the lance wrenched free and he was fighting to restore breathe to his body. A horse thundered by Eglon and the Israelite who had stricken him was suddenly staggering about with blood gushing from a sword wound in his throat. A few paces to his right Sered lay still, a gaping wound torn below his ribs.

Bela was crawling about on his hands and knees, blinded by the lance that struck his temple. An Israelite stood over him with a dagger poised high for the downward thrust that would extinguish Bela's life. With a bellow of anguish Eglon raised himself and drew the axe from his belt. The Israelite turned to Eglon in time to see the axe bury itself in his forehead.

Then Eglon looked down at the blood pumping in spurts from his shoulder. "Contempt breeds carelessness and carelessness is the mother of defeat," he muttered. Then he slumped to the ground as consciousness left him.

After the first rush of horse warriors had passed Joshua raised his sword high to rally his men for the return of the cavalry.

"Blow the call to assemble, Anani. Then come beside me and be anointed with the clamor and blood of close battle."

The Edomites were returning now, enraged by the ruse for which they had fallen and the heavy losses they had suffered. Joshua took a spear from a fallen horseman and stood waving it high as the desperate tones of the ram's horn shattered the air. The Israelites massed together as the cavalry struck again. This time the horsemen drove through the Israelite lance men as a sickle through wheat and many fell before them. Joshua struck a horseman's shield with his spear but it glanced away and the man rode off, stopping Only to help the fallen Bela to his horse's back. Then suddenly they were gone and Joshua was left with the dead and the cries of the wounded. He looked up at the high place and Moses stood there still. When the men that were on the field looked up to him he raised his arms in blessing. And they were greatly heartened.

Joshua walked then among the fallen, those who were of the people and lived were carried back to their tents to die or heal. Those of Edom that still lived were struck with a mace that they died quickly. For only the grievously wounded of the Edomites remained, all others were taken by the retreating horsemen.

Scarcely had the Israelites bound their wounds when the foot soldiers of Amalek came. And now when they were close, their archers loosed arrows upon Joshua and his warriors so that they fell upon the bullhide shields like the hail had fallen upon Egypt. Many were stricken but Joshua waited to send the trumpet signal to his own archers until the army of Amalek passed near the hills. Then Anani blew hard upon the ram's horn and the archers of Joshua sent their arrows behind the shields of the warriors of Amalek that they fell in great numbers.

Now the Israelite warriors with swords and axes ran forward and the fighting became that of sword to sword and spear to spear. Above the battle Moses raised his arms in blessing so that the warriors of Israel might know that the hand of God was with them. Still the Edomites were not conquered for the horsemen came again and trampled the ranks of Joshua's swordsmen so that the warriors of Edom broke through and escaped the trap of Joshua.

Thus the day was spent. Sahed renewed his attacks until his warriors and those of Joshua failed in strength and the plain was stained with blood.

Then when the sun was low the remnants of the army of Amalek drifted into the wilderness and Moses blessed the warriors of Israel. The battle of Rephidim had ended.

CHAPTER 7

Jethro, priest and chief of the clan of the Midianites, rode slowly, though the old chestnut mare, Areli, chafed at her enforced plodding. Jethro smiled at Areli's enduring spirit so like his own. *We two have aged together and well,* he thought. Beside Jethro rode his eldest grandson, Gershom, on a young stallion, a foal of the chestnut mare.

Areli had given Jethro three such foals, sired by a rugged stallion stolen from a warrior of Joktan, and Jethro was pleased with her. Zipporah had been pleased too and claimed rights to the red mare born of Areli. Now she was riding it beside Eliezer, who had somehow gained control of a large, irascible stud donkey.

The boy has a way with animals, Jethro thought, a true Midianite though somewhat too gentle for a nomad. He glanced at the boy now, he was tall for his age, reed straight and well muscled for a youth. His curly, brown hair had a reddish cast to it and his eyes were not brown but had a gray green tint to them. Jethro wondered idly where such a strange eye color had come from—he was startled from his reverie by Gershom.

"Grandfather, ...riders come!"

Jethro squinted, forcing his aging eyes to focus on what was already clear to Gershom. There were riders indeed, a handful at most, but he bellowed a warning to the herdsmen anyway. One never knew these days when innocent riders would be thieves. He halted the mare and pushed his cloak back from his dagger so the hilt stood out in open view.

"Are they of Joktan, Gershom?"

"They are not of Joktan, Grandfather, but there are men only without women or children. And their horses are caked with sweat and dust as though from a hard ride."

Jethro was glad for the eyes of the youth beside him. To his own tired eyes the riders were only blurred forms.

"Do they wear the headdress of plains people, Gershom?"

"They do, with bindings and trim of red."

Jethro relaxed somewhat, but he kept his hand near the dagger.

"They are Edomites, whose people have an agreement of peace and sharing of the land with us. We will ask them to break bread with us."

As the riders neared they became more clear to the eyes of Jethro. By the time they had drawn up their horses he had noted the red-brown stains on the clothing of two or three and the stained binding around the head of one who rode slumped over the withers of his horse. He gave orders that a canopy should be set up that the riders might rest in shade.

"Hail, men of Edom! ...I am Jethro, a chief of the Midianites. You look as if you have ridden long and hard. Would you rest with us and break bread?"

"Hail, Jethro, Chief of Midian! ...I am Elika of the tribe of Sahed of the Amalekites. You say well, for we have ridden far and are weary. And we would ask the kindness of some water, for our waterskins are long empty and we thirst, as do our horses."

Jethro unslung the waterskin from about his shoulder and handed it to the rider, then gave orders that a little water be given to the tired mounts.

"You have one among you who seems badly hurt. Bring him down from his mount and place him in the shade. My daughters will tend to his wound if you so wish."

"For that we would be most grateful," Elika said. "Bela is grievously wounded that he is blind and may yet die."

He ordered the riders to dismount and carry the wounded man to the canopy that the family of Jethro was raising. Then he clumsily dismounted and Jethro saw that he walked only by using the broken shaft of a lance for support.

"It would seem that you also have suffered injury, Elika. Would you have my women tend it?"

"It is nothing, a trifling scratch...it will mend. But if your women would see to Bela we would be greatly indebted to your kindness."

"It is done."

Jethro motioned to Zipporah, who was already bending over the prostrate form of Bela. Then he gestured for the five other riders to sit on the camel hair mat that had been spread beneath the broad canopy. When they had settled, Maai and Eshton, daughters of Jethro, brought wine and food.

"How then did you come upon your wounds, Elika? Did the bandits of Joktan waylay you?"

Elika shook his head. "It was a thief that ensnared us, but one of a different breed. One of our own relatives of ancient times now come upon us to destroy our livelihood."

Jethro looked at Elika curiously. "How so...one of your ancient kin? I know of no such tribe that wanders the wilderness."

"They have newly come to the wilderness—you know of them as the servants of the king of Egypt, for such they were. They are the Israelites and they have streamed into the wilderness in greater numbers than all the tribes of Edom and Midian joined together."

At these words Zipporah straightened herself from her ministrations to Bela.

"Who leads the Israelites, that they have been freed from Egypt?"

Elika spoke as though he had something evil in his mouth and must spit it out.

"Their leader's name is Moses. They regard him as a prophet of God and follow him as sheep follow their shepherd."

Zipporah's mouth moved as though to speak, but Jethro motioned that she should keep her silence.

"You fought with the Israelites?" asked Jethro. "With what numbers and where in the wilderness did you encounter them?'

"We gathered all of the close tribes of Edom together behind the banner of Amalek. We set upon the Israelites at Rephidim."

"And you did not prevail with such a force of valiant fighting men? Were these not servants, shepherds and laborers?"

Elika shook his head as one who has been humbled—his eyes avoided Jethro.

"They were rallied behind a young warrior called Joshua who entrapped us and fought with great valor. When the sun was low we gathered our wounded and left the field."

"And they still remain at Rephidim?"

"At the springs of Horeb—and may they be cursed forever!"

Zipporah bent over the young man, deftly cleaning his wound, but her thoughts were of Moses. Beside her was Ribai, her youngest sister. Bela lay on his back, his eyes open but unseeing.

"He is young," Ribai whispered. "He is very nice to look at."

A fleeting smile crossed Bela's face and he spoke in a weak voice.

"I am not that young, for I have passed a score and five summers. I shaved my beard so I would be nice to look at."

Ribai blushed. "I didn't know you could hear me."

"It is my sight that fails me, not my hearing...but the voice I hear is sweet...who is it that speaks so?' The words were said slowly, barely audible to the women.

"I am called Ribai, daughter of Jethro."

"Youngest daughter of Jethro and yet unmarried," Zipporah added. "Have you a wife, Bela?"

Ribai struck her sister so sharply on her back that the men turned to look—the corners of Bela's mouth lifted in a wan smile.

"There are women among our people who fancied me but I thought little of them.... But now I am blind and it is they who will despise me."

Zipporah spoke gently as she applied an ointment to the wound on Bela's temple.

"Don't despair so soon. Your sight may yet return to you. But you must rest and have your wound cared for, it reddens and fills with foulness."

"But I cannot rest, I must ride and return to the tents of Amalek."

"If you ride you will die," Zipporah said sternly. Then she rose and spoke to Elika. "Is this young man kin to you?"

Elika nodded. "He is the son of my sister."

"And do you have concern for him?"

"He is my sister's only son. Her elder son...and her husband too...died at Rephidim. It grieves me as it will grieve her."

"Then if you want this one to live on he must not ride today," Zipporah said. "His wound turns foul. If he is not cared for he will die. And your wound also must be properly dressed. Even now blood seeps to the earth where you sit."

Indeed a patch of red had gathered beneath Elika's injured leg. He moved it with effort and despite his stoicism his face betrayed his pain.

"Zipporah has a wonderous healing talent," Jethro said. "We nomads sometimes deny the dangers of our wounds over much and pay a greater price because of it. It would be a good thing to submit yourself to her care."

Elika was, like all nomads, very conservative in his sense of morality. The thought of a strange woman, particularly a handsome, still-young woman touching his body did not set well with him. And yet he sensed that the injury to his leg was somewhat more than a simple flesh wound, for the bleeding continued and the color about the wound was not good. Reluctantly he took his place beside Bela and submitted to the immodesty of allowing Zipporah to look at his uncovered leg. (This, of course, was subject to the presence of one of his men at the examination, as well as the exclusion of Ribai.)

The javelin that had found Elika's lower leg had not been intended for him at all but had been thrown by one of his own men. The fact that it was an error in aim during the heat of battle did nothing to lessen the damage it had caused. Zipporah's forehead tightened into a frown as she assessed the severity of the wound

"The leg will be forever weak," she said, "for the blade cut some of the flesh that works the foot. But that is not the greatest concern at this moment. The blood flows from your body and though it may not kill you it causes your foot to become cold and pallid. I have seen this before and the men so affected died if their leg was not taken from them."

As befitted a warrior, Elika's face was expressionless as Zipporah talked to him. But when she said the last his eyes betrayed his fear. For, to a nomad the loss of a leg threatened his manhood and to do that was to kill the man within.

"You will not take the leg," he said. "Do that which you can and the rest leave in the hands of the gods."

"I can stop the bleeding and I can dress your wound with a salve that may prevent the foulness that will otherwise come. Do you stand pain well?"

"The sons of Edom are weaned on pain. I fear it not."

"Good, then your men will not have to hold you when I sear the wound! ...Rest easy, I will have Ribai bring you some strong wine. It will dull your senses against pain."

When she had built a hot fire of charcoal and the heavy bronze spoon was heated she gave Elika a piece of bullhide to clench his teeth against. Then she beckoned to his companions and spoke quietly to them.

"Hold tightly his arms and legs. For no man can bear the pain of the searing, despite the numbness caused by the wine."

When it had been done and the screams of Elika had subsided Zipporah spread a soothing balm upon his wound. Then she wrapped it with a poultice of healing herbs and linen and covered the whole with soft goatskin. In time she brought a gruel of barley cooked with dried dates and fed Elika and Bela that they might renew their strength.

In the early morning of the second day, before the sun had driven the chill from the desert air, Zipporah arose and tended to the wounds of the two men of Edom. Though the danger was not yet gone healing had begun. She thought slow travel safe for Bela, though he had not yet regained his sight. So the warriors of Amalek left to go to their people and a bond of debt between them and the tribe of Jethro was formed.

As the Edomites rode away Jethro spoke to his daughter.

"We are but three days from the camp of the Israelites. Would you go there and seek to make amends with Moses, your husband?"

It was a thought that had been on Zipporah's mind since she heard the account of the battle at Rephidim. But her last memory of Moses had been one of fear and loathing and she was unable to erase it from her mind.

"He is not a husband to me nor a father to my sons. Why should I seek to amend that which I do not desire?"

Jethro stroked his beard as was his habit when he was in earnest thought.

"It may be that Moses has shed the shadows that lurked within his mind. He is now the leader of a people that may one day be a power in the land. It would be well that his sons stand beside their father then to support him and share in his glory."

Zipporah's eyes were troubled as she faced her father.

"I fear him, Father. I fear for my sons and myself. Moses fancies that his god speaks to him. I have neither heard nor seen his god. But Moses would do anything this god demands, even take his own son's life."

Jethro's face grew somber. "That is a bad thing. I have heard of it among the children of Ben-Ammi.... It may be that it was but a moment's madness that is long past. Yet, I love my grandsons as my sons and I would not put them in the way of harm. Perhaps we should go to visit Moses and make our judgements then."

"And if he rejects his wife and sons or is any way hostile to us?"

"Then we shall bid him goodbye and be the better for making an end of it."

Past midday of the third day of their journey through the nearly barren hills of Paran a scout sent forward by Jethro returned.

"We will reach the camp of the Israelites by early evening," he said. "They have armed men upon the high places and their numbers are great."

"Take another with you and leave your weapons that they know you come in peace. Fly my banner upon a staff that Moses may know that Jethro comes.[32] Bid him peace and tell him that his father-in-law comes and his wife and sons also."

As the sun hung at the edge of the western hills, Moses watched Jethro's caravan reach the outer bounds of his encampment. At his order herdsmen went forward to see to the watering of Jethro's animals, while others helped the family of Jethro raise their tents. Moses himself strode down the path where but a few days before the warriors of Israel had marched. To his right, just below the rocky bluffs a long row of burial mounds reminded him of the cost of the victory against Amalek.

Though Zipporah often walked beside her father she left that place to Gershom now and just behind them the boy Eliezer. She herself walked behind the men of her family though Eliezer was still a boy and Gershom, though tall, was still a beardless youth. Within her uneasiness made her heart beat as though it would leap from her breast and her stomach threatened to spew its contents upon the path. She lowered her head and kept her eyes downcast as Moses approached, not out of respect for her estranged husband but because of the uncertainty of her emotions.

"Hail, Jethro, Chief of Midian!" Moses spoke loudly with an assurance his father-in-law did not remember.

"Hail, Moses, son of Amram!" Jethro returned. "But do I speak to you wrongly? I perceive that you are the leader of a numerous people."

Moses embraced Jethro, kissing him on the sides of his bearded face.

"I am but a servant of the Lord. As a hireling shepherd is to his master's flock, so am I to the chosen of God. Do you and your family enjoy good health and prosperity?"

"We do and your sons grow strong and tall as the cedars of Canaan."

Moses turned to Gershom and Eliezer.

"In truth they have grown closer to manhood since last we were together."

He moved to embrace Gershom but the lad stepped back, his face stormy with hostility. The younger boy cowered behind Jethro, his eyes wide with apprehension.

"Here, Gershom. Is that how you greet your father who loves you?' Jethro asked.

Gershom took another step back.

"A father who seeks to kill his sons," he spat.

Jethro put his arm around Gershom's shoulder and drew him near.

"It may be best for all if you take your mother and Eliezer back to the camp. I will return to you in the night."

But Zipporah took no notice of Jethro's words for she saw the heaviness in the eyes of her husband. She went to Moses and put her arms about him and she kissed the man that had saved her from the shepherds of Joktan. Then she fled back to her tent with her sons.

Moses took Jethro by the arm and led him to his tent where he dwelled alone.

"The boy is young and does not understand the things of manhood. He does not know that a man is sometimes driven by forces he cannot control," Jethro said.

Moses nodded forlornly. "Nor did I until the day I saw the burning bush. Until then I was a free man and happy, except for a certain melancholy of spirit."

"And now, ...are you happy now, my son?"

"It is not mine to know happiness as other men know it. I have been chosen to lead this flock of slaves out of Egypt and to make of them a great people—the Lord wills it thus."

"And what of your wife and your sons? It is perhaps the time to make amends."

"I lie alone in the darkness of this empty tent and long for Zipporah by my side. I whisper her name to the night and I am greeted by the sighing of the wind. In the day I see boys at play or learning from their fathers and I am alone."

"Do you then want them to join you?"

"I want them most earnestly but I fear I have already lost them because of the people. This multitude is a hard mistress that is jealous of my own needs, of kin and home."

"Will you at least talk kindly with Zipporah? ...She is still young in spirit and misses her husband by her side. Such a thing happens in time of war or by a sickness but she should not be bereft of a husband who lives."

"I will pray to the Lord that he may show me the path which I must walk and I will speak gently with Zipporah. But I cannot tomorrow for it is the day on which I must judge. ...So it is ever with me, my spirit is not my own but belongs to the people."

The two men talked then of the exodus from Egypt and the war against the Edomites. But Jethro spoke not of the coming of Elika from whom he knew the presence of Moses at Rephidim. To honor Jethro, Moses made an offering to God with him and they called the elders so that a peace might be made between the Israelites and the people of Midian. Then Jethro returned to his tent and spoke with Zipporah.

"My eyes tell me you still have a woman's care for Moses, my daughter. Yet you fled from him before he could make proper greeting to his wife."

"I fled because I feared he would reject me in the presence of my sons. I knew not whether my husband of Midian still lived or if this man is another, a stranger to my love."

"He spoke of his love for you. ...But he is torn between his need for you and the duty his god has put upon him. He is as two men in the body of one," Jethro mused.

"Is then his god so jealous that he would take a good man from those who love him? ...Moses casts us aside like a spoiled fruit or a lump of moldy bread."

"Do not speak carelessly of Moses' god, Zipporah. He had the power to bring Pharaoh to his knees. It is not for us to judge the goodness of his works."

"Perhaps you are right father, though I wish he had found another to perform them. Will Moses speak to me tomorrow then?"

"Not yet tomorrow, for it is the day on which he judges issues of the people. But the next day he will visit with you. Perhaps then you can amend your differences and join together again."

On the day following Moses sat before the people to hear their disputes. All day the people came before him with all manner of issues. When it was done, Jethro took Moses aside from before the people and advised him that he should not be able to rule the people if he must tend to their minor bickering.

Said Jethro, "Choose wise men from among the leaders of the tribes and let them make judgements on their own people.[33] Thus you will not be overburdened, nor will you face the anger of those who are ill satisfied by the judgement put upon them. And beyond this make of your brother Aaron a high priest and make minor priests of his tribe that you shall have control of the priesthood. And make of your warrior captain, Joshua, a general over the captains of all the tribes and over all the fighting men. When you have done these things your position shall be secure that no man may put you down. Then sit you down with the judges and make laws whereby the people may be governed."

Moses looked at Jethro thoughtfully and a look of gratitude lit his features.

"Truly I am blessed by your wisdom, My Father. For I am a man who is guided by my wish to do for all and so I lack prudence. Indeed I see that a candle that is lit both during darkness and time of light will not last. But many candles each lit in its turn will cast light for many days. I will do as you counsel me before a moon has passed."

In the morning of the day following, Moses went with Zipporah to the high place from which he had blessed his warriors in the battle against Amalek.

"It is from this place that I watched Joshua defeat the warriors of the tribes of Edom," Moses said. "I bring you here that you may know the power of the Lord. For it was not likely that peaceful men, new from their bondage in Egypt, should defeat the Amalekite horse warriors. But with the help of God, who gave great cunning to Joshua, we drove them back to the desert."

Zipporah looked down across the battlefield and her eyes came to rest on the rows of new burial mounds beneath the rocky bluff.

"And for what cause did the warriors of Amalek make war against your people, that brave men lie beneath those piles of rock?'

"They sought to drive us from this wilderness because we would not leave at their dire warning."

"But was not this land that of Esau who left Canaan to Jacob, your forefather? And is it not the land which gives them sustenance? Why do you trespass without the leave of Prince Sahed or fail to resolve your difference peacefully?"

"We do not trespass for we travel at the bidding of the Lord. It is by God's command that we fought the Edomites."

Zipporah shook her head violently. "I cannot believe that your god would so trample on peaceful people. Were not the Edomites also descended from Isaac, whom you revere?"

Moses regarded his wife coldly. "We Israelites are the chosen people of God. The sons of Esau dwell in wickedness. Therefore God has directed that we make war on them."

"Wickedness? ...What is this wickedness of which you speak, Moses? ...They scratch for life upon this hard land. They herd goats and sheep and they raise up children who wander the wilderness with them. I nursed two of these evil men—one a warrior too brave to give care to his wound—the other a young man who lost his sight to one of your lances. I saw nothing evil in these men."

"You nursed my enemies in the house of your father! ...It would have been better that they had died in the desert that we will not have to fight them again. Their evil is not in your sight but in the sight of the Lord. Only we of Israel are the Lord's chosen—all others will be driven from our path!"

"All others? ...You seek to drive all others from the land you covet? ...What of your wife and Jethro who was as a father to you and also your sons? We are of the people of Midian, who was a son of Abraham, our common ancestor. He was sent into the desert by his father because he was a son of Abraham's lust! He was cast off from his house because he was born to a concubine instead of a wife! Is this the way of your mighty god, to raise up the lustful and spit upon the children of their lust?"

Moses looked at Zipporah darkly and the arteries at his temples pulsed with his anger.

"Have a care that you do not invoke the wrath of the Lord, woman! He is righteous in his anger and terrible in the execution of his judgements. He will glorify the righteous and lay waste to those who despise him."

"And what must we do to be counted among the righteous?"

"Submit yourself to the commands of the Lord."

"And how will we know these commands?"

"I will tell them to you as the Lord directs me."

"And if we do not submit, ...my sons and I?"

"Then you are children of wickedness in the eyes of the Lord and he will visit sorrows upon you."

Zipporah breathed a long sigh, then searched deep in her husband's eyes.

"And you, Moses...do you still love your wife and your sons? Do you desire your wife in your arms in the night and your sons by your side by day? Or do you think us children of wickedness, unfit for the company of a prophet?'

Moses' face softened. "Your husband longs for you, Zipporah, in the hours of the night and in the light of day. And I dream that the sons you bore me might one day lead these people as a great nation. For these things I pray."

"Then why did you not send a courier to bid us come, that we might join together?'

"Because the demand of the people is great upon me. They ever fret and whine like little children and cry unto me for every cause, so that my spirit groans with vexation. I did not know if you would abide with me in such a turmoil or curse me and return again to your father."

"Oh, my husband, you are wise and yet a fool! ...You know of the ways of your god and lead great numbers—yet you do not know your wife! But for the fear of your god I would follow you across all of the deserts of the world.... It was fear for my sons that drove me from you, not want of love. Can you not give me an assurance that I and they, will not be in peril of your god's anger if we return to you?"

Moses averted his eyes from Zipporah and gazed across the field below.

"God's name is Yahweh—all that is or will be is of him. What he will ask no man can know...or refuse."

"Then if he asked the lives of your sons, you would give them to him?"

"I must do his will."

"And if he asked you to kill all of the Edomites and the Midianites and all of the people of Canaan?"

"Then I would slay them."

Zipporah stared at her husband in astonishment.

"I cannot live with so bloody a man, nor can I make obeisance to a god who brings death to proclaim his glory—I will return to Midian with my father and my sons. But I ask of you one thing—give me a pronouncement of divorce—that I may not be looked upon as a woman who has lightly forsaken her husband."

Moses turned to Zipporah and the warmth had left his face.

"So it shall be, Zipporah. You are a wife to me no more."

So ended the marriage of Moses to Zipporah. The family of Moses returned to Midian.

CHAPTER 8

In a while the fields of Rephidim became barren and Moses led the people close to Mount Sinai. At the mount Moses made a council with the elders who worried because the cattle which were fatted at Elim were growing gaunt and there was neither cheese nor fat to put upon bread. But Moses put down their grumblings with severity and spoke to the elders that the God of Abraham, Isaac and Israel should speak to them from the mountain. Then Moses charged Joshua and his warriors to set a line about the mount that none should cross.[34] This Joshua did then he and certain others departed about the foot of the mount, for they went into the wilds on a quest of the spirit.

On the second day thereafter, the mountain shook and rumbled deep within its depths and fire rose from it with much smoke. The people's eyes rolled wide with fear and they fell on their faces. Then a sound was heard like a great trumpet and a voice of great majesty called for Moses. Then Moses and Aaron went beyond the line which the soldiers of Joshua had made about the mountain and climbed high upon it until they were gone from the sight of the people.

After three days they returned from the heights and made a great show of blood sacrifice to the Lord. Then they made promise before the people that the land of Canaan should be wrested from its inhabitants and be given to the sons of Israel. Also they spoke to the people many laws given them by the Lord, which they must obey without question.

Upon completing his admonishment of the people the prophet took Joshua and returned to the heights of the smoking mountain to commune again with God. And when they were gone the people murmured anxiously for they feared that Moses and Joshua would not return again to lead them.

And so, after the days of The Prophet's absence had lengthened to a fortnight certain among the assembly whispered rumors that Moses would not retum.[35]

Hur sat on a low stool beneath the awning of Aaron's great tent. He sipped tentatively at a bowl of herb tea that Miriam had placed in his hands.

"I long for a cup of wine or a horn of good strong beer." Hur glanced at Aaron, who sat on a camel hair mat. "Your sister tries hard to entertain a guest, but this bitter water does not set well on my stomach."

Aaron gave Hur a puckish grin. "In Egypt you complained about the roughness of the beer and the sour taste of the wine. That you no longer are disturbed by these annoyances should please you well."

Hur snorted. "A man should have something better than bitter leaves cooked in water to wash this desert dust from his throat. There is some wine left. Could we not drink just a little that we might remember its taste?"

Aaron shook his head. "It is to be kept for drink offerings to the Lord. Moses would be much angered if we drank of it."

"Since you mention your brother, it is time the great prophet shows himself. The people are hungry and that makes them restless. They want to move the cattle while they can still walk. I swear by my father's beard that you can see the light shine through the hides of some of them, they're so gaunt."

Aaron sighed. "I know, he should have been back by now. It is nearly the return of the full moon since he left. It could be that something has befallen him and Joshua."

"What could have befallen him? There are no great beasts or serpents high on the mountain, nor is it so sharply ascended that they might have fallen to their deaths."

"There are always bandits, those cast out from the tribes of Midian. Or perhaps some warriors of Amalek have bided their time to take revenge on Moses and Joshua."

Hur grimaced as he sipped a little of the bitter tea.

"Whatever the cause, Moses had best return soon if he wishes to remain as leader. The people are like children. They pout and grumble when times are hard and they will readily follow those who promise them sweets. There is talk in the camp that another would take the place of Moses and lead the people to better pastures."

"You speak of that one—the great bull with the surly temper?" Aaron pointed across the encampment to a group of men led by Ethan, who were striding purposefully toward them. "I think that he has gathered followers and from them has gained courage. He comes now to spew his anger and contempt upon us."

Hur frowned. "What shall we do if he seeks to take your brother's place?"

"We will hear him out and attempt to reason with him if he wishes to usurp the rightful station of my brother."

"And if he does not listen to reason, do we draw swords?"

Aaron smiled grimly. "If we lifted our swords with those scoundrels we would be stuck like fatted calves before we drew a drop of their blood. We are more good to Moses alive than buried beneath the sand. And in truth, I much prefer the role of wise priest to that of a dead, valiant warrior."

"So be it then, though to bend my neck to Ethan would set poorly on my stomach. But now let us smile civilly. Ethan and his cronies draw near."

The two elders raised themselves to their feet and walked forward to meet the approaching men. Aaron raised his hand in greeting as was the custom to show he held no weapon.

"Hail, men of Israel! We are honored by your presence. Would you take a bit of refreshment beneath the shade of my canopy? I can offer you little in these days of hardship, but Miriam makes an invigorating drink from herbs she gathers."

Ethan looked at Aaron and Hur sourly, his black eyes smoldering in his dour countenance.[35]

"Trouble your sister not. We come not to while away the parched hours of afternoon, but to speak of matters of urgent concern to our people."

"Then, do you speak for the people? ...It was my understanding that Hur and I stand in that office until the return of Moses, yet none have come to us for counsel."

"Perhaps it is because the people have a diminished faith in their leaders that they come to us with their complaints, Aaron. We come to ask what knowledge you have of Moses and Joshua. There are rumors that they have gone to the land of the Philistines to live a life made full by Pharaoh's gold. The people murmur that we are left to die in this accursed place."

"If indeed it is the people who murmur so, they speak idly. Moses is chosen of God—he cannot be bought by the gold of man or turned from his purpose."

The cold eyes of the priest fixed on Ethan and for a moment he felt as though he faced the angel of destruction. Then he remembered his purpose and took courage from the presence of the elders with him.

"If that is so, Aaron, might you not tell us the nature of your brother's purpose? Is it to starve our cattle and our children while he sits on the mountain dreaming dreams of coming greatness? Does he speak to God and hear answer from the mouth of the Lord? Or does he plot to craft the eternal subjugation of the people to himself?"

"It is not for me or any mortal man to know the thoughts of God or his purposes. But Moses stands in The Lord's favor. By God's bidding he led us forth from Egypt and by his bidding he will lead us to Canaan!"

Aher, an elder much respected among the tribes, came to stand beside Ethan.

"This man, Moses, came forth...from where we do not know. He stirred the people up to discontent and moved them to rebellion against the Lords of Egypt. There are those who say he stood in league with Pharaoh and his councilors to seduce Israel into departing from Egypt. It is known that Pharaoh disliked us and wished us gone."

Hur snorted. "That is the thought of fools and simpletons! Why would Pharaoh wish to drive out the very people who build his cities and till his soil? And why then did he deny us leave when the land was so besieged by plagues, each forewarned by God himself through his prophet, Moses?"

"The Egyptians have long stood in fear of the strength of Israel," Aher said. "Yet they dared not drive the people out for fear of an insurrection that may well have gone against the throne of Pharaoh. What better way to rid his nation of our numbers than to foment rebellion and so cause the people to leave of their own accord? How else would the people leave the comfort of house and hearth with full pots of meat and drink to give solace after the work of day? Nay, they otherwise might have kept the land and drove the Egyptians out from their sumptuous courts."

"There may be truth in what you say, Aher," Aaron said, "but you do not give answer to the scourge of plagues that swept the land. Why did Pharaoh so resist the warnings which I myself spoke at Moses' instruction? Why did he send us from his presence instead of hearkening to our words, that the people should go to the wilderness to worship God? I myself have witnessed these things and say to you that Moses spoke truly to the people."

"You and Moses are as two feet on the same body," Ethan snarled, "where one goes, so must the other! ...We do not know what discourse was held between Pharaoh and Moses in those days. We do not know what pretext you make to veil your real purpose for bringing us into this barren land. Of the plagues, I say that they were no more sent by God than was the drought that first brought our people to Egypt in ancient times."

Aaron regarded Ethan coolly. "If that is so, why were only the firstborn of the Egyptians killed on the night of the Passover?"

Ethan looked at Aaron blankly for his wits were as slow as his temper was quick. But Barnabas, his crafty brother, spoke subtly.

"We know indeed, wise Aaron, that a sickness came upon the houses of the Egyptians. But we do not know that those who died were only firstborn for who among us ventured among the houses of the plague? ...Then too, the children of Israel do not consort in the courts of the Egyptians.

Therefore the evil vapors that caused the Egyptian deaths did not abide with us."

Aaron stroked his beard thoughtfully. "If that were true, Barnabas, why did the king so desperately drive us from the land?"

"It is known that a daughter of Pharaoh died, whom he loved greatly. The Egyptians are a people who set great store in superstitious beliefs. It may be that Pharaoh believed that one of his many gods was angered because he allowed Israel to remain in the land of the Nile. Therefore, he made haste to expel us lest more misfortune be dealt upon him by his own gods."

"Enough, priests!" Ethan shouted. "We do not stand here to discuss the motives of Pharaoh but to devise a means to our own survival. Moses and Joshua are gone and our cattle will die and we with them if we do not leave this place. I will lead the people to a better place. In that, many of the elders stand with me." Ethan turned to the men behind him, who nodded their heads in affirmation.

Aaron's eyes met those of Hur, then returned to Ethan. "If you have already agreed to usurp the leadership of Moses why do you speak to us?"

Barnabas responded. "We have no need of you, Aaron, for we will lead the people forth without you. But wisdom would tell us that it would be far better to lead a united people then to lead a people beset by political disagreement. Therefore, we seek a resolution of our differences that we may join together as one people in peace and harmony."

"I understand that you wish us to ally ourselves with you and so betray Moses," Aaron said. "But what reward awaits us if we refuse your most reasonable proposal?"

Barnabas shook his head sadly. "That would be a most unfortunate decision. We might not be able to restrain the people if they sought to stone you."

Hur stepped forward and made as if to strike Barnabas, but Aaron held his arm and calmed him. He fixed his eyes on those of Ethan.

"What would you have us do?"

Aaron had sought out Mahar the maker of jewelry and put him to work on a task of great difficulty. Aaron and Hur had required gold of the people, not just any gold but the gold of their earnings.[35] This had been a device of the crafty Barnabas. The earnings were marks of personal identity of each of the people. And so, if they were fused together it would be a potent symbolic joining of the people into one. Thus, the melting of the earrings into a single mass was one with the joining of the tribes into a united nation.

Mahal had weighed the pile of personal adornment and had calculated the size of the figure he would make. Then Dara, who had made pottery figures of the gods for Pharaoh's court, made a clay figure of a bull with great shoulders and outstretched horns. This bull was covered with beeswax and tallow and a jacket of clay. Then Mahal baked the whole in an oven so that the clay hardened and the wax ran out through a hole in the belly of the cast. Next he poured molten gold into the still-hot cast. When the thing had cooled Mahal struck the clay off the outside of it leaving a rough figure of a bull about the size of a small camp dog.

It had taken Mahal days to smooth and engrave the figure so that every detail was perfect, from the glowering eyes to the hairs of the tail. But now it was ready, an idol that represented power and potency. The power was that of the united nation of the Israelites. The potency was the sexuality of the people that had caused their numbers to swell, to the dismay of the Egyptians. Ethan had chosen the symbol of his leadership well.

Aaron was pensive. He regretted having given in so easily to Ethan and his cronies. Yet, there had been little else he could do except to die for his ideals. That was something he admired in others but considered a bit extreme for himself. The fact was that Moses had been gone a long time and the people needed to get away from the slab of rock and sand they were camped on. So he had bent to the will of Ethan and tonight was to be the feast of obeisance to the great bull of Israel. Aaron would no longer be the chief priest and sage orator of Israel, Barnabas would likely be that. But at least his head was on his shoulders even though his honor was tarnished.

"It is time!"

Two of Ethan's men appeared at the door of Aaron's tent and beckoned him. He followed the men to a flat ledge that jutted from the abrupt rock face of the mountain like a dais above the surrounding field. The people were already milling about below, sniffing the smell of roasting beef and mutton with anticipation. Aaron noted that the jars of wine that Moses had reserved for drink offerings were set out near the roasting spits in preparation for the coming feast. Barnabas and a few elders were already at the place of honor along with trusted warriors of their tribe. Before them on an altar of stone, draped with a tapestry of rich purple cloth, stood the gleaming, golden bull of Ethan.

As Aaron ascended the rude stone steps to the dais a silence fell over the vast assembly. So quiet it was that the solitary cry of a restless infant seemed to echo from cliff to valley and back and the restless lowing of a distant ox came to his ears as clearly as the blast of the battle horn. His eyes met those of Barnabas, smoldering with hatred as his lips curled in a thin sneer of triumph. There was death in those eyes, Aaron thought. There was death for him and Hur and for Joshua and Moses also, if they ventured into the encampment after the obeisance was accomplished. But he wondered at the absence of Hur and Ethan as he turned to face the people.

As if in a preconceived answer to Aaron's question, one of Ethan's warriors strode briskly through the parting crowd followed by a bearer with the banner of Ethan raised high. Behind the flag walked Ethan and Hur, followed by two warriors. It was a show of solidarity ingeniously put together by the crafty Barnabas. Its effect was immediate. For as Ethan and Hur mounted the dais to stand beside Aaron, Ethan's tribe began to shout as with one voice, "Ethan! Ethan! Ethan!" And so they continued, ever gaining voices as those of other tribes joined in, until Ethan himself raised his hands to silence them, that he might speak.

"People of Israel! ...Moses, our leader, ascended the mountain a moon and better past. He has not returned and many fear he will not, or ill happenings may have befallen him.... Or perchance our Lord, The Living God, has taken him to his breast.... We have great concern for the wellbeing of Moses and Joshua. Yet it is a greater concern that we leave this place while we may, lest our cattle die of starvation and we with them.... I and Barnabas, with elders of the nation, have consulted together on this matter with Aaron and Hur, who stand in the stead of Moses. In their great wisdom they have agreed to leave Sinai and in the absence of Moses have chosen to embrace me as your new leader."

The people began again to chant for Ethan. But those far back of the tribe of Levi which was the family of Moses stood grimly silent. This time Ethan did not raise his hands to silence them but reveled in the adulation, turning from side to side to acknowledge the crowd. At length he turned and extending his hand to that of Aaron he drew him to his side and motioned for silence.

"I find humble pleasure in the strength of your approval for what we do today my kinsmen, my friends all. Yet I cannot be your leader without the solemn pledge of every man to our mutual cause. There is a thing which must be done to bless my investiture as your leader, lest I stand guilty of usurping the rightful office of Moses. In this act I cannot officiate, but Aaron, brother of Moses and priest of the people, shall."

Ethan placed his free hand on Aaron's shoulder, while he grasped his sword hand in a crushing grip. Then with a last look of warning Ethan stepped back and left Aaron standing alone before the people.

Aaron stood before the congregation of Israel, acutely aware of Ethan's warriors staring at him watchfully, swords slung purposefully at their sides. He glanced at Hur and saw what the people could not, the short knife held by Barnabas just below Hur's shoulder blade. The people were silent now, looking up at Aaron expectantly. The men of Levi stood frozen in rapt attention, their faces hard, their eyes angry.

"Children of Israel, people of the living God," Aaron began, "it causes me great agony of spirit to install another in the place of my brother, Moses, ...yet I will because I must! Every man among us must pledge himself to the leadership of Ethan, that we may safely travel to a fertile land without strife and division among us.... Before you stands a golden bull. It is a symbol of the strength and potency of our people. And as such it will lead us in our travel. Every man must pledge obeisance to the leadership of Ethan by kissing the golden bull in the presence of this company. Thus will we know the friends of Ethan.... But before we perform this solemn rite let us feast! Let us drink to Ethan and let us throw off our girdles and cloaks and dance to the newness of life that will be Israel's!"

There was a great roar and instantaneous tumult within the crowd as the mass of people surged toward the roasting spits and wine vessels.

Ethan took hold of Aaron's arm roughly. "We agreed to have the ritual of obeisance before the feast. We should do it before wine dulls the people's wits."

Aaron smiled benignly. "And that is to your advantage, Ethan. There are many who have little taste for what we do and will balk at kissing that idol of yours. A few drafts of wine will perhaps make them less reluctant to join your venture. And a belly filled with good meat will do much to convince the hungry of your fitness as a leader."

"He is right, Ethan, I would it were my plan to do it so." Barnabas chuckled. "It is far easier to gain the good will of a man who has supped well than one whose empty stomach gnaws at his spirit. And behold the dancers, their nakedness can hide neither sword nor dagger. Thus they must accompany us in our undertaking."

Ethan laughed. "By my beard, Aaron, if you were not the brother of Moses I would think you had a sincere interest in removing him from the leadership. But I know that your hatred for me presses so strongly against your ribs that you can scarcely gain breath and so you are a danger to me. Even so, Ethan does not betray those who have served his purposes. So you will be safe to pursue your life as you will and ponder your own betrayal of Moses, your brother."

Aaron shook his head. "To do that which you must for the welfare of the people is no betrayal. The leadership of the people wears greatly on Moses and often he wished for its weight to be lifted from his shoulders. Perhaps it is God's plan to use you to fulfill Israel's destiny."

"Perhaps it is and well put. It becomes clear why Moses used his brother's tongue to speak to Pharaoh. Your words flow smoothly as the flight of a bird. And like the flight of a bird, all trace of your words is gone once spoken."

Ethan took then a silver cup of wine brought to him by a fair young woman, a concubine of Ethan's. She was rumored to have certain occult powers which were bestowed on her by Osiris, the Egyptian god of the dead, and his wife Isis, the goddess of fertility. It was Thesa who nurtured Ethan's ambition and it was now she that brought the ritual wine that would seal the pact between Ethan and Aaron.

Ethan raised the cup to Aaron. "I drink to the wedding of our tribes by the coupling of our purposes. The people of Israel will achieve greatness thus yoked for the common good."

It was in that moment, when the destiny of a nation was so poised as to change the history of the world, that an act performed in the anger of a single man intervened. As Ethan brought the silver cup to his lips, one of his guards was struck down by an object which hurtled from above then shattered upon the rock dais. It was immediately joined by a similar object which struck near the feet of Ethan, sending shards of broken stone rattling against his sandals and onto the men nearest the dais.[36]

As though touched by the finger of God the thousands of the assemblage fell silent, their eyes fixing above the group on the stone ledge before them. Surprise tinged with the first shadow of fear froze their faces and silenced their mouths. There on the high bluff above the festivities stood Moses, his face convulsing in dark fury. Behind him and at his right side stood the angry figure of Joshua, mighty warrior and general of the Israelites.

Ethan turned his face upward. In turn, surprise, fear and the anger of frustration altered his features. Beside him Aaron stood pale and rigid as though his body had been turned to a statue of salt like the wife of Lot at the destruction of Sodom.

Moses slowly descended the precarious pathway down the rocky face until he stood at a point a little distant and above the group on the dais. Joshua followed like Moses' shadow, the hilt of his sword just inches from his hand.

"What do you perpetrate here, Ethan?" Moses shouted, his voice clear and sharp in his anger. "Do you hold assembly in place of Aaron and Hur, whom I have appointed to lead the people in my absence?"

Ethan had regained his wits and spoke belligerently. "The people do seek that I should lead them from this place for you have not, but you go to dream upon the mountain while they and their flocks wither like severed grass in the summer sun!"

"I entered the mountain mists at the bidding of our Lord, The True God, to receive his commandments! ...It was his commandments, written by his finger in stone, that I cast down upon you because of your great unfaithfulness! ...By Yahweh's ordination I lead the people and at his bidding they shall go forth from this place!"

Ethan spat upon the pieces of broken tablet at his feet.

"You say, oh, stuttering prophet, that you visit with God. Yet we know not of these visits for only you record their history! ...You say that these stones which you so angrily cast down upon us were written by the finger of God! ...Is then the finger of God so sluggish that the inscription of those tablets might require these forty days? Is it not said by the men of old that this same god created the world in six days? I think perhaps that the hands of Joshua bear callouses from this handiwork!"

"No man may scoff at the handiwork of God and live, Ethan! Have a care that the Lord does not strike you down for your disbelief! ...Is that golden bull before you of your creation—an idol to lead the children of Israel astray from The True God?"

"It is not an idol to be worshipped but a symbol of the coming greatness of Israel, which shall require the allegiance of every man. It shall go before us as we leave this place and lead us as we subdue the nations of Canaan!"

"It is an idol and an abomination unto the Lord! It must be destroyed and the people must be punished for their profanity against the Lord. For they do dance naked before you as the sons of Molech do!"

Ethan laughed. "The people dance for joy at their liberation from your hand which causes them to starve in this barren place. They will not follow you, neither will they be punished because they dance for joy. With whose hand will you punish them if they follow me?"

"The hand of God! His hand will not be stayed by those who would rebel against me! Let those men who stand for the Lord come forth and number themselves with me!"[37]

Many of the men nearest the bluff began drawing back in their reluctance to take sides in the confrontation. Some others and the tribe of Ethan stood uncertainly, glancing from Ethan to Moses.

In the back of the multitude there was a stirring as the Levites, who had thus far refrained from joining Ethan, moved forward. These men, who stood to lose the power they wielded under the leadership of Moses, now joined in a solid front before their leader and tribesman. In the confusion of the moment Aaron and Hur quietly joined the ranks of the Levites despite the scowls of many who had listened with disapproval to Aaron's acceptance of Ethan. As the ranks of Moses grew many of the celebrants simply disappeared from the plain in the hope of neutrality.

But many of the house of Ethan and of other elders who had supported him formed ranks below the dais where Ethan stood. By evening the ranks of Ethan were swelled by those who feared retribution by Moses, so that there was no clear majority of numbers supporting either man. However, many men who stood with Ethan had no strong desire to join in battle against the Levites in order to remove Moses from the leadership. Their alliance was one of self-preservation. Therefore, they would fight to defend themselves but not as an offensive tactic. So when night fell, there was a stalemated struggle for power. The deciding factor would take a very simple, yet insidious, form.

In the dull light of a campfire built from a few sticks of desert scrub banked with dried animal dung Aaron faced a truculent Moses.

"How is it that my brother betrays me!?[38] ...By what cause do you join in league with Ethan!?" Moses' voice cracked sharply, clearly.

It seemed Moses could only speak clearly when he was angry, Aaron thought. Now he directed his cool hazel eyes into those of his brother. He was painfully aware that when Moses was in the grip of one of his fits of rage not even his brother's life was safe.

"The people were hungry and restless so that they listened hopefully to the false words of Ethan. I joined with Ethan and Barnabas falsely that you might be returned to your rightful place on your return, My Brother."

Moses' eyes narrowed. "Your glib tongue works desperately to save your neck from Joshua's sword, Brother. How would you return me to my authority after Ethan usurped it?"

"I sought to make those of Ethan drunk on offering wine that the sons of Levi might defeat them. Even now they drink of it to celebrate their saving numbers."

Moses turned sharply to Hur, who stood with Aaron as a traitor. "What say you to that, Hur? Did you and Aaron conspire to defeat Ethan and Barnabas?"

Hur raised his hanging head and looked into the angry eyes of the prophet. "Your brother speaks truly. He called for feasting before the rite of obeisance for he knew the sons of Levi would not join in it. Thus might they overcome Ethan's tribe before loyalty was sworn to him."

For several moments Moses stared at Aaron as though he could peer into the mind of his brother.

"What you say might absolve your guilt of treason. But, why then did you make the idol? ...God has commanded that the people shall not make idols to worship. To do this is to stand in danger of stoning."

"I made no idol, Brother, nor did Hur. Ethan ordered that a statue might be made as a symbol of the people's strength and potency and of his leadership and this I did. I had no choice if I were to thwart his plan, for I could not speak for you with a throat that was cut from ear to ear. But Hur and I worshipped no idol nor did we bend our knees to Ethan."

Moses' anger was cooling and he could feel the unsureness of his speech returning to his tongue. He knew he needed the glibness of his brother both as a priest and as a political orator. He turned to his general.

"What think you, Joshua?"

"Your brother and Hur are not the enemy for they stand with you. But Ethan and Barnabas are like scorpions in your tent. You will never be safe from their sting."

"Well said, Joshua. A scorpion must be destroyed and his nest also, lest there come forth more of the creatures in his stead." He turned to Aaron and Hur. "You stand free of guilt in this thing. But pay heed that you never again test my justice for you may find me in a more vengeful humor. Now let us plan what course we may take in restoring the people to the fold of the Lord."

"Ethan's people drink deeply from the offering wine," Aaron said. "When their camp becomes quiet with sleep we will easily capture Ethan and Barnabas and so strike off the head of the serpent that threatens us."

"That is well," Joshua said, "but we deal with a nest of scorpions, not a serpent. Another elder of this conspiracy will rise in Ethan's place. We must take all of the elders who oppose us." He looked to Moses for approval.

"You both are right but your knives do not cut deeply enough." Moses' eyes glittered black in the firelight and his face took on a look of manic fervor that created a coldness in Aaron's soul. "We must destroy all the scorpions in their nests—bring all the elders and captains that stand with me."

Joshua and Hur went out, Joshua to the captains and Hur to the elders who stood with Moses. When they had all come and seated themselves before Moses he spoke.

"You well know the threat that stands before us. If the house of Ethan gains the leadership of Israel the tribe of Levi and all that stand with us will be cast into the dirt as the sweepings from a house. He will lead the people away from our Lord, The True God, and into the presence of strange and evil gods. Yahweh has spoken to me that this shall not be. We must put down this rebellion in a way that will give others cause to think well before they rise against their god."

There was a murmuring and a nodding of agreement among the elders and captains. Elizaphan, a cousin of Moses, spoke quietly, questioning him.

"Will we then punish the leaders of the tribes that stand with Ethan?"

Moses nodded. "We will punish them."

"And by what means? Shall we lash them for their treachery?"

"They are as scorpions, they will survive the lash and sting again."

Another elder, called Kamri, spoke. "If the lash should not suffice to curb their rebelliousness what would you have us do? Should we cut out their tongues that they cannot speak against us again?"

"Nay, that will only serve to martyr them so that those around them will plot again. There is but one way to end their treachery," Joshua said, "with the sword."

Again there was a murmur among the elders and one among them, whose name was Joram, rose angrily.

"Can we take the lives of our own so easily? I have a sister who is married into the family of Ethan. She is dear to me and I would not hurt her or cause her to grieve!"

"I speak the will of our God, the God of our forefathers! All men that do not bend to his will stand in the way of judgement! We cannot choose only those who have no ties to us!"

Joram made as though to answer with anger but instead cast down his eyes and spoke softly.

"The will of God is that we strike with the sword all of the elders who stood with Ethan?"

"The elders and many more."

Joram winced and looked again at Moses. "There is yet more blood to be shed? Who then shall the sword seek? Speak you of Ethan's mighty men, the captains of his guards?"

"They also."

The murmuring now grew loud among the captains and Elizur, a warrior known for great strength and courage, stood and fixed Moses with a fierce glare.

"We who fight to protect our tribes have no taste for killing our own for following the commands of the elders. We make no laws nor do we choose those who command us. We do nothing but obey the orders of the elders, for that a man should not be executed!"

Moses looked at the captain grimly. "As a warrior captain you can be executed for refusing to obey the justly given commands of your leader. It is then your choice, to kill or be killed. For if you would remain in favor with your god, you will obey!"

Joshua stepped forward and motioned for the captain to sit. Then he gazed at Moses and spoke.

"We grow perplexed at guessing the true extent of God's will, Great Prophet. What then is the entirety of what we must do to redeem this people?"

"Far into the night when the men of Ethan sleep deeply from the drinking of wine we will exact the vengeance of the Lord.[37] All the men of weapons that stand with us will creep into the camps of Ethan and they will strike with sword or knife every man who stands against us! ...Let not friendship or kinship, youth or agedness, wife or family stay your swords. Slay all men surely and swiftly, all but Ethan and Barnabas, you shall bring them to me!"

In the camp of Ethan, twenty-four-year-old Enaim reached to fondle his new wife, Helah. He had not drunk as much wine as many after the confrontation between Ethan and Moses and now the spirit of his loins was rising within him.

Enaim was a carpenter so the lack of forage for Israel's cattle didn't affect him directly The lack of good wood and the greater lack of customers affected him greatly. He had become a regular at the dole tent where particularly needy people could get a little food. So Ethan's promise to move to a better place appealed to him as it did to many. Today he had joined the ranks of the rebellious elder, standing directly opposite his friend Raschan, who had become one of Joshua's warriors. It bothered Enaim that they should be on opposite sides in a struggle such as this, after all they had grown up together. But Enaim wasn't thinking about that now. He had waked from a sound sleep and now the feel of Helah's warm body sent his heart pounding. She didn't respond to the gentle stroking of his hand on her thigh so he raised himself just enough to be able to bend his neck and kiss her.

Enaim was too startled to make a sound when the strong hand gripped his hair and pulled his head back. The knife tore through the muscle of his neck severing the carotid artery and jugular vein and slicing into his windpipe. The shocked exhalation of his breath caused blood to spray across his bed and sleeping wife. It took only a few moments for him to lose consciousness and a few more for his heart to stop.

Raschan stood for long moments outside the tent holding the knife. It and his hands were sticky with blood, his friend's blood. It shouldn't be like this, he thought. But then what else could he do? It was ordered by God through his prophet and he must obey. He looked at the bloody knife. Then he bent over and retched violently. Three days later Raschan threw himself on the blade with which he had killed his friend.

The woman quietly raised herself from the rough bed where she lay awake beside her snoring husband. She crept quietly to the front of the tent and opened the flap. A breath of fresh air would clear the fumes from her nostrils. Eziel had eaten and drunk too much and the air in the tent was fetid with his bodily vapors. She had no way of sensing the presence of the man about to enter her home, so when she drew back the flap she was silent in her surprise. A second later she started to scream but by then a heavy hand had clasped her mouth in a forceful grip and a dagger had entered her back just below her shoulder blade. She slipped silently to the ground and the assassin stepped over her body to plunge the dagger into the chest of her snoring husband. Ephah walked quietly and swiftly away to find his next victim. He would later become a captain in Joshua's army.

Ishmael stood outside the tent of the silversmith. He didn't know the man though he had often walked by his tent where he sat quietly working at his trade. The silversmith simply had the ill fortune of allying himself with Ethan. Now one of Joshua's captains had ordered Ishmael to kill him. He steeled himself for he was a man of peace himself, a simple merchant. He bought things from the eastern caravans and sold them, silk, furs. rugs, pottery and household goods of every sort and the knife he held with its long slim blade of Philistine iron. Ishmael put his hand on the tent flap but he thought of the man's cheery lithe wife and dimpled children, four of them. He withdrew his hand and was about to leave when he heard the low voice of the man.

"Is someone there? It is late. Who are you?"

"It is I, Ishmael the merchant. Come out, it is a matter of importance."

"What matter could be of such importance that you must wake an honest man in the middle of the night?" the man grumbled.

He emerged and his eyes opened wide as the Philistine blade passed cleanly through his heart. A few moments later his eyes were fixed sightlessly, his face frozen in an attitude of surprise.

Ishmael hurried away to his own tent. Though he had been assigned other killings, a drover of cattle and a miller of flour, he could not. Trembling, he cleaned the knife in the sand and rubbed most of the blood from his hand before rinsing it with a little water from the hanging waterskin. He laid himself down on his straw mat and waited wretchedly for the first cries of anguish to come.

Moses' features shone bronzed and hard in the firelight, much like one of the statues in Pharaoh's temple to the gods. He wore an expression of resolute confidence that was almost joyful in the knowledge of the slaughter he had ordered. But Aaron's face was troubled to the point of melancholy. He stole furtive glances at his brother, as though he wished to avoid the younger man's eyes for fear of what he might see in them. Aaron was a man of words who dealt with the ideals of human nature and the wishes of a god whom he feared but did not fully understand. He wanted no part in the mass destruction of people who had been acquaintances and neighbors, if not actually friends, but he had no choice. Once again he was caught in the meshes of the ambitious plans of another, unable to deter the thing that filled him with revulsion. Again his weakness made him the pawn of another. His silky voice would, in the days to come, clad the innate evil of this thing in a garment of righteousness.

The first piercing scream of a woman's terror brought Miriam and Elisheba out of the tent. Elisheba took hold of her husband's arm and looked into his distant eyes.

"What was that scream, Aaron? Why do you stand so silently with Moses in this forsaken hour of the night while a woman cries out beyond?"

Another wail rang into the night, closer than the last. Helah, wife of Enaim, had awakened at the sound of a woman's scream and reached in the darkness to awaken her husband. Her touch found a wet stickiness that caused her to recoil. "Enaim?" She whispered his name tentatively, then when she received no answering grunt she reached to shake him forcefully. He made no movement or sound beyond a muted sloshing as his body rocked in the congealing blood that soaked their bed. It was this that brought Helah her first comprehension of the hideous thing that had happened in the warm darkness of her tent. She recoiled in the mute, starkness of her fear. Her hand went to her breast where her sleeping garment clung to her with a chilling stickiness. It was then that Helah fled into the night screaming in uncontrolled terror.

Elisheba released her husband's arm and listened to the fading scream. It was no sooner ended then another began elsewhere in the camp. Soon the sound was not of single walls, but many, a chorus of terror and grief rising in intensity until the entire camp of Ethan seemed immersed in the hysterical cries of terrified women. Elisheba looked at Aaron's face and saw there a painful melancholy that brought a tightening to her throat and a shivering chill to her body. She turned to Moses, her face twisted with contempt.

"It is you is it not, Great Prophet? ...I prayed to hear the last of women's cries in the night when we left Egypt. But horror follows you like a hunter follows his hound. What evil have you done that these screams foul the sweet stillness of night?"

Moses spoke evenly without condescending to look at Elisheba. "What is done, is done at the command of the Lord.... I am but a tool in his hand."

"You are a tool of evil spirits that seek to destroy our people! You brought us out of the comfort of our houses to mill about in a wilderness where we are set on by fierce tribes, starvation and thirst. You desert us in the depth of our need to sit upon the mountain and dream of laws with which you might belabor our spirits. And when one comes that would deliver us from our adversity, you seek to strike him down—you are of evil, not of good, Moses."

Moses turned to Aaron. "Bridle your woman's tongue, Brother, lest the Lord take grave offense against her! The sword of Joshua will not be blinded in seeking out those who conspire against God!"

Miriam had been silent, but now she put her arms around her sister-in-law.

"Moses, brother whom I cared for amid the reeds of the Nile, why do you speak so to your own? For what cause do those women scream? Have you sent Joshua and his captains to murder among the tents of Ethan?"

Moses did not look at his sister but stared down the pathway that the men of Joshua had taken.

"The Lord has called for vengeance upon the idolaters. For they seek to lead the people from his righteous paths. Their blood must wash away their sin. Joshua does naught but exact the justice of the Lord."

"And how many must die before this justice is served?"

"As many men as stood on the side of Ethan."

"But thousands were there—for what good purpose would God, who created all, make so many widows and fatherless children?"

"It is not our place to question God's commands but to perform them. His people must be as one—though half the wives of Israel be clothed in sack cloth and ashes."

Miriam looked at her brother with disbelief.

"Yet not all of us, but only you, have heard these commands. Must we then believe such things as this that we have not witnessed?"

"The Lord has vested his power in me. You must believe and obey him, through me. Take Elisheba now and retire to your tent for Joshua returns."

In the barely perceptible glow of light before the sun breached the blackness of Sinai's horizon figures appeared dimly. Joshua led a trudging column of men, not talking as men do in their travels, but in a heavy, dispirited silence. As they came closer Aaron saw that they pressed two captives in their midst. They were bound to a rude yoke that crossed their shoulders, their arms held high against the beam by cords wrapped tightly at their wrists. Aaron immediately recognized the burly form of Ethan and guessed the other to be Barnabas.

Aaron felt a sickness of his belly as the men neared him. For the warriors were haggard and smeared with blood like priests who cut the arteries of oxen for sacrifice. There was none of the bravado of men returning from battle, for none bore wounds to justify with their own blood the blood of the men that they had so coldly killed. Rather, there was the sullen demeanor of men who have done an irreversible evil that would forever haunt their living souls. The bloodiest of them all and the only one that seemed to relish the grisly parade was Ephah, who led the column with an air of triumph.

The two men lashed to the yoke were prodded to the fore and ordered to kneel. When they angrily refused, two warriors delivered kicks at the back of their knee joints so that they fell prostrate on the ground, unable to rise because of the beam lashed to their shoulders. At Joshua's sign they were roughly lifted to a kneeling position before Moses.

"So end those who would usurp the power of the Lord, Ethan," Moses said. "His valiant warriors are courageous and mighty in enforcing his justice."

Ethan snorted contemptuously. "Your warriors are cowards who murder men in their sleep! They weep with fear at the sight of a warrior with a sword! And you are a viper that strikes with his poison without danger to himself!"

Ethan's words were halted by a sharp blow across the mouth delivered by Joshua's hand.

Moses glowered at him. "You talk foolishly—your captains are dead and you will follow them! Yet there is a chance that you might live to raise your grandsons, though your sons have died with the rest.... You and your brother will stand before the people and confess your great sin against the Lord! You will cry out to The True God for forgiveness and bend your knee to me in the presence of the people!"

"If you stand as prophet for the Lord, I want no part of him! You are a murderer and a lunatic who dreams of greatness but stands as a stuttering fool!"

Ethan then raised his head high and spat, so that the drool from his bloodied mouth found a resting place on Moses' beard, where it clung like a scarlet ornament.

The face of the prophet grew livid with rage and his eyes grew wide.

"Kill them!" he screamed. "Kill them!"

The two mighty men of Joshua brought down their great axes as one and the heads of Ethan and Barnabas fell to the ground. Because of the heaviness of his hair, Ethan's head turned face up and the eyelids parted so that for a moment his eyes stared into those of Moses before life left them.

The warriors of Joshua carried the bodies of Ethan and Barnabas beyond the borders of the camp to be left for hyenas and vultures. Their heads were impaled on battle lances and placed at the gateway of Ethan's camp. For all of that day grieving families carried their men past the grim trophies to an unhallowed burial ground. When the day was over, Moses declared his unchallenged leadership.

CHAPTER 9

It was some time before Moses had consolidated his complete control of the people. But finally he broke camp and ventured into the greater wilds of Paran. It was there that he met a young woman from the people of the other nations that followed with Israel.

It was in the morning of the day of alms, the day when Moses and Miriam and certain of the elders gave of the meager stores of Israel to those in great need. It was their custom that Miriam should consider the needs of the women who approached the doorway of the prophet. In that way no implication might be made that the prophet might be swayed to greater benevolence by a smile or a knowing glance. On this day, though, there were many women with baskets outstretched that they might receive food for their families. So it was that Moses deigned to help in the giving also for Miriam was hard pressed and sorely worn by their numbers.

Among the many that sought alms of Moses there came a young woman[39], clothed in a worn tunic of blue linen and sandals of twisted grass. She was tall, about as tall as Moses, and walked with the dignity of an Egyptian princess despite her desperate poverty. Her skin was very dark and shone with the luster of polished ebony. Her features were as his, the nose prominent, the cheekbones high, the forehead straight and broad. Her mouth was full, framing perfect, gleaming, white teeth, which gave accent to an expression that was at once sensuous and regal.

The prophet looked at her and for the first time since the departure of Zipporah he thought of a thing other than the guidance of the people. Her eyes met the intent study of his, not in a way that was ill mannered nor coquettish, nor did she avert her gaze. But she looked at him directly and the slightest hint of a smile formed around her mouth.

"What is your need, woman?" Moses asked.

"Sustenance that my body might live, My Lord," she said, "and food for my spirit."

"Sustenance for your body I can give you. But should you not seek this spiritual food at the tabernacle of women?"

"It is not that food of the spirit that I seek, My Lord, but another.... Forgive me for my boldness of speech, Lord. But I have neither husband nor family to soften the hard ache of loneliness within my spirit. So sometimes I seek a word of kindness before I think well."

Moses smiled, a thing he did seldom in these days, and he felt the string that tied his tongue tighten. For never did a woman such as this speak to the prophet in such a fashion. He forced himself to speak with a calmness he did not feel, that he should not stumble in his speech and appear a fool.

"I too have need for this food for the spirit of which you speak. For I have this great multitude of people which I must nurse, yet there is none to give me solace nor hold me to her bosom."

The woman looked at him steadily. "It is a sad thing for a man so well favored to live in solitude. You are not without years. Have you never taken a woman to wife?"

Moses grew somber. "There is much of which we might speak. But there are many who await my attendance. Would you not come in the evening hours and share my poor meal, that we might give solace to our mutual loneliness?"

"I would, My Lord."

"Go then to the larder and draw what you will and leave me until the cool of evening. But then, come to the courtyard of my tent and we will sup together."

Throughout that day the mind of the leader of Israel was drawn from the matters of the people. He saw always in his mind's eye the regal, dark face of the woman. Only once before had he seen a woman who had excited his inner yearnings in such a way, he thought. But perhaps it was the months spent without Zipporah that had multiplied his need. Yet, he saw many fair women in his walks throughout the encampment, women who smiled at him shyly but with obvious favor. Many were young women whose parents would gladly see to the betrothal of their daughter to such an illustrious man as he. Strangely, these did not stir his fancy except to return their smiles in a momentary flush of warmth, which dissipated by the time he had taken ten paces forward.

But now he was mooning over a woman to whom he had spoken but a few words. A woman whose situation was unknown to him except that she was poor and alone. She had been direct in making her feelings known. But he, like a young stripling who first looked on a fair young woman, had hidden behind the demands of his office. He could have had others dole out alms to the people. He could have taken her hand and led her to a secluded place and talked with her. Perhaps he might even have had his way with her. But in the shyness of his inner nature and the difficulty of his speech he had put her off until evening without inquiring of so much as her name. If she did not come how would he find her among the thousands of Israel? Would he send out couriers to search the outer nations and thus let it be known that the prophet lusted for a woman not of his own people?

There was another perplexity to deal with. Miriam and Elisheba would chide him if he took a woman to him. They had been vocal in their disapproval of his treatment of Zipporah and would be adamant in their refusal to accept another woman in her place. Aaron would not be a great problem except that he took his priesthood seriously and would probably balk at a women of a different nation in the prophet's bed. But his sister! Miriam might be difficult.

Moses worried throughout the day until he went to the solitude of his tent. But then his spirit brightened and he spread his dinner upon a new mat of woven reeds in honor of his expected guest. Elisheba had cooked his food that day and had looked at him strangely when he asked that certain herbs and spices be used. But she had not questioned him. In truth she was loathe to converse with the prophet casually. It had been that way since that night in Egypt when he had sent away her friend with the dying child. He sighed, tonight he had no desire to ponder on the enmity of his sister-in-law. At last, though, he went to the back of his tent and returned with a small jar of sweet wine that had escaped the depredations of Ethan's renegades. It would be a fitting pleasure to share with a woman of such beauty.

Adanah, the Ethiopian woman, walked in the cool twilight of the shadows cast by the mountain. As always, she strode straight and proudly, oblivious to the leering appraisal of the groups of young men scattered along the pathway. Though inwardly she wanted to run and hide among the broom bushes that stood in little clumps at the border of the camp.

She had been too forward in her admiration of the prophet and now she went to his tent with a feeling of apprehension. Why would one as great as he ask her to his tent? Perhaps he wanted her as the young men along the path wanted her, for a night's usage, to be cast aside with the coming of the sun. Adanah thought that if such a thing happened she would surely kill herself. For she was only tolerated, not respected, by the Hebrew women about her. For them to have call to consider her a whore, the plaything of the men of power, would make life unbearable for her. And there was the prophetess, Miriam, to consider. She had looked at Adanah in an unkind way when she spoke with Moses.

Adanah pushed her uneasy thoughts to the back of her mind as the tent of Moses came into view. The prophet stood at the door flap of his tent, his hard muscled arms crossed upon his chest, his carefully trimmed, reddish brown beard providing a perfect setting for his strong mouth and piercing eyes. He was a strong man, some said cruel, but that was not a thing that bothered her. Her life had been spent amid cruelty of every sort and she accepted it as a natural part of life. And beyond this the halting manner of his speech betrayed a certain vulnerability that made Adanah feel akin to him. For she held her own insecurity within her breast, shielded by an aloof show of confidence she often did not feel.

Moses took the arm of Adanah and led her to sit on a low stool that had been made for him by the carpenter, Enaim. He seated himself on a camel hair mat and extended a bowl of pistachio nuts to Adanah.

"I am fond of these. I gathered them once to sustain myself as I crossed the wilderness alone. Without them my bones would be bleaching in the desert now or perhaps ground to chips by hyenas."

"Pistachios have always been a great favorite with my people," Adanah said. "My father said they would gather them in great baskets to provide for the times of drouth."

"I know not of your people nor do I even know your name," Moses said. "Of what lineage do you come?"

"I am Adanah, daughter of Goram of Ethiopia. I did not know my mother for she died when I was but a child. Goram carried me to Egypt where he served in the army of Pharaoh. When I was still a girl he died in battle and I preserved myself by serving in the household of a rich Egyptian."

"Were you then indentured to him?"

"So I was for five seasons, until you came to the people. When Israel entered the wilderness, I came also."

"Would not your lot have been more prosperous if you had stayed in Egypt? My people came on command of their god, but you could have remained to live in the richness of the land."

Adanah shook her head violently. "He to whom I was indentured sought to use my body and so let others use me. I would not be indentured into whoredom, therefore I came."

Moses surveyed her. "Indeed I see the reason for his lust, for you are very comely. Indeed my own heart leaps within my ribs because of your beauty. But I have difficulty in speaking and the gentle paths of courtship are long gone from my memory. Thus I must talk to you earnestly but plainly as one who is used to authority but not the subtlety of women."

Adanah smiled. "I perceive that you are not yet so aged that you are foreign to the ways of women. For you speak gentle flattery while you deny the subtleness of your own nature. Why then is your tent empty of a woman? It would surprise me greatly if no woman had comforted you in the warmth of your bed."

Moses became grave. "Indeed I have married a woman who bore me two sons and is now gone from me."

"Why is she gone? ...Are your sons gone also?"

"She could not abide my fealty to the Lord. I must walk in his path and perform his will, which is sometimes hard to understand. All else in my life is at the Lord's sufferance. My sons abide in Midian with her and their grandsire, Jethro. It was an issue of our unlike wills."

Adanah's eyes met his. "I do not understand that a woman would leave her husband for such a cause. Our lives are bent by obligations, bondsman to master, master to king, king to nobles, nobles to freemen, freemen to slaves. And all of us stand at the mercy of the gods."

"There is but one god, Adanah, The Lord of all, The God Almighty! He rules in glory overall and crushes the gods of the nations under his heel."

"This is the god which you serve?"

"He is The True God who lives! He delivered us out of Egypt and he leads us to defeat our enemies.... But let us eat now, for I did not bring you here for purpose of religion, but because my heart longs for the company of a woman. My table is poor, as are those of my people. But there is a certain shepherd who made blood offering of a lamb. The carcass is the just rewards of the priests that they may live. But it was given to me. So we feast tonight upon it and a little sweet wine which I had saved."

He uncovered an earthen tray and the aroma of roasted lamb permeated the air about them. In a basket were loaves of wheat, their brown crusts shiny with fat. Beside it all was a large pomegranate, split to expose its ruby red capsules. There were two silver cups in which Moses now poured wine.

Adanah's eyes grew bright with excitement as she breathed deeply of the rich aromas. "I have not partaken of such food since I left the courts of Egypt. And there it was as a servant eating of the scraps after the feast had ended."

"Here you are my honored guest, so feast," Moses said. "And I feast also on this lamb for the hunger of my body and more greatly on your beauty for the hunger of my soul."

Adanah smiled as she tore a piece of flesh from the Iamb and savored its aroma.

"My Lord speaks as sweetly as the poets of Noph. It touches my ears brightly like the flutes of Joktan for I have known little but coarse enticements and curses for my refusal of them."

"To curse such a woman as you is the mark of a fool and a rogue."

"But are not your gentle words spoken for the same cause, My Lord?"

She looked at him with a smile in her eyes that bewildered his thoughts and yet gave promise to his heart.

Moses laughed softly. "In truth, never have I known a woman who spoke so deftly and so humbled me with her perception. But I say to you, Adanah, that man smells not a hot loaf from the oven but that he thinks to eat. Nor does he feel rich clothing but that he touches it to his skin. Of what then does he think when he regards beauty such as yours?"

Adanah laughed and Moses thought it was like the sound of harps in the halls of Egypt.

"If he is indeed a man of virile nature, he would think not of loaves or garments. But he would think of tasting of her lips and feeling her body against his."

"And if he were a man of power would she think his enticements to be a command, a perversion of his power?"

"Not if she looked with favor on him. She would say, 'I am yours, Lord, do with me as you will.'"

Thus it was that Moses took the woman of Ethiopia to his bed and she took him to be her husband. Not since the happy days of Midian had the tent of Moses known the scent of man and woman. Nor had his heart known the exultation that he now felt. For Adanah was a woman of strong desire and she bore the prophet to great heights of rapture.

Elisheba had returned from milking her she-goats when Adanah walked from the tent of Moses—hastily she put aside the milk and went to the tent of Miriam.

"The Ethiopian woman who talked with Moses leaves his tent even now!" she told the prophetess. "Your brother, the prophet, takes a whore to his bed—which he has said a priest should not!"

"Do you indeed know that he has bedded the woman?"

"For what other cause would she leave his tent at the sun's rising?"

"It is true. Let us go to Aaron that he may know of this matter."

The women went to Elisheba's tent, where the priest was making his morning ablutions. "Husband," Elisheba said, "Moses causes grave concern among us."

Aaron's eyes were still dim and puffy from sleep and he faced the women grumpily. "How could Moses cause concern among us when yonder camels still chew the night's cud? Has he dreamed a bad dream that he cries out from his bed?"

"It is not what he dreams in the night that is of concern," Miriam said, "but with whom he dreams!"

Aaron frowned. "What do you mean? My brother sleeps alone as he has since parting with Zipporah."

"Not last night!" Elisheba said triumphantly. "He took to his bed a whore from the encampment of the nations!"

"How so? The prophet consorts not with harlots. Have you seen her within his tent?"

"Not in, but walking away on the pathway—it was the Ethiopian woman who sought alms before us yesterday."

"If indeed he beds a women we must know the circumstance," Aaron said. "For if others have seen what Elisheba speaks of, it will not bode well for the sanctity of the law. But, my wife, speak to no one of this but let Miriam and I speak to him privately that we may know the truth."

Moses stood in the doorway of his tent as Aaron and Miriam arrived. He was free of mind and fresh of body as though he had become much younger in the night. Yet when he saw them he felt his spirits plunge, for the anger on Miriam's face and the worried furrows on Aaron's brow spoke of their knowledge of Adanah.

Aaron bowed as he faced his brother, proper and respectful as befitted a priest conversing with the chosen leader of the people.

"Are you well on this morning, my brother? We would speak with you on a matter of some importance."

"I am well and I perceive that you are also for you are abroad before your usual hour. What is this important matter that requires such urgent attention?"

"It is not so much a matter as the presence of a person that provokes our interest!" Miriam snapped. "Elisheba saw that young Ethiopian woman as she departed your tent this morning."

Moses raised his eyebrows. "Is the prophet of God required to ask leave of his sister and sister-in-law before he might consort with a woman?"

Aaron raised his hand to silence Miriam. "We neither give leave nor forbid it, my brother. But we ask whether you may abuse the law of God by taking this woman to you. For it would cast an evil rumor if others saw it and knew this woman to be unfit for the prophet of God."

"It is said that she is a whore!" Miriam burst in. "Would my brother put away his wife and sons for such a one as this? Would you profane the law of God which you yourself have spoken? For the law demands that no priest might take to him a whore."

Moses face became dark with anger. Once again his temples throbbed and his eyes became piercing black points of rage.

"Adanah is not a whore, but a virgin that I rightfully take to wife! Nor do you do well in raising up Zipporah before my face. For it was she that asked for a pronouncement of divorce, which I gave her from the compassion of my heart. Therefore, leave me be sister—I do no wrong before the eyes of God or people."

"That may well be, Brother," Aaron said gently, "yet she is of the nations who worship other gods and not of the people. Therefore it would ill befit you to take her to wife, for has not God forbidden it?"

"I take her to God as I take her to wife, Aaron. For his hand has reached out and brought her to me that I might have the joy of her presence. For the Lord knows that even his righteous servant needs sustenance for his spirit. Now go you both and leave me in peace. For this is not a thing of your concern—but of God's."

So Aaron and Miriam left Moses. But Miriam would not leave him in peace, for she had an enmity against Adanah[40]. She went then among the elders and spoke against Moses, that the elders might compel the prophet to put away the woman. But they would not but instead told Moses. When he heard about it he was more angry then before and called Joshua to bring Miriam before him.

"I know that you meddle in my affairs which do not rightly concern you, Sister. Furthermore, you speak against me among the elders that you might cause them to rise up against me....I am chosen by The Almighty God to lead the people! Therefore what you do is treason against Israel and against God. For that you should be stoned until death before the people. Do you have reason that I should not so pronounce sentence?"

Miriam stood before Moses with lowered head. Tears ran freely from her reddened eyes to streak her aging face.

"What I wished was for your good and that of the people, My Brother, My Lord. I feared that the woman would do you wrong and so I spoke foolishly that the elders might bid you to turn her away. I was wrong for I do see that you most truly love her. I beg that you might spare your sister's life for the sake of our dead mother and father who perished in the wilderness."

"Because I see that you are contrite I will spare my sister's life. Yet punishment is required that others do not seek to do as you have done. You are cast out from the camp of the people to the camp of the nations, that they may see your shame!"

So Miriam was driven from the camp of the Israelites to the fringes occupied by the lesser people of other nations. Nonetheless, after a week Moses repented and brought her back. Never again until her death did Miriam raise her voice against Moses.

CHAPTER 10

After months of encampment at Paran grazing for the cattle became ever shorter and the trek between forage and a dwindling water supply became ever greater. The encampment was foul with offal and the dung of animals and the air stank with the accumulation of garbage and the shallow latrines of the people. As in previous encampments flies bred in great numbers so that the air was abuzz with them and neither food nor drink could be left uncovered in the hours of light. The sieges of disease that plagued Israel were ever more frequent and deadly, with typhoid, cholera and virulent strains of dysentery taking a heavy toll, especially among the very young and the aged. No day passed that it was not hailed by the sound of pipes and anguished wailing as yet another Israelite found rest beneath the soil of Paran.

So it was that the elders beseeched Moses to bring them to a land where they could disperse their numbers and return to a life of normalcy. Moses, for his part, knew he had reached a point in his leadership where assurances would no longer suffice to appease the people. He was forced therefore to make bold plans and a show of action. Accordingly, he called a council of the princes of Israel and the generals under the command of Joshua.

On entered the meeting place Aaron silenced the muttering conversation of the leaders with an imperious wave of his hand.

"Your leader, God's Prophet Moses, has called you that he might advise you of God's plan for Israel. It has long been promised by the Lord that we, his chosen people, shall enter into the land of Canaan and claim it for our own. That time has come!"

There was an intense hum of excitement among the convocation. Then one of great wisdom, an aged patriarch, rose to speak.

"If indeed it is time to enter Canaan it is a welcome thing. For we die in this wilderness of plague and hardship and our spirits sicken with the monotony of our existence. But how shall we go into Canaan? Will we walk along the high roads under the face of Sahed, trusting that in his benevolence he will accept us?"

A grim chuckle sifted through the ranks of the elders but Aaron was undisturbed.

"Indeed Sahed's remembrance of us may embrace a certain bitterness in his spirit. But we shall not ask leave of him, neither shall we enter without circumspection. But we shall enter with strength and with a full knowledge of the land and the peoples therein."

"And have you secreted among this company some of Pharaoh's diviners, that you will know the secrets of Canaan?"

"The secrets of Canaan and the lands about will be ours by surer means than a diviner's dreams, Revered Elder. Let our Lord Joshua, General of the Armies of Israel, speak now. And mark his words well for they are commanded by your Lord, The God Almighty."

Joshua raised himself from his place and stepped to the front of the assembly. Whether to stress the serious nature of the meeting or simply to accentuate his dominion as high commander, he was dressed in battle garb. A coat of bronze scales covered his tunic and was pulled tight at his waist by a bronze-buckled belt that carried an Egyptian sword. His feet were shod with heavy sandals and greaves of bronze covered his feet and lower legs. His unsmiling mouth drew a hard line between his short, raven-black beard and his mustache. Joshua's penetrating stare fixed on the old man who spoke so boldly.

"It is said that age imparts wisdom to those who listen and learn. Nonetheless, a fool remains a fool always, for he prattles on witlessly and remains a stranger to wisdom."

He looked out at the generals who ringed the assembly of elders, battle-hardened men who had long chafed at their inaction.

"It is indeed time for the people to enter Canaan and take it for our own. But we shall not spill the blood of our valiant men foolishly. We will learn the ways and the might of the people of Canaan and those about. Then we shall take the land that Yahweh has promised us."

A low hum proceeded from the elders rising in intensity until it was not unlike the sound of flying locusts. Then the old patriarch rose with some difficulty and spoke again.

"Forgive this old fool for prattling on, Most Revered General. But the promise of Canaan is ancient, more so than even I. For it was spoken to me as a child and to my father and to his father before him. So it is a wonderous thing that raises the spirit of ones such as I, that in my lifetime I might yet see the fulfillment of the promise."

"Well, we know that Moses speaks to Yahweh, ...and perchance his conversation is attended by the Lord. But will Yahweh now go before us, that we shall strive against the armies of the nations and conquer their multitudes? Have you yourself heard the Lord's command and promise that we should be assured of Moses' prophesy? For well we know that the prophet dreams many dreams...but lo, in these many months little has come forth from them to comfort the people."

The statement enlivened the hum of conversation, which was accented by many grim faces and nodding heads, especially among the older members of the assembly.

Joshua raised his hands for silence. "I am not privy to the mouth of Yahweh for he speaks through the heart of Moses and the mouth of Aaron. But my arm is the Lord's and my sword is also his. Therefore I say, what God has spoken to Moses is a command unto me and unto Israel! He that would rebel is not of God and shall be driven out from his people! But the fire of Yahweh shall lead us and he that follows shall enjoy the richness of Canaan!"

"So will we do then, noble Joshua," the elder continued. "My sons and their sons will follow your banner to the promised land. And so would I if the years had not weakened my stride and the might of my arm.... But tell us how we shall gain intimate knowledge of Canaan that we fall not into the jaws of the wolves that reside there."

"We will send a party of spies into Canaan and all the lands about.[41] They shall march beneath the curtain of night and they will abide in the crags, amid the rocks and beneath the bushes by day. They will study the fertility of the lands and the strength of the cities and their battlements along with the people and their armies. Then when they know all, they will return and we will make our plans to conquer Canaan."

The old man looked at Joshua thoughtfully. "It is a good plan indeed, albeit a perilous one. Have you then decided who shall go on this adventure and who shall lead them into the very maw of the lion?"

"Twelve men, the bravest and most cunning, one of each of the twelve tribes will go. I shall go with them, as befits the trust that my lord Moses has placed upon me."

So it was that Joshua and Caleb trekked together from the land of Paran and above the eastern shore of the Dead Sea, along its rough and barren hillsides. Caleb was younger by several years than Joshua, but he was of a gentle strength that appealed to Joshua and the two had become fast friends. Thus far there had been little to excite their desire for the acquisition of this land because they had not yet entered into the fertile plateau to the east. The rocky hillsides were no better than Paran and the two warriors had seen neither fish nor fowl in the shallows of the sea. This caused no wonder, since the water was so heavy with salt that a man could float on it like a dried reed. Neither fish nor the food of fish could exist in it, nor the creatures that preyed upon them.

"Is this in truth the land which the Lord has promised us?" Caleb asked. "I see no cattle that might provide milk, neither do I see fragrant blooms, that bees might make honey. The sea below is as dead of life as the tomb of Abraham."

"Be of faith, friend, the Lord's promises are as sure as the rising of the sun," Joshua said. "Never have jewels been found on caravan trails, but far from those who would seek them. We will go further, to the river that pours its water into this sea from the north, the River Jordan."

"You think then that we will come yet on this land of goodness? Here even the streams that run down from the heights taste of salt. Is there not a better land to the east that is fit for fields and flocks?"

Joshua nodded his assent. "The others go there and to the west. We will spy out the great jewels, the River Jordan and the sea of Chinereth. In those waters, it is said, lies the wealth of Canaan."

They travelled on until the hills fell away to lower land at the north of the Dead Sea. Gradually, like the emergence of a great snake, the shining serpentine of the River Jordan came into view. Its banks were green with dense thickets of willows and poplar trees which gave way to a barren mid-land of salt laden sediment. In turn this relatively level area merged into a rocky hillside, barren but for an occasional scrubby broom tree or acacia. The hillside rose to a plateau of arid soil that bore enough vegetation to sustain a flock of wild sheep that scattered in fear at their approach. Miles further, the rocky hillside gave way to a greener landscape on which domestic sheep, goats and cattle grazed. Along the riverbanks small patches of tilled ground were poked here and there in the unruly growth of trees and shrubs. On the hillside the parallel green lines of a vineyard cast shadows on the clean earth.

Joshua smiled at Caleb. "The promises of the Lord are as true as the rising of the sun."

"In truth," Caleb nodded, "here I see the source of milk and honey, as well as beef and mutton and the bread to eat with it."

"And melons, onions, garlic and cucumbers such as we ate in Egypt, from the fields by the river. And wine from the vines on the hillside to drink with stout cheese from the goats that those boys herd." Joshua grinned.

"They do not know that soon their charges will be ours and they will be our slaves if they live at all."

Caleb stole an anxious glance at his commander. "It is true, though I had not pondered upon it. To build our place we must destroy theirs, a pity since they do well here. I see women working in the vineyard. They look to be young and well favored, much as my daughters."

Joshua turned to Caleb and spoke soberly. "Think not upon it, for of such thoughts are born the phantoms of failure. We will take this land for our people as the Lord commands. It is true that blood will flow. The life force of our mighty men will mingle with that of the warriors of Amalek and the Canaanites. It will be washed from the earth by the tears of widows and orphans. But in the end the children of Israel will inhabit the land. It is the prophesy given to Moses and from him to us."

Caleb nodded dubiously. "I know it must be done for our people sicken and starve. They have been too long among the plagues of the wilderness. And yet, it is not in my heart to destroy a people who do me no harm."

"Would you rather that the bones of your daughters bleach in the desert sun?" Joshua snapped angrily. "For they will in time and you will never ride their children upon your knee or know their comfort when you are old. I would also that we could enter this land in peace. But it cannot be so—we will take our swords and kill or be killed—for if we do not we are already dead."

Joshua's words had found their intended mark for Caleb seemed to fill with a new resolve.

"I will not be the cause of my daughters' deaths by some wretched desert plague," he said. "Let us go back now and make plans to subdue this land."

Joshua smiled. "I am heartened to see your spirit so renewed, my friend. But we will rest now beside the river. When our legs are fresh we will explore yet a while along this river to the fertile Sea of Chinnereth and you will see richness beyond your dreams. Then, when your heart beats fast with desire for this land, we will return to the people."

The elders of Israel watched expectantly as the twelve warriors stooped to splash water on their faces from the trough at the sheepfold.[4] Behind the elders were massed the princes and warriors of Israel. Behind these stood the women and children. In the rear milled a diverse crowd, the people of the unhallowed nations. Word of the spies' return had come by the lips of a young camel driver hours before. And now the elders sat in the scant shade of the scrubby acacia trees that were sprinkled about the meeting ground. Apart from them, to the front of the assembly, Moses and Aaron stood talking quietly.

In the forefront of the weary band walked Joshua and Caleb. Each paced with a walking staff, polished smooth by their dusty, hard-callused hands. Behind them were Shammua, lean and tall and with him Nahbi, the silent one. Then came brawny Ammiel and following him, mighty Geuel. These two labored beneath a staff that bent between them with the weight of an immense cluster of grapes. Shaphat, short and muscular, carried a basket of pomegranates upon his shoulder. Abreast of him Igal, the red-bearded, bore a like basket filled with plump figs. Behind these Gaddiel and Sethur, the hardened graybeards, marched laboriously. To the rear walked Patti and Gaddi, younger warriors who smiled happily at the admiring giggles of young women along the way.

As Joshua halted before Moses he bowed slightly then raised his hand in salute. "Hail, My Lord, do we find you well?"

"You do, Joshua—all went well? I see twelve warriors return and none seem ill used. It would also appear that you bear trophies from Canaan."

"Yes, we bring fruits of the land. Tell our Lord Moses of that which you bear, Ammiel."

Ammiel grinned. "We saw these grapes on our northward journey in the lands of Amalek. On our return we plucked this cluster as we passed in the night. There was a vineyard so great that wine from its grapes would fill all the jars of Israel."

At that there was an excited chatter of amazement from those nearest that ran back and across the entire multitude.

Geuel shifted the staff on his shoulder and nodded vigorously. "Never have I seen such vines, nor fruit in such great clusters. It is truly a land of milk and honey."

"And of wine of exceeding sweetness. Let My Lords taste of Canaan's bounty." Joshua broke off two small clusters of grapes and gave them to Moses and Aaron.

Moses placed a grape in his mouth and savored it.

"The promise of God is true.... And what do our kinsmen Shaphat and Igal bear upon their shoulders?"

Shaphat stepped forward and placed his basket before Moses.

"Pomegranates as big as a babe's head, Lord."

He cut through one with his dagger and handed the halves filled with bright red berries to Moses and Aaron.

"In Egypt none were as sweet as these, nor were the seeds so thickly covered with flesh. But come Igal, bring your burden, for Lord Moses would taste of the treasures which you bear."

Igal knelt behind his basket and proffered a brown, softly ripe fig to the prophet, who broke it open and tasted its sweet flesh. Then he ate the fruit slowly, savoring its rich flavor. Those nearest him watched expectantly, like camp dogs waiting for a morsel that the master might discard. It had been long since most of them had tasted a fruit of any kind except the occasional dried dates and figs purchased at a dear price from wandering traders. At length Moses motioned to the men who carried the fruit to distribute it among the assembly of elders and captains.

"Share these few fruits among you," Moses said to the elders, "that you may taste the purpose of conquering Canaan. And that you may know that the Lord's promises through me, his servant, are not in vain." Then he turned again to Joshua and Caleb.

"Are the other fruits of the land as abundant as these?"

"The land beyond the Sea of Salt, along the River Jordan until the Sea of Chinnereth, is exceedingly rich," Caleb said. "There are cattle of every sort and fields and vineyards beyond our dreams. It is truly a land flowing with milk and honey."

"It is that and a land planted upon the caravan routes from the east to Egypt in the west," Joshua agreed. "I say that we should gather our warriors and take the inheritance God has promised us."

There was a hum of excitement among the elders. Some nodded their heads in obvious agreement, other faces were grave with consternation. But all became silent when Shammua stepped forward and spoke.

"Let us not be hasty, Lord Joshua. There are grave considerations that we must make before we invade those lands.... Near to us now lies Amalek, like a lion ready to pounce."

"We have met the warriors of Amalek before and bested them."

"But that was in the desert at Sinai," Shammua retorted. "Here the lion is in his lair and it is we that must attack him—that is quite a different matter."

The greybeards, Gaddiel and Sethur, now emerged from the ranks.

"Prince Sahed is not alone here, Valiant General," Sethur said to Joshua. "But he is joined by the Amorites, the Hittites and the Jebusites behind him and all the way across the Jordan. If we vanquish the Amalekites we must then join all the others in battle before Canaan is ours!"

"And to the north, along the Great Sea dwell the Philistines," Gaddiel interjected. "Their land sets upon the trade routes from the countries to the north. They will not sit quietly while we overcome Amalek."

What had been a hum of excitement among the elders now became a deeper rumble. The faces that had been grave with consternation now were nodding angrily. Those that had nodded with jubilant anticipation of an easy conquest now listened somberly.

Caleb drew his sword and raised it high until the assembly fell silent.

"Are the warriors of Israel suddenly afraid?" he roared. "Do we suddenly quake like little children at the thought of battle? We will not fight all of these at once, but we will conquer one at a time, growing stronger with each battle. I saw nothing that we could not easily overcome—say as Joshua, let us attack Amalek now!"

But Sethur pointed a sinewy hand at Caleb and spoke with an ominous tone.

"You and Lord Joshua chose the route to the east of the Salt Sea where there are few cities and no garrisons defended by archers and stone throwers. If we went there we would surely conquer it. But you speak of overcoming all the peoples from the Salt Sea to the Great Sea. I myself have seen great walled cities wherein the inhabitants would defy our poor army with laughter."

"It is true!" Shaphat now joined in the protest to Caleb and Joshua. "Besides the walled cities they have companies of soldiers, regulars skilled in the arts of battle. They are all big men, twice my size and armed with Philistine swords of iron such as the one you carry! Many wear armor and helmets and carry bucklers of bronze to ward off our swords. Our weapons are poor except for those we took from the dead soldiers of Amalek at Sinai. To come against them would be for many of our men to die without gain or glory!"

Now his companion Igal, not to be outdone, spoke loudly.

"We walked through the land of the children of Anak.[44] And when I saw their men I felt like a grasshopper, that they might step on me to destroy me! For they are huge people, giants who carry spears greater than tent poles. We hid until they had gone, then we ran away a great distance, for we were filled with fear for our lives!"

Again the rumble of voices began among the elders and spread like a wave over the entire multitude. But now it would not be quelled though both Joshua and Caleb raised their arms for silence. Then a figure, old and frail, rose among the elders. It was the patriarch who had spoken against Joshua before the spies were sent to Canaan.[45]

"It is only I, the witless fool, who speaks to you, Brave General and Wise Prophet," the old man began. "For in the slowness of my wit I do not yet understand how our poor company of homeless wanderers can overcome the might of the wealthy nations before us.... Forgive my doubts, Lord Moses, for though I speak daily to the Lord, he has not spoken to me as he does to you. Therefore I ask what purpose the Lord had in bringing us forth from the comfort of our homes in Egypt to this desolation? ...For there old men such as I can while away the little time before our deaths attended by our grandchildren. While here, it seems to me, we men will all die by the swords of Amalek or the Philistines. Then our children will be sold into slavery and our women into whoredom, to grieve forever over the great evil that has befallen them.... Would it not be better to return to Egypt and beg Pharaoh for his indulgence, that we might live in his land and serve him as before?"

"You say in truth that the Lord God Almighty does not speak to you," Moses said, "but to me, his chosen servant. And I say to you that as long as I live I will not lead the people back to Egypt!"

The Patriarch bowed in mock reverence, then continued. "It is not my choice, Revered Leader, ...but if it were, I would think on electing a captain who would do the wishes of the people rather than command them to ruination!"

At that the voices of the people erupted in a deafening uproar.[45] The thousands of common people now clamored that they should make a captain and return to Egypt. In their frenzy, they began throwing cattle dung at the group of leaders. At that Moses and Aaron fled to the tabernacle for refuge, but Joshua and Caleb remained. They took their swords and threw them down on the ground and tore the collars of their rank from about their necks and stepped them into the dust. Then the people quieted, for they wondered that Joshua would throw down his sword, because he was lord general over all the tribes of Israel. When all the people were silent and their eyes were fixed on him Joshua turned about and spoke.

"Hear me, brave people of Israel! We know the richness of the land before us. We also know the strength of its peoples and of ours. Many cry out that we will die if we enter Canaan and that we should return to Egypt. ...I stand here now, not as a general but as one of you—the truth is that we cannot return to Egypt! Look about you! Are not many sick and frail? The old man who so boldly speaks of his grandchildren and Egypt knows he will not live across the wilderness a second time. Look at your cattle and your flocks! They are hungry and thin so that their bones will bleach on the desert if you go! Think on it! ...Will you die as men making a place for your families? Or will you die babbling with a parched tongue on the sands of the desert, to be carrion for the vultures that circle overhead even now?"

The people looked up at the wheeling dark shapes that were ever a part of the wilderness sky. Caleb saw looks of indecision where but a moment ago the frantic desire to flee had ruled. He raised his arms and spoke.

"Joshua speaks the truth—we cannot return—therefore we must fight! We will win because we have the blessing of the Lord! Go then to your tents and pray and rest for tomorrow we will gather before our general to train for war."

The people began leaving the field, but a group led by Shammua gathered together and pressed toward Joshua and Caleb, shouting, "They will destroy us all—stone them, stone them!"

Then Joshua made a sign to the captain of his guards and they drew their swords and drove the rebels from the field

"Will they fight, or will they try to make it across the desert?" Moses asked.

"They will fight only if they see the hand of God pointing the way," Aaron replied. "They are like little children who are brave only while clutching their father's hand."

"Yes," Joshua agreed, "they have lost their faith in us. Their weariness and sickness rules them. We could have united them if Shammua and the others hadn't spoken against us."

Moses made no answer. He was staring across the emptiness of the wilderness. his face devoid of expression, his eyes shining black and distant. Suddenly he turned to Aaron.

"They have sinned against the Lord and they must receive the judgement for their sin—God has spoken to me."

"How shall they receive judgement? We cannot command them, lest we create greater dissention in the camp."

"Let their Lord Joshua call them to us this evening, that we might talk to them privately for the reconciliation of the people. I will show them that they err in their judgement."

When the light of day slipped into the shadows of night, the ten warriors led by Shammua arrived before the tent of Moses. Their disagreement with Moses was now a visible belligerence and they swaggered forward to halt without greeting at the edge of the firelight. Moses, Aaron, Joshua and Caleb had already gathered and sat near the fire savoring cups of wine.

"Hail, brothers!" Aaron said, echoed by his peers. "Come join with us in a cup of wine."

"Why bid your adversaries to come and drink with you?" Shammua asked. "We will not change what we have seen and said by virtue of a warmed stomach."

"No, you will not, for you are strong men and true," Joshua said. "Yet we have a common need that we must address, thus we offer you drink from our jar as honorable men and just."

"Indeed? And what is this common need we have? I see nothing common in choosing to invade a land or refusing so to do."

"Our common need is the good of the people," Moses said. "That you cannot dispute—nor would you seek to do so. Come, sit and have a cup with us on that pledge."

"On that pledge we will drink, Lord Moses." Shammua and the others came forward and settled heavily beside the fire. "But we will not drink on one that commits to the deaths of my companions and their sons for purposes futilely undertaken."

"Then we have common purpose for our endeavors, Shammua," Aaron said. "Take each man a horn from which to drink for we have too few cups for such a company."

Shammua took one of the carved bullock horns from the basket that Aaron offered, then passed the basket to his companions. "If that is a common purpose, Lord Priest, do you say that you will not seek to enter Canaan?"

"What Aaron means, Shammua, is that we will not embark on a futile endeavor," Moses said. "Adanah, pray pour for our guests."

The dark Adanah emerged from the tent and poured wine for each of the men seated before Moses.

Shammua looked at Moses suspiciously. "I know that you are a prophet who lives by the command of God. But how do I know that the Lord has not commanded that some substance other than wine be put in that jar?"

Moses smiled benignly, then he stood up and held his cup out to Adanah.

"Pour, that our guests be reassured of our good will, for the wine is sweet and bears no evil."

Shammua emptied his horn in one draught and held it out to Adanah to be filled again. "It is often said that prophets and priests enjoy the best wine. But before now I would have disputed it. Does this come from Egypt?"

"From Canaan, I bought it from a caravan going to Edom. It may be from the very vineyard which you so craftily sampled. But drink it more slowly, my friend, that you savor its vapors."

Shammua laughed and drained the horn. "My father said, 'When you drink your own wine, drink slowly, when you drink another man's, drink much.'"

Adanah returned from serving the others and bent to fill his horn again and the scent of her touched Shammua.

"I do not know if it is your wine or the perfume of your wife that intoxicates me, for my head rests lightly upon my shoulders, Lord Moses. Let us talk of our common concerns before drowsiness overtakes me."

But indeed, Shammua never spoke further, for his eyes took on a glazed look and he slumped to the ground. In a few moments all of his company lay inert before the tent of Moses.

Adanah was staring at the men with horror.

"They are dead!" she exclaimed. Her voice was tremulous, verging on the edge of uncontrollable terror. "But how...was it the wine?"

Moses put his arm around his wife and comforted her.

"No, we all drank of the wine. They sinned against the Lord in their disbelief—it was a plague by the hand of God."[46]

Quietly Joshua gathered up the horns from which the men had drunk and cast them into the fire. Then he ordered that the bodies be carried out so that their kin might claim them. And it became known throughout the camp that those who had spoken against the invasion of Canaan had died by a plague of God.

When all but Joshua had gone, Aaron sat beside Moses. He stirred the embers of the fire idly, turning the remnants of burned horn over in the coals. Then he threw the smoking remnant of acacia stick into the fire and looked at Moses.

"You have won again, little brother—your adversaries are dead and will trouble you no more. But what have we gained by it?"

Moses stared into the fire. "We did what we did at God's will. It is not for us to profit by it, but to obey."

"And the people...will they profit by it? Or do they only make more graves to weep over?"

"They will gain a new land for their children...but not now."

Joshua looked at Moses sharply. "What do you mean, 'not now'? ...Ten good men lie dead because we sought to enter Canaan and they opposed us. And you say 'not now'! Would you that I tell their widows not to grieve because their deaths were a mistake?"

"They died because they spread dissention among the people—it was God's will. But we cannot invade Canaan because the people are not as one. They have faltered in obedience and now they are like scattered sheep. God is not with them, Joshua!"

Aaron nodded. "The armies of Canaan will slaughter them as the wolves slaughter sheep. Sahed waits to wreak vengeance on Israel for his losses at Rephidim. We must wait until we are again united."

"We have spied out the land and it is not so strong that it cannot be taken," Joshua fumed. "Caleb and I have exhorted the people that they gather in the morning to make a swift strike on Amalek. We cannot retrace our steps now that Shammua and the others lie dead because they opposed us. Let us at least send a small force to test Sahed's strength."

Moses turned to Joshua angrily. "If you will not abide by my counsel send a force toward the Sea of Salt where there may be fewer of his warriors. But The Ark of the Covenant will not go with them—nor will I bless them! They have doubted his prophesies, therefore the Lord is not with them and the tribes of Amalek will destroy them."

"Would it not be your duty that you give them your blessing as a prophet of God?" Aaron asked. "Will you so abandon those you lead?"

"The strength of my blessing is not come from me, but from The Lord. Therefore such blessing as I give without his grace is as an empty husk from which the kernel has fallen. Send those whom you may well afford, Joshua, for they will fall by the sword. But you yourself will not go—I forbid it!"

CHAPTER 11

Elizur, The Bull of Rueben, studied the ranks of his army, tightening his legs as the stallion from Joktan pranced beneath him.[47] They were not nearly enough in number or in experience. Two thousand foot soldiers, most bearing crudely fashioned bronze spears and axes. Not more than two hundred wielded iron-bladed swords taken from Amalek's dead at Rephidim. Most were well shielded. The large bullhide frames gave better protections against arrows than the small bronze bucklers the Edomites carried, though they were cumbersome in sword fights. He wished he had more archers and of greater skill. Sahed had ranks of bowmen, both on foot and mounted on tough Joktan ponies.

Elizur shuddered when he thought of the thundering waves of Edomite horses that had overrun them at Rephidim. He had been one of the lancers then, standing with sharpened tent poles against the onslaught of mounted lancers. He wished he had a thousand mounted lancers, but he had scarcely three score men on horses and many of those were captains of foot soldiers. He would have more horses but they were bought dearly and the prophet disliked the fact that they ate much forage he considered better used for the flocks and herds of Israel.

Elizur looked up at the grim face of his commander, who stood on a rock outcrop high above him. Moses the prophet was not with Joshua, nor were the musicians who were to blow the silver trumpets that sent Israel into battle. Were they to go against Amalek without God's blessing? Elizur's back chilled with uneasiness at the thought. He had served his god and his general well. He had been among those who carried children and aged from the Sea of Reeds. He fought shoulder to shoulder with Joshua at Rephidim and he had drunk wine with his general on many evenings. But now, Joshua looked away from him. He had seemed uneasy when he told Elizur he had been named to lead this raid on Amalek. It was as if Joshua had not made the decision.

Who had named him if Joshua had not? Was it Moses the prophet, the right hand of God? Only he would have a power greater than Joshua. But what ill will could he have against Elizur? His mind went back through the months past and came to rest on the slaughter of the dissidents at Mount Sinai. He had spoken against the prophet then—the chill in his back deepened and crawled up the nape of his neck.

It was Moses then—he who had ordered the killing of Ethan and Barnabas and the thousands who stood with them! And there was that thing last night. Shammua and the others had spoken against Moses and Joshua and now they were dead! A plague by God's hand, Caleb had said. But Caleb stood next to Joshua and Aaron now. He would speak as the mouth of Moses, like Hur had once, before he fell from favor with the making of the golden bull. So did I fall from favor, though I had no part in the making of the bull, Elizur thought, and now? Was this a mission from which he would not return?

Elizur had wondered why the greater of Israel's mighty men had stayed back and the lesser warriors were sent. Actually, most of these men were untested or misfits. Except for a few young and brave novices, these were men that would be better placed at gathering dung for the campfires or slaughtering sheep. But it was done, the lots had been cast and now he must enter the maw of the lion. A sound came upon the air then, not the sound of Moses' silver trumpets, but the sound of the ram's horn of Rephidim. The army moved forward as one, to greet the warriors of Amalek.

Elika, first captain of the cavalry of Amalek, rested his horse at the brow of the highest of the hills that ringed the desert plain south of Beersheba. His leg pained him as it always did when he rode. Now he crossed it over the withers of his horse and rubbed the scarred muscle gently. He turned to the young warrior beside him and spoke.

"They come, Bela, the dogs of Israel come. Their dust rises from the south, half a day's journey by foot, less if they ride."

Bela nodded. "They ride upon their own two legs, they have no horses save those they stole from us."

Bela turned his face and smiled at his uncle. A leather patch covered the eye that Zipporah had tended. For though his sight had returned he now saw two where one should stand, without the patch.

"We will return these afflictions they bestowed upon us, twice over and more."

"Aye, but have a care that your desire for revenge does not lead you to take foolish risks and so lose all. The Israelites fought with courage and determination at Rephidim and we paid dearly for our contempt for them."

"That is true, Uncle. But they were cornered and had nowhere to run. Even a jackal will fight savagely when he is backed into a hole. Here they must attack us where we stand upon the hilltops. But they will not—they are too few."

Elika stared out at the plain below. "They are but two thousand, three at most, the scouts said. We have a thousand archers to rain arrows down from the heights, nearly that many mounted lancemen and five thousand warriors on foot. All of these are poised to pounce on the Israelites as they climb the hills. Joshua is not such a fool that he would attack us with this handful. Perhaps he sends his main force elsewhere and seeks to strike us from our flanks."

"Perhaps," Bela said, "but perhaps he misjudges our strength or thinks we are not wary of his presence. If so he will fall to us as the drinking antelope falls to the leopard.... It matters not, for they will not come today. If they come, it will be in the morning before first light that they will seek to ascend these hills."

Elika spat disdainfully. "Then they will die at the dawn of a new day!"

Daniel could all but smell the fear of those about him. He was seventeen and a goatherd until the slaughter at Sinai. It was then that he first stood in the ranks of the prophet. It was then that he had fallen under the spell of Joshua and had sought to learn the art of war. He trained with a group of young men much like himself, recruited from among the herdsmen and tradesmen of Israel. They took up their weapons and trained in the arts of war when their daily labors were finished, because Israel was too poor to pay its soldiers.

The recruits spent hours with sword and lance under the watchful eye of veterans who had first learned the military arts as conscripts in the army of Pharaoh. As young men then and ever after, the recruits were proud of their skills in mock battle. They took with pained good nature the swift and true blows delivered to them by the wooden swords of the cadre. For it was not a matter of death they faced on those evenings, but only the mocking insults of the veterans and the soreness of bruised limbs.

Daniel had developed into a passable swordsmen over the weeks of practice. He was good enough to best most of his fellow recruits, but not good enough to catch all of the blows of the veterans on shield or sword. Once he had been engaged in a double match against Joshua and Elizur. His ally against the two mighty men had been a tall but slight young man who was as unassured of nature as he was fragile of build. The two veterans had separated the novice swordsmen within seconds and the tall one fell with a less than gentle blow to the neck by Elizur. Daniel was left to deal with Joshua and was doing a fairly adequate job of defending himself when a heavy blow to his back drove him to the ground. Sprawled in the dust, he looked up indignantly at the grinning face of Elizur, who stood with his thick neck arched like that of a herd bull.

The warrior extended his hand and pulled Daniel to his feet, then led him a distance from the others.

"I smote you thus to teach you that you may live through war, for you bear promise to be a valiant soldier," he said. "There is no honor in the heat of battle—only life and death. When you fight alone your back is open to sword or spear and you will die by the hand of one when you fight another. Therefore, when you go to war choose a comrade who is as strong and brave as yourself, that you might stand back to back if you are enveloped by your adversaries. Thus you may win the battle and live to fight another day."

Elizur motioned with his thumb to Daniel's partner. "He will be among the dead on the first day of battle and likely he who stands with him also—a pity, since he plays well upon both lyre and flute and sings as the angels of The Almighty. He should grace the tabernacle of the Lord with his music, rather than futilely pouring his blood upon the ground."

Now, standing in the shallow darkness that comes before dawn, Daniel glanced at the stalwart young man whom he had chosen as his comrade to share the fury of the coming day. He was staring at the fading stars as they melted in the first slight glow on the eastern horizon. Near to them were the dark shapes of bouldered bluffs. These hid the soldiers of Elizur from the prying eyes atop the high hills a few hundred yards away.

"Are you afraid, Joha?" Daniel asked, feeling ashamed for his own fear.

Joha's eyes met Daniel's for a long moment before he answered.

"Elizur says that only fools are not afraid when death awaits. Yes, fear bites into me like a venomous serpent. It makes my belly cold and sick within me."

"I too feel so...I hope that the first swordsman I meet is a novice such as I—I fear I will not stand long against a mighty man."

"Don't think so, Daniel. Elizur says that you must build a fierce anger and hatred for the enemy within yourself before a battle. It fuels the forces within that make the blood run hot and the sword arm strong. Doubt weakens both a man's arm and his courage."

"I know, ...he says also that fear is not cowardice. A brave man fears but meets danger with courage despite his fear. I think I will fight despite my fear, but there is a thing that fills me with foreboding, Joha."

Joha nodded grimly. “I feel it also, the prophet did not give us God’s blessing before we left. At Rephidim he raised his arms in blessing as long as the battle raged and so we triumphed. Nor is Joshua with us to give courage to his warriors—it is an evil omen, I think.”

Daniel shrugged. “Perhaps, ...but it may mean nothing. Joshua’s place is with the greater body of the people, that’s why Elizur leads us. And in that we do not fare poorly, for he is indeed as brave and strong as the bull for which he is named. The prophet may have had concerns which he could not defer, or perhaps he is ill. But look! The banner bearers take their place before the ranks. We go to war now, Joha!”

“Yes, soon our strength and courage will be tested. But mind you, Daniel, stay close that we may guard each other. I wish not to die by a spear between my shoulder blades.... See now! The banners beckon us forward! May the blessings of the Lord protect us this day!”

No strident ram’s horn summoned them, no hoarse shouts of grizzled captains drove them forward. In the dark stillness before the forces of nature greet the day a whispered command from Elizur drifted down the ranks of Israel. Shadows glided forward on soft-shod feet, their shields and swords held tightly close to muffle metallic sounds. Each man walked quietly, intent on the dark summit before them. Each man whose thoughts of family were held close with apprehension in the night, now left these thoughts behind in the singleness of fear. All knew that within the hour many of their company would lie dead or dying on the limestone slopes before them.

Thus they ascended the first gradual slopes toward the inevitable fierce greeting of Amalek. Then the incline became steeper and suddenly stealth was lost by the clattering of a small rock dislodged from its ancient resting place by a hasty foot. Elizur cursed silently and covered himself as best he could with his bullhide shield. The arrows will come soon from above, he thought. Yes, arrows and perhaps rocks thrown from the heights. Many of these men will fall before they reach the summit and they will be the lucky ones. They will not have to face the javelins and swords of the Edomites.

He smiled grimly—at least Sahed couldn't use his cavalry on this rock strewn hill.

Elika, Captain of Amalek, stood behind a hastily constructed rampart of rock slabs, peering into the dim shadows below. Behind him the skyline was lightening as an awakening sun crept toward the eastern horizon. Off to his right Bela stood, yellow tunic setting him apart from the rest. To his left was Badar, the Syrian mercenary, in bronze chain mail. All along the rampart were massed a solid line of archers. There were three ranks in all, the first kneeling, the second standing, the third as a reserve. Behind them swordsmen were poised to throw piles of stones down on the climbing attackers. Before the light was strong enough to betray the Israelite warriors whom Elika knew were near, he heard the solitary clatter of a dislodged stone bounding down the hill's barren face. He turned to the trumpeter at his side and held up two fingers—the stones would fly before the arrows.

Daniel and Joha were perhaps fifty paces from the rampart when the first stones came. A large one struck Daniel's shield with a force that thrust him back against the unyielding surface of a rock outcrop. Another spun Joha around and sent him crashing headlong over a low ledge he had just ascended. Suddenly the predawn stillness came alive with the clatter of falling stones and the cries of strickened men. Then a voice roared above all. With a bellow like that of a great bull, Elizur urged his army forward.

"Up, warriors of Israel!" Elizur shouted. "To the crest before light guides their arrows! Raise your swords against the spawn of the evil one, for the glory of Yahweh!"

Up and down the ranks of climbing men their arose an uproar of masculine shouts melded together with the insistent trumpeting of the ram's horn. Joha emerged from his accidental sanctuary below the ledge, rock cuts on his face dripping splotches of scarlet across his blue tunic. The fear was gone from his countenance. Instead, his eyes glittered black with hating anger in the dim light. He drew his sword and with a shout to Daniel he began a running climb toward the ramparts captained by Bela the Edomite.

Elika clearly heard the roar of Elizur and smiled that he might think the shadows would protect his men at such close range. And now the first sun rays of dawn broke through the gloom to reveal the figures of warriors scrabbling up the treacherous slope. Elika raised his forefinger to the trumpeter. In an instant bows were bent and the air was alive with the whizzing sound of feathered shafts. An instant more and many of the approaching forms had slumped to the ground and there were new cries from below. Before there were roars of pain and curses at the crushing impact of the stones. But now there were piercing screams as arrows found their marks and bit deep into living flesh. These cries did not end abruptly, but continued with dreadful anguish until death silenced them.

Daniel and Joha were untouched, though their tough bull-hide shields were pricked with arrows, much like needles in a tailor's cushion. Some of the warriors who had started the climb with them were no longer there. The two young men did not notice—their complete awareness was on the mass of soldiers before them. There were rank upon rank in what appeared to be an impenetrable wall of death spewing bows, backed by spears and swords. But then there suddenly appeared chinks in the wall as a lethal flight of arrows found their prey. Daniel glanced to the rear. Well below him stood the motley archers of Israel. They were loosing high, arching, volleys of death over the ascending warriors against the ranks of Amalek.

With the first rain of barbed shafts upon the Edomites the warriors of Israel took heart and charged forward with lusty yells. The archers of Amalek, thus confronted with death from both sky and earth, broke ranks and fell back behind the protection of shielded warriors with swords and spears. in but a few moments the Israelites were swarming over the ramparts at the brow of the hill.

The battle became a melee of hacking swords and thrusting spears. But most deadly were the iron, Philistine axes that chopped through shield and bone with fearful efficiency. It was one of these that was Daniel's first blood trial. Wielded by a great Hittite with a bronze helmet and a fiercely evil countenance, the axe drove through Daniel's shield with ease. But when the Hittite would have drawn back the axe for another blow it was caught securely in the tough hide of Daniel's shield. And so, he was now attached to the warrior he sought to kill. Roaring with fury, the Hittite pulled so mightily that the shield was wrenched from Daniel's arm. It was a happenstance of battle, a fluke with which fate decides who will live and who will die. Thus freed from encumbrance, Daniel thrust his poor bronze blade forward beneath the wildly flailing ax and shield with all his might—it was the first time he felt the resistance of a leather battle tunic give way to the lesser opposition of flesh and inward parts. With a momentary feeling of sickness he jerked back the blade as the Hittite dropped to his knees, the look of battle rage changing to one of astonishment. Then as his blood gushed from the mortal wound in his heart, his grip on the axe loosed and he fell sightless and still.

"Take it!" A voice behind Daniel roused him from the shock of his first killing and he saw Joha, bloodied sword pointing to the Hittite's ax. "Take it or I will! It is a better weapon than your poor sword."

Obediently Daniel returned his sword to its scabbard and picked up the axe. The long haft felt alien to his hand but it would be better than a short bronze sword, especially since his shield was broken and torn beyond usefulness. Another Hittite confronted him—young like him—just emerged from boyhood. He holds a sword as though it is a cattle prod, Daniel thought. His eyes were wide with terror as he looked wildly at Daniel over the top of his bronze shield. Then, as though he had resolved to die, he raised his sword high and charged. Daniel swung the axe and saw it impact on the shield, then glance to strike the warrior's sword arm. The boy-warrior's sword flew, making coppery spins in the air and he clutched the terrible wound in his arm. His eyes fixed on the axe in Daniel's hands as though it was a cobra about to strike. Then his newly gained manhood left him. His face contorted and he broke into tears—Daniel turned from him and met a new adversary.

Joha's blood had indeed grown hot, for he bested all that confronted him. Three times he met swordsmen and stood unflinching before their attack. Each time his adversary fell by his blade or retreated with a grave wound. Together, he and Daniel fought into the very midst of the Edomites. There in the tumult of battle they drew apart. It was then that Joha came upon a warrior who wore the helmet of a captain and a bronze breastplate over a tunic of mustard yellow, now spattered and streaked with crimson stains.

The warrior wore a patch over one eye, but there was a coldness in the other that struck to the heart of Joha. He grasped an iron sword that was bloodied to the very hilt and beyond to the fist that clenched it. In an instant he engaged Joha, striking at the youth with the calculating blows of a veteran swordsman. He never allowed his bronze shield to be drawn away from his body, nor did he ever slow the unrelenting blows he delivered to Joha's sword and shield. Twice he delivered blows that would have severed the throat of Joha, except for the agile retreat of the young warrior. Then in an instant the contest was resolved. Joha's bronze blade parted from its haft and fell uselessly to the ground.

Joha's eyes widened momentarily—the boy yet within him froze in terror. The captain's iron sword flashed high in the early sun to deliver yet another blow. Then Joha did a thing that was so senseless as to be judged insane, were it not done in the heat of battle. He dropped his shield to his side and stood before the captain, stolidly awaiting the bite of his sword. The captain's arm stopped in its downward arc and the cold menace of his face softened into a grim smile.

"By the swords of Amalek, I have found a stripling who knows how to die!" he said. "Where is Joshua? ...Speak, young warrior!"

The sword hung over Joha's head, menacing, with strands of its earlier victims' hair stuck to the bloodied iron and to the fist that held it.

"He is not here, Elizur commands us," Joha said in a weak voice. He looked into the cold eye of the captain and thought of bringing up his shield. But he knew that the sword would be swifter and so he remained motionless.

"Then tell Joshua that Bela who fought at Rephidim spared your life. And I give you now what his lancers gave me!" The sword dropped swiftly, but not with its full force. Joha felt the tip of its cold blade strike his temple, then he fell senseless.

Daniel swung the Philistine axe until it and he, stank of blood and gory bits of flesh and inward parts. He hacked at his opponents with the mindless fury of battle rage. Oblivious to his own blood oozing from a wound on his thigh, he drove forward with insane screams and flailing axe until the Hittites fled from him in terror. Then only did he stop, as the battle swept past him over the crest of the hill. Joha was no longer with him, only the dead and the dying lay in twisted, moaning heaps about him.

Daniel was about to follow the battle, when there was a movement among the fallen where the fighting had been the most furious. A blotch of blue moved, then sat upright. Daniel ran, leaping over men writhing and crying out in agony, until he reached Joha's side. His friend was sitting numbly, blood running from a hideous wound that bared his cheekbone and his skull at the temple. He did not turn as Daniel crouched beside him, but stared dumbly ahead.

"It is Daniel, Joha!" Daniel took Joha's bloody face in his hands and looked into his staring eyes. "Do you hear, Joha! It is Daniel!"

Joha spoke feebly. "I hear, though I see but a shadow. An Edomite captain struck me, Daniel. He could have killed me, but he spared my life."

Daniel took a sash from a dead man and began binding the wound on Joha's head.

"I will get you down to safety, Joha. Can you walk?"

"I think so, if you guide me. Where are the others?"

"They drive the forces of Amalek before them. The battle rages on."

"Then we may win?"

"That only Yahweh knows. Come, I will lead you to safety. Then I must return to Elizur. He will have need of me."

At the bottom of the hill there was a cleft in the limestone, the mouth of which was screened by a thick growth of stinging nettles. Daniel and Joha had discovered it when they were searching for night shelter. But they had rejected it then because of the obnoxious weeds. Now Daniel led Joha into the darkness of the narrow crevice, disregarding the burning of the weeds on his skin. He looked about in the dim light. Joha would be safe here, safer by far than he would be on the battlefield.

"I go now, friend," Daniel said. "If I do not return, wait a day. Then return to Joshua if you are able. I leave you my waterskin and a few bits of bread, for if I do not return l will not have need of them."

"Daniel."

"Yes?"

"The protection of Yahweh be with you."

After Daniel left, the silence and darkness of the crevice closed on Joha like a tomb. An intense throbbing pain was pervading his cheek and temple, where before there had only been a dull numbness. He squinted his eyes close in an attempt to see. It is better, he thought. It seemed that the shadows he saw before were taking on solidity and the light at the entrance of the crevice was brighter. Exhausted by battle, pain and loss of blood he closed his eyes and fell into a nightmare-filled sleep.

Joha came awake to a hand roughly shaking him. His startled exclamation was silenced by another hand on his mouth. His eyes opened and he saw dimly the face of Daniel.

"Speak quietly," Daniel whispered. "They are all about."

"Who?"

"The armies of Amalek, the Edomites, Hittites, Canaanites, all of them—Israel is vanquished —those of Israel that live flee for their lives."

Joha sat up with a start. "How so? Did not our army drive them back upon the hill?"

"It was a trap. They drew us back until they could attack us with their mounted warriors. They were swift and terrible. Israel died by the hundreds within the hour."

"Will not our army rally about Elizur?"

Daniel shook his head grimly. "Elizur is dead—killed by a mounted lancer—by now his head adorns a spear at the command tent of Sahed."

"What must we do? Are there none we might join with?"

Daniel shook his head again. "The warriors of Amalek hunt those who remain. We are not yet safe.... We will wait. If we are not discovered we will make our escape in the night.... Your sight returns?"

Joha nodded. "I see but dimly and from one eye. The other is swollen shut. The cut from the captain's sword pains me greatly."

"It should be sewn shut and covered with a poultice of crushed rue leaves, but we have nothing. Pray that we reach the camp quickly."

The two huddled in the crevice for all of the day. Several times they heard the sound of horses' hooves or voices and once an unseen warrior stopped to urinate at the nettle clump outside. But when dark came there was no sound. They arose stiffly from their rocky bed and crept into the night.

A bright moon and stars illuminated the field on which they walked. Everywhere were strewn shields, packs, water flasks and other weighty accoutrements of war. It was obvious that those who had passed were fleeing for their lives. They had shed all but their weapons and sometimes those, to gain swiftness over their pursuers. For many that had been in vain. Their bodies displayed wounds in their backs that they had received from mounted lancers. Some had turned at the last moment and so received the blessing of Amalek (as it was later called) in their chest or belly. The latter, if they were fortunate, received a second thrust to the breast or a swift sword blow across their neck or head. Others were left to die slowly in great agony as the contents of their ruptured bowels slowly corrupted their bodies. These finally succumbed from loss of blood or their hearts stopped because of the contagion inflicted upon it.

Thus the two young warriors made their way through the dismal remains of the ill-fortuned battle. The one was armed only with a sword, having long past thrown away the encumbrance of the heavy Philistine axe. The other, weak from loss of blood and half blind, carried only a nearly empty water skin. They walked quietly, listening ever vigilantly for a sound that would betray to them the presence of a lurking enemy.

"Hark!" Daniel whispered. "A sound comes from beyond that clump of desert weed. Like that of music, softly sweet, yet faint."

"I hear no sound made by man," Joha said. "It is but the whistling of a night bird singing to its mate."

"No, there it is again. A sound like that made by a shepherd's pipe."

"But what shepherd would be out here in this newly bloodied land?" Joha asked. "Neither sheep nor goats would abide the overwhelming stench of death upon the air."

"Even so, a sound like music floats through the stillness of this night. Let us seek out the source of it."

"Dare we? It might be a soldier of Amalek."

"No soldier alone would dare to make such a noise and so betray his presence," Daniel said. "And more than one in the night would make comradely talk or snores of sleep. Let me look."

Daniel crept silently to the clump of weeds, peered over it and beckoned to Joha. Then he knelt beside the form lying in the sandy niche sheltered by the weeds. His throat tightened with recognition—it was the slight young man who had been his training partner in the sword match against Joshua and Elizur. He held a shepherd's pipe in his hands which now rested on his chest. His face was creased with pain and drops of perspiration formed on his forehead despite the chill of the night. His mouth twisted in a half-smile of recognition as he looked at Daniel.

"Daniel?" he whispered.

"It is Daniel...and Joha."

"Yes...Joha, the warrior who took my place." The voice was weak but faintly bitter.

"We were cast together, it was not by intent."

"Yes, I know...it was Elizur who scoffed at my skill. But I bested him, Daniel...he died on the hill. I lived 'til here."

"Is it that bad? I will look."

"There is nothing to be done.... It was a lance, an Edomite horseman, ...he laughed when he pulled it out of my belly.... Then he left me like this—I'm so thirsty."

The voice was pained and hopeless. Daniel could think of nothing to say. He motioned to Joha for the water skin and dribbled a few drops on the young man's lips. It seemed to ease his misery, for he spoke again.

"Daniel?"

"Yes?"

"There is a girl, ...her name is Sara, ...her father is Ishmael the potter.... Will you find her and give her my pipes?"

"Yes, I will find her."

"Tell her...tell her...I died thinking of her love."

The young man exhaled his breath and his eyes fixed on something beautiful, for he smiled and was gone. Daniel and Joha scraped a shallow grave in the sand and buried the young musician. Then they covered his grave with rocks against the visit of jackals. Daniel carefully wrapped the pipes in his sash and the two warriors returned to the encampment of the Israelites.

CHAPTER 12

After the defeat of Elizur's army, the tribes of Israel drifted further into the hard land of Paran. Moses became ever more withdrawn and severe with the people. He spoke continually to God and translated the Lord's words to him into ever more restrictive and harsh laws. The fierce, unbending, religious fervor of the man became his primary nature and he meted out swift and merciless justice to those who transgressed his laws.

Gunai awoke to the light of dawn with a pounding headache. He had drunk too freely of the cheap wine offered by the innkeeper Ebaliah and now he suffered from its sickness. He was a driver of donkeys and led caravans for the merchants of Israel into the nations about. His life was hard and had grown harder since the foolish invasion of Canaan. He had always driven caravans there in danger of both robbery and death, but now the danger was far graver. Though he was from Joktan and not an Israelite he was considered one by the Edomites, because he camped among them. His only passport among the nations of Canaan was the heavy tribute he now paid them. Because of the tribute, this trip had brought him only a small pouch of silver pieces to show for the months away from his wife and family. And so he had drunk too much to ease his frustration.

"Mari, rise up and get me some porridge," Gunai said to his wife. "And put a little goat's milk on it to ease my stomach."

Mari turned over on her sleeping mat and looked at him peevishly.

"There is no porridge because I had no fuel with which to cook. The fields around the camp are stripped bare and the children have the stomach sickness so I could not leave them."

Gunai scratched for the lice in his unkempt hair and regarded his wife sourly.

"Is there then some bread? ...My belly cries for food."

"There is nothing but a little cheese and some raw meal. I told you I had no fuel with which to cook or bake. I expected your return much earlier."

Gunai grunted. "Umh, a donkey grew lame, so I and Shalum had to carry his load upon our own backs. A man was not made to carry such burdens swiftly."

"Even so, I could not get wood or even dried cow dung for fuel, so I could not cook for you."

"Never mind," Gunai sighed. "I will take a donkey into the wilderness and gather some wood."

Mari sat up fearfully. "Have you forgotten that it is the Hebrew's Sabbath? Moses has decreed that no work must be done on this day—on pain of death."

Gunai snorted. "That maniac does nothing but cause us trouble with our neighbors and dream up laws to make a poor man's life harder. I am not a Hebrew. Why should I abide by his foolish laws?"

"Because he will kill you if you don't!" Mari's eyes were wide with fright. "He has spies everywhere and the swords of Joshua and the Levites to do his bidding."

"You worry too much. Our camp is not even close to the Levites. They would not dirty their sandals walking among the tents of the nations on the Sabbath. I will go out by way of the Ethiopians and into the brush beyond. Moses will never know, nor would he care about such a one as I."

"Don't go—death is too great a price to pay for a full belly, Gunai! If you care not for yourself, consider me and the children. We have need of you!"

"Umh, and the children will soon awaken. They will have need of their porridge, just as I. Would you have me listen all day to crying children for lack of a little firewood?"

"My impatience with crying children is less than my fear of the Levites, Gunai. I beg you, husband, stay!"

Gunai waved off her fearfulness impatiently and went to get a donkey.

Six men of Levi strolled quietly in the wilderness.[48] It was their custom on the Sabbath to breathe the cool morning air and meditate on the precepts which Moses and Aaron had given them. They were elders of strong religious belief, dedicated to the teachings of the prophet and the ancient histories of the patriarchs. These things together utterly ruled the minds and spirits of these men. They could no more deviate from their religious morals than a donkey could shed its ears. So it was that when they saw Gunai packing sticks upon the back of his donkey they stopped walking in horror.

Then one known as Gad called out to Gunai. "What do you there, foolish fellow?"

Gunai turned to face them. "If I am foolish because I bring fuel that my wife might cook for me, then so I am. For I am just returned from a long journey and I have not that which I might eat."

Gad answered, "You are foolish because you violate God's law. It was given to us through the prophet Moses that none shall labor upon the Sabbath."

"I have heard of that law, but I am of the people of Joktan not of Israel. Therefore I need not abide by the law of Moses."

Another said, "The law is given that all who live in the encampment of Israel shall abide by it. Those who do not shall be punished by the judgement of Moses. We are Levites and it is within our office to enforce the law."

A shadow of apprehension settled on Gunai's features. "If you are determined that I do wrong I will cease my gathering and depart to my family. For I would not willfully violate the just laws of the prophet."

Yet another spoke. "No, it shall not be so! For by your own admission you knew of the law and yet you held it in contempt." He turned to the other

Levites. "This man scoffs at our law and disobeys it flagrantly. Therefore he must be judged and punished."

The others nodded their heads solemnly.

"You have disobeyed the law," Gad said. "And for that you must be judged. Come with us now to Moses."

Fear overcame Gunai for he knew the dreadful judgement that was cast upon those Israelites that violated the Sabbath. In his fear he tried to run. But the Levites laid hands on him and took him back to the encampment of the Israelites.

Moses and Aaron sat before the congregation, teaching them the law, when Gunai was brought before them.

"What manner of thing is this that you bring a man before us on the Sabbath?" Aaron asked.

"We knew not what to do," Gad said, "for this fellow was gathering wood on the Sabbath. Therefore we brought him that Lord Moses might judge what to do with him."

Moses observed Gunai, who was on his knees trembling violently.

"You are not of Israel, are you?"

"No, Lord, I am a poor donkey driver of Joktan."

"Did you know of the law of the Sabbath?"

"I heard there was such a law, but I knew not that it was for the people of the nations. There was no food prepared and we hungered. So I went out to gather sticks for a fire that my family might eat."

"The law is of Yahweh, The Almighty God. Well it is known to be for all that live in the encampments of Israel. You place yourself in grave peril by violating it."

"I beg forgiveness before God, My Lord. I did not violate the law out of contempt, but for the need of my family."

Moses gazed at Gunai impassively. "I must ponder your transgression. You have made a sacrilege against the law of Yahweh—your judgement is with him." He turned to Joshua. "Take him from me and hold him. I must pray over this."

Moses and Aaron consulted together within the tent where the priests rested themselves. With them were Joshua and Caleb and a few of the high elders.

"What will you do with the donkey driver?" Joshua asked. "It seems to me he is but a fool who should be soundly flogged and set free."

"He broke the law and for that the punishment is set," Moses said.

"That is true but he is not of our people and so he is not blessed by God," Aaron said. "Is it then right that one who does not share in the blessing shall bear the weight of the law?"

"A thought well spoken, Brother," Moses said. "Yet, though not blessed, he is created by God, therefore he is subject to his law."

Aaron looked into his brother's eyes. "True also, yet there is another consideration. The man has a family, a wife and two young children, I am told. He begs for forgiveness. It might be well to show him mercy and so gain the affection of the nations."

Joshua interrupted. "But if we allow one to break the law others will also. And if we show him mercy so must we do with others. Then the law becomes as a eunuch, full of words but impotent."

Moses looked at one and then the other. "You are filled with love and mercy, Brother, and you, Joshua, know only justice. It is a hard thing to decide the death or life of a fool and to carry the weight of justice upon one's spirit. Therefore, Aaron, draw forth the stones of judgement from your breastplate and let God speak through them, that we may be absolved from responsibility in this onerous decision."

Obediently, Aaron thrust his hand into the breastplate pocket of the opulent costume he wore as high priest and withdrew two glowing gemstones. The stones, pale blue-green and opaque, were cut flat and in an oval shape about two inches long. They were deeply engraved on both sides and the characters so made were filled with gold. The first read simply "without blame" on one side and "judged erring" on the other. The second carried two terse inscriptions, "the law prevails" and "God gives mercy."

Solemnly Aaron flipped the first stone, catching it deftly as it spun in the air. He laid it on Moses outstretched palm, then read the characters that shined with baneful beauty. Reluctantly he made ready the second stone, which must now make judgement because of the condemnation of the first. The stone spun upward and was caught but nearly dropped by the nervous hand of the high priest. He reached his hand out over Moses' palm and released the thing as though it was a burning coal that was searing into his flesh. The three great men of Israel stared at the glowing stone on Moses' palm—none spoke for there was no need. They turned and walked back to the assembly of the people.

When the three emerged there was a great hum of voices, which ebbed to absolute silence as the Levites brought Gunai before Moses. In the extreme of terror, he threw himself headlong at the feet of the prophet, trembling and weeping.

Moses' face was an impassive mask as he regarded the pitiful creature before him. He made a sign to Joshua, who stepped forward and raised Gunai to his knees.

The prophet, the supreme judge of Israel, spoke slowly. "Gunai of Joktan...you have disobeyed the law of Yahweh, the Lord Almighty, by laboring on the Sabbath day.... For this you must surely die at the hands of the people!" He turned to Joshua. "Let the Levites take him out of the encampment that the people may stone him until he is dead."[48]

The Levites took hold of the begging, weeping man and dragged him to the field at the pathway to the encampment of Israel. There a jeering mob threw a rain of stones upon the simple donkey driver until he died.

From that time forth many of the people of Israel and those who abided near them feared and hated the prophet because of his cruelty. And now there was hunger among the people because of the poor pastures for their cattle and because the thin, dry soil of Paran could not bear crops.

Too long now, the people who once had known the rich abundance of the Nile were forced to wander as poverty stricken nomads. Their basic source of livelihood was their flocks and herds, which provided the bulk of their food as well as and wool, leather, cheese and meat to trade. Because of their great numbers, little subsistence could be gained by foraging in the arid countryside. Nor were there precious stones, metals and rich woods in abundant supply for the artisans of the land. Thus the people were ever restless, dreaming ceaselessly of the land of plenty promised them by Moses.

As time passed the people murmured more, though secretly, for they feared the law of Moses and the sword of Joshua. Their state was more evil than in the days of their servitude to Pharaoh. Leanness and hunger stalked them and death stood with Amalek on the one hand and the plagues of the wilderness on the other.[49] In their fear and misery they cried out to Korah, who was a great prince of the Levites.

"Lead us forth from the wilderness," they cried, "and free us from the stern hand of Moses. For we would be your subjects and swear obeisance to your hand."

Having compassion for the hardship of the people, Korah counselled with many of the princes of the people. Then he came to Moses and Aaron and challenged them, that they should yield up the leadership of the people. But Moses dealt subtly with him and bid the princes that they might gather to pray to God for a solution to the crisis. But when the princes had laid aside their swords and taken up censers with incense for the time of prayer, Joshua fell upon them with his warriors and put them to the sword. So ended the rebellion of the people—and the plight of Israel worsened.

Aaron had been summoned from his duty at the tabernacle by the urgent entreaty of his wife, Elisheba. Now he knelt beside the bed of Miriam,[50] stroking back the graying hair from her pallid forehead. Her aging temples burned with a fever Aaron had seen too often during the years of Israel's exile and her eyes seemed small and sunken.

It had indeed been many years now since they had left the security of their labors in Egypt. How long they had wandered he couldn't bring to mind, but it had been too long. Now, here in this desolate place, he had somehow become an old man before his time and his only sister lay dying of yet another plague.

"Brother...raise me up, that I might look into your eyes." Miriam's voice came faintly as though spoken from a place far distant.

Gently Aaron slipped his arm beneath her emaciated shoulders and raised her so that he could place cushions beneath her back.

"The hotness lessens," he lied. "Perhaps your illness abates."

Miriam looked at him lovingly with eyes that shined feverishly in her careworn face.

"I die, Brother. I will not see Canaan nor will you or Moses. This land turns us all to withered corpses."

"Speak not so, My Sister. You will regain your strength when the fever lifts."

"This fever lifts only when the heart stills, Brother. I have seen it often, as have you. Spare me your well-meant denials—I do not fear death. It brings welcome relief from this accursed pilgrimage."

Aaron sat quietly and reached to hold his sister's frail hand.

Miriam gave her brother a tender smile. "You are such a gentle man, Aaron. You should be a priest in happier times."

"Happier times will come, Miriam, we must have faith."

"Not for us, Brother, except there be another life. But my heart cries out for the young, your children and your grandchildren."

Miriam hesitated and pressed Aaron's hand weakly when she saw a deep melancholy appear in his eyes.

"Forgive me, Aaron. In my sickness I had forgotten those of your sons who died in the ministry of Moses. Yet there are many young who need not die—press Moses to take the people from this terrible land."

"But where shall we go, Miriam? The warriors of Canaan are too mighty for us and Pharaoh would drive us away even if our people had the strength to cross Paran."

"Does not Moses have a wife and sons and a father-in-law in Midian? Is it not a large land and better than the wilderness? Take the people there." Miriam closed her eyes as though to sleep.

Aaron stroked his beard thoughtfully. "It might be a possible way. I will talk to Moses about it. But I see that you have grown weary. You should rest now, Sister."

Miriam's eyes fluttered open. "I will rest soon, for the ages—bring Moses, I would make peace with him."

Moses raised himself from the bench beside his tent flap as Aaron approached. He had visited Miriam in her illness, but the tightness in Aaron's face told him that his sister's condition was more grave than before. He extended his hand to Aaron and gestured for him to sit. Aaron lowered his body with a deep sigh.

"Is she worse than yesterday?" Moses asked.

"She weakens and the fever does not abate. She asks to see you. She says she would make peace with you."

Moses' eyebrows raised. Though he had spoken to Miriam many times since he had so impulsively banished her to the camp of the nations, she had never forgiven him. And he had never apologized to her. It was a thing between them because they were both prideful and headstrong. Miriam must be ill indeed if she wished to make peace.

"I will come," he said.

Moses called to Adanah. "Make a soup of barley and beef that I might take it to Miriam."

"Why? Would she do as much for me, My Husband? She has shown me nothing but enmity since I entered your tent."

"What you say is true, My Wife. But my sister dies and though she might not touch a spoonful to her lips, I would do this to reconcile our spirits."

"I will do it then, since it is an evil thing to die with regret in one's heart. But if she wishes to find peace she should repent of the sorrow she has caused me."

"That also she may desire, especially since you are with child of her blood."

Adanah smiled. "It will be a son for you, My Lord, to lead the people after you."

"And if it is not?"

"Then I will bear you a son."

In the still, quiet time before the sun yielded its last rays of warmth to the desert, Moses kneeled beside the bed of his sister.

"I come in obedience to your wishes, Sister. I bring you a rich soup to restore your strength."

Miriam gave Moses a wan smile. "It has been long since my brother has obeyed anyone, save his God.... I thank you, Moses, for your gift and I will taste of it. But first we must talk, for there are things which weigh heavily on my spirit and I must speak of them."

"If it is about our disagreement over Adanah, I offer you my regret that I dealt so harshly with you."

Miriam waved her hand feebly. "That is of no matter, I was jealous of the woman and acted foolishly. She is a good wife to you and I bless her for that."

"And she brings you a nephew or a niece to be your protector in your old age."

Miriam looked at her brother with surprise. "I thought the prophet too intent on the Lord's commands to sire a child. I am glad, Moses and I wish I could see the child grown—but I will not see the birth of the babe, much less its maturity."

"Do not speak so, Miriam. If you but trust in the Lord you will surely be healed."

Miriam raised her hand a few inches in mild protest. "I am dying, Brother, that is the Lord's will and I do not have disdain for it.... But I wish the babe to be born and to live in peace—and that is your burden."

Moses frowned. "The child will live such a life in Canaan—the Lord has promised it."

"It was promised before either of us was born and we are old.... No, my brother, you must take the people out from this desolate place now."

"But we cannot face the armies of Canaan. That is why we wander in this wilderness."

"You will wander in the wilderness until the people are consumed by it.... Can you not take them to the land of Jethro? You can make a pact with the Midianites and live among them."

Moses turned and looked out of the doorway to the west, where the last crescent of red sun was slipping below the horizon. *It is an omen,* he thought. *Surely the Lord speaks to me through the mouth of Miriam.* He turned to Miriam and gently stroked her face.

"It will be so, Sister. Rest peacefully now, for I have given you my promise that I will take the people out of the desert."

In the morning, when Elisheba went to her, Miriam had given up her spirit and found her peace. Then the elders of all the tribes of Israel gathered together and paid homage to Miriam and they buried her with a great show of grief at Kadesh.

"Behold, Brother," Aaron said, "the people come now in a great rabble and those who would lead walk purposefully before them."[51]

Moses nodded somberly. "We have just buried our sister and already another sorrow rests upon our shoulders.

"The people have cried out against us because the wells are empty and the cattle low for water," Joshua said. "They bemoan the death of Korah, the rebel and claim him to be a martyr for the people. It is commonly said that were he alive Israel would follow him. It is but a short time until an ambitious warrior prince will take his place and they will rise to open rebellion."

Even at a distance the voices of Israel made a hostile droning. When they drew near, the angry voices were made more ominous by the ill-tempered scowls of the people. As they reached the tent of Moses, Elah, who was a well-respected prince and a formidable warrior, planted his staff angrily on the hard earth.

"Moses, son of Amram," he said, "you hold yourself up as a prophet and God's chosen leader of the people. Yet you have brought the children of Israel into this forbidding desert where we cannot plant, nor can we feed and water our cattle—is it your prophesy that the people of God shall die in the desert?"

"The prophesies of Moses are by the Lord's command," Aaron said once again. "It was by God's command that he brought us forth from Egypt. It will be by God's command that we enter into the promised land."

"So says Moses, but the people did not hear these commands, neither in Egypt nor here in the desert. It was by his beguiling promises that we left a land that was free of hunger, to die in the desert."

At this there were angry shouts of agreement and even a few shouts of "Stone him! Stone him!" But Elah raised his hand for silence and continued.

"For these many wanderings Moses has struck down those who would offer salvation to the people, even until the very desert was awash with blood! ...Behold, Ethan and Barnabas and three thousand men died by his bidding at Sinai! ...Then those who warned us of the strength of Canaan were struck down. Also those who fought Amalek to gain Moses' favor died without his blessing.... When the people wearied of his cruelty and begged Korah that he might deliver them, he too was killed and a host of princes with him—now we stand without water in this burning sun. Will his prophesies bring us water or will our carcasses feed the jackals and vultures?"

Moses drew himself up and faced Elah. "Many times I have stood between the people and the wrath of God. Otherwise every man, woman and child would have fallen by The Lord's plague. You dare to chide me for the deaths of those who sinned against the Lord. But know you, that were I not on my face before God you would have died.... Still, I will take Aaron into the tabernacle and we will seek the grace of The Almighty. Pray you that he is not angered by your rebelliousness, that another plague does not fall upon you!"

And when they had entered the tabernacle, into The Holy Place, Moses cast his eyes upon the golden altar and prayed. Aaron in his priestly vestments lit incense and prayed also in an earnest voice, that The Lord's presence might be visited on them.[52] In time Moses fell down before the altar and became as one in a deep sleep. Then Aaron ceased his praying and prostrated himself beside his brother. Thus they stayed until Moses recovered his senses and rose to his feet. Together the two men, with heads bowed, backed out of The Holy Place. For they had been in the presence of God and dared not turn their backs on his altar.

When Moses gained the courtyard he stood as one who was struck dumb, staring into the infinity of the heavens. After a time that seemed interminable, though it had been but moments, he turned to Aaron with his brow furrowed with distress.

"I had a dream, Aaron, and I know not if it is a message from the Lord or if it is but a fantasy of my spirit. I am sorely pressed by the wants of the people and I fear that I swooned from weariness and fear and that the message of my dream is not true."

"Always before your dreams have been true, Brother," Aaron said. "What was different now, that you distrust this message?"

"Always before, when the word came to me, I knew it to be a truth revealed to me in might and glory. When the storms struck Egypt I saw the hand of the Lord and so I did when the chariots of Pharaoh pursued us. When we sought water at Rephidim there were signs that the water was behind the rock and the Lord showed them to me. But here there is nothing but the stones and the barren hillside. Yet the voice within me tells me to speak to the stone and water will come forth."

Aaron shrugged. "Then speak to the stone and water will flow from it. I have often seen that the Lord's hand works through you."

"But what if I fail?" Moses asked. "What if my dream is not the word of the Lord but only a delusion of my mind's affliction? Surely at that moment the people will stone us and after all that has happened we will die in vain. The people will never enter into the promised land, but in their lack of direction they will dwindle and die in the desert."

Aaron's face clouded, always he had trusted his brother, but now fear cast a cold sickness of doubt into his belly. He looked at Moses grimly.

"If you fail, My Brother, we will indeed die and your wife and mine and all of our households will die with us or be driven from the congregation."

"There is nothing to be done but to hope that my dream is true," Moses said. "Bring your staff, Aaron, for it has done the wonders of the Lord. Perhaps it may once more perform a miracle before the people."

Then Joshua called the princes of the people and they followed Moses and Aaron to a place where a great sheet of limestone stood out from a hill. Gathered behind the princes and elders was a great throng of people watching the prophet with skeptical interest. Of late nothing but laws and admonitions had come from the prophet and the people's patience had worn thin. The life or death of the people as well as their flocks and herds depended on water, not a trickle or a shallow pool but thousands of homers. At this moment there was little trust that Moses could provide such a flood and Israel waited to vent its rage on the prophet.

Moses now stood before the wall of rock, searching the dry, impervious surface with his eyes. His spirit sank within him. He hesitated for long moments, trying to summon the courage to command the rock to give forth water. At last a man behind the solemn front of elders spoke in rude jest.

"Will the prophet piss on the rock and thus bring forth water?"

The crowd snickered and Moses felt a wild rage rise within himself. He turned to the princes and screamed so loudly that the echoes of it came back from the high places.

"If you would have water, you rebels, God's hand will bring it forth from this rock!"

Then he seized Aaron's staff and drove the butt of it hard against the brittle stone. The place it struck cracked and a wetness showed. Moses drove the staff against it again and a stream of water sprayed into the air. Then Moses fell in a faint and they took him and laid him in the shade of the rock. Aaron kneeled by him and bathed his forehead until his eyes opened.

"Are you well again, My Brother?"

Moses blinked and shook his head as though to clear his mind.

"The faintness leaves me."

"God has blessed you again, Moses. Your dream was true."

"The dream was true indeed. But I have earned a curse rather than a blessing."

"How so? You brought water from the rock and the people drink of it."

"No, God brought the water despite my doubt. I did not believe in his revelation to me, nor did you, Brother." He stopped speaking and Aaron thought he saw a solitary tear form at his stern brother's eye.

Aaron lowered his gaze then and he felt a deep shame creep through his heart.

"It is true, I doubted God and for that I deserve his wrath. Has God spoken to you again because we did not believe?"

Moses nodded. "He has declared his judgement for our lack of faith."

Aaron looked up into his brother's eyes. "A curse?"

"Yes, it is a thing most hurtful. Yet he permits us to abide in our station."

"He does not cast us out?"

"No."

"And he will allow us to lead the people into Canaan?"

Moses breathed a deep sigh. "We will never enter Canaan, not I nor you. That is the judgement for our doubt."

In the days that followed the three leaders of Israel spoke of how they might escape from the desert to a more hospitable place and so placate the people.

"Perhaps it would be best if we gathered our forces and invade Canaan again," Joshua said. "We could go by way of the plains of the Philistines instead of the hills."

"Is it better to die by Philistine swords rather than by those of the Amalekites?" Aaron asked. "No, our people are starved and weary. They are no match for the Philistines or for Amalek, much less the two united against them. And that is what they would face if we attempt to enter from the South."

"Aaron is right," Moses said. "We cannot fight now. We must try another way."

"There is no other way with Amalek," Joshua said.

"I was not thinking of Canaan, but of what Miriam said before she died. It might be that we can go to Midian, if Jethro can persuade his people to accept us."

Aaron looked at Moses thoughtfully. "But there also lies a hazard, Brother. We must pass through Edom, where live the kin of the Amalekites. Though they are of many tribes and loosely joined, I fear that the blood that joins them to Amalek will set them against us."

"That may well be, but I see no other course. The king of Edom is blood kin of Prince Sahed, yet it is said no love lies between them. I will send messengers to plead for safe passage through his land."

Moses sent messengers out of Kadesh and into the land of Edom to search out the king and deliver to him the petition he had written.[52]

CHAPTER 13

Kybar, aging prince of the eastern tribes of Edom, looked up peevishly from his breakfast as his priest-minister entered. He took a bite of a hard barley cake filled with soft cheese and washed it down with soured goat's milk before acknowledging his presence.

"What matter is of such urgency that you disturb me before I have broken the night's fast, Shaddim?"

Shaddim bowed low. "A foot messenger awaits your pleasure, Lord. He beat upon the gate in the early light of dawn, then fell senseless at the feet of the guards. He was faint with thirst, but given a little water he was soon restored. He seeks an audience with your eminence."

"And could you not hear his words and act on them as my minister?"

"I sought to do that, Lord. But the petition which he brings is of such a serious nature that it must be considered by your eminence alone. He waits in the courtyard. Would you have me bring him in?'

"No, wait—of what nation is this messenger with the weighty burden?"

"He is an Israelite named Joha, Lord."

"An Israelite? A follower of that scoundrel Moses? Is he not the one who so foully set upon the Edomites at Rephidim?"

"The same, Lord. Though I might remind Your Greatness that it was the Edomites that attacked Israel—the messenger brings a petition from the prophet."

Kybar threw the remnant of his bread to a great brute of a dog chained by the doorway. "Of what nature is this petition, Shaddim?"

"The Israelite desires passage through your lands, Lord."

Kybar raised his eyebrows. "He desires passage! ...for what purpose?"

"I am unsure, Lord. The messenger said that this Moses would go to Jethro, the Midianite."

"Ah, yes! ...I know of Jethro. He had an Israelite son-in-law who left his wife and went to Egypt. Would this Moses then be the same?" Kybar smiled at his minister's nod. "Bring in the messenger, this issue interests me."

Joha adjusted the patch over his left eye and followed the priest through a heavy wooden doorway and into the courtyard of the stuccoed brick and stone house. The two stories of the flat-roofed structure carried vines of grapes along its walls and two fig trees shaded a bench where a time weathered and scowling man sat. At the priest's sign Joha prostrated himself before the prince and awaited the command to rise.

"Rise, Israel, and let me see your face."

Kybar spoke sternly in a dialect that was strange, yet fairly understandable to Joha.

"Ahh, you are a warrior—your young face carries the signature of the blade. Tell me who you are—and for my pleasure divulge the cause of the patch you wear."

"My name is Joha, warrior of Joshua, General of the Armies of Israel. The patch I wear and the scar beneath it were given to me by a captain of Amalek who carried a like inscription. Bela was his name."

Kybar laughed heartily. "I know the man of whom you speak, Joha of Israel. Everything in this world must come in a full circle. He received his patch at the battle of Rephidim, so he returned the favor to you. Rephidim was a battle that sorely bruised the pride of my cousin, Sahed. But surely you are too young to have fought at Rephidim. How did you come on Bela's sword?" Kybar was suddenly serious, his black eyes piercing Joha from beneath bushy gray brows.

It was the thing that Joha feared. Now he must give account of the recent attack on Amalek and the Canaanites.

"There was a conflict with Amalek east of Kadesh. I was in an army led by Elizur, who was known as 'The Bull of Rueben.' It went ill for us—Elizur was killed and we were driven back into the desert."

Kybar looked at Joha grimly. "It is well that you told the truth, for I knew of this thing. Indeed, I saw the shriveled head of Elizur upon the lance of my cousin. But enough of these unpleasant remembrances. For what cause does Moses, your prophet, send you?"

"To seek passage through your lands, My Lord, as is written upon this scroll." Joha produced a small roll of papyrus wrapped in goatskin and gave it to the priest.

Shaddim unrolled the document and studied it. "My Lord, this Moses requests safe passage for his people through Edom that he might go into the land of Midian."

Kybar scowled and spoke to Joha. "The prophet wishes to pass through with all his people, old and young, warriors and women, cattle and belongings?"

"That is true, My Lord. The wilderness wears heavily on the people and they would go to the land of Jethro, the Midianite, where they might graze their herds in peace."

"Your people are many, even as the locusts of the plains and they strip the land bare wherever they go, young Joha. That is why Sahed struck them at Rephidim and that is why he stands with the peoples of Canaan against them, that they might not enter. Yet Israel would attempt trespass nonetheless and that is why you wear that patch."

"The people hunger for food and a place to live in peace, Lord Kybar. In the broad plains of Midian the tribes might spread themselves as the sands spread in the desert. Thus their presence would not be grievous to your people or any other."

Kybar shook his head. "Tell Moses that you are too many. The cattle must eat and drink and when they have gone through there will be nothing left for our own. If the people of Israel wished to eat and drink they should have stayed in Egypt."

"But, My Lord, the people were slaves in Egypt and that is why they fled. If they went swiftly and stayed to the camel roads they could reach Midian without trespassing on your fields or draining your wells. Pray send word to the chiefs of Midian. Ask them if they might accept Israel for the sake of the sons of Moses, which are the grandsons of Jethro and live with him as Midianites."

Kybar looked at Joha and breathed a sigh of resignation. "Very well, young Joha, because our bloods are intermingled I will send word of the request of Moses to the chiefs of Midian. Until my couriers return you will remain in my home and rest, for I see you are an earnest young man and I like that well."

In the days of waiting until the return of the couriers Joha visited with the prince or wandered the dusty streets of the walled village. The settlement sat at the crossroads of caravan routes and the inhabitants were accustomed to people of many nations in their midst. Though they regarded him curiously because of his Hebrew dress, they were friendly and passing the time of day was not difficult. Because of his handsome features and his good-natured way he received many smiles, especially from the younger women. Thus the days passed quickly until one morning the couriers, tired and dusty from days of camel riding, returned.

"I have done your bidding, young Joha," Prince Kybar said.

He scratched the ear of his great dog, which rumbled its pleasure, then he continued.

"The chiefs of Midian care not that they are joined to Israel through the sons of Moses, Gershom and Eliezer. It is said that the grandsons of Jethro despise Moses because he deserted their mother, Zipporah. Because of this the chiefs deny the blood tie even as they reject the ancient ties between your ancestors. For is it not written that Abraham sent out Midian from the good land and let Isaac remain to claim the inheritance? They will not accept Israel as brothers. Therefore I cannot let you pass through Edom."

"And if Israel comes despite your refusal, My Lord?"

"Then the issue shall be settled with the sword."

When Joha related the words of Prince Kybar, Joshua gathered the principal officers of Israel and rode to the edge of Edom, near the city of Prince Kybar. Then he sent a courier to the prince asking for a meeting wherein he might seek to pacify the tribes of Midian. But when the prince came out there was a great horde of warriors with him, both on foot and mounted on camels and horses.[52] Kybar rode forward of the army with his minister and certain of the warlords until he was but the length of a tent pole from Joshua.

"Why do you come, Warlord of Israel?" Kybar asked. "Is it not enough that I have told your messenger that Israel shall not pass through the land of Edom?"

"I come to assure you of our peaceful intent, Lord Kybar," Joshua said. "We wish only to pass through your kingdom harmlessly, keeping to the road. We will take nothing without your grant whether it be a drop of water or a blade of grass. And for that which we may require we will pay in gold."

"That may well be, but where would you go then? The chiefs of Midian reject your plea for refuge because you are altogether too great a nation. They know of your battles against my cousin, Sahed of Amalek. They do not trust your intent and fear that they will be driven from their land. Therefore, they stand behind the army of Edom to repulse your advance."

Joshua colored with suppressed anger. "If Midian will not offer us succor perhaps the king of Moab would be more charitable and accept the hand of our friendship."

Kybar's face twisted with contempt. "Do you think me altogether a fool? You would pass through Moab that you might strike at the back of the Amalekites and enter into their lands. From there you would also control the caravan routes to the east, which carry our life blood and so you could strangle Edom."

He turned and pointed to the army massed behind him.

"No! Warlord, Israel shall not pass through Edom without first passing through them!" The prince of Edom abruptly turned his mount and galloped back to his army.

"In time we will overcome and destroy them!" Moses shouted. "They will regret their refusal of our simple request! In the days to come we will put to the sword all who stand against us. We will take their lands and their chattels and we will put the torch to their cities. Thus will all the nations near and far know that Yahweh is The Almighty God and Israel is his people."

"Will I then gather the warriors and go forth against Kybar now?' Joshua asked. "In truth my spirit smarts from the man's arrogance."

"Not yet, Joshua, for we must first make offerings to the Lord, that we might gain his full consent and blessing. And in that we must wait, for Aaron lies abed with a fever and cannot lead the priests in their ministrations."[53]

"Is Aaron gravely ill then? I saw Elisheba and she wept when I spoke of it."

Moses nodded solemnly. "He is, ...I fear my brother will travel no further on this pilgrimage. His bowels expel all that is put within them and he grows weak and wasted."

"Who then will stand as high priest if your brother is taken to the Lord? It must be a priest who upholds our purpose."

"I have thought on that—Aaron's son Eleazar covets his father's place and he will not test my commands. If my brother dies I will place the mantle of the chief priest on him."

Elisheba lay beside her dying husband, cradling his emaciated face against her breast. *When he dies,* she thought, *I might as well, for my life will be an empty husk. Miriam was a true friend and she is gone, taken by the plagues of this forbidding wilderness. Two of my sons, my favorites, died in the service of Moses—because they displeased God, he said.*

But who knows with Moses? He is different than Aaron, always so stern and frightening. He seems not to have love in his heart—always it is the law before all else. I wonder how Adanah fares—how could a woman, even an Ethiopian, lie with such a man? But it is said that she carries his child now, so there must be something I do not know of in my brother-in-law. A sound came from the lips of her husband then and her mind returned to Aaron.

"Elisheba, my wife, cover me with the robe of sheepskin for I am cold."

Elisheba touched her husband's forehead with the back of her hand. For days it had been as hot as the desert sands with the fever that raged within his body. But now his brow was cool, almost cold. She dragged the soft robe over him with the fleeces against his body.

"The fever has broken, my husband. Soon you will be well again."

Aaron's mouth curved in the smile that had made her love him when he was a young man.

"The fever relents because it has won the battle. Soon I will go to be with Nadab and Abihu."

"Hush! Do not speak so, Aaron. Our sons can wait for you a while yet. I do not want you to leave me."

"Nor do I wish to leave you, Elisheba. I have loved you from the time when I first saw you as a young girl. You were too young to marry then," Aaron's eyes sparkled, "but two years later you were not."

Elisheba looked at her husband and his image was blurred by the tears that misted her old eyes. "Even though I was too young I told my mother you would be the man I would marry. She grew impatient and told me I was too young to marry, but when I was old enough she would decide my match." Elisheba smiled tenderly at her husband. "She did make my match and it was you."

"Life was good then, though we were bonded to the Egyptians." Aaron looked at her with eyes that were suddenly haunted. "Did I do wrong in joining with Moses to free the people? But for my dreams of glory for Israel our sons would still live and thousands of others, who have perished in this wilderness, would sit by their fires in Egypt."

"We must not doubt that Moses is the prophet of the Lord, My Husband. You were chosen to aid Moses and to be a priest before the people.

You are a good man and a servant of our God. You could do nothing less than his bidding."

"Your words are balm to my sore spirit, Elisheba. For it would be a hard thing to die, doubting the worthiness of my life. But you have spoken truly...I could do nothing but serve the Lord. I can give up my spirit to the company of the patriarchs in peace."

Aaron died and was buried on the heights of Mount Hor. With him died the last restraint on the ambition and harshness of Moses. The new Israelite era of bloodshed and conquest was about to begin.

During the passage of thirty days, which was the required time of mourning for Aaron, Adanah birthed Moses' son before the child was able to sustain life. Moses was filled with a dark grief at losing his heir to the leadership of Israel before he had breathed life and he hid himself within his tent for seven days. When he stepped forth again it was the end of the nation's mourning for Aaron and the prophet wore the harsh visage of a warrior king.

Then Moses commanded Joshua. "Go to the warlords of all the tribes and order them to conscript all men of strength and courage. All from sixteen to thirty-five years shall train in the arts of war."

"Do we then venture onto a campaign that we will need so many warriors?" Joshua surveyed Moses thoughtfully. "Will it not do us harm to take all of the able-bodied men from their many labors?"

"We will not take them all for every hour of every day, but all will train in the arts of war. Your guards will instruct them in companies, each for a portion of a day and each with a captain over them."

"And when we have trained them in war with what will we arm them? We have few weapons and battle garments to make a proper army of them."

"Those conscripts who work in the skills of metal we will set to the task of making swords, spear points and all manner of battle armor. Our carpenters will make bows, spear shafts and the frames for bullhide shields. Those skilled in the working of hides will fashion skirts and greaves of bullhide and covers for the shields. And last, the weavers and tailors along with the women of the tribes will make tunics, sashes and banners for the warriors of every tribe. Each of a different color and device so that they will be known by them."

"I know My Lord has a purpose for the creation of such a mighty army. It is a campaign of conquest, is it not?" Joshua smiled with anticipation.

"Yes," Moses said, "the people wither and die in this wretched wilderness. It is time we go to a better land where they can live fit lives."

"Then do we enter Canaan, the land of the promise?"

Moses shook his head. "Not Canaan yet, but close, to a better place. And if we are not granted entry we will take it by the might of our warriors."

When it was done Moses gathered Israel up and departed from Kadesh. The multitude marched then through the wilderness past the land of Edom. For Joshua would not provoke the king of Edom because he had many exceedingly fierce warriors mounted on swift camels and on horses and mules. But he went by way of the Sea of Salt into the edges of Moab until the River Arnon and camped there. Israel went no further, for the land beyond was governed by King Sihon of the Amorites, who had fought beside Sahed of Ammalek.

Then Moses requested of King Sihon that the people might venture peacefully through his lands and so enter into Canaan. But Sihon distrusted Moses and he had made an alliance with the Canaanites for their common good. So he forbade Israel to pass through his land. Instead he gathered his army, which was a foolish thing because they lacked greatly the numbers of Israel and he took them to the far side of the River Arnon and stood there that Israel might not pass. For Sihon did not know the strength of Israel, supposing the people to be but slaves, herdsmen and farmers.

When he saw this, Moses was greatly angered that Sihon sought to keep him from Canaan. He ordered forth the armies of Joshua and they killed the Amorites with a great slaughter. And those who could fled into Ammon and Canaan and to the northward. But Joshua took Sihon and some of his captains and executed them.

It was in this manner that Israel settled into the land of the Amorites and they took all that the Amorites had. The men of Israel took the virgins for concubines and they made slaves of those who remained. Though Joshua drove the Amorites from all their lands he did not pursue them into Ammon, for it was strong and had many tribes of fierce warriors. Nor did he cross the Jordan into Canaan because all of the nations were as one there and stood against Israel.

But it was not enough. The chieftains of Israel looked to the north to the rich lands of Bashan and coveted them.[55] There Og ruled as king over three score Amorite cities, fat and content, not given to war but prosperous from trade and the goodness of the land. And Moses drew Joshua and the council of elders about him that they might plan the destruction of Og.

Then went Joshua with all of his mighty men of war into the borders of Bashan. In answer Og went forth with all his war chieftains, proud in fine battle dress. Before him strode his warriors gripping fine swords of Philistine iron and shielded by helmets and bucklers of burnished bronze. But they were soft and weak from good living and they were as fatted sheep against the lean and hungry wolves of Israel. In the passing of a moon Og's armies were vanquished and he and his sons, royal princes and generals, were put to the sword. All who had not fled, though they fell to their knees in supplication, were slain without mercy. For Moses was jealous of the wealth of the land that only Israel might live within it.

CHAPTER 14

Now the ministers and elders of great Moab and far Midian, along with Edom and Ammon, whose strength Joshua would not yet test, conspired against Israel.[56] For they looked with dismay at the armies of Joshua and the cruelty of the prophet's conquests.

Thus it was that they sought to retain a soothsayer, a magician of great renown and mysterious power, whose name was Balaam. And Balak, the king of Moab, offered him gold and great honor to lay a curse on Israel. But Salaam looked on the vast host of Israel from the heights of the altars of Baal and he refused to curse them. But instead he blessed them for he feared for his life if they should triumph. Also Balaam prophesied many dire things that Israel would bring upon the nations about them. And therefore the fears of the nations about Israel were greater than before.

As time passed, the people of Israel spread like locusts upon the lands that had been of the Amorites. They rested and ate of the fruits of the land which other peoples had labored over, growing in strength of body and in number.

But then, the men of Israel took unto themselves the daughters of Moab and of Midian as Moses himself had done (for he never took a wife of Israel, but a Midianitess and an Ethiopian). And they pleasured themselves with these women and followed in their ways, which were of the false god, Baal.[57] For the women's ways were seductive and licentious, irresistible to the nature of men who chafed under the zealous, stern dictates of Moses.

Moses and the judges were much provoked and jealous for the sake of The True God and for the security of their stations as leaders of Israel. Then a sickness descended on the people of Israel and the judges and priests counselled for the cause. They charged it to the sins of those men of Israel who had abandoned their faith in favor of the lascivious worship of Baal. In their righteous indignation they brought a complaint to Moses, demanding that he take action against the transgressors and so end the plague that was raging among the people.

So it was that The Prophet counselled with Eleazar, son of Aaron and high priest of Israel, and with Joshua, Israel's warlord.

"What say you of the pestilence that walks among us, Priest?"

Moses' piercing gaze scanned the shifting eyes and well-oiled beard of Eleazar.

"Young and old die by three risings of the sun and those who were hardy but a few days before lie pale and wasted in their beds."

"It is a condemnation by God against the unfaithful, My Lord, as the judges have spoken," Eleazer asserted piously. "It is a curse against those joined to Baal-Peor and a penalty exacted against the faithful for tolerating the presence of the evil one. The pestilence will not pass until the false worship of Baal-Peor is destroyed!"

"Many of the nations about us worship Baal and have not suffered this pestilence. If false worship is the cause, of which nation does this curse come, Lord Priest?" Moses paused and fixed the high priest with a stony frown. "Is it of Moab, the forbidden seed of Lot? Behold, we live among them! Or perhaps it is of Edom, or of the barbarian Amorites that remain, or of the people of Midian?"

"It is of all," the priest ventured cautiously, "but most greatly of the Midianites."

Moses frowned. "Why of Midian? They are no worse than any of the others and perhaps better, for they are distant kin of Israel as are the children of Edom. I myself took a wife of Midian, a good woman who bore me sons, as you well know."

"And who are long gone from you and from the true God," Joshua said dryly. "The plague first began in the tents of Midian and descended through them to the houses of Israel."

Eleazar was bobbing his priestly head in concurrence, his black eyes shuttling back and forth between Moses and Joshua.

"The plague comes from the houses of the Midianites whose young women tempt the men of Israel. It is a judgement from God against the harlots and their evil worship of Baal-Peor, with which they corrupt our young men and draw them from the Lord's temple."

Moses regarded Eleazar doubtfully. "The priest of Midian, Jethro, did not seek to corrupt my faith or sway me from following the true God. Indeed he gave me prudent counsel and bowed his own head within the tabernacle of the Lord. I think, Eleazar, because the thistle blooms first in one field does not make it the source of the infestation."

Eleazar smiled slyly. "That is true, My Lord, but would not a farmer hoe where they are first seen to bloom? Thus Midian must first feel the sharpness of the farmer's blade."

"Perhaps, but the thistles must be hoed from all the fields lest they spread with the wind. Would the farmer hoe far and wide and so weary himself that his own fields become corrupt with the weed?"

"Your wisdom is great, My Lord," Joshua said with a dour look at Eleazar. "The priest dances about with many words but evades judgement. All the thistles must be cleared from the fields of Israel and destroyed, lest they infect the greater part."

"You also dance about with words, Lord Joshua—make your meaning clear—would you have us fight all the nations about us and drive them from their lands?"

Joshua shook his head. "We must first purge our own fields, not those of our neighbors. We must destroy those of our own who have fallen to Baal-Peor, lest we lose all of the congregation to the nations and so forfeit alt that we have striven for."

Moses nodded somberly. "You speak words that are true, but they are severe in their consequence. Once again, as at Sinai, we must sacrifice the few to preserve the greater part." The prophet's shoulders seemed to slump as if with a great weight. "We will make a proclamation of compulsory obeisance to Yahweh in a congregation of the tribes. Then we will issue a judgement of death against all men of Israel who bow to Baal-Peor."

Joshua studied the prophet's eyes. "It is the right thing to do but I think it is not enough. If the sheep stray into the bushes and are taken by wolves is not the fault of the shepherd greater than that of the sheep?'

"Speak not in parables, Joshua, but clearly in your exact meaning!"

"We must make a terrible example of the tribal chieftains who have allowed this false worship to happen. Quite simply, Lord Moses, they should be bound naked to poles beside the road until they perish in the sun.[58] Thus will it be known that the God of Israel will not endure the infidelity of his people."

Moses regarded his general thoughtfully. As severe as he himself had become, he was concerned with the change in the earnest young warrior who had carried old women from the Sea of Reeds. It seemed that the man Joshua had become bore altogether too great an acceptance of the pain and bloodshed of others. And yet he held the armies under his control as no other could and was resolutely loyal to Moses. It was something essential to the leadership of the prophet, even as the priestship under the fawning Eleazar was irritating, but necessary.

He thought for long moments about the men Joshua urged him to destroy. They had supported him in past crises and now they were merely guilty of nothing more than moral negligence. Yet that negligence could well cause the dissolution of the Hebrew nation. He drew a deep breath that he exhaled in a quiet sigh, then he spoke reluctantly.

"Very well, Joshua, blow the trumpets far and wide, that all of Israel must come to a meeting of the tribes. Then arrest the chieftains quietly and confine them where others will not see. When the people come we will make our proclamation and seize those men who consort with women of the nations and bow to Baal-Peor. The judges will try them for profaning

The True God by worshipping false idols—those condemned will be slain with the sword. Thus we will purge the tribes of Israel of this plague that afflicts us."

"It shall be done," Joshua said. "But what of those who refuse to obey the summons?"

The thought angered Moses, so that his temples throbbed with pain. Must he forever coddle this stiff-necked people as though they were wayward children?

"Slay them!" he barked.

In the days that followed, a massive encampment grew once more about the tabernacle at the acacia grove. Tents were pitched in whatever shade could be found and the pathways rang with the playing cries of sun-browned children. The adults were subdued, wondering among themselves what urgency, in this time of sickness, would cause the prophet to summon all of Israel. Only the very old and the immature were left behind to tend the fields and flocks. If it were war, Joshua would summon the warriors and leave the rest to care for their homes. But this was different and a sense of foreboding developed.

There were whisperings that some of the princes had been taken by the Levites to an unknown place. So now the people were brought close together in an uneasy swarm of humanity, some without leaders to direct them. Sick mingled with those that were well and the seeds of plague that were in a few spread among the multitude.

On the day following the second Sabbath after the calling of the tribes, assembly was called by the trumpets of Eleazar. The people came to the field at the entrance to the tabernacle, which was now made small by the crowding of tents about its borders. They pressed close about the long stone terrace on which the senior judges now sat, protected by a cordon of Levite guards.

When the tents had emptied and the congregation was gathered the soldiers of Joshua quietly encircled the field. The people glanced at their guards uneasily and a low hum of concerned voices sprang up from the crowd. But then their attention was drawn forward as Moses, flanked by Eleazar and Joshua, emerged from the tabernacle and mounted the terrace.

The prophet, with a countenance as grim as the angel of death, stepped forward and spoke.

"Children of Israel, The Lord's wrath is great against you! ...For in his benevolence he has taken you out of the desert to lands of goodness. Yet instead of thankfulness for his great blessings you turn your backs on his righteousness and bow down before Baal-Peor. The Lord has long endured your unfaithfulness but his patience is come to an end!"

Moses paused and glared at the faces beneath him, which now stared up in fearful expectation.

"The Lord has spoken words of vengeance against those who are joined to the false god and his vengeance is...death to idolaters!"[59]

There was a horrified sound from the multitude, not a cry but a startled drawing in of thousands of breaths at once. Then the multitude fell silent, save for the quickly muffled cries of a few infants. Among the thousands many men shifted uneasily, while others edged away from their heathen women, as though the minute space between them would give them immunity from the judgement they knew would come. A few made as if to leave the congregation, but sight of the stony-faced guards encompassing the field caused them to halt.

"The God of Abraham, Isaac and Israel has spoken to me in his righteous wrath!" Moses was screaming now. "Turn from your unfaithful ways and bow down before him, that you may be spared! For the pestilence is sent as a judgement against you because you take women of the nations and follow their evil ways!"

Some women were weeping now, while many men stood with downcast eyes. Others stared up at the judges belligerently, as though trying to gather the courage to rebel against them. One of these now spoke with an angry voice. It was Zimri, a young man of an influential family of the Simeonites.

"How is it, Lord Moses, that you have taken a women of Midian as I now do and still abide in good health?" He put his arm about the woman who stood beside him. "Did you justify yourself with the Lord by sending her back to her father, ...and your sons as well?"

Moses' face darkened with a rage so intense that his tongue was hindered and he could not bring forth words.

Zimri laughed. "Is not the wife you have now taken also of a foreign people? It seems that My Lord is intent on binding the people with proclamations that he himself ignores. Behold! ...Cozbi, whom I hold close, is the daughter of a chief of Midian just as Zipporah was. If such was good enough to bed the prophet himself should not this one be a fit match for me? ...I care not for the ravings of a madman—for such you are, Lord Moses! Leave me in peace to love my woman as I would!" With that Zimri turned and walked past the stunned guards to enter his tent with Cozbi.

Phinehas, son of the high priest, had been watching with intense interest.[60] He, like his father, followed Moses with a fanatical zeal and the insulting rebuff to Moses was like a slap to his own face. He had never liked Zimri, who was handsome and influential and much more popular than he. And now he saw how to ingratiate himself with the prophet while eliminating an annoyance to himself.

In an instant Phinehas leaped to his feet and tore a javelin from the grasp of one of the guards. Then he raced into the tent after Zimri and Cozbi. Zimri's eyes grew wide with surprise and fear at the javelin in the hands of Phinehas and the malevolent darkness in the young man's eyes. Instinctively he turned away from Phinehas as though to shield Cozbf with his own body, for he thought her to be the target of this threat. It was a futile move—the fanatical young man plunged the weapon through Zimri and into the woman he held before the startled guards could lay hands on him.

Then the kin of Zimri drew knives from their belts and would have struck down the murderer where he stood, but the guards took him and began to drag him off to the prison pits of the malefactors. But Moses raised his hand and halted them, then he spoke in a loud voice so that all could hear.

"Release him —for Phinehas does the service of the Lord this day!"

He turned to the kin of Zimri, who had pulled out the javelin that held the man and woman together like two roasts upon a spit and were now attending to the dying man and the mortally wounded woman.

"You minister to these two in vain for they are stricken by the hand of God! Therefore, take heed that their lot shall not be your own and seek not to avenge these deaths upon Phinehas. For I say to the congregation of Israel that this day Phinehas has done the work of the Lord and he shall be a priest until his death.[61] And again I say repent and put your heathen women and their idols from you! Fall on your faces before the Lord and beg his forgiveness that death may not visit you on this day!"

Then many of the men of Israel who had sworn themselves to Baal-Peor cast their women from them and fell down on their faces before Moses and the judges that forgiveness might be granted them. Others stood courageously, holding their weeping women to them in defiance of the judges. It mattered not which course they took for the informers among the Levites knew all and the guards of Joshua swiftly laid hands on those who were joined to Baal. Swiftly also the judges tried the idolaters, giving without exception the simple judgement of death.[59]

On that day so many fell to the swords of Joshua that the earth of the field of death could not drink in the blood but it lay upon the land in a fetid, fly-ridden slime. And yet those that fell to the blade were the fortunate ones. For now the judges passed sentence on the chieftains whose tribes were corrupted by Baal. Because they were entrusted with the enforcement of the law and neglected it their punishment was more severe than the quick death of the sword. They were stripped and bound to stakes in the fierce sun and the cold of desert night until they died.[58] So did Moses and the judges deal with those who displeased them.

Driven by grief and anger, Zur, father of Cozbi and prince of the northern tribes of Midian, gathered about him a hundred of his best mounted warriors. With them he rode to the encampment of Moses at the Grove of Acacias in Moab. Daniel was captain of sentinels on that day and it was his keen eyes that first saw a heavy haze of dust rising with the wind. He watched it closely for some moments, not wishing to give the alarm for a simple desert whirlwind. Then he put the ram's horn to his mouth and blew the alarm. Instantly there was a frantic scurrying in the encampment below the bluff on which Daniel stood. In moments the mighty men of Israel were running to answer the summons of the ram's horn with Joshua and Joha already clambering up the steeply pitched slope to him.

"What causes you to blow the alarm, Daniel?' Joshua's breath came in harsh rasps for though he was not yet old the endurance of his youth had fled with the graying of his head.

"A company comes, Lord General. There...to the south below the hills, the dust rises as from a group of horsemen."

Joshua squinted to see what the younger man's sharp eyes were watching.

"I see the billowing dust but little else. Perhaps it is but the wind playing tricks on you."

Daniel shook his head. "The dust cloud grows legs and flying manes and tails. It is a troop of mounted warriors riding swiftly. They come toward us."

Joha now stood beside his friend, looking out across the plain with his one good eye.

"Daniel's eyes do not deceive him, My Lord. It is a troop of lancemen but not enough to attack us, more likely a prince's guard."

Joshua grunted. "Umph, I see them now but my eyes do not reveal their identity. From what nation do our swiftly riding guests come?"

"They are not armored but ride in flowing robes as people of the plains do," Daniel said. "They carry slender lances and bows, not swords and heavy shields. I think they are Midianites."

Joshua spat disgustedly. "That bodes evil for us. The people of Midian have little reason to extend us friendship." He turned to Joha. "Tell the prophet that visitors come. He may wish to greet them personally."

Soon the prophet came hurrying with faltering steps from the tabernacle, flanked on either side by Eleazar and Phinehas. He had aged with time and travail and the strong stride of the warrior prophet was no more. Yet, Joshua thought as he descended the bluff in deference to his Lord's infirmity, he has the spirit of an eagle and the menace of a cobra. The prophet would rule until death claimed him.

By the time the trio of holy men reached Joha and Daniel the riders had halted their mounts just beyond the reach of arrows. They sat motionless on their horses—sullen, shadowy figures silently observing the warriors now grouped behind Joshua. Then one rode a few paces forward. He was smaller than the rest, dressed all in a black except for a red band around his headpiece. His mount, as though chosen to compensate for the compact build of his rider, was tall, black as ebony where sweat had washed the dust from its hide and judged by his prancing, a stallion. The rider now turned the lance he held so that the point was down then fixed a large white cloth to the haft. He rode forward proudly with his makeshift banner held high.

Moses watched the advance of the warrior unperturbed. He had met too many crises of frightening circumstance to be disturbed by a handful of Midianite lancers. The warrior was close now, his sun-darkened face scowling within a beard and wildly flowing locks of gray-streaked, black hair. Above him his banner flapped in a quickening breeze. Moses stared at its curious emblem of red-brown, trying to decipher the strange symbol. Then his eyes fixed on a small tear at the center of the device and the meaning came to him. It was a woman's undergarment, stained with dried blood and torn by a javelin—the javelin of Phinehas. In spite of the self-control that had become a facet of his personality, he shuddered. He glanced toward Phinehas just as the priest's face blanched and his eyes took on fear.

The rider paused, paying no mind to the bent bows pointed at him or the javelins held at the ready by Joshua's warriors. He looked hard at the group before him, finally bringing his hate-filled eyes to rest on Phinehas. He sidled the black stallion to within a few paces of the priest and suddenly drove the lance into the earth before him. Then he turned to Moses and spoke with a voice that was filled with rage and pain.

"I am Zur, Prince of Midian and father of Cozbi, who was murdered by this dog in the tent of Zimri! Give him over to me so that I might slit his throat and watch his blood flow onto the ground as did the blood of my daughter!"

Moses was calmly aloof. He studied Zur for some moments, then spoke scornfully.

"I will not give him over for he did the will of the Lord on that day. For your daughter was evil and led Zimri to do evil. Therefore, Phinehas is cloaked in the mantle of the priesthood forever that no man may lay hands on him."

"Your priest is a murderer of women, the lowest of dogs, a coward fit only for a coward's end!" Zur screamed. "Give him to me, that I may avenge my daughter who was young and dear to my heart! She was but a young woman of high spirit who loved a man and for that no woman should die!"

"She led Zimri to the altar of Baal and for that he was condemned by the righteous wrath of The True God and she with him! ...Phinehas was an instrument by which the Lord did his will, therefore he is glorified and I will not give him over to you!"

Zur glared at Moses with an anger that permeated his deepest being.

"Then hear you well, Lord of dogs! Cozbi will be avenged! ...If she is not avenged by the blood of her murderer she will be avenged by the blood of Israel.... If you will not give me justice, Lord Moses, then I will give you war!"

With that, Zur wheeled the stallion and galloped back to his warriors. In a moment nothing was left to speak of their visit but dust hanging in the oppressive heat.

That evening, as the land of Moab put on the chill mantle of night, Moses and Joshua with his lieutenants, Joha and Daniel, crouched around a crackling fire of acacia branches. In attendance to the prophet were Eleazar the high priest and his ignoble son, the priest Phinehas. The threat made by Zur had been taken very seriously by the hierarchy of Israel. The Midianites were a people endowed with a fierce pride and Moses' refusal to hand over Phinehas as retribution for the death of Cozbi would force them to seek other revenge.

"Even now Zur is sending messengers to gather the tribes of Midian," Joshua was saying. "When he has assembled them he will overrun the far settlements in Bashan. And then, having conquered our people in the plains of Bashan, they will gather the tribes of Edom and the people of Moab with them and they will descend upon us with thrice the strength they now have."

"But surely the sons of Baal cannot prevail against the people of The True God," Phinehas said. "We have the ark of the covenant to carry into battle to insure our victory."

Joshua regarded Phinehas scornfully. "Alone, Zur cannot stand against us. But if we must do battle with all of the plains tribes we may taste the bitterness of defeat. For they will not come at us with foot soldiers alone, but with hordes of archers and lancemen all mounted on the swift horses of Joktan—our warriors will be as chained dogs standing against wolves—they will be cut down and the ark will be taken to Zur as a trophy. And you, ...you will wish you were never born before at last death releases you from the agony Zur will inflict upon you."

Moses looked at his general and his words held the sharp edge of anger when he spoke.

"Do not misjudge the courage of our warriors or the strength of our God, Lord Joshua. For if ten of our mighty men stood with the Lord against a hundred Midianites the ten would prevail if they but believed in his power. Yet...if one must stand against a lion there is no wisdom in waiting until the whole pride comes forth. Strike at Zur now, before he gathers the other nations to him."

"That is easily done. I have but to send messengers to those tribal princes that remain and they will obey my call for warriors. Those that live after the purging of the followers of Baal have little desire to end their days naked upon a stake in the sun. I will send messengers this night and my army will be assembled within three days. But my captains must know what is to be done. What course shall we take if the warriors of Midian are defeated and throw down their weapons before us?"

"There is but one course—the command of the Lord is that all idolaters shall die!"

"But My Lord, does that not speak of the children of Israel?" Eleazar asked. "To slay all idolaters would put us in mortal struggle against every other nation of the world."

"The Lord has called us to avenge him against Midian. The Lord commands that we must utterly destroy them, that they shall not rise again to do battle against us. Therefore kill every person that might bring forth seed to rise against us."

A fleeting shadow of aversion crossed the face of Joshua, then disappeared into its usual stoicism.

"So it shall be done, My Lord—but what of the spoils of war and Zur's great city?"

"Take all that you can of the riches of the land and that which you cannot carry or drive before you...burn! And when you have burned the houses topple the stones that remain."

"But, My Lord," Phinehas interjected, "would not their homes be fitting dwellings for our people? I myself would rather live in a fine house of brick with ceilings of wooden beams than in the moth-eaten tent that shelters me now."

"It cannot be. We seek to destroy the nation of Midian. As long as their idols and temples, their shops and houses and even their sheep pens and granaries remain we have not destroyed them. We will raze every proof of their civilization so that they will never again corrupt our people. And you, Phinehas, will oversee the destruction in my place. For you will take the silver trumpets and lead in the battles, that all may know that Phinehas is not a murderer of women, but a great warrior priest."

So it was that Joshua conscripted soldiers from every tribe, a thousand from each.[62] Six thousand mighty men of war whose strong arms wielded swords of iron or axes that cut through armor or shield. Four thousand spearmen with lances and javelins tipped with Philistine iron that could pierce the leather-and-bronze armor of Midianite horsemen. And two thousand archers with strong bows of wood and horn and arrows tipped with iron.

When they were assembled, there stood upon the plain of Moab the most fearful army that Israel had yet mustered. Though they were fewer in number than those who stood against Amalek at Rephidim their weapons were no longer crude and those who stood in the ranks of Israel were warriors of might. At their head were Joshua and the young priest Phinehas, appointed by the aging Moses to attend the warriors as the instrument of God. Before these two stood the twelve warrior princes, the most stalwart of the mighty men of Israel and each a captain over a thousand men. Subject to each of them were ten lesser chieftains or captains over hundreds. Among these last were Daniel and Joha of the ill-fated battle against Amalek at the hills of Beersheba. Also a captain was Ephah, who murdered many of the rebels at Sinai and whose nature was as his name, which means "darkness."

These warriors stood in the early light to receive the blessing of Yahweh by the hand of his great prophet, Moses. And when the Lord's blessing had been given, Moses sent them forth to conquer the high plains of Midian, where he had once fled from Pharaoh.

CHAPTER 15

Zur was in a black mood as he surveyed the encampment at the fringes of his city. It was a milling swarm of people, horses and camels, but it was pitifully small. He had sent messengers far into the desert and south to the sea in an attempt to rally the many scattered tribes of his people. Now, a fortnight later, he had succeeded in enlisting only four tribes to his cause. What would five tribes with less than as many thousands of warriors be against the swarming hordes of the Hebrews? Were it not for the insolent judgement of the prophet against Cozbi he might forget his rash threat of war.

Yet Cozbi had been his youngest and the favorite of his daughters, though she had gone to an Israelite man against his wishes. It was true that no woman was worth a war—but he had to kill the dog, Phinehas, or be labelled a man of little honor—a coward among his people. How would he do it? That was the question that had perplexed him since he left Moses standing in the dust of his horse's hooves. The answer still eluded him and four tribal princes awaited him in his palace. The sun was hanging near the western horizon and the trails from the desert were still—and barren of riders.

Zur heaved a heavy sigh of frustration. He turned and walked down the dusty path to the brick and plaster structure that housed his family and served as a meeting place for occasions of state. As host and prince of the largest tribe he made his appearance at the banquet hall last, bending low and grasping the sword hand of each of his guests as he greeted them. The four princes were already seated on cushions around a low, carved table of acacia wood, drinking strong red wine from silver cups while they visited.

Their aides, crouched in a cluster just beside the doorway also sipped wine, though from pottery cups rather than silver. Shafts of light still streamed in through the westerly window slots from the descending sun and reflected from the whitewashed walls, giving an unusual brightness to the otherwise plain room.

After settling himself on the ornately carved chair that served as his throne Zur clapped his hands. Two of his servants entered bearing silver trays of wheat cakes, dried dates and figs, cheeses and various meats. When all of the princes had been served, two musicians with flute and lyre appeared and began playing.

After a few moments a seductive female dancer of many veils—a priestess who danced at the rites of fertility before Baal of Peor—undulated to a point directly in front of the princes. The voluptuous movement of the dancer drew lascivious smiles of approval from the men as she began a sensuous and erotic dance. There was no sound at all now except for the feverish music of flute and lyre and the rhythmic padding of the dancer's bare feet on the flagstone floor. Even the trays of food were forgotten as she whirled and swayed, shedding fine linen robes of different colors as she danced. As the last colored robe fell away she was covered only by a very fine white cloth that revealed every feature of her body as she danced in a frenzy of erotic movement. Then suddenly she leaped to an inner doorway and was gone.

Then the men reacted with loud and crude applause, showering the floor with silver coins which the musicians quickly retrieved.

"For such a one as that I would give over my best stallion. Indeed, I would give my best stallion and five choice mares for her to share my bed and bear me children."

The speaker was Reba, prince of the tribes that wandered the lands east of Bashan and who therefore was intimate with the plundering ways of the

Israelites. He was a large man, somewhat younger than Zur and gregarious to the point of boisterousness.

"Had the Israelite prophet taken her to his bed he would be less zealous in persecuting the priesthood of Baal and we would not have this problem." Reba laughed with a rumble that emanated from deep within him.

"The prophet's desires for issues of the flesh have departed him as his member has shriveled with age and righteousness," Zur grumbled. "The man has desire only for power and his lust is for the torment of those who defy him."

Tall, lean Evi, whose tribes rode the plateau to the south of Reba and adjoining Zur, nodded his head in assent. His Adam's apple bobbed up and down as though it would break through his skinny neck as he spoke and his watery eyes peered out over a formidable nose so that his profile resembled that of a bearded vulture.

"Though Reba and I had no great love for the Amorites we have given many of them sanctuary among us. Though they were barbaric they were better neighbors than the vermin that have driven them out. For these do not defeat and enslave...they annihilate all that stands in their path! Never has a greater destroyer walked the fair fields of Bashan than Joshua, their general!"

Rekem, the eldest of the princes and much respected, had been listening attentively. "All that I have heard is true," he said gravely. "But I have not thus far heard mention of what course the peoples of Midian should take. Surely we do not come with our entire tribes to feast and leer at dancing girls."

Zur colored at Rekem's remark. "We gather to see if we might put a snare about the prophet's feet or a noose about his neck. We well know that no nation is safe from the greed of these people, not even our people who gave Moses refuge when the guards of Pharaoh sought to kill him."

"And who befriended him and gave him a good woman for a wife," interjected Hur, the strong and fierce prince of the tribes east of Edom, who was in his prime and feared no man. "For my father was a friend of the priest, Jethro, who helped this Moses when he would have died in the wild plains. He befriended the man and gave him his daughter as wife. The woman, Zipporah, bore him two sons, Gershom and Eliezer, now grown into fine Midianite warriors."

"By the beard of my father!" Reba exclaimed. "The sons of the Israelite prophet ride among us?"

"They ride with my people, encamped here this very day. The mother is still straight and strong and is the queen of Jethro's family. She is wise and kind but with the heart of a female leopard. She has raised her sons with those of her sisters—they bear no love for their father, who rejected them."

"We cannot trust our welfare to such a man, nor can any of the nations about him," Rekem said. "The bull that gores a cow and her calves cannot be trusted among the herds. My heart is sore for Zur, who has lost a daughter because of this man's evil judgement. Nor is he alone, for we have received many women and children who were cast out by their Israelite men or whose men were slain because they would not cast out their wives. This, Moses does in the name of his god and speaks of righteousness!"

"That man's righteousness is as hollow as a gourd for it has no wholesome meat within it, but it rattles with the seeds of murder, rape and theft. He must be stopped before he takes the whole of the world and leaves us to rot in our own blood!" Hur exclaimed.

Reba agreed. "I find no fault with that—but how will we do it? Our warriors are as handfuls against the heaps of Israel. Our men are valiant and we have swift mounts, yet Joshua has ten warriors for every lancer we might send against him. Are there no more tribes that will join us?"

"I have sent messengers as far as the Red Sea and the deserts of the people of Joktan. Some cannot be found in their wanderings and others feel no duty to fight against a people who are far from them," Zur said.

"What of the peoples of Edom and Ammon?" Evi asked. "They are very strong—will they not stand with us against Joshua?"

Hur shook his head. "Kybar of Edom has already refused Moses passage for his people and he won the issue. He feels secure in his position and will not send his warriors and so arouse Joshua against him."

"It is so with Ammon," Evi said, "they are strong and Joshua will not violate their borders. Though they wish us success and let us travel through their land they will not provoke the lion, Joshua, by pricking him with a spear."

Reba struck the table with his fist. "Will none join us to stop this scourge? What of Moab? The Israelites already stand upon Balak's land—will he not fight with us?"

Rekem pursed his lips and stroked his silver beard with a gnarled hand.

"Zur and I spoke with Balak when first the Israelites came and destroyed the Amorites. Even then his fear of the Israelites was great, because he knew they might take all of Moab. Balak is a very superstitious man and consults all manner of priests, diviners and sorcerers. Thus he knew of a diviner of great wisdom, a magician who has wonderous powers.

"We sent emissaries to Pethor where this man, Balaam, dwelled," Rekem continued. "These men brought him a heavy purse to entice him to come and lay a curse on Israel that they might fail in battle. Balaam came then and we built the altars he required on the hills above the encampment of Moses that he might make a strong enchantment against Israel.

"But when he looked out on the vast numbers of Israel the magician's legs shook with fear and he refused to curse them.

"Even so, to lessen the anger of Balak against him he counseled Balak that Israel might be defeated through its young men. He told us to inspire our young women to seduce the young men of Israel and lead them to the temples of Baal. Thus the strength of Moses and Joshua would diminish in time, so they would no longer be a threat."

Reba chuckled. "I had heard something of that. It would have worked because of the female wiles of our women and those of Moab. Beside them the Israelite women are as geese beside swans."

Zur smiled sourly. "It is because of the strictness of the judges that the women of Israel are so. Yet the old fox might not have seen the dangers if he hadn't been so jealous of his tabernacle. He is overly zealous in the service of his god. It makes me fear that he may be right and we who worship Baal are wrong. It angered him greatly to see his young men fall away from the worship of Yahweh."

Rekem nodded. "Even so, he might not have done anything if it hadn't been for his priests and the judges. They are a suspicious, devious lot and they found out from a Moabite traitor about Balaam's counsel to Balak and the elders. That happened at the time when the fever came among our people and those of Israel. The priests and judges said the plague was a judgement against them by Yaweh because of our women and Baal. That's when they had the blood purge among their people."

"That is when my daughter, Cozbi, was killed by the coward Phinehas," Zur said. "And that is why I must kill him and why we must go to war. To avenge a blood crime against our people and to stop these evil hordes who will destroy our lives and those of our children."

"But you have not said whether Balak will stand with us against the forces of Joshua," Reba said. "Or will he stand wringing his hands like a woman while the Israelites take his land and his livelihood as they took that of the Amorites?"

Rekem regarded the men at the table soberly. "After counseling us to use our women to overcome the Israelites, Balaam made predictions that Israel will rule the land and the nations about would fall. And when he left, Balak was more fearful of Israel than before. I think Balak will not join us against Joshua's warriors unless he thinks we will surely win."

The men at the table fell silent, each immersed in his own grave ponderings. A few ate without interest in their food like cattle chewing straw. At last Zur raised his silver cup.

"I drink to you, Princes of Midian. Though we may die in the coming war, we will die fighting. And though our women may grieve, they will grieve for brave men."

The princes drank to the toast and when all had put down their cups, Zur spoke again. "We cannot go alone against the army of Joshua. But we can sorely hurt Israel where his army is not massed. What think you, Princes of Midian? Let our lancers swiftly strike Moses' settlements in Bashan while our people and our warriors on foot follow behind them. Thus we can attack them quickly that none may escape to warn Joshua. When we have taken the fields of Bashan Balak and others will join us in the battle against Joshua."

There were strong words of agreement among the princes of Midian, words that were the prelude to many hours of planning that night. In the late hours of darkness a plan had been conceived that might drive the Hebrew invaders back to the wilderness of Paran.

In the predawn gloom six young women of the tribes of Hur walked quickly to a yard where their livestock would be waiting. They must milk the she goats, a few gaunt brindle cows and the ewes whose lambs had found the roasting spit, so that the herders might take them to pasture. Behind them lagged Ribai, daughter of the priest, Jethro—now wife of the Edomite warrior, Bela. He had left Prince Sahed of Amalek to wed her after the battle at Beersheba. Beside her was Mara, second wife of Prince Hur himself. Both women moved laboriously, being great with child. The younger women, twelve to sixteen years of age, chattered happily about young men they admired who rode among the lancers of Hur. Beyond the little niche of field that bedded the sheep shepherds dozed in wraps of goat hair while armed sentries yawned at the top of the encompassing rocky bluffs.

"Hur told me this morning that we will soon attack the Hebrew settlements in Bashan," Mara confided. "He says we must before the Israelite general, Joshua, has time to send his armies against us. Moses has sworn vengeance against us because of the trouble at the acacia grove."

Ribai frowned. "Bela has told me that it is our obligation to Prince Zur to avenge the death of his daughter, Cozbi. She was killed by a cowardly Israelite named Phinehas in the tent of one named Zimri. It would be a shame for men like my husband to die for such as her. She is known as little more than a common harlot and she had bedded many men before Zimri."

"It is true that Cozbi and others like her give their bodies freely to the men of Israel. But were not our women told to sacrifice their bodies to lead the men of Israel to the temples of Baal?" Mara's voice took on a scandalized tone. "The chieftains sacrifice their women to weaken the rule of Moses."

"Perhaps, but would it not be better to give our young women as wives rather than have them raped by the Israelites as the Amorite women were?"

Mara nodded. "I suppose so, but it's shameful to give such as those before us to the savages of Israel when our own young men are wanting for wives."

The gossiping conversation of the women was halted abruptly by the startled cry of a sentry as an arrow plunged into his chest. There was another cry, quickly muffled by a strong hand, as a dagger found another sentry's throat. Then in the half-light a succession of human figures appeared against the reddening sky, leaping from the rocky bluff to the field below. In front of Mara and Ribai the screams of frightened milk-girls rose into the air in a piercing chorus of terror that was swiftly muted by the blows and grips of heavy hands. A masculine curse followed as sharp young teeth found a purchase on one of the offending hands, but it was swiftly followed by a pained female cry, then silence. Then as if by some miraculous design of providence the clear, piercing call of a ram's horn trumpeted into the heavens, the final sacrifice of a sentry not yet discovered. It was followed by the chaotic, frenzied cries of men in battle, diminishing as one by one the outnumbered sheepherders courageously gave up their lives.

Mara and Ribai abruptly turned and scurried back toward the encampment as swiftly as their bulky bodies could traverse the rough path. As they neared the jumble of tents they were met by a scattering of warriors just emerging from interrupted sleep. Twice they encountered still-drowsy men who pointed slender, sharply tipped, javelins at them until recognition lessened the wildness in their eyes and they rushed on to meet the true terror of the dawn. The women split up then, each running more swiftly than they themselves could imagine, all the while screaming a warning to close encamped neighbors, until at last they found the empty seclusion of their own tents.

"Run!" An old man, clumsy with infirmity, poked his head through the flap of Ribai's tent. "Run, get inside Zur's walls if you wish to live, the Israelites have come."

With that he disappeared to deliver his frantic message again and again, until at last his aged heart refused the unaccustomed labor and he slumped silently against a solitary donkey standing indifferent to the mounting pandemonium.

In the darkness of her tent Ribai fell to her knees at the bed she shared with Bela, hoping halfheartedly that by some quirk of fate he might yet be there. It was empty, but still warm to her touch and she knew that by now her warrior would have mounted his fiery Joktan horse and would be rushing to victory or to the veil that would forever separate them.

Unconsciously she seized a little carved chest that held her wedding jewelry and some gold and silver pieces. She wrapped it in their wedding blanket and ran. Outside, women and children and those men too infirm to fight were rushing to the gates of Zur's city. The last carried weapons as decrepit as themselves, which if defeat came, would more likely be used for self-destruction than defense against the Israelites. For all manner of horrible stories were told of the agonies endured by those who were taken by the Israelites.

At the gap in the rugged stone wall that served as a gateway to Zur's city a group of armed men were struggling to close the heavy plank gate that, long unused, sagged heavily on its huge wooden hinges. They finally succeeded, but they left a little opening that could be quickly closed. Through it came a trickle of stragglers who were slow in finding the dubious safety of the walls. Leaving a few men to close the gate the last few cubits and place the huge bar, the soldiers took up their stations on the defense walkway of the wall. They peered anxiously over the top, watching for the first sign that the Israelites had routed the foot soldiers who had answered the call of the ram's horn. The men on the wall were not truly warriors, but more a sort of home guard, comprised mostly of merchants and craftsmen who did their daily business within the city. Their skill with arms was poor and so there was little hope of withstanding a siege unless the warriors returned.

CHAPTER 16

Zur's horse warriors—strong, fierce, valiant men—had already dashed to the night holding where their horses were kept. It was on the side of the high city wall where attack was less likely because of a steep gorge that formed a natural barrier to intruders. In moments they had found their mounts and were thundering past the city gate, a swift procession of fierce fighting might, led by Zur on his black stallion.

From the men on the walls and from the citizens gathering in knots on the flat rooftops overseeing the plain, a spontaneous cheer exploded, enheartening both the riders below and the people within the walls.

In the field beyond, more mounted warriors were grouped in loose brigades behind the banners of their leaders. The bulky form of Reba was already riding his great, gray stallion at a furious gallop toward the battle. Blue ribbons adorned his lance, held high as a rallying symbol for his warriors—at his side hung a vicious curved sword with a hilt of carved ivory.

Hur, the fierce one, followed with the Edomite, Bela, close by his side. Both carried lances flying red ribbons, the color contrasting sharply with the yellow of Bela's battle tunic. Behind them in the first rank of lancemen rode two young warriors, Gershom and Eliezer, sons of Zipporah. They were straight and lean, darkly bronzed and taut of muscle—both wore the red sashes of the tribe of Hur about their battle tunics.

Then rode the gaunt Evi, tall and formidable in battle gear. If before he gave the appearance of a bearded buzzard, the resemblance was now akin to a fierce eagle, its beak pointed toward battle. His banner, a trailing device of large feathers fluttered from the lance of his captain, a young chieftain wed to Evi's daughter.

In the rear rode the archers of Rekem. They followed his son, Medan, the best bowman of the tribes of Midian, who now wore the silver breastplate of his father as his sign of leadership. Rekem himself, his body now too infirm of muscle and bone for battle, stood among those on the walls of the city. But still, the proud veteran of many battles wore his bronze sword sheathed at his side. It had been his companion in the wild rage of mortal combat, but like him it was no longer fit to stand the tests of better blades and younger men.

At the livestock hold, which spread for a great distance between the encampment and the bluffs that faced the city, pandemonium met the sunrise. Cattle, goats and sheep, crazed by the smell of blood and the tumult of battle, raced in all directions, as attacking warriors weaved their way among them. A huge bull, incensed by this violation of his domain, chased a group of Israelite soldiers until it impaled one on his massive horns. It stood goring the screaming man until he became still, then turned its attention to others chasing them with the intestines of the first unfortunate fluttering from his horns like a grisly banner. The bodies of the slain herdsmen lay scattered among their crazed animals, their blood mixing with the urine and excrement of the wildly dashing creatures.

Within minutes the first Israelite warriors had found their way through the cattle yards and were engaging the leading Midianite foot soldiers, driving them before their onslaught. But as more Midianites joined the battle the Israelite progress stopped and they began to give way before the savage defense of the Midianites.

As the sky lightened, Joshua watched from a high bluff. His first wave of foot soldiers were about to bolt and run. He nodded his head to Phinehas and the priest put the silver trumpet to his lips. Two thousand sword and spear men rushed down the bluff just as the first wave of Israelite warriors turned and ran. The pursuing Midianites, now tiring, ran into a greater force of fresh soldiers who quickly overpowered them and drove them across the field to the edges of the encampment. Frantically fighting overwhelming numbers, the Midianites gathered in encircled clusters to face a certain death.

It was then that the Midianite lancemen descended on the warriors of Joshua. Crouched low on the backs of their galloping horses they were a sight that drove terror through the minds of foot soldiers. For when they attacked side by side with lances extended there was nowhere for a foot soldier to go. To stand and fight was to face the speeding point of the long lance or be trampled beneath pounding hooves. Even if the warrior's shield took the blow he would be driven to the ground by the force to be trampled by another horse or feel another lance or the edge of a sword. To flee was futile for a man could not outrun these swift horses and would only die by an unseen hand as point or blade caught him from behind. The lancemen cut through the soldiers of Joshua as the hail had cut through the fields of Egypt.

Joshua watched the swift change of fortunes with frustration. If only Moses wasn't so stubborn about raising horses, he thought. If his lancemen were mounted this battle would already be over. He turned to Simeon, a commander of bowmen.

"The archers...loose the arrows."

Simeon looked at him with surprise. "Are you sure, My Lord? Our men are mixed among the horsemen."

"Those men are already dead!" Joshua snarled. "Loose the arrows on the horsemen of Zur!"

Prince Zur wheeled his horse and his bloody sword flashed downward yet again. Beneath the blade Daniel warded off the blow with his shield and struck with his sword at the black-robed warrior who grinned so evilly at him. *It is most surely the evil one I fight,* he thought, *for no man's face is so filled with desire for another's death.* Again the sword fell from above and this time the force of it drove Daniel back until he stumbled over a body and fell heavily to the ground, shield and sword spread wide. Above him the warrior raised his sword high to strike a lethal blow but his hand stilled in the air and his face took on a perplexed look. Zur raised upright on his horse then fell to the ground, a feathered shaft protruding from his back. The black stallion leaped as an arrow found his haunch, then it bolted through the melee, leaving Daniel staring into the desolate eyes of Zur.

The arrows came in dense flights, like angry wasps in buzzing pursuit. Where they alighted they left their stings of death. It mattered not if it was horse or horseman or swordsman holding up his shield as scant protection for his life. The arrows of Joshua's archers fell in a rain of death. Daniel jumped up and ran, with those of Joshua's warriors who still could, to the bluffs where they scrambled up the rocky slope like men possessed. Desperately they climbed with shields before them, seeking shelter from the swords of the enemy below and the arrows of their compatriots above.

Now, onto the bloody field where men and horses groaned and uttered shrill cries of pain, came the bowmen of Rekem. Dismounting in leaps they drew fully the long bows of the nomads, crafted to find a mark in bounding antelope or distant sheep. Far stronger were they than the clumsy devices the Israelites drew, launching flint-tipped shafts high onto the bluffs where Joshua and Phinehas stood, so that they were forced to retreat to a safer vantage place. The ranks of Simeon's archers thinned in the face of the nomads' arrows and finally all withdrew in panic because their own shafts fell short of Rekem's bowmen.

The battle stilled and the warriors of Midian gathered their wounded and carried them to the safety of Zur's city to be tended until they died. The dead they left, for fear of the Israelites, except for two Princes. Prince Zur, toppled from his horse by an arrow, and Prince Evi, pinned beneath his stricken mount amid the bodies of ten of Joshua's swordsmen. The princes who still lived sent the remaining foot soldiers and Rekem's archers within the walls of Zur's city and old Rekem stood as warrior-prince in the place of Zur. The mounted warriors, who now numbered little more than half their former strength, gathered behind the banners of Reba and Hur and rode off from the city so that they might fall on the flanks of Joshua's soldiers if they came again.

The hours of midday passed into evening and Joshua did not come. With the evening came the lowing of cows and insistent bleating of the she goats which wandered with overfull udders about the milking place. The sounds pained the ears of those milking girls who had been tardy in their duties and so had escaped capture by the Israelites. Some of these sat sniffling in miserable huddles, weeping for friends who had been taken. But also they wept because their goats suffered, for they had an affection for the animals in their care. They called each gently by a name bestowed in a laughing moment and sometimes gave a favorite some small tidbit of grain or perhaps a crust of bread.

But at this moment there were no gay laughs or giddy chatter. For some, though yet too young to have a hearth of their own, had formed love bonds with dashing young warriors who would not return. Others grieved for a brother, father or favorite uncle who had not come through the gates after the battle. These still lay upon the bloody field, tended only by buzzing flies which already laid their eggs in oozing wounds.

Ribai did not grieve, for those who had died among the lancers were not yet known, save Zur and Evi. She had thought she saw Bela's yellow tunic among the riders as they regrouped behind the two banners which were still raised above the field. With a warrior's superstition her husband believed the brilliant tunic had kept him safe at Beersheba and so he wore it always when he carried a lance or sword. Now Ribai lumbered gently among the wounded with her friend Mara, who was overjoyed at the sight of Hur's banner upon the field. Mara was younger than she and was despised by Reumah, Hur's first and older wife. So the young woman had been attracted to Ribai, who like an older sister gave her love and sympathy.

Ribai bent to assess the wound of a young warrior who was crying out, then shook her head as she looked at Mara.

"It is a lance wound in his belly. Already it becomes foul," she whispered. "Give him a little syrup of the poppy that he may die without such pain."

"I know him," Mara said, "he cared for his old mother...it is sad."

"War is always sad. The youngest and strongest die and the old are left," Ribai answered. "But it may be different now."

"What do you mean?"

"Your tribes were far distant when the Israelites took Bashan. They killed all the men who could not get away and nearly everyone else."

"Even the old people?"

"Especially the old people—they could do no work for the Israelites and so...they were worthless to them," Ribai said. "And of course the little boys had to die since their mothers would raise them to be Amorite men."

"And they kept the young girls, I suppose."

Ribai nodded. "The men of Israel had use for them."

Mara shook her head violently. "And those girls stayed? I think I would run away, rather than be a bed slave for such as them."

"They had nowhere to go except to the desert and perhaps to others who would treat them as badly." Ribai looked at Mara pensively. "When we could still mix among the Hebrews did you not see women of your own age that looked very sad?"

Mara thought for a moment. "Yes, I did and I wondered why they did not smile. Those were women taken as young girls?"

"Yes, ...it is a thing that robs a women of her life, though she yet lives. Home, husband and kin—all are lost. Pray that you do not see it. Pray to Baal that the Israelites do not conquer us."

That night there was little sleep in Zur's city. Those that did not stand upon the rampart stood about the palace of Prince Zur. There his body and that of Prince Evi lay upon biers of stone. They were clad fully in battle dress with their swords laid upon them, hilts in folded hands and points downward to symbolize their battles' ending.

Already, in the square that was the daily place of trade, firewood brought from the valley of the Jordan to sell was being piled in two great stacks. When it was done the sons of Zur and Evi came. They carried the two warriors and placed them on the pyres amid the loud wailing of the family women and the more restrained cries of the populace. Then the eldest son of each took torches and set the pyres ablaze. This they did to protect the princes' bodies from desecration if the city should be taken by the hordes of Israel.

At the top of the bluffs the soldiers of Joshua watched the walls of the city with interest. All evening they had watched certain horsemen enter the gates and listened to the distant wailing of the bereaved—but Midian in its anguish did not grieve alone. Even now graves were being dug and bodies of Israelites were being placed in the shallow trenches as they were readied. The camp followers, many of whom were wives of the deceased, put up an anguished lament that pressed harshly upon the ears of the resting warriors. But then suddenly the anguished cries within the distant city were stilled and the glow of fire flickered against the sky. It grew brighter until the tongues of flame leaped higher than the walls and seemed to lick at the very stars. The Israelites upon the bluff grew silent and even the wailing of the women ceased as all eyes watched the distant fires.

"Zur has escaped the wrath of Moses," Joshua mused aloud. "I had thought to tie his body upon a stake or place his head upon a spear. Yet he was a man of courage and the pyre that burns so fiercely is a fitting end to such a man."

"Brave he was indeed, My Lord, and fearful," Daniel said. "Never have I looked into a man's eyes and seen such hatred. But for one of Simeon's arrows, I would be sleeping in a grave tonight instead of him."

Joshua glanced at the warriors around him. "It was but one of the turns of battle. I chose right and so you are alive today to fight again tomorrow. That Zur died was a happenstance of battle—but there are two fires in the city—what prince of Midian lies upon the second pyre?"

Joha spoke. "It was Evi, the prince from the land south of Zur, My Lord. His horse was felled by arrows and he was pinned beneath it. A swordsman took his life but he had killed many of us before he fell."

"It is well then, that Lord Joshua ordered me to loose the arrows," Simeon said. "Of my own accord I would not have and all those who faced Zur's lancers would have died when the Midianite archers came."

Daniel nodded. "And Zur and Evi might both still live to lead their warriors.... For myself, I think your arrows were less deadly than the lancers. For a man cannot hold a shield against a charging horse. And arrows come from one side only, while the horses whirl about like the desert winds. You speak truly, for when the Midianites loosed their arrows we would have died as we fought or as we climbed the bluff. It would have made no difference which we did."

Joshua had turned his attention back to the city. "Listen, my warriors. It is well for Zur that his ashes now ride the winds. For after tomorrow his city will be no more and his people will face the wrath of Moses. Phinehas, the priest, has sworn an oath before Moses that Midian shall be utterly destroyed. Therefore make your hearts hard that you will be able to do what is required of you."

Shupham, one of the princes of a thousand warriors, crossed his arms upon his chest and spoke.

"What nature of thing is it that Moses requires of us, My Lord? Must we destroy those of Midian who lie wounded in battle?"

Joshua did not turn his gaze from the city. "Put them to the sword, Shupham, and save them a lingering death."

"We will give them a swift death, My Lord. For no brave man should lie upon a field and slowly die in agony. Often I wish I could give my own stricken warriors so kind an end. But we will defeat the Midianites because our strength is much greater than theirs. What shall we do when the last warriors throw down their arms and plead for their lives?"

"Phinehas has sworn an oath before God and Moses that every man among them shall die, that Midian will not rise up against us again."

Shupham, who was a prince among farmers and herdsmen, looked down and idly turned a stone with his foot as though he were considering a field that must be harvested. "It is a hard thing that you ask, Lord Joshua.

To coldly kill a brave man with whom I have no issue, save that he fights for his nation, is not the path a warrior wishes to take."

Joshua looked at Shupham impassively. "It is not a thing I ask of you, Lord Shupham, but I command you and all others in the name of The Almighty God. For Moses has spoken to Yahweh and it is his command. You will give the Midianites no mercy!"

Rekem stood on the high tower beside the gate of the city. His long, silver beard was ruffled slightly by an early morning breeze and he frowned as his time-weakened eyes strained for sight of Joshua's army.

Again he inquired of the young warrior beside him, "Do they come? Look to the bluffs, Reu."

"I see nothing, Lord Rekem, save a few sheep and a tent which sets on the plain."

The warrior was not more than seventeen and his face was taut with fear.

"Will we die today, My Lord?"

Rekem looked at the lad beside him. He was scarcely more than a boy, with wispy beard just starting to form about his mouth. *How I wish I could give my life as ransom for his,* he thought. *His life is just starting and mine is nearly ended, yet this day may see the finish of us both.*

"It is in the hands of the gods," he said gently. "Our warriors are valiant and we still have mounted lancers. We have better bows than they, with archers that can pluck down a swift antelope. We may keep them from the gate. Be brave, my son."

The boy was about to reply, but his mouth froze upon the words and he could only point to the bluffs. There, as far as one could see, the frightening figures of Joshua's warriors lined the horizon. Then, in answer to the command of the priest's trumpet that echoed even to the city's walls, they surged down the bluff and converged into a column, perhaps forty warriors wide and seemingly without end. As they advanced Rekem saw that they carried with them the long tent which the lad had seen. He cursed softly to himself and glanced at the young warrior who was watching the column move across the cattle yards as though he were mesmerized.

"It is a ramming log," he said, "run and tell your captain to ready the hot oil and fire."

The boy ran, glad to get away from the awful sight before him. Rekem watched the huge column advance, quickly, inexorably, like a winter flood washing down a wadi. When it had reached the encampment two bands of horsemen suddenly appeared and fanned out into a line of lancers on either side of the Israelite column. They charged then, perhaps a thousand mounted lancers following the banners of Reba and Hur, against eight times as many of the best warriors of Israel.

Rekem watched, fascinated, yet filled with a strong foreboding as the distance between the forces lessened. The outer ranks of Joshua's column turned to face the horsemen and knelt, shields forming a solid wall, lance butts planted in the ground with point's thrust outward. Then the second ranks took their place behind the first and yet another close behind them. Bowmen! The sight exploded in Rekem's head as his foreboding raced toward reality. Too late, Reba and Hur saw what had happened. But to turn would put their horses broadside to the arrows that would come and all would be lost. With lances poised the riders raced into the flurry of shafts and suddenly all was mayhem. Men of both armies died then as lances and arrows found them. Riders fell with their stricken horses and managed to gain their feet, only to be dispatched by swordsmen of Joshua. Others fought with their swords, wheeling their horses about, killing until either mount or rider was stricken.

In the end, perhaps a hundred riders escaped, a beaten remnant of the once proud force. Among them a warrior in a bloodied yellow tunic stopped and surveyed the slaughter that continued as Joshua's swords began dispatching those who still had breath. Bela, the only captain who still rode among all the lancers of Midian, turned away because he could no more stop Joshua then he could prevent the rising of the sun.

Prince Shupham witnessed with a sickened stomach as the Midianites were executed. He was accustomed to the slaughter of sheep or bullocks but these were men as noble and courageous as he. Most were severely wounded and with those he ordered death without remorse, for it was to them a release from hours or days of agony. It was a mercy he could not grant his own wounded. But a few had wounds from which they might well recover and these watched him with accusing eyes as he touched the hilt of his sword in judgement.

The captain of the executioners was Ephah, a man much attracted to killing. He had volunteered for the post to the priest, Phinehas, whom Shupham despised as a murderer. Ephah had brought the bodies of Reba and Hur, the princes of Midian, to him and offered to cut off their heads as a present to Moses.

"Where are their wounds?" Shupham had asked.

"A lance wound in the chest for the one," Ephah told him, "and a sword wound in the neck for the other. I see not where it makes a difference."

"And where are your wounds, Ephah?" Shupham wore a rough bandage over the sword gash on his own bloody arm.

Ephah looked at him unsurely. "I have none, My Lord."

"Not even a scratch or bruise?"

"I was fortunate, My Lord."

"Were you fortunate or did you hide from the battle?"

"I fought as you but with greater skill, thus I am untouched! Lord Joshua knows well of my courage," Epha said insolently.

"To take the head from a brave man's corpse requires no courage, Ephah, to die well does. Put their bodies among those who died with them and let them be!"

Ephah was about to reply angrily when two of his warriors brought a Midianite lancer to him.

"I know this one," one warrior said, "I saw him at the camp at Rephidim. He was but a boy then but he is the same one. I wondered whether he might be granted clemency."

"Is he not a Midianite?" Ephah asked.

"He is so."

"Then kill him!" Ephah shouted angrily.

Prince Shupham looked closely at the young warrior before him. Then he held up his hand to stay the execution.

"Bring him with me to Lord Joshua," he said. "And you, Ephah, finish your evil work."

Joshua looked sharply at Shupham as he approached. "What do you bring to me?"

"A Midianite lancer."

"Have I not told you what must be done with them?"

"You have, but look at this one—do you not recall his face at Rephidim days after the battle—though he was still a stripling then?"

Joshua looked closely into the defiant eyes burning into his. "What is your name?"

The eyes blinked and the warrior licked his parched lips. "It is Gershom."

Joshua looked at the warrior more closely.

"It is true, your hair and face are the same as his—the prophet is your father!"

"I have no father!"

"Perhaps, ...but Moses has a son. Were there not two of you?"

The warrior swallowed, then said in a hoarse whisper. "His name was Eliezer, he lies among the dead."

"And your mother, Zipporah, does she still live?"

Gershom's head lowered. "She is in the city of Zur."

Joshua studied Gershom—at length he turned to Shupham.

"Take him to find his brother that you might bury him. Then put this one on a horse and send him away. We cannot take him to Moses alive—because he himself made the judgement against the Midianites—nor will I kill the prophet's son!"

Then Joshua surveyed those that stood about him and spoke again.

"Let no man speak of this to Moses.... It shall be unknown among the people. This I command you for fear of death by my sword."

At his place on the tower, silver-haired Rekem watched the destruction of the proud lancers of Midian. They had been mauled by Joshua as jackals are mauled by an angered lion. And now nothing would keep the fearsome throng of Israel from the gates of the city. The column had stopped, but Rekem knew the purpose. He stood with his head lowered out of sadness and respect for the valiant men that had died before him. Then the column moved again and the men on the walls grew tense. Some nervously fiddled with their bows on which arrows had already been fitted and refitted many times. Others, gripped by the fear that haunts men who face violent deaths, moved their lips silently, praying to whatever gods they worshipped. But most simply waited, gazing impassively at the awful sight before them, thinking whatever thoughts unfold in the minds of men who are about to die.

The column was nearly within bowshot when perhaps ten ranks of men split off either side and marched to the right and left, encircling the city. They halted then, shields readied against the arrows of Rekem's archers. Their own bows, at least a thousand more, were strung to receive their iron tipped arrows.

The men on the wall watched with awful fascination as the long tent at the column's center crawled forward like a huge, bleached caterpillar. At last it was so close that the men above could count the raw bullock hides that covered it. They were sewed coarsely together with the entrails of sheep, creating a broad, stinking canopy that stood against both arrows and fire. Inside, it shielded the awesome engine that could splinter the mighty beams of the city's gate.

As the thing drew within a few cubits of the gate Rekem signaled and men threw pots of hot tallow out upon the loosely stitched top. They were rewarded with cries of pain as the burning substance trickled down on the men within. Then fire pots were thrown and the melted grease burst into flame, raising a choking stench as it charred the green hides of the canopy. The progress of the thing stopped. Some men ran from the flaming structure with their clothing spewing oily fire. Inside, men with wetted sack cloth beat at the fires franticly.

Archers darted out through flaps at the sides of the canopy to send arrows at the men above the gate. In turn, Rekem's archers on the wall sent their own shafts into the easy targets that emerged, so that at last the Israelites dared not show themselves.

The canopy drew back, for the moment defeated by the terrifying assault from above. Inside, fresh men clothed in mantles of raw hide took their places at the ram. The thing was a log of oak cut from the forests of Bashan, ten times a man's arm length and more. It was hung by thick ropes to a framework of poles on which forty men labored. A crude device it was, but deadly. For once the log was swung forward its force was more than enough to burst the gate of Zur's city. Outside now, men labored at adding skins to those charred by Rekem's fire and cutting small holes from which the archers might launch their missiles.

The thing advanced again and now the archers inside sent their arrows freely to the wall top in a deadly duel with the Midianite bows. The stinking tent was brought up against the gate despite the burning oil that roared furiously in blackening clouds and the first strokes of the ram thumped ominously against the gate.

Prince Rekem shouted to the warriors above the gate. Now they tipped down huge rocks which had been pried from the battlement itself and balanced precariously above the gateway. The poles that supported the bullock skins splintered and brought the canopy down upon the ram and the men who carried it, crushing them beneath the massive weight of stone and hide. And again, Joshua's men withdrew the thing from the city's gateway.

Inside the city the full force of Rekem's warriors was clustered behind the gate, except for the bowmen who stood on the walkway near the top of the wall. Many were battle-scarred veterans, a hardened, fierce lot, who endured danger and pain without a sign of fear. They would fight until the last man had fallen, not holding back the sword out of pity, nor asking that it be held from them. These rugged warriors seemed to radiate an aura of invincibility about them, giving heart to the younger and the more mild warriors in the company. And so they waited for the return of Joshua and the onslaught that would decide the very existence of Midian.

The remainder of the city's inhabitants had sought refuge in their clay-brick houses or on the rooftops. There, women, old men and young boys gathered with timeworn weapons, sickles and clubs to make a last desperate defense if the Israelites should overrun the city. There was little of the impassiveness here that was displayed by the warriors. Many of the women endured their fears quietly, by strength of spirit, for the sake of their children who cried in frightened clusters around them. And some simply submitted themselves quietly to the will of the gods, because of the tired hardness of age or because they saw no other course. But many, already aggrieved by the death of warriors within their family groups, wailed loudly until they were silenced by the hard hand of another.

The thing below the gateway began to move again. But now the long lines of Joshua's archers that were strung out along the wall ran toward the gate. They swiftly mobilized a mass of bows that closed upon the battlement, unleashing volley after volley upward felling the defenders of the wall surely and relentlessly. Now Joshua's ram found the gate with little resistance and the defenders within the city steeled themselves before its relentless, rhythmic pounding. Then with a wretched, cracking sound the cross bars broke and suddenly the massive planking of the gate fell askew.

As Israel's horde surged through the gateway, Rekem himself drew his bow and loosed arrow upon arrow into the swarming tide of Joshua until a warrior of Israel scaled the wall and thrust a dagger through his heart. The battle, though fierce, was quickly won, as the valiant defenders of Midian fell before the overwhelming host of Joshua. Swordsmen of Zur and Hur, Reba and Evi, backed into corners and alleys of the city and hacked at the swarms that beset them until their own blood spilled upon the earth. Rekem's archers that still stood upon the wall set their last arrows into flight, then drew their daggers and fought until they fell to arrow or sword. Thus they died, the defenders of the city of Zur, avengers of Cozbi, woman of Midian.

In the farthest room of the dark castle of Zur, eyes wide with fear, women and children watched the doorway for those who soon would come.

Mara and Reumah, newly bereaved wives of Hur, clung to each other, finding in their common grief a solace and affinity they had not shared before. About them clustered the children of Reumah. There were five in all from a toddling boy of two to the eldest, Pasach, now fourteen and the image of his father. With them were two daughters of Zur who were pretty like Cozbi, their murdered sister, but older by several years. Like Reumah they were mothers of little children who snuggled close to them, whimpering with fear.

The curtain that hid them from view abruptly sped aside and two men in battle garb stood in the doorway. They were frightening, unsmiling creatures, with beards and hair in wild disarray, sweat soaked and bloodied, so that they seemed to be apparitions from an insane nightmare rather than men of flesh and bone.

The boy, Pasach, took a step forward, uncertainly brandishing an ancient bronze knife. Reumah clutched at his arm in a desperate attempt to take the knife from him and so give him some chance to live. But he tore his arm from her grip and advanced on the soldiers with the same stubborn courage that had made his father a great warrior. Suddenly he lunged, making a clumsy thrust at the first soldier. The warrior deflected the flimsy blade with his sword, then he struck the boy viciously, not with the sword edge, but with his fist and the hilt of the weapon. Pasach fell back in his mother's arms, dazed and helpless.

"The stripling has spirit," the soldier laughed, "if he were my son I would teach him to be a great warrior. What say you, Ephah?"

"He is not your son and we cannot let such a young wolf live. Already he bares his teeth at us. When he is grown he will bury them in our throats—kill him!"

The first soldier stepped forward and raised his sword. But with a scream, Reumah leaped in front of her son and in an instant she had plunged his knife to the hilt beneath the soldier's breastbone. The soldier looked down incredulously at the thing protruding from his sternum, then he sagged to his knees and balanced for a moment before he quietly fell prostrate on the floor.

Ephah, Captain of a Hundred, stared at the dying soldier. It would defame him that his warrior had been killed by a woman. The other captains would laugh him to scorn beside the campfire that night.

"The bitch bites more savagely than the whelp!" he cried.

Angrily he stepped across the man and struck Reumah so hard with his sword that her neck was nearly severed. Then he grabbed the still-senseless boy by his hair and, with a quick slash, cut his throat.

"So we deal with the spawn of Baal!" he shouted. He raised his sword to the other women and took a step forward.

"What do you here, Ephah?" The voice was angry and filled with authority.

Ephah turned about, looking at his commander belligerently.

"I but destroy a nest of serpents, for one has killed an Israelite warrior, Lord Shupham."

"And would you not have done the same, Ephah? The woman protected her own and for that she died. And the lad was nearly a man, so he must be killed by the order of Moses. But why do you raise your sword at these women and little children?"

"They are all serpents of the same nest. We will do well to destroy them before they release their venom against us again."

"We are warriors and do not degrade ourselves by murdering women and suckling babes!" Shupham shouted. "Get them out into the square and from this moment kill only the boys who are near manhood and the old and infirm who cannot march to Moab!"

Mara gathered Reumah's children about her as they were driven like sheep to the market square. Now there only remained women of child-bearing age and some beyond who were strong, as well as young girls and small children. The old people, both men and women, and the adolescent boys lay dead where they were found.

Joshua sat on his horse, a tall sorrel, as the captives were herded into the market square. A short distance away was Zur's castle, a building of mud-brick that would have been a stable beside the palace of Pharaoh. Four soldiers were coming out of the gateway leading a man in fine clothing between them. They stopped before their captain, Joha, who in turn brought them to Joshua.

"What manner of pretty bird do you bring me, Joha? Indeed his plumage is as fine as that of a peacock."

Joha smiled grimly. "He was a guest of Prince Zur, for we found him in one of the bedchambers clutching a purse filled with coins. He claims to be a friend of our people."

"A friend of Israel? Indeed, ...what would a friend of Israel be doing in Zur's castle? Speak, son of Baal! Who are you and how do you come to be in Midian?"

The man pulled his arms away from the soldiers and puffed himself up haughtily.

"I am Salaam, soothsayer and servant of The True God."

Joshua looked at the man incredulously. "I know of no soothsayers in the Lord's bond. Moses, the prophet, speaks to Yahweh and hears him. But I know of no other. Lord Shupham, do you know of this man?"

"I have heard of him. He is a sorcerer and a diviner of fortunes. He lays curses and blessings for a price and he bows down to the god that pays him most."

"Is that true, Balaam? Do you serve both Baal and Yahweh?"

"Let My Lord Joshua hear and believe.... I was once a servant of Baal but your god has spoken to me and I now know him to be The True God. Therefore, I serve him faithfully and I am a friend of his people."

"Then being a steadfast servant of the Lord and a friend of our people, why do you hide with much money in the castle of Zur?"

"I was called by King Balak to Moab and I went there for fear of refusing him. He asked that I lay a curse on your people, which I would have done. But God Almighty spoke to me and forbade me, so instead I made a blessing on your people. From that time I have visited among the people of Moab and of Midian that I might spy on them in the service of your god."

Joshua laughed harshly. "You took money from Balak to curse us and instead you blessed us?"

Balaam smiled ingratiatingly. "I blessed your people, that you might be victorious in battle. And you have conquered Midian.... Perhaps you might wish to reward me." Joshua stared at Balaam coldly. "I will have Joha give you just reward for your treachery." Then he turned to Joha and touched the hilt of his sword.[62]

The murdering had been done and now the warriors sacked the city, the encampment and the corpses of those who had died defending them. They gathered great piles of goods of every kind. Gold and silver, jewels and finery of every sort they placed in baskets and urns before the watchful eyes of Joshua and the priest, Phinehas. The weapons they had taken were placed in great stacks before the warrior princes, along with shields and helmets of bronze. Food was gathered for both the warriors and the prisoners, great pottery jars of wine and oil, woven sacks of wheat and barley and great baskets of dried fruit and bread. In the field, among the bloating bodies of slain Midianites, the cattle, goats and sheep still wandered. These were gathered together in herds and flocks and the young women of Midian were made to milk those with full udders, so that their milk should not dry up before they were divided among the people of Israel.

The hours of the day were nearly passed when they had made an end to the looting and nothing of value remained, except the houses and gardens of the city. Then quickly the soldiers cast the dead of Midian into the houses. This they did so they would burn with the houses and be buried in the ashes and the rubble. For Phinehas wanted nothing to remain for those who lived to worship as a memorial to the princes of Midian. Then Phinehas made a torch and poured holy oil on it and lit it from the holy lamp he carried with him.

"Take this flame," he commanded Daniel, "and from it light the many torches of the captains, then put your torches to the city. For it is the holy fire of the Lord, which will destroy the city of Zur, who was a servant of Baal. And when the city burns, cut down the olive trees, the trees of fruits and nuts and the vines of grapes and cast them into the fire along with the carved images of their gods. Let nothing remain that others might raise houses from the ashes of the city."[62]

Daniel took the torch and from it lit the torches of the captains. Then they put the torches to the houses of the Midianites. And in the light of the flames, the soldiers cut all the living wood and took all things good and threw them into the fires. By the midst of the night the city of Zur was consumed and nothing stood but smoking walls of brick and stone.

In what had been the market square the young women and the children watched numbly as the fires devoured the last vestiges of their lives. Within the leaping flames, everything and everyone that had mattered was consumed and the last miserable remnants of their people now huddled together wretchedly. Theirs was the deepest of despair, for the losses were not only of dear ones and property, but the very essence of their lives was taken from them forever.

CHAPTER 17

From a distance, Daniel and Joha stared at the glowing embers of the city. Again they had survived the vicious frenzy of war and with battle weariness they were slipping into a state of depression. They had fought and killed as warriors must do to stay alive in the pandemonium that is commanded, but not experienced, by men of power. But now, in the quiet of night, they were visited by specters of those who had died beneath their blades. These images of frightful terror died again and again within their minds, giving them no peace or respite for their tired bodies. So now they sat with arms clasped about their knees, talking quietly to hold back the melancholy that afflicted their spirits.

"My bones ache with weariness, yet I cannot rest," Daniel said. "Does your spirit groan within you as mine does?"

"Aye, my body cries for sleep, yet I cannot," Joha's expression was dismal. "I hear the sounds of death within my ears."

Daniel nodded pensively. "I do also—the cries of the dying scream within my head—the faces of terror show themselves before my eyes. After Beersheba I only fought with the remembrance of fear, not with such apparitions as these."

"Why should this be?" Joha asked. "Is this not a mighty victory? Were we not commanded by God to destroy the Midianites because of their wickedness?"

"So the prophet has decreed. Yet I look about at the awful devastation we have brought and sickness overtakes my spirit. To kill armed men in battle is the purpose of a warrior. Yet against the Amorites and now again, we kill all before us with no regard for women, aged or youth, or pleas for mercy. Is this truly the command of our mighty God?"

"Moses has proclaimed it and he speaks with God as one man to another," Joha said. "Yet when the defeated warriors were put to the sword something within me cried out against it, though Moses said it is God's will."

Daniel returned his gaze to the ruined city. "I felt the same then—and when a beardless lad and his grandmother were killed before me I wanted to vomit. I think such things cannot be the duty of a warrior."

"Perhaps you are right, my friend. But it is not our place to judge what shall or shall not be done. We must obey our superiors. Yet, I wish that those who command it would look into the eyes of those we kill.... But sleep peacefully if you can, Daniel. Soon we will return to Moab and we will kill no more."

Phinehas, the priest, smiled with satisfaction as he watched the procession of animals, captives and warriors set out on the road to Moab. Where the city of Zur had stood nothing remained but ashes and rubble. In the field where the dead of Israel had been buried, a huge altar, blackened by the atonement sacrifice of seven bullocks, stood as a memorial to the brave men who had perished there. In a few years weed growth would cover the ruins and the existence of the city would be stricken from the earth.

Phinehas had been given a mission by Moses and he had accomplished it well. In addition, the plunder had been much richer than he and Joshua had expected. The cattle alone would have been worth the campaign. But Zur's city had been a trading center and the spoils in terms of rich goods, gold, silver, bronze and jewels had been enormous.

And slaves! There were enough healthy women and children to provide slaves for much of Israel. It was too bad the prophet had insisted on killing all of the men. But then, they were a wild, rebellious lot. They would have been no end of trouble if they had lived. For even if they were castrated so that they could spawn no more of their kind and they were chained to the grist mills or forced to quarry rock, they would look always for a chance to kill Israelites.

Only one thing bothered Phinehas. He had seen Joshua turn a Midianite lancer loose, but when he asked him about it Joshua refused to answer him. For that matter, neither would any of the warriors. Phinehas supposed the lancer might have been related to one of the warriors. Perhaps it might be something to mention to the prophet—he would think about it.

That evening Joshua walked slowly among the prisoners who were gathered for the night in dismal clumps. He had ridden his horse past the long column of captives as they marched, but he had not seen the one he sought. Now at the end of the day's trek he was searching again. It was difficult to tell the women apart, they looked much alike with their loose, flowing robes. The one he sought might have died at the city. Yet she wasn't so old and infirm that she would have been killed. If she was still alive he must find her before they returned to Moses. Her presence would create a very difficult situation for the prophet.

Now and again Joshua stopped at huddled groups.

"I seek the mother of Gershom and Eliezer," he would say. But the answer would always be the same, shaking heads with stony glares of hatred and a mumbled negative response in the dialect of the plainsland. Then as he asked the question again a woman looked up sharply, as though startled by the question, then turned and walked quickly away. He overtook her and grasped her arm.

"You know of the woman I seek," he said.

"I do not know of the woman you seek."

"You know, ...why else did you leave?"

"To take care of my young sister, she is with child and I fear it will come in this desolate place."

Joshua grasped her with both hands and shook her.

"Do not lie to me! I must find the woman of whom I speak."

"Why? ...So that you might kill her as you killed her sons...and mine?"

"So that she might live! ...I have word of her sons. Are you her friend?"

The woman hesitated, searching his face, then she answered.

"I am her sister, Tirrzah. I will take you to her."

Joshua knew the woman the moment his eyes came to rest on her. She still stood proudly as she had at Rephidim, though her face was lined with past hardships. Sorrow showed in her eyes as she looked at Joshua, but she did not turn her gaze from him.

"It is you, Zipporah," he said.

"It is I. And you are Joshua, the murderer of my people." She said it calmly, as though placing a long-lost relative.

The quiet condemnation struck at Joshua more savagely than a Midianite sword and he colored with surprise and anger.

"Be more careful of your tongue, Zipporah. I am but a general who answers to your husband, Moses."

"I have had no husband for these many years," she said. "And now, because of Moses, I have no sons. I do not fear you, Joshua. You can do nothing to me except send me to my sons."

"I can do that, Zipporah—I can send you to one or the other, whichever you favor."

"What do you mean? Are not my sons among those that burned in the city?"

Joshua shook his head. "One still lives, the other we buried safely on the bluffs above the city of Zur."

The woman looked at him and for the first time Joshua was forced to look closely into the sorrow of a mother whose son he had killed. She fought to keep the calmness with which she had greeted him, but in the end her composure crumbled and her proud face was laid waste by grief.

"Which of my sons died?"

"It was Eliezer."

"I had not thought it would be the gentle one," she said. "But I thank you, Lord Joshua, for telling me.... Where then is Gershom?"

"We put him upon a horse and set him free," Joshua said.

"You set him free?"

"I could not take him to his father because Gershom denies him, nor would I allow the prophet's son to be executed. Nor will I bring his wife or any of her family as captives for I know that the family of Jethro gave Moses refuge when he was hunted by the Egyptians.

"But it could go ill with me if the elders of Israel learned of it for they are adamant that all of your people must be killed or made captive. So you must go to those of Midian that remain and ride to the far plains beyond the reach of my warriors. My captain, Prince Shupham, is a kindly man. He will give you mules that will take you far and fast. If you wish to live free of bondage take your sisters and your children and be gone this very night!"

Moses rested himself on a bench in the shade of the acacias. There was an incessant pain in his joints and his recurring headaches were stronger, bringing a throbbing hurt of such fierceness that it caused him to fall into a rage at the slightest provocation.

It had been so with the murder of Cozbi and Zimri. He had made a serious error in judgement, one that he would not have made earlier in his life. His elevation of Phinehas to the priesthood, rather than punishing him and the subsequent execution of the idolaters, had caused deep and needless rifts in the congregation. Moses was getting too old and impaired to rule, he knew it and he often thought of ceding the leadership to Joshua.

Gathered around him now were the seventy elders of the council of Israel. Like him, many were old and infirm and nearly all were jealous and distrustful of Moses. Those who had lost relatives in the purging of Baal were becoming militant in their opposition to his leadership, particularly the younger members who considered him to be an insane despot.

Others who had supported him in the past drew away because they disliked sending warriors to wage what they considered an unnecessary war, one which was likely to be unprofitable both in terms of lives and plunder. Moses rubbed his aching temples and looked at the men around him talking quietly in little clusters. He needed a major victory to bolster his declining leadership and now it appeared that this had happened.

Just days ago one of the Israelite princes to the east had sent a courier who said that Zur's city had fallen to Joshua. The man could tell no more because he knew only what a wounded Midianite lancer told the prince before he died. The next day a camel caravan from Aram had stopped at the settlement for water. Rasha, the chief of the drivers, excitedly told of a huge column of people moving slowly across the plainsland toward the acacias.

"They are followed by herds and flocks of such a great number that the dust from their hooves rises wide as a desert storm," Rasha said. "But I did not venture near in hopes of making a profit in trade. I feared that my goods might be the price exacted for my neighborliness, that and perhaps my life."

Moses had asked then, "Of what land are these warriors, Son of Aram? Are they of Joktan or perhaps of an eastern people who come to wage war against us?"

"You jest with me, Lord of the Israelites," Rasha said. "They are not of the east nor are they of the people of Joktan or others of the desert lands. This I know because the greater number of warriors walk instead of sitting astride horses and camels."

"Nonetheless, might they not be of Edom or Ammon? These nations have great numbers of foot soldiers. Might they not march toward us intent on subjecting Israel to their rule?"

Rasha grinned craftily. "It is not so, My Lord Moses. The greater number of the women and children walk in a swarm guarded by warriors. They do not journey in family groups with donkeys and camels carrying their household goods. I think they are prisoners being led to slavery and whoredom by their captors. They are part of the spoils of war as are the vast herds that accompany them. Thus, the warriors do not march to subject the people of Israel but to be glorified by them. Your General Joshua returns in triumph, Lord Moses."

It was almost certainly true that Joshua had overcome the Midianites. But if what Rasha had said was true, the returning army brought another problem with them. Moses felt anger creeping into his belly. It knotted his vitals tight and sent a throbbing torment to his temples. He wished he could leave the never-ending problems of his unruly people and go somewhere with Adanah.

Yet he smiled despite the pain in his temples. Adanah, woman of the nations, how well she had pleased him with her dark beauty and guileless love. Yahweh had given her to him but their union had not been blessed with a child—nearly, but only nearly. Perhaps they were too old, or perhaps if they had more time alone—a farm with a vineyard in Bashan....

Moses' reverie was dispelled by the rhythmic clatter of a galloping horse. With nostrils flaring and its body caked with lather and dust the beast coursed along the road to the acacias and slid to a stop at the sheep trough. The rider leaped down beside his mount, which already had its muzzle deep in the trough and splashed the tepid water into his mouth and over his head. Then he turned and ran toward Moses.

"They come! They come!" the rider shouted as he ran. He was small, wiry and young, more boy than man, but already the fastest of Joshua's couriers. Now he halted before Moses and fell to his knees as a sign of respect for the old prophet, trying desperately to contain his excitement until Moses bid him speak.

For the second time within the hour Moses found himself smiling despite his pain.

"Who comes, lad?"

"Lord Joshua and the army, My Lord! We have vanquished the Midianites! They are all put to the sword or fled. Five tribes met us at the city of Zur and all are destroyed."

"Five tribes? I would have thought Zur could rally more. Of which princes were they?"

"Zur, Evi, Reba, Hur and Rekem. Fierce they were in battle, My Lord."

Moses nodded. "The tribes of the plains are a valiant people but they are corrupted by the priests of Baal. What of the princes?"

"They are all dead. Four died upon the battlefield and Prince Rekem died defending the city."

"I know of him, though I had thought him too old for battle. It is fitting that an old lion should die defending his pride. And the captains and warriors?"

"Most died fighting and those who did not Ephah executed, except for a few mounted lancers who escaped and the one that Joshua re—" The young courier stopped abruptly, looking flustered.

Moses looked at him sharply. "You were going to say that Joshua released one. What of that?"

The courier turned his eyes downward. "I am sworn to silence under peril of death, My Lord."

"Which oath you have already broken and for which I would have you flogged if you were not so youthful. Who was this lancer that Joshua released? Tell me or the whip may yet taste your back."

"He was the son of one of our people, My Lord. I know no more."

Moses studied the lad's face. "I see that you speak truly and so I grant you pardon for hiding this thing from me. Tell me of the city and the spoils of war."

"The captains bring great riches and much goods of every kind, My Lord. There are cattle of such numbers that they cannot be counted. The weapons of the Midianites we took for our own as well as their shields and armor. And there are thousands of women prisoners and many thousands of children to be our slaves.

"As for the city...it is no more. When it was emptied of its wealth we piled the dead of Midian within it. The priest, Phinehas, made a holy torch and from it the captains lighted their torches, then put them to the city. And when nothing remained that would burn we cast down the walls that it should be altogether destroyed. Thus we buried the princes and people of Midian and the city of Zur."

"And you fought no other battles?"

The courier shook his head. "None would stand before us. Twice we saw riders in the distance but they vanished like shadows in the night."

"Of the twelve thousand warriors who went with Joshua, do you how many will return?"

"Men of Israel died, My Lord. But I cannot tell how many because it was not given to me to know. It was said among the warriors that a tenth part of the army died and that for every one that died two more were hard stricken."

"And Phinehas made an atonement sacrifice for those who died?"

"We dug graves for our dead and when we had buried them we built a great altar on the field where they lay. The priest, Phinehas, burned seven bullocks upon the altar as an atonement to Yahweh for their spirits."

Moses nodded soberly. "It is well that he did so. When will the company reach the acacias?"

"Joshua says they will arrive two days hence."

"The congregation will greet him upon the warrior's field. You have done well. Go and refresh yourself and rest. I will send another to tell Joshua we await him."

That evening Adanah chided her husband because he did not eat well but nibbled absently at his food.

"What ill humor overtakes you, My Husband? The lamb is young and cooked well with the spices you like yet you do not eat. Surely the elders no longer upbraid you now that Joshua returns victorious?"

"No, Adanah, they are content now that the smell of riches is in the air. It is another thing that causes me perplexity."

"It must be a very grave thing for your face is drawn as though you faced the angel of death."

"Perhaps I do, for God commanded me to destroy the people of Midian because they led us to the altar of Baal. Yet Joshua and the captains have not destroyed them all but they bring the women and children back to live among us. In that I will have disobeyed the Lord and for that he may again cast a plague upon us."

"But My Husband, Joshua and the captains are warriors and it profanes them to kill women and children who cannot stand against them. Therefore should we not show them mercy? I also was of the nations before The True God touched me. Will these not follow him also?"

"You were of the nations, Adanah, but you were taken by love not violence. These women will hate us until they die and one day their spawn will rise up against Israel as we rose up against Egypt."

"Even so, it would be a terrible thing to slay them. They are people just as we, not dumb brutes to be slaughtered. Were they not created by Yahweh just as we were? Will he not forgive them their false worship if they turn from Baal and follow him?"

"You go too far in your pleadings, woman. It is for the Almighty to judge who shall live and who shall die. I will go to the tabernacle and pray and the Lord will surely give me answer."

For six days Mara, young widow of Prince Hur, plodded heavily with the prisoners of Joshua. On the night of the sixth day she gave birth to a baby the newest son of the slain Prince Hur of Midian. She was attended in birthing by Jana, the twelve-year-old daughter of Reumah, first wife of Hur, who died by the hand of an Israelite soldier. In the morning Mara rose and joined the pitiable procession as it trudged toward the acacias of Moab. Beside her walked Jana and the other children of Reumah who still lived.

"How far is it yet?" Jana asked. She hunched herself to shift the weight of her two-year-old brother on her back.

"A day, two at most," Mara said.

"I'm glad, I don't think I can carry Reu much longer. Is the baby well?"

"He is well and very, very hungry. I am glad I'm fat because I can make milk for him even with little food."

"That's good. Can I see him again? He is my new little brother, you know, since we both have the same father. Seeing him makes me less sad that they killed Pasach and Mother."

Mara opened her cloak so that Jana could see the naked baby sucking hungrily at her breast. The girl managed a fleeting smile, then looked into Mara's eyes.

"I'm glad that father married you, Mara," she said. "You're like a big sister to us and I love you. I don't know what we'd do without you."

Mara took the girl's hand in hers. "I love you too, but I don't know if the Israelites will let us stay together. You must be very brave if they part us and you must take care of the little ones if you can."

"I don't know if I can, but I'll try.... Mara, why do they hate us so and kill all our men?"

"I'm not sure. I think it's because we worship different gods in ways they do not worship their god."

"Why should they care what god we worship or how we worship?"

"I don't think they really do.... They became angry with us because some of their people started worshipping Baal instead of their own god. And so they began disobeying their king."

"But why did they have to come and kill everybody and burn the city? We weren't hurting them!"

"I don't know, Jana. I don't know. These things are brought to pass by warriors and kings not by poor women like us."

At the sound of the trumpet the elders and the princes of Israel gathered on the warriors' field. At the front of the eminent assembly Moses stood with the high priest Eleazar. All night Moses had prayed to the Almighty God for a divine command or a sign regarding the prisoners from Midian but had received none. He was drained in strength and spirit and his temples pulsed with pain. Now he felt the first burn of anger touch his belly as the huge mass of people and animals crept slowly toward him.

Behind the warriors and in front of the herds a great horde of bodies plodded in the billowing dust dislodged by the army and driven by the wind. They moved as a huge blot of indistinct shapes creeping across the field. These did not walk with the cadenced stride of the warriors, but weakly and stumbling, sometimes falling to feebly rise again or lie prone to await the club of a guard.

These were the women and children of Midian, weak and trembling prisoners of Israel—yet a terrible threat to its solidarity. As they drew nearer the hordes of Israel cheered the coming of Joshua and the riches he brought. But Moses' features became ever more dour as the multitude approached.

At the front of the broad column of soldiers the warlords, mounted on fine Joktan horses, rode proudly. Joshua and Phinehas first, then the warlords of the twelve tribes and finally the captains of hundreds. These rode within an arrow's flight of Moses then stopped and waited. The column of warriors split and marched one half to the right and one half to the left before the elders and princes. When the warriors stopped and faced the assembly the prisoners were driven up between the two armies and made to kneel in a great show of glorious triumph for Israel. At this the multitude of the people who had gathered behind the elders cheered loudly, calling out the name of Joshua and praising Moses.

Now the warlords rode forward until they neared Moses, then they dismounted and approached Moses and the elders with heads bared to receive the prophet's blessing. In the fore were Joshua and Phinehas who now bowed low before Moses and the high priest, Eleazar.

"Your servants return victorious, Lord Moses," Joshua said, speaking clearly in the manner of a soldier, neither pridefully nor with false humbleness. "We have met the forces of Zur and they are destroyed."

Moses regarded his general sourly and when he spoke it was not with a blessing of fatherly approval.

"Have you also destroyed Midian that it shall not rise again?"

Phinehas, not being accustomed to the prophet's moods, drew himself up pridefully.

"We have destroyed all that was Midian—the warriors, the elders of the people both men and women and the groves and vineyards—the walls and buildings of the city of Zur we cast down in ashes, so that not one stone stands upon another. Thus we have destroyed Midian forever!"

The color came to Moses' face abruptly, as the stem features tightened with anger.[63]

"What folly do you spew, Phinehas? If you have obeyed my bidding and destroyed Midian as the Lord has commanded, why do these now stand before me?"[59]

The prophet pointed a gnarled finger sharply at the wretched assembly of women children kneeling dejectedly before him.

"They are a prey of war, Lord Moses, we bring them as a prize to forever serve the people of the Lord," Phinehas said. "Will not their labors increase the prosperity of the people and bring riches to the house of the Lord?"

Again Moses pointed his finger angrily, this time at a group of younger women at the front of the prisoners.

"It was women such as these who led the young men of Israel to the groves of Baal!" he roared. "You say you seek to do the Lord's will, yet you pay little heed to his commands! ...The Lord was greatly angered by the faithlessness of his people and he sent a plague to destroy us for our perfidy. You yourself thrust a javelin through a priestess of Baal and the son of Israel whom she corrupted—because of that, the Lord relented and stayed the plague and the people returned to his temple. Now you would bring the same ones that caused our anguish to live among us and corrupt our people with their idolatry again?"

Joshua stepped closer to Moses as though to confer privately with him.

"They will be nothing but slaves and the children of slaves," he said quietly. "Before they were free people living around us as equals and so their fair maidens easily led our young men to Baal. For as the ram pants for the ewe so our young men panted after the seductive harlots of Baal. But not now, ...these women are but slaves subject to their masters. Whether they be in field or bed they must provide that which their master seeks. And so they cannot lead our men to the temples of Baal by promising them carnal favors if they would do so and withholding favors if they refuse."

"You fail to credit these women for the guile which they learned as little girls," Moses returned. "Were not the heads of powerful Egyptians turned by daughters of Israel who were slaves to them? ...How then will the men of Israel differ? ...Think you they will not be turned from the righteous way by those whom they bed?"

"I see that you are right in your judgement, Lord Moses," Phinehas said. "But it would seem that there is a simple remedy to this difficulty. If you decree that only those who are virgins may be taken to an Israelite bed, it shall be law. Thus the women who are a danger to us will have no chance to seduce our men."

"Phinehas speaks truth, Lord Moses," Joshua said. "The females who have not yet slept with men are still pliable in their ways and can be brought into the congregation without risk of corruption. The others will end their days as slaves in various labors outside the households of Israel. Will that not satisfy the command of the Lord?"

Moses started as one who had slept and suddenly awakened.

"Do I counsel with fools?"[63] he shouted. "It will in no manner satisfy the command of the Lord! ...Has he not judged that we should destroy Midian? ...How then shall we destroy Midian—which is not a land but a people—when we thus take them to our breasts? You have saved the little boys and brought them among us. Will not their mothers raise them to hate us and rise up against us when they are men? It is for this cause that the Lord has ordered their extermination."[59]

"What you have said may be so and if we have erred it is on my head and that of Phinehas who have commanded the warlords," Joshua said. "But we have brought these people this great distance and now they kneel before us meekly as sheep before shearers. Therefore, what would you have us do with them? It is not fitting that valiant men of war should raise their hands against such as these."

Moses pressed the heels of his hands to his temples to ease the pain that pounded at them relentlessly, then he screamed at the warlords.

"Are you all witless fools that you cannot obey my commands? You must do as you should already have done—kill them!!"[63]

The warlords stared at Moses in astonishment then Prince Shupham strode forward. His face was set in an expression of angry contempt.

"What say you, Old Prophet? You would have these valiant warriors who have faced the lancers of Midian defile themselves by murdering these captive women and children? ...At the city of Zur I myself ordered the death of many brave men, who had done nothing except defend their people, because you commanded it! ...When the city fell we executed all the men, from aged patriarch to beardless stripling. We killed the women who were too infirm or too old to march and some who stood between us and their kin.... We struck with our swords until the earth was slimy with blood and hardened warriors puked with the stench of it! ...Has there not yet been enough blood spilled upon the plains to satisfy your enmity toward the princes of Midian?!"

There was a sober, almost imperceptible nodding of heads among the warlords that reflected the disgust that these veteran warriors felt. The younger captains remained at rigid attention behind their princes, but their eyes and the set of their mouths mirrored their revulsion toward Moses' words. Yet none, except for Shupham, dared incur the wrath of their aged leader and risk a hard death at the hands of the fanatical Levite guards. Joshua himself glanced nervously from Moses to Shupham, caught between his loyalty to Moses and his respect for Prince Shupham. As it was, the high priest Eleazar took hold of the arm of the prophet, who now looked as though he might expire with the violence of his rage and spoke to the warlords.

"Let the princes and the captains consider that the words of Moses are but an echo of the voice of Yahweh," Eleazar said. "Therefore to challenge Lord Moses is to challenge the Lord Almighty and is just cause for a judgement of death on he who does so. Regard carefully then what Lord Moses says to us, for it has come out of unceasing prayer and the greatest distress of his spirit. Lord Moses is a kindly man, not given to evil or vengeance, but the hand of the Lord rests heavily upon him and he must obey. Listen then to his words and do his bidding for you also must obey."

Thus pacified, the prophet regained his composure and again spoke to the warlords, though he now did so discreetly that the people should not hear.

"The Lord has commanded me that Midian must be destroyed. Though it may seem an evil thing—all those who might renew the seed of the princes of Midian must be destroyed. Therefore take all of the male children out into the wilderness and kill them.... Also, know you that the women who have slept with men may carry male children in their wombs. Those such as she," he pointed at a young woman who was near to birthing, "will bring the spawn of Baal back into our midst. Because of this you must take them out into the wilderness and kill them. Only the girl children who do not carry the mark of betrothal on their foreheads may you save. These shall be taken into your homes and shall become new blood of the nation of Israel. Go then and let it be done swiftly."

Prince Shupham turned as if to leave, but instead he took his swordbelt from about his waist and the chain and medal of leadership from about his neck. Then he strode swiftly to Ephah, who stood stolidly in the ranks of the captains and thrust the warlord symbols into his hands.

"These are better worn by a coward who delights in the shedding of blood!" Shupham roared at Moses. "I cannot do what you have decreed, Lord Moses, for my spirit protests within me! Therefore do as you would with me for I will not kill these innocents!" He turned and walked away, but before he had gone beyond the edges of the crowd a cluster of Levite guards encircled him.

Fearing that the other warlords would join Shupham in open revolt, Joshua walked to Ephah. He drew Shupham's sword from its scabbard and thrust the hilt into the captain's hand.

"You will do the deed that Prince Shupham refuses. But give me the medal of his rank, for one such as you shall not wear that which was won by a warrior such as he." Then Joshua turned to the warlords.

"Let each man of you choose a captain best suited to this work and send him with a hundred men such as himself. They will take the prisoners deep into the wilderness and divide them according to the command of Moses. Take care that none but girl children and virgins return. Let the rest of the warriors cleanse themselves from the filth of war and return to their families. Then when you have refreshed yourselves, let the warlords join me again in the grove of the acacias. It is expedient that we give notice to The Prophet of certain happenings of the campaign, lest others cause him to err in his knowledge of them."

CHAPTER 18

"Mara, why do they march us away from the village? I am so tired I can scarcely carry Reu. He sleeps and he slips from my grasp."

Jana staggered under the weight of her little brother, then finally put him down to be towed by his hands between Jana and her younger sister Ahni. The child cried his protest at being so rudely awakened, but he was forced to run on his stubby legs as the crowd pressed them along.

Mara looked at the young girl who was just a child herself yet struggled with a woman's task. She tried to reassure Jana but her face betrayed her own fear.

"Perhaps they have readied a camp for us away from their own people. We will rest soon."

"Do you think they will separate us? I don't think I can take care of Reu alone."

Mara clutched her baby beneath her robe with one hand and squeezed Jana's hand with the other.

"I don't know, Jana. But you must be brave and live, whatever happens. You are a daughter of Hur. He was a mighty warrior and through you, your sisters and your brother Reu he lives."

They came now to a place among the scraggly brush and rock where there was an open sandy flat. The village of the acacias had disappeared, leaving only the hostile wilderness and the endless pale blue sky in the prisoners view. Here Ephah, who had been chosen to lead, raised his hand to halt the pathetic procession.

Mara edged close to the daughters of Zur and their children and these women in turn drew their children close about them. It was as though the simple act of clustering together eased the terrible fears that they held within their breasts. Deep within they knew that their march to this place held some awful purpose. Yet they drew their children to them, soothing and consoling them as best they could, as mothers do, even in the face of overwhelming adversity. And so they watched mutely as the guards entered the fringes of the crowd of women and children and began dividing them into two groups.

The guards had been chosen for their unrelenting truculence, men known for their love of brutality. This the captains had done because true men of valor might rebel against the task which had been assigned them, even as Prince Shupham had defied the command of the prophet. Now these men moved through the mass of helpless prisoners, roughly pushing the women who wore the marks of betrothal upon their foreheads to one side, along with the babes too young to leave their mother's breasts.

The children were divided by sex, each having his or her genitals exposed to view lest a mother protect a boy child by dressing him as a girl. The boy children were allowed to rejoin their mothers, the virgin girls were dragged within a circle of guards where they began a subdued wailing of grief and fear.

Mara stood bravely even as the men approached. She gave Jana and her sisters a last squeeze before brutish hands were laid on them and they were subjected to the indignity of exposure. Then they were dragged, crying, toward the growing group of girls. Jana broke free and ran to her little brother, who lay screaming on the ground where he had been thrown by a guard. A particularly vicious guard jerked the girl to her feet and slapped her hard across her face so that she stumbled blindly back to her sisters. Then he turned back to the boy with a malicious expression, but Mara had already drawn the terrified child to her. Her black eyes penetrated those of the guard with angry defiance.

"Beast!" Mara hissed. "Son of a sow!"

The guard stared at her in disbelief then raised his fist to strike her, but another more humane guard stepped between them and hurried Mara and the boy away. So it continued for what seemed to Mara enough time for the sun to have set and risen again, though in truth it was but a short space of time that would be burned forever on the souls of those who survived it.

Then the last girl child had been sent to the pen formed by guards and they were ushered away, back toward the Israelite village, where they would begin their new lives as prey of war. The older girls would be claimed by various of the elders and more prestigious warriors to become concubines and mistresses after their allotted time of mourning had passed. The young would be assigned to various houses as slave girls until they passed puberty, when they would be used in the same manner.

Mothers and brothers watched stolidly as the girls were led away, their emotions numbed by the knowledge of the fate that awaited them. They huddled together, some praying to their gods, others staring at nothing, desolate, dazed to near insensibility by shock and fear. Then Ephah drew his sword and the guards advanced with clubs and swords, the screams of pain and terror began, raising in a horrible medley that etched itself indelibly on the minds of even the most hardened of Moses' butchers.

Mara watched, mesmerized by the overwhelming evil that now destroyed the lives of women and boy children whom she had talked and laughed with in the good days of Midian. She saw the wives of Zur fall to the sword and little Reu die by the club of a guard who laughed as he splattered the boy's brains on the ground. She clutched her robe tight about her, hoping that by some odd chance or intervention by the gods, the child she pressed to her breast, this last heir of Prince Hur, might be overlooked and live. Then suddenly it was her time. The guard she had cursed stood before her, blood spattered, grinning evilly. For a brief moment their eyes locked again, then the sword he raised high bit deeply into her neck and she fell dead. The babe she clutched within her robe fell free and lay crying on the bloodied ground. The guard reached down and picked the child up by the legs. Then he bashed his head upon a rock, killing him as casually as though he had been a rabbit or a goose for his dinner.

Ephah looked about him with satisfaction, there was not a twitch of life among the bodies strewn on the ground. The guards wandered about, sickeningly spattered and smeared with the blood of their victims. A few of the most scurrilous ones laughed and made crude jokes about the butchery while they searched the bodies for an overlooked ring or a piece of silver. But most stood with their eyes downcast, not wanting to look at the foul thing they had done. A few had run into the bushes and were vomiting violently.

After the scavengers made an end to searching the dead and had given a portion of their gains to Ephah he ordered the return to the acacias.

When Joshua and the warlords had assembled about the prophet's bench beneath the acacias, Moses came out from his house with Eleazar and Phinehas. He beckoned to Joshua.

"I would speak with you privately, Lord Joshua. There is a matter of some concern that has fallen upon my ears."

Joshua joined with the old prophet, supporting him with his arm as they reentered the house of Moses.

"I suspect I know what the rumor is, My Lord, and also from what source it issues forth."

"Then you admit to an irregularity in the handling of a certain prisoner?" Moses asked. "There were two occasions on which I felt it the best part of wisdom to depart from my orders, My Lord."

"Twice! You admit to disobeying me twice? Were you not as my very right arm I would have you tied to a stake for that, as Lord Shupham will be!"

Joshua looked somberly at the gaunt old prophet before him and wondered whether the Levite guards or the soldiers of Joshua would triumph if put to such a test. But now he spoke quietly to Moses.

"I beg you to hear me out, Lord Moses. For both Lord Shupham and myself did only that which we thought our God would desire us to do. For the thing which comes to your ears is of a young man of Israel, a lancer in the army of Hur, a warrior of courage and bravery whom Shupham brought to me and I set free. It was a thing for which I knew no other course."

Moses looked at Joshua sharply and when he spoke the hard edge of anger was in his voice.

"If this lancer you freed was of Israel he was a traitor to his nation and should have been executed."

"Not so, My Lord, for this warrior was born of Israel and of Midian also, thus he served Midian rightly despite his Israelite blood."

"Was then this man driven from his Israelite home that he served Prince Hur? What is his name? I would know of whom we speak."

Joshua looked deeply into Moses' eyes. "I do not know if he was driven out from Israel or if he left for some other cause—he was a boy then and gained his maturity among his mother's people—his name is Gershom," he said quietly.

Moses stared at Joshua, at first not comprehending, then he exhaled deeply and seemed almost to collapse within himself.

"It was Gershom, my son of my wife Zipporah?"

"It was, My Lord. But for Lord Shupham, Ephah would have killed him."

The Prophet seemed to age before Joshua's eyes and his face grew troubled.

"By the command of Yahweh he should have died yet as his father I rejoice that he lives—do I do wrong, Eleazar?"

The chief priest placed his hand on Moses' shoulder and spoke gently to him.

"Gershom was of Israel, flesh of your flesh and blood of your blood, therefore the order of death to the Midianites does not extend to him. You do no wrong nor did Joshua and Shupham."

Moses sighed. "It has been so long since I held my sons in my arms that I had near lost their memory.... I thank you, Lord Joshua, that you spared

Gershom for he is indeed flesh of my flesh and blood of my blood.... But have you knowledge of his brother Eliezer? ...He was the favorite of his mother. He bent toward poems and gentleness of spirit."

Joshua thought of Gershom's denial of his father and wondered if Eliezer would also have done so. The old prophet was looking at him intently, waiting for his answer. Joshua spoke gently.

"We buried him in a safe place. He died in the charge of Hur's lancers against us."

Moses thought of young Eliezer on his lap when he lived with Jethro's kin and despite his dour nature his eyes misted. Then he shook his head as though to dismiss the thought from his mind.

"Once again I thank you, Lord Joshua, for though the news you carry presses heavily on my heart you have been of great service to me. But what was the second thing of which you speak? I have heard of nothing else from those who inform me." He glanced at Phinehas, who lowered his eyes sheepishly.

"It was after the fall of Zur's city, My Lord. Zipporah, the mother of Gershom and others of the family of Jethro were among the prisoners. We set them free in the night—I and Shupham —for I knew that they had been your salvation when you fled from Pharaoh. Thus it is that their goodness to you has been repaid."

Moses sat as one who had been struck dumb. He turned his face inquiringly to Eleazar.

"Joshua did well to spare the families of Jethro," Eleazar said gently. "They were instruments sent by God to save you that you might lead our people from Egypt. They are blessed by God and holy in the sight of Israel. Therefore I pray you, Lord Moses, to dismiss doubts of the loyalty of Joshua and Shupham and to return Prince Shupham to his rightful place among the princes of Israel."

Moses nodded his head wearily and spoke. "So it shall be—that it be known that Moses, servant of God, does not repay goodness with evil."

Zipporah and her sisters had ridden the mules given them by Lord Shupham for two days now and it was late in the afternoon. They were well into the high, arid country shared by the Midianites and the nomads of Joktan. The region was unfamiliar to the women for they had long lived at the fringes of Moab. They did not know whether any of their own band survived or if other Midianites roamed the area, nor did they know where the far-flung wells were. Their water was gone and without it even the desert-tough mules would lie down and never rise again. Zipporah glanced at her youngest sister riding near her side. Ribai's face was pale, her jaw clenched tight, she rode rigidly like a wounded warrior who must endure pain at every step of the mule.

Zipporah reined in her mule. "Are you well, my sister?"

Ribai shook her head reluctantly. "The water has come. It is early but the babe will be born."

Zipporah now saw the darker patch that had further wet the mule's sweat dampened ribs. Below it water was dripping from the animal's belly.

"We will find a place to stop," she said calmly. She gazed about the arid plain for a possible refuge. To the east there were great blocks of stone and what appeared to be a gorge. She turned her mule toward it, beckoning to the other women who rode with small children clinging to them. As they neared the place, she saw that there was indeed a gorge that had been hewn from the rock by ancient waters. If the gods were kind there might still be water as well as shelter there. She rode to the brink of the gulley and looked down. It was shallow, not more than ten arm lengths in depth. And praise the gods!—in the bottom was a tiny pool of water fed by a trickling spring that measured but a handbreadth in width. Wearily, Zipporah dismounted and helped her sister down from her mule and into the skimpy shade of a huge block of stone.

"Bring us water, then tend to yourselves and the mules," she said curtly to her sisters, who were now clustering around Ribai. "Then find something to make a fire—we will need its light." She said this as an afterthought because the sun was low.

"Are the pains close?" Tirzah asked Ribai. She was only two years younger than Zipporah and was slow to do her bidding.

“They are not very close,” Ribai said, but her face tightened as she spoke.

“Close enough to ready a bed for you to rest on after the babe comes,” Tirzah responded.

Then she set the small children to gathering bits of grass and leaves to make a mattress of sorts and brought two of the tattered blankets that the kind Lord Shupham had given them.

It was not a swift delivery for the birthway had not properly opened. But in the midst of the night Tirzah held a baby boy up to the light of the fire for all to see. An irate wail came from the small form in her hands.

“Is the baby all right?” Ribai asked, her voice faint and worn.

“He is a fine boy,” Tirzah said. “He is small, but strong. Praise the gods that you have given Bela a fine son.” She placed the child against Ribai’s breast and pulled her cloak over him against the chill of the night.

Ribai smiled, then whispered, “Midian renews itself.”

To the west, sharp eyes read the flickering glow of Zipporah’s fire against the great boulder that sheltered Ribai.

“It is a campfire,” one said from his perch on a high rock. “It must be of the people of Joktan.”

“How do you know that it’s of Joktan?” asked the other.

“There are no others but us here, save those of Joktan.”

“None...unless Israel follows us.”

The eyes of the one on the rock narrowed. “Joshua would not take the bother to follow our pitiful band. But nonetheless, call the captains.”

In a few moments two warriors came—they wore the leather breastplates of Midianite captains and about their waists the red sashes of the lancers of Hur. The elder of the two wore a stained tunic of yellow and a patch over one eye. The other was taller and lean as a leopard, his thick mane reddish in the moonlight. Together they climbed the rock on which the sentry stood staring at the distant glow of a fire.

“What think you, Gershom, do the riders of Joktan come to call? Or perhaps Joshua thinks to destroy us utterly and so sends riders to pursue us?”

"Neither, Bela, there is but one fire and it is far too small to warm a fighting force or cook its food."

"Perhaps they are spies, come to search us out," the sentry said.

Gershom shook his head. "Nay, spies would light no fire. A lone hunter perhaps or an outcast such as us fleeing from the swords of Israel."

"You are right, I think," Bela said. "The fire may not bode ill for us. Yet it would be good to know who camps there and for what purpose."

Gershom nodded. "We must spy them out now, while darkness hides us—I will go."

"I will go with you."

"No, Bela, it is not good that two captains leave the camp. For if evil befalls us there would be none to lead our people."

"Then I will go and you will stay!" Bela snapped. "I am your senior and I declare it."

"And that is the reason you must stay, Bela. Your skill and strength is greater than mine. So you must lead the people, should I not return."

Bela drew back from his irritation and laughed. "Perhaps my skill and strength exceed yours, my friend, but not my craftiness. Go then, but take a few good men with you."

"I think not, for if there is danger in the night silence is a better protection than clattering swords. I will go alone. I go to spy, not to do battle."

'Then so be it and may the gods protect you, my friend."

Gershom unbuckled his sword and kept only a dagger as a weapon. He cut a hole in a large piece of brown sack cloth. Then he drew it over his head as a mantle to cover his armor and tunic and tied it about him with a leather cord. Last, he took a piece of charcoal from the dead campfire and rubbed it on his face and hands. Then he walked into the night.

Gershom silently cursed the brightness of the moonlight as he made his way through the sparse cover of thorny shrubs and occasional thickets of tamarisk or broom trees. Despite his precautions he knew he could easily be seen if anyone watched. Still, it was more likely that he might be heard than seen so he moved slowly with the stealth of a leopard. It seemed that it had taken hours for him to come the short distance that lay between the camp and the strange campfire, though the time had been much less. At last he was close enough to make out human forms sitting by the fire. One or two moved about. There were small forms lying near the fire which now and again stirred. Children! There were children in the group and that of a certainty meant it was not a war party. Gershom studied the moving figures for signs of weapons but could see none. He moved closer, much closer, until he could see the figures clearly. They were women! There were no men unless they stood guard in the shadows away from the fire. But then not all would be sentries at once, some would sleep. These were women, dressed in the long loose-fitting robes of the nomads. Not women of Joktan surely, for they would not be without flocks or tents. These could only be women of Midian!!

Zipporah was exhausted. Settling the women in for the night had taken the last of her energy and now she was sinking into a depressed stupor. She thanked the gods that Tirzah was a practiced midwife. She herself had always been good with the ewes of her father's flock, but birthing a child was different and she felt ill at ease with it. She glanced at Ribai, now peacefully sleeping with her son. The Israelites had destroyed most of the men of Midian and the women and children were in captivity, but already her tribe was renewing itself. On the edge of sleep, she looked up from her musings and her eyes widened with horror. A dark figure had emerged from the shadows and was running toward them. It was almost shapeless and Zipporah could make out no features where a face should have been. It was a faceless dark blob carried on long plunging legs with arms and robes flapping like the wings of some macabre bird. Surely a demon descended on them, ...Zipporah screamed a rending cry, born of the grief and terror she had so recently endured.

Her sisters leaped up to face the apparition, shaken by her scream. And then, suddenly they were attacking it, flailing it with their arms in wild desperation. But no, ...they were not beating the demon, but embracing it all at the same time, vying for a place to hold onto the thing. And then it was striding toward her in great, swift steps and the black mask became a face with a mouth that opened, showing strong white teeth. Then she heard the sound coming from it, "Mother-r-r-r!" and suddenly strong arms folded around her and the black blob became the face of Gershom. Zipporah closed her eyes and collapsed into the strong arms of her warrior son.

The reunion of the women of the tribe of Jethro with the remnant band of the lancers of Hur was a bittersweet time. For while a few embraced loved ones thought to be dead there was a deep sadness also, for many faces were missing, both of warriors who had died and also of women and children taken captive by the Israelites.

But even so gladness overflowed for Bela and Ribai. For with their reunion had come a new son, to be named Hur, after the valiant prince who had given his life for his people.

Yet, of the five proud tribes who had defied the might of Joshua only a few hundred souls remained. Those of sparse white hair and toothless mouths no longer dwelt among them. For the old had all died at the city of Zur and with them died the history and legends of the tribes. There were no stripling boys making their first unsure steps to manhood for they had met the same fate and with them had died a generation of future warriors.

Only a few hundred warriors, sullen and scarred in body and mind, stood watch. Less than a hundred women, aged too soon by grief, young girls who would never again smile at the swagger of stripling boys and toddler children who did not laugh and play, remained.

For all but the families of Jethro had been taken to the place of the acacias and there had met the hard fate decreed by Moses. The people that remained of the five tribes had been stripped of their kin, their belongings and their identity as a nation. Yet, these few would join the tribes of Midian who had not been destroyed at the battle of Zur and they would multiply.

But for now, Jethro's people were helpless and when they heard of the slaughter of the innocents at the place of the acacias, all they could do was weep and hate. In time the grandchildren of Gershom and Bela, the great grandchildren of Moses and Zipporah, ingrained with hatred for what

Moses and Joshua had done to them, would return to trouble the people of Israel again.[65]

CHAPTER 19

After his terrible judgements following the war with Midian the old prophet lost his taste for conquest. During that bloody campaign he had been at that age when the body has already fallen into decline and the spirit grudgingly follows. Now, knowing he had passed the peak of his service to the people as a warrior-prophet, he chose to be spiritual mentor and educator to them. And so, his last years were spent teaching and admonishing the people in the way in which they must live as the chosen nation of God. That and spending what peaceful hours he might with Adanah, his wife.

In their early years in Moab, Moses and Adanah had longed for children to fulfill the union between them. But after the loss of an unborn child Adanah's womb remained barren though she took her husband to her with willingness and vigor. And yet, after his first mourning for the lost child the prophet did not chafe at his wife's infertility, but instead accepted it as the will of his God. Still, though Moses had prayed much over it, The Almighty had made no discourse either directly or in a dream, concerning Moses' failure to produce an heir to his leadership. So the prophet was left to ponder the cause of this burden. Not infrequently he wondered if it were not a punishment for putting aside Zipporah and her sons.

In that, he bore a keen pain within his breast. For he knew that Eliezer, the gentle one, lay dead in a grave somewhere in the hills of Midian. More distressing, he knew that Gershom, the warrior, disavowed Moses as his father and Israel as his people. Though Moses wondered why God had not led his sons to follow in the steps of their father he assumed no blame for it himself. Perhaps God did not wish his sons by Zipporah to lead the people because their blood was not pure of Israel, but was mixed with that of Midian, some of whom had followed Baal. If that were so, then Moses was blameless. After all, he had done everything since he left Midian many years before at the command of his God. He had no other course open to him but to obey regardless of how harsh the orders were. And if his family rebelled because of it the fault was theirs, not his.

Then too, if the blood of Gershom and Eliezer was not pure enough for them to become the leaders of Israel, might that not also be the reason God had denied him a son by Adanah? For though Moses loved his wife dearly she was a woman of the nations and therefore would always be inferior to his sisters of Israel. He was at fault in this for he had followed his lust in taking the woman to him. He had not prayed to God for guidance concerning Adanah. He had prayed, but only in thanksgiving to his Lord for the gift of the dark woman's love. His neglect had been foolish, but the grape once crushed cannot be made whole. God had not chastised him for it so perhaps his trespass had not angered The Almighty.

Nonetheless the years were heavy upon his shoulders and his temples were racked with pain more often than not, so that he wished for release from his burden of leadership. When one evening the old prophet felt the presence of the Lord, he was not fearful but spoke with joy to his God. His God spoke to him then and made him to know that his days upon the land were few and that Joshua should lead Israel in his stead.[64] Then also the Lord told him that though he might view the fruitful plains of Canaan he would not enter them, but would die in Moab. Only then would Israel again take up the sword and conquer the promised land.

Moses accepted this final edict with resignation, even with gladness. He began to draw the scattered threads of his life together that they might be woven into a flawless whole before his passing. In this Adanah joined him with a gentleness and patience that spoke well of the dark woman's nature. Thus it was that Moses turned for counsel and friendship to the woman he had loved with such great passion. For no other person near him, save Joshua, knew him not only as a prophet but as a man.

Adanah had watched the decline of her husband these last years. She had thought of him as an ageless warrior-prophet of God—not a god himself—but certainly very near to it. And so it was perplexing to her to ponder this waning of body and spirit in the man who had been so strong and robust. For he had been in his prime, all hardness of muscle and mind, when she as a young woman joined herself to him. But they were no longer a seductive young woman and a virile mature man. The age difference was still the same but now she was still strong—though past child bearing—and he was aging, with the pains and weaknesses that afflict the aged. Adanah placed bread and some of the soft goat cheese that he liked before her husband, along with a hot tea that he had come to favor since the coldness of old age had descended upon him.

"Has my husband slept well? You rose in the night and I knew not the cause, so I kept my silence." She took a piece of bread and began spreading cheese on it.

Moses gave her a rueful half-smile. "Only ten years ago I would have stirred in the night because of your body against mine, Adanah. But now I rise in the night to gaze at the stars and piss and that painfully slow. My body no longer does my will, but rather I obey its dictates."

Adanah laughed. "You are still strong, My Lord. It was but a night or two past that you joined with me as a young man would."

Moses grimaced. "You soothe me with a woman's deceit, my wife. The days of which you speak were passings of the Sabbath. And the joining of which you speak was cut short by my loss of breath and that before I had sown my seed."

Adanah kept her silence for she knew that though he joked with her about it the gradual loss of his once surging potency did not rest easy with him.

"God spoke to me last night."

"It has been long since he has come to you."

"That is because he has no more need of my service."

"What do you mean? Do you not serve him every day? You teach and write down the law and you sit as high judge over Israel."

"These things I do. But could they not be done by any one of the judges or elders? ...No, Adanah, my purpose was to bring the people out of Egypt and make of them a mighty nation. ...That I have done."

"And has God told you that your service has ended? Must you not yet lead the people into Canaan to conquer the nations and claim the promised land?"

"Must you question me thus?[64] One answer will not suffice for both things you ask.... God has indeed told me that my service is near an end and my life also—he grants me the indulgence of seeing the goodness of the land of promise—but I will not lead in its conquest. Joshua will do that when my time has passed."

"Perhaps it is well that Joshua should take the leadership. You have carried the burdens which the people thrust upon you for too long."

"Too long indeed, the princes and elders entreat me to pass the leadership to a younger man. Soon they will be clamoring for my removal and I am too tired to rebuff their challenge. The burden is indeed heavy, yet it fills me with melancholy that it passes from me—for the people are my children—I have no other."

"It fills my heart with bitterness that I bore you no sons and daughters. Why has God so cursed me that 1 cannot bring the fruit of my womb to ripeness?"

"It was but once that the little one died, my wife. That you did not conceive again you cannot fault yourself. For when the millet does not sprout does the farmer blame the field or the seed? ...No, I do not blame you for the lack of children around me. For I had sons and I turned my back on them. Had I given them but a portion of what I have given the people I would now have their sons and daughters flocking about me."

"And you would have Zipporah by your side instead of me—does that distress you, My Husband?"

"Zipporah is a good woman and strong, if yet she lives. But her heart remained with her people and her gods and she could not embrace our ways. I bear her no ill will, nor do I regret the years I have spent with you. The Almighty brought you to me to warm my bed against the chill of night and to comfort me in my travail. Were it not enough God would have given me more."

"We will spend many more years together, My Husband. It will pleasure me to have you with me instead of always tending to the needs of your unruly people."

Moses gazed at Adanah for a moment, then he spoke gently.

"I think not, My Wife.... There has long been an uneasiness in my breast that grips me and my temples often threaten to burst with pain. My breath leaves me when I would walk swiftly, so that I must sit and gather my strength before going on. God has spoken that I must die and Aaron and Miriam call to me from their graves."

Adanah turned away from him so that he would not see the grief in her eyes. She had already seen in her husband the things of which he spoke, but she had denied them in her mind.

"It does not distress me that my time comes," Moses continued. "Yet I would not leave you alone."

"Do not fear for me, My Husband. I am strong and I lived alone before I joined myself to you. I can do so again though it will be harder now."

"For that you need not fear, Adanah. For I have laid aside a store of wealth with Eleazar, the high priest. He is sworn before God to provide for you."

"I bless you, Moses, for your care. But it was not that of which I spoke—without you, My Lord, there will be an emptiness that no other can ever fill—for though I was sometimes frightened by the things you did, I loved you always."

"And I you, My Wife. Yet the time swiftly comes when we must part. Now I would go to see the lands of the promise. I have never seen them because I thought the Lord might relent of his judgement against me, that I might one day walk in the fields of Canaan. But it is not to be—Joshua will lead the people there and I will die here in Moab."

"If you cannot go into the land, then how might you see it?"

"I will have Joshua and Eleazar and the princes of the tribes take me to the very summit of the mountain, Nebo. From there I will see the lands beyond the Jordan and I will appoint them to the princes, that each might know the just portion for his tribe. For some will stay in these lands and others will go beyond the river. But all must join in the conquest so that if blood be shed, it be shed by all."

"And when you have done that, My Husband, will you then rest?"

"Then I will rest, My Wife."

So Moses was carried to the top of Mount Nebo. From its heights he looked out upon the lands that he had conquered and upon those which yet stood against Israel. To Jericho and Gilgal and all the lands beyond the River Jordan and beyond the Salt Sea he raised his arm and charged Joshua that he should overcome the nations that dwelt there. And he marveled at the richness of the Lord's gift to his people.[64]

"It was for this land that I brought the people forth from Egypt, Joshua.... And now I will die at its very threshold, for I am ill with a great sickness that will not be stayed by potion or prayer. You must lead the people now, my friend and bring Israel to greater glory. King of nations will Israel be—guardian of the Ark of the Covenant—destroyer of Baal and Dagon and protector of Yahweh's law."

"But will the people follow me as they follow you? You are the maker of the law who has spoken to God in the midst of his holy fire. I am but a warrior, who is subservient to God's prophet."

"God wills it so and the princes petition me that another should lead them.... Who is better tested than you, Joshua? God will fill you with his fire and put down those who would stand against you. You will lead with your bloody sword and the people will follow. They will devastate the cities of Canaan and you will hang their kings upon trees.... So the Lord has spoken and so shall it be."

"As you command, so will I do. I will point my lance to the land of the promise and we shall not lay down our swords until the thing is finished—but what of you, My Lord?—is there a boon with which I might honor you, that will give pleasure to your last days? Perhaps some fine wine or rare fruits or meats cooked with rich spices?"

"Things of the flesh I have in abundance, Joshua. But there is a thing that you might do."

His face was lined and brown from exposure to the wind and sun. The still-thick mane of hair, once a red tinted glossy brown, was now mixed with coarse strands of white like the coat of a roan stallion. Gershom sat at the crest of a hill overlooking the first scant flow of the River Jabbok in the lands of Ammon, north and east of Moab. He was captain of the watch on this day, a watch that was kept diligently because the tribe of Hur ventured too close to Bashan and the warriors of Joshua. They came for water and the rich grazing that these borderlands afforded the Midianite herds. But danger was always near and so riders patrolled the hills around the camp. On this day, the patrol was tardy and Gershom grew anxious.

In the years since the slaughter of their people at the city of Zur the Midianites had recovered a portion of their former strength. Some of the warriors of Midian who had survived that disaster had married wives among the more distant Midianite tribes, others had sought women of the nomads of Joktan, where women were regarded as chattels suitable for barter. These unions had strengthened the blood of Midian, for the wanderers of Joktan were a fiery, indomitable people, a trait passed on to the children of these marriages. The couplings had also served to cement a bond between these nomadic peoples reducing the enmity that had existed between them for centuries.

Other Midianite men, including Gershom, had married women of the Amorite clans that had been scattered to the countries around Bashan during the decimation of their nations by Joshua. Here too the people of both nations were strengthened by the mixing of blood and a common sentiment—their hatred of Israel.

Gershom rose to his feet impatiently. The riders were young and had probably lost track of time, intent on discussion of some romantic adventure. He smiled and thought of his own children. Jethro, the oldest was now twelve, growing tall and wiry, and soon would be riding beside his father. The two girls next, named for his mother, Zipporah, and aunt, Ribai, were images of their Amorite mother, small and slender with delicate oval faces and glistening black hair. The youngest was always cause for pondering. Already his head shone with the coppery tint of his father's—and that of his grandfather before him. He was very much different from Jethro who had the heart of a warrior. Named for Gershom's brother, the lad was gentle in his nature as Eliezer had been and slow, halting in his speech even now as a small child.

Gershom's reverie was interrupted by the appearance of riders from the west. As they drew closer he counted five. The patrol had been four and already he could make out the white horse that young Hur rode. They had another with them, either friend or captive and now Gershom made out the long ears of a mule. The strange rider was not of Joktan, they hated the homely, ill-tempered creatures. As they drew closer Gershom saw the blue trimmed fringes on the cloak of the stranger, a young man of perhaps twenty years. He grew tense as the realization came to him that the man was an Israelite. Instinctively his hand went to his sword although there was no need for it.

The small procession drew up their mounts before Gershom and he saw that the stranger was not bound. He carried only the least of weapons needed to travel alone, a short sword and a bow of horn and wood. He carried no shield or armor, just a small bag for food tied by a nearly empty water skin. He dismounted and spoke to Gershom and his dialect confirmed what Gershom already knew—the man was an Israelite courier.

"I am a messenger sent by Lord Joshua of Israel—I seek Gershom, son of Moses."

"I am Gershom, grandson of Jethro, son of Zipporah —is it I that you seek?"

Confusion showed in the young man's eyes, but he spoke again.

"I was told to seek the son of Moses. I know not the Jethro of whom you speak."

Gershom ignored the messenger's statement. "You are an Israelite. You take idle risk with your life by riding into the camps of Midian. My people are sworn to kill all Israelites with no concern for the purpose of their coming."

The young man looked at Gershom without fear. "It is for that reason I was chosen. It is said that Gershom of Midian will not do me harm."

Gershom raised his eyebrows. "How so? Does your god ride with you to shield you from our swords and arrows that you do not fear us? What is your name?"

"I am Elihu, youngest son of Prince Shupham of Israel."

"It is as you were told," Gershom said quietly. "A son of Prince Shupham is safe within all the lands of Midian where I am known. Joshua, in his cunning, chooses his messenger well. For what reason do you seek me?"

The courier drew a tightly rolled piece of goatskin from within his cloak.

"Do you read?"

Gershom nodded and took the scroll. It was small and the message was terse.

"MOSES, YOUR FATHER, DIES. HE WISHES YOUR PRESENCE. JOSHUA OF ISRAEL."

Gershom stood there as one whose tongue is tied from birth. He reread the words before him and still he stood mute as a torrent of conflicting emotions was released within his soul. At last he turned to young Hur.

"Take this man and give him to eat and drink. Spare nothing, for without his father my bones would lie with those of Eliezer, my brother."

Still strong, though more scant of flesh and creased by age the face of Zipporah was emotionless as she listened to her son.

"I thought that he was gone from my life forever," Gershom said. "He would have killed me except for you, then he left us alone and but for grandfather we would have perished. Then when we came to him in the wilderness he sent us away. He is a man of evil who destroyed the lives of thousands of our people and killed my brother—I hate him as I have hated no other— even the butcher, Ephah, I would take to my breast before him. Yet, now that he dies he calls for me and I think that I must go to him.... But I cannot! I am a Midianite and he is the murderer of my people. What folly of mind causes me to think thus?"

Zipporah had thought that she had long past shed her last tear on Moses' account. But now she felt the familiar sensation rise again in eyes which had long been dry. She sighed a heavy, tired sigh and took her son's strong, calloused hand between her dark veined and withered ones.

"It is because you are your father's son," she said. "Every time I look at you I see him driving off the shepherds of Joktan at the well where my sisters and I watered my father's flocks. He was a splendid man then, as you are now and I loved him with such a fulness that I thought my breast would burst from it."

"I remember that he was strong and fearless," Gershom said, "and that as a boy I wanted to be like him. But then he began changing as if his spirit was desolate and anger was his constant companion. We grew fearful of him and suddenly he went to do his god's bidding and I never had a father again.... I did not understand why he left us and I hated his god for making him do it."

Zipporah nodded sympathetically. "He was often withdrawn as though he missed his people and I thought it might pass. But one day he came from the hills as one possessed by a demon. He said that his god had spoken to him from a burning bush—not just a bush that was on fire—but one that was not diminished in the burning!" Zipporah rolled her eyes. "The man I had loved was gone then and I never saw him again. In his place there stood a wild-eyed zealot who wanted to bring his people out of their bondage in Egypt.... In time he brought many of them out—by miracles of his god, it was said. Others said that Moses and his followers were driven out because he caused unrest among the slaves, which angered Pharaoh.

It mattered not because many left Egypt with Moses and he gathered many more to him in the wilderness of Paran, along with the poor and hopeless of other nations who had nowhere to go. He became a hero to these people and he made a mighty fighting force out of thousands of slaves and wanderers."

"I know of that and it could have been noble, Mother. But why did he start to kill and destroy everyone and everything in his path?"

"I don't really know. I think it began when Sahed of Amalek attacked the Israelites at Rephidim. He had nowhere to go and it angered him that Sahed would have driven him back to Egypt. When we went to him with your grandfather he was changed. He told me then that he would drive out all the nations in the path of Israel, even us.

"After Rephidim he attempted to enter Canaan but he was driven back by the people of Amalek—you know of that because Bela fought there. Then he thought to come to us, to live as he did once in the lands of Midian. But Kybar of Edom denied him passage through his lands. After that he made a great army of Israel and destroyed everyone who opposed him.

"But we were not at war with him when he set Joshua against us, nor were we even hostile to him! Many of our people lived among the Israelites, but that is all."

"I know, but our women led many young men out of his authority by their worship of Baal. Moses had already put down several insurrections among the tribes and he saw us as a threat to his power. So he sought to frighten his own rebellious people and other nations by destroying us. I'm sure his intent was to subjugate all the nations between Ammon and the great sea."

"But he has failed in that if he is dying."

"He has not failed—while Joshua still lives."

"Then perhaps I should go to Moab to see Moses. I might have a chance to kill Joshua and so end the menace."

"Don't talk like a beardless youth, My Son! You would only lose your own life upon a stake and further weaken Midian. Another would rise in Joshua's place, ...perhaps more malevolent than he. No, ...one warrior cannot stem the storm that is Israel. Raise many sons, that in time their sons might take up the sword against them. We shall not battle them again in our time—But we shall defeat them one day."[71]

"Then there is no cause why I should go to The Prophet, for he sought to kill me and he killed Eliezer and many of our kin. Might I not go to a death that is planned in malice?"

"I will not tell you to go in reverence to your father's side, though your sire he is—but be it known in your mind that when he sent Joshua upon us it was a quarrel among nations. He did not know the people of Jethro would be among the tribes gathered by Zur—nor did he know that his very sons rode against the spears of Joshua—he will not put his son in danger, nor will Joshua, for he has once spared your life."

"That may be true, My Mother. But they killed our people without justice or need. To kill men in battle is the way of war. But to kill women, children and feeble old men is the way of evil. It is not the way of brave men but of cowards and beasts of the field."

"That is the truth as my father taught it to us—but Moses believes that his god calls him to destroy the nations because they worship other gods. He says that all gods but Yahweh are false and that all ways but that of the Israelites are corrupt. The children of Israel stand alone in righteousness. Therefore his god has commanded him to utterly destroy the nations about him, throwing down their gods, burning their cities and killing their citizens, even to the last of their kind!"

"If that is righteousness I quake at the thought of evil, Mother. For if such a one as killed the innocents at the place of the acacias be the emissary of The True God, there is no cause, except fear, to worship that god. When I think of the scourge of death that the prophet ordered against our people I am filled with anger and revulsion. The desire to deride Moses for his vile deeds at the very nearness of his death clutches at my heart. I will go to him as he asks, but it will not be to venerate him as a good and wise father, nor to make peace with him so that his death may be easier. But I will go to condemn him for what he has done and put my curse upon his head!"

"Then go, My Son, to do that which you must. But you may well discover that your hate for him is not so great as you now believe. Go to him, Gershom. I will burn incense candles to Gad and to Remphan that you should be safe within the encampment of Israel. And I will pray to Yahweh, the god of Israel, that he should look with compassion on the son of Moses. For if indeed he be the god of all the world and Moses is his seer, it may go ill with you to so denounce your father."

CHAPTER 20

"Two men come out of the east!!"

The young rider flew from his mount and knelt on one knee before Joshua.

"One is Elihu, I think, for he has his bearing and he rides a mule. The other I do not know. He rides a black horse like those of Joktan."

"And his dress...," Joshua said, "what of his dress?"

"He wears the black cloak of a nomad with a red sash and a headdress tied with red cord. He carries a lance, a bow and a shield upon his horse's shoulder."

Joshua smiled grimly. "He carries a sword as well and wears a breastplate beneath his cloak. He is a lancer of the tribe of Hur of Midian—I know them well. He is the one we await. Go to him and say that he is welcome in Abel Shittim, the place of the acacias."

As the scout remounted Joshua turned and strode briskly toward the house of the prophet. He could see no good that would come of the young Midianite's visit. And yet, he saw and felt the anguish of the man he had so long served when he spoke of his sons. And that was enough reason to welcome this young warrior, the only remaining son of Moses. It was a mystery that Yahweh did not give his prophet many sons and daughters too. It was a tragedy for the blood line of one as great as Moses to end so abruptly. And yet, ...was it about to end or was it carried on by this warrior of Midian?

Was the line of Moses to be carried on by those he sought to exterminate? Joshua ceased his pondering as he approached the house of Moses. The old man sat on a rough-hewn chair in the shade of a grape arbor, leaning forward in anticipation of news. His piercing eyes, a thing that had not aged, were already fixed on Joshua and his expression betrayed the question in his throat, though he remained silent.

"A rider comes," Joshua said. "A man of the nomads—I think it is your son."

Moses settled back. The severe mouth softened and something very near a smile touched its corners.

"I will have Adanah prepare a meal. He will be hungry after his long ride."

"No, others will make food, My Lord. Let Adanah prepare herself and you to greet your son. Comb out those great white tangles that still mass about your head, wash your body with soap and rub it with scented oil. Then put on your finest robe and your rings of gold. It is not proper that the Lord of Israel be dressed like a bondsman to meet a warrior of Midian—though he be your son."

"Do not treat me as a child or a servant," Moses grumbled. "I know well that my countenance is that of Israel, though I dress in rags. Nonetheless, I will dress myself as befits a servant of the Lord and a prince of his people. And will you attend to my son, that he may cleanse himself after his journey?"

"For that and every need he may have preparation has been made. But we have thus far dealt with his coming secretly. When he, a lancer of Hur, rides into the city questions will be upon the lips of the elders. What then shall we make of his presence?"

"Tell them that he who is a son of Moses comes. Tell them that he is blessed by the hand of the Lord and comes at the bidding of the Prophet of God. He shall come in peace and receive the hospitality of the princes of Israel."

Moses stopped speaking and fixed Joshua with his piercing gaze.

"And he that would do him harm shall die upon the tree!"

The bath was a wonder to Gershom though it was small and built plainly of stone in the manner of the Amorites. He had been brought to a courtyard that bordered it by Elihu, who immediately left him to the care of serving slaves. They had fed him cold beef with cheese and bread washed down with a strong red wine and now he lounged in the bath. Never had he submerged himself in such luxury, nor had he ever had anyone serve him as a lord.

When the slave women tugged at his cloak Gershom was embarrassed and he refused to strip before them. But when the women tittered and ran to fetch a piece of linen goods for him to cover himself with, he obeyed their demands and peeled his dusty garments off and entered the bath. The water was tepid, though rather murky from the baths of those who had preceded him. But it served to make his privates less conspicuous as he sat in the little pool and Gershom was soon at ease as one of the women energetically scrubbed his pale body with a coarse sponge.

The woman was not old, perhaps in her late twenties, perhaps in her early thirties and darkly handsome like his people. He wanted to speak to her, though speaking to a strange woman and worse yet a slave, was a thing looked upon with disfavor. He might not have but Elihu the courier had proved to be a reticent travelling companion. Gershom had learned next to nothing from him about the settlement at Shittim and certainly nothing about its people.

"From where do you come? Are you of the Amorites, or perhaps you are debt bonded of Israel?" Gershom asked.

She looked at him with startled eyes. "It is forbidden to speak to those I serve."

"I know of that, but I am not of Israel though Israelite blood flows in my veins. Speak freely for I will not give your master evil report. From where do you come?"

"I come from the land near to the desert of the east. I was brought here as a girl with others of my tribe. Captives of war we were."

Gershom started, his muscles tightening beneath the pale skin of his shoulder blades. His brown, burnt face turned to the woman standing beside him and his piercing eyes sought hers.

"I am from that land and as a young warrior I fought in a terrible war against the army of Joshua. Of what nation were your people? Were you of Midian?"

A shadow settled on the woman's face. It seemed to dull the brightness of her eyes and she answered wistfully.

"Yes, we were of Midian—of the plains and hills where sheep grazed in great flocks and our warriors rode swift horses. It has been so long but yet I remember it well."

"Of what tribe were you?" Gershom asked excitedly. "Were you of Zur or perhaps Reba or Rekem?"

"Of none of those, I am Jana, daughter of Prince Hur, who led the lancers at the battle of Zur's city. My mother was Reumah, his first wife."

Gershom, oblivious to his nakedness, lurched upright in the waist deep pool and grasped the woman by her shoulders.

"You are a lost daughter of Hur!! ...I rode with his lancers at Zur's city. I saw your father die.... His horse was killed by a lance and Hur fought like a lion among jackals, thrusting and swinging his sword at the host of Joshua. But there were too many swords and one found his throat, ...and he died."

Jana looked up at the tall warrior and fought back the tightness in her throat.

"For these many years I never knew if he died or perhaps he yet lived. I feel a sadness but it is a good thing to know at last.... But you said you rode with my father. What then is your name?"

"It is Gershom, grandson of Jethro, son of Zipporah."

"I remember, ...you were very much the warrior and you had a brother who rode beside you. He seemed gentle and more the poet than warrior, I thought. I was a young girl then but fancied that when I was grown he would marry me."

"His name was Eliezer and he died with your father in a battle that won us nothing. What of your mother and your brothers and sisters? You had a brother who was not yet old enough to ride with the lancers. Your father spoke of him often."

"He and my mother were both murdered within the house of Zur by the hand of one called Ephah. They both stood against him...and both died by his blade."

Gershom's face grew dark and he returned to his seat in the bath.

"I know of Epha, he butchered the captive lancers before the city fell and took pleasure in it. He would have killed me also but for Lord Shupham."

"You know Lord Shupham? It is his household that I have served since the killing of the innocents."

"I know him indeed, he stayed the sword that would have claimed my life. And at Joshua's bidding he released the family of Jethro from the march to Shittim."

"We wondered what had become of them," Jana said. "Your mother cared for everyone around her. She gave of her strength to help those who were weak and to rally those whose spirits flagged. Then one morning she was gone and all of her family with her. We thought that perhaps Ephah had done more of his foul chores."

"No, by the guidance of the gods they came upon us in the distant plains and brought with them an heir to my grandfather's bloodline. Ribai, youngest daughter of Jethro, bought forth a son by Bela, warrior of Amalek. He is a true son of Midian, born in hardship and blessed by the stars of those endless plains."

"It is good that a few escaped to carry on your family," Jana said quietly. "My father's young wife, Mara, gave birth also on the march of the captives. She birthed a son, an heir to Hur.... But they and my younger brother Reu died at the field of death. My two sisters and I were given to families of Israel as spoils of war."

"Then your sisters live?"

"I do not know. I never saw them again because they went out into the distant settlements. I was fortunate because Lord Shupham is a kind man. He did not force me to be his concubine nor that of any other and for that I serve him gratefully."

"He is a man of kindness and compassion, virtues that I fear are uncommon in Israel. How fares the prince? He must now be of an advanced age."

"He is, infirmity grows on him and he is shunned by many of the elders because he stood against Moses in the killing of the innocents. Yet as age takes his might as a warrior from him his gentleness becomes greater, it seems."

"And The Prophet, ...what of him?"

"I know little of him except that he murdered my people and yours. He dies soon, they say—though not soon enough, I say.... But perhaps I speak things that should not be spoken. You have said that Israelite blood flows in your veins. Forgive me, Lord, if I offend you. The loss of my people has put bitterness in my mouth."

"And also in mine, but I carry the heavier burden—for I also carry guilt, through my blood, for the losses of our people."

"How can it be that you, a warrior of Midian, should feel guilt for our people's anguish? You have not spoken of your father. Is it because of him that you carry this burden?"

"Yes, it is because of him—he is an Israelite!"

"Was he perhaps a warrior in the army of Joshua or one of the elders?"

"No, it is greater than that. He has a position of great authority. It is because of my father that I come now to Shittim."

Jana's eyes widened and the raw edge of fear crept into her words.

"Surely, your father is not Joshua himself! ...The swordhand of Moses! ...I could die for what I have said!"

"You have no cause for fear. Joshua is not my father." Gershom's voice ebbed to a whisper. "My father is Moses."

Jana's features froze and she stood motionless for a moment then the knowledge of Gershom's lineage overwhelmed her and she fled from the bath.

"We of Israel did an evil thing to the people of Midian." Shupham peered at Gershom with mild eyes set below craggy gray eyebrows.

"If it had been at my command that vile campaign would not have been waged. But Moses said it was God's command and some saw that great plunder was to be had from the city of Zur. And so Joshua smashed the city and massacred its inhabitants and we of Israel claimed a great victory."

Gershom shifted himself in the alien discomfort of a straight-backed chair set across a richly carved table from Lord Shupham. He had been brought to the prince's house after the bath at his own request. Now he studied the old man before him whom he still remembered as the strong warrior who had given him a reprieve from death.

"It is the way of war, Prince Shupham. Those who win garner wealth and hatred—for those who lose captivity and death are the rewards. Had Joshua lost, ...his head would have adorned a lance at the gate of Zur's city. But we warriors of Midian lost and so our elders, our boy children and all the women except the very young died. And we who survived were driven to the edges of the desert before Joshua, as the desert sands are driven by the winds of Joktan. I come to thank you for my life, Lord Shupham, and for those of my mother and the family of Jethro."

"Your thanks are received with pleasure, Captain. I regret that I could not extend amnesty to the rest of your people. But Moses in his fervor became most unbending in his judgements. He said that the extermination of Midian was the will of the Lord Almighty." Shupham pursed his lips as if in deep consideration of his words. "That, I cannot either argue or support. For he speaks to the Lord alone and seats his judgements on the commands so given. So it was that the women and boy children who were brought captive to Shittim died.[63] It was a thing that brought no glory to our warriors and brought shame to all.

"We heard of it and anger ran hot against the prophet, though nothing could be done. Those of the rashest nature wanted to raid the outlying settlements of Israel and shed blood for blood. But we knew that it would only bring the might of Israel upon us and no matter how many farmers and shepherds we killed, Moses and Joshua would still live. So we quelled our desire for blood—but not our hatred—and someday our grandsons will again raise the sword against Israel."

Shupham nodded. "The shedding of blood begets more of the same—but the report is given among the elders that the son of Moses comes to see his father. Some say that Moses seeks to install his son as king of Israel. Already there are murmurings of rebellion among the tribes if such a thing should come to pass."

Gershom snorted with contempt. "The Israelites are like vultures, ever ready to pick the bones before the ox is dead.... Though the blood of Moses runs in my veins, contempt for him runs in my heart. My people are those of my mother, who still lives, by your grace and that of Joshua.... Let Joshua lead Israel in conquest of its neighbors. I have no desire for such greatness as he has gained. I come at the request of my sire, who dies, to rebuke him for his misdeeds. Father he has been to his people but not to me. Therefore let them comfort him at his death, for I will not!"

"I thought as much," Shupham said, "nor do I find fault with your contempt for Moses. But have care that you do not too greatly offend your sire—or his general. I cannot protect you here at Shittim. I have little influence among the younger elders and they would kill you as easily as they kill a lamb. But if there is a thing which I might do for you, ask it of me, for my spirit seeks to make amends to your people."

`There is a thing which I might ask...if you can do it."

"Then ask it and if it can be done, it is."

"There were three women, girls then, among the captives of Midian. One is in your service, Jana is her name. The others were sent into the settlements far from Shittim. They are the sole living blood of my prince, Hur, who died in the battle of Zur's city. I would take them back to their people."

Shupham looked at Gershom thoughtfully. "I have given you my promise and so it shall be, though there is a prohibition against freeing slaves of Midian. Jana has been a good and faithful servant and is a virgin yet. She can go back with you though it give me the ill will of Joshua and the elders. Her sister, younger next to her, is no more. She died of a plague the same year in which she was taken. I kept this knowledge from Jana for it would have caused her greater pain than was already her lot. The youngest of the three was sent to the eastern borders of Bashan. She was but a small child who had little knowledge of what had befallen her people. She is grown now and married to a young farmer, with children of her own—it is best to leave her as she is, for even there the bloodline of Hur continues."

Gershom nodded. "Though she is in Israel the blood of Hur flows in her children's veins as the blood of Moses flows in mine. It is good to know that his line will not die for Hur was a brave warrior. After I have visited with my sire I will take Jana back to Midian with me. Perhaps there may yet be an heir of Hur who lives free."

"He comes, Lord Moses."

The Levite guard saluted stiffly then retreated to escort the visitor into the prophet's house. Despite his age and temperate nature Moses felt excitement flush through his spirit. He called to his wife who was fluttering about the courtyard where slave women were cooking a meal in Gershom's honor.

"He comes! ...Attend me Adanah, Gershom is here!"

Adanah straightened her blue tunic about her and hurried to stand beside the couch of her husband. Several bracelets of twisted gold strands adorned her wrists and ankles and a chain around her neck was splendid with precious stones. Her sandals were of soft leather held on with braided thongs of goatskin. She was splendid in her dress and still comely in appearance. Now she stood quietly as she had done so many times before, ready to offer hospitality to her husband's guest. To worry about whether her stepson would approve of her did not enter her mind. Moses was her husband and lord and this son of his was of little concern to her, except that Moses longed to see him before he died.

The man who entered and stood before them was tall and well muscled. He was recently shaved and only a stubble of red sprinkled with the first white hairs of middle age stood on his strong jaw. He wore a knee-length tunic of goatskin with a breastplate and apron of polished bullhide. About his waist was wrapped the red sash of Hur's lancers and hanging from his neck was the bronze medallion of a captain. His feet were protected by bullhide sandals with leggings of goatskin after the manner of the nomads. In the laces of his right legging an empty scabbard bulged, made devoid of its dagger by the cautious Joshua.

The warrior raised his fist to touch his breastplate in salute as lancers did, while staring hard at the old man reclining before him. Was this worn and feeble creature before him the terrible despot who had caused his people so much misery? He had fueled the fire of his anger and hatred toward this man from the moment he had received his call. And now suddenly, in but a moment, his anger was cooled and he, seasoned warrior of Midian, was a confused boy again.

"I am Gershom of Midian," he said simply, forgetting the mocking sarcasm he had intended to greet his sire with.

With a touch of his own gnarled hand to his breastbone, Moses returned the salutation. "I bid you welcome, Gershom. I thank you most earnestly for honoring my request."

"It had nothing to do with honor. I come at the command of my sire and the wishes of my mother."

The old man ignored the insult. "Your mother? She still lives then—it gives me pleasure that she does. But let us not stand in strange formality as though our lives had never touched. Come to board with me, there is much I would speak of with you, My Son." Moses lurched to his feet unsteadily and would have fallen had it not been for the strong grip of Adanah. Then he put his hand on Gershom's shoulder and with tottering steps guided him to a seat at a table, which was already set with delicately worked pottery bowls and cups of polished silver which had once adorned the house of Zur.

Adanah helped her husband to his chair—its ebony was heavily decorated and polished to a high gloss and color not unlike the skin of Adanah. The prophet sat down on it heavily, gripping the ivory ram heads of the arms to steady himself. With her husband and guest seated, Adanah immediately poured wine and offered delicate cakes sweetened with honey to tease their appetites. Then she went to oversee the completion of dinner, leaving the two men to renew their acquaintance.

"Adanah is a wonderous woman and a faithful wife," Moses said, offering an introduction he dared not hazard while his wife was present, for fear that Gershom would rebuff him.

"I took her to me when we were in the wilderness after your mother returned to her people. I was alone and so worn with the cares of the people that I asked the Lord at my evening prayers to take me to him. Instead he gave me Adanah, she has given me much love and solace."

"You were alone because you abandoned your wife and family and the people who took you in as their own. You lacked for nothing within the family of Jethro. But you left us so that you might gain great power."

Moses shook his head. "I obeyed the command of the Lord, nothing more. I was content in Midian but I could not refuse The Almighty. Though I asked him to free me from his command, he would have no other but I to lead his people, I a poor, stammering shepherd of Midian."

"So you left wife and family, goods and flocks, all the abundance with which my grandfather, Jethro, blessed you and went to Egypt at this strange command?"

Moses nodded. "I was commanded to bring the people out of bondage and that I did. And with the Lord's guidance, I made a nation of the rabble that flowed forth from Egypt."

"And when we came to you in the wilderness with my grandfather, your father-in-law, Jethro, could you not have taken your wife and your sons to you? Could you not for one day forsake the people, as you had forsaken us, so that peace might be made and your family might be reunited?"

"I would gladly have taken your mother and my sons to me. But Zipporah would not bow down to The True God, whom I must serve. Therefore I could do nothing but let her return to Midian."

"Mother told me of that. She would not bow down to your god because your god would destroy all those who stand in his path. That is why she left and that is when you took this woman to give you solace for your woes. Has she also given you sons to carry you to your crypt?"

"I do not lack for those who would gladly do that service. But we have not been blessed with children. You and Eliezer were the only sons born to me."

"And now there is only I. Joshua's warriors claimed the life of my brother in a war that you waged to increase your dominion. And now only I and my sons and daughters remain to carry on the bloodline of Moses."

Again Moses ignored the unpleasant portion of Gershom's words. He smiled as though he had been given a costly gift.

"You have sons...and daughters too?—by what woman?"

"I have two sons and two daughters, born of Riblah, a woman of the family of Sihon."

"You took a woman of the Amorites? They are the bitter enemies of Israel!"

"As are the people of Midian—my people! Israel is friend and ally to none and fearsome enemy to all! I could not take a wife to please you, except of Israel. And by your own decree your people must not marry to those of Midian, whereof I am."

"But you are my son, a son of Israel, Gershom and thus a union to a maiden of Israel would have been blessed. But even so, your wife and your children would be welcomed into the tribe of Levi if they embrace The True God. I would that the family of Moses should grow with the greatness of Israel. Therefore I give you my solemn entreaty that you gather your family to Israel and pledge their veneration to the altar of Yahweh."

"I am not of Israel—though I carry your blood! I fought against your army and your god, for my people—the people of Midian. I will raise my children and they will raise theirs under the banner of Hur and they will worship the gods of our people. For indeed, what would move us to worship before a god who commanded the unmerciful murder of our people? Or what folly would cause us to live among the people who extirpated our tribes?"

The face of Moses lost its sickly pallor and took on a threatening darkness as anger crept into him.

"You and Midian shall yet kneel before the altar of Yahweh, Gershom!

His awful power shall move you and you will sing his praises before the congregation of Israel!"

"We will not kneel to the oppressor, nor will we sing praises to him though we are stricken to the last of our kind!" Gershom spat. "Nor will the grandsons of Moses ever know the face of the prophet!"

"Then your people will be destroyed by the hand of The Almighty as a man would kill a nest of vipers! You will go down into the pit unhallowed and your remembrance will be stricken from the face of the earth!"

Gershom rose abruptly, so that the table before him was shaken and the fine setting on it rattled discordantly.

"You have already sent many of our people to the pit but you will not destroy their remembrance! For the grandsons of Midian shall come again to raise their swords against the grandsons of your princes! And they will cry out with fear because of the slaughter that Midian shall make against them! And in their woe they will bring forth the remembrance of the evil you have done against my people!"

Having said these things Gershom turned his back on Moses and strode from the house.

In the space of days, Gershom with Jana, daughter of Hur, had returned to his people. In time he took Jana as his second wife and she bore him three sons. Of these three sons, the grandsons of Hur, would come the fierce chiefs that joined with the people of Amalek to rain a devastation on Israel in the time of Gideon. Zipporah, matriarch of the Midianites, lived to see the tribe of Jethro grow to a powerful nation.[65]

Moses then took to his death bed and died in the arms of the faithful Adanah. He was buried in a valley in Moab in secrecy so that his enemies should not defile his grave.[66] The people of Israel made a great show of mourning for Moses for thirty days. And when the time was over Joshua became Israel's leader and the conquest of Canaan began.

THE JOSHUA YEARS

CHAPTER 21

"The princes whine endlessly for their portions of Canaan now that Moses is gone to his resting place. They will not tarry long before their grumbling grows to rebellion," Joshua spat. "They are like fat steers which having had good pasture covet that which is greener still."

Caleb considered his response carefully. He had long been Joshua's friend and had been content to serve as the general's adjutant. But now, since his own ascendancy to the leadership of Israel, Joshua had made Caleb commander of the Israelite armies. It was no longer enough to agree with Joshua or mildly suggest some minor adjustment to a strategy. He must make his own judgements and present them to be approved by the high prince of Israel.

"They are restless indeed, but they have waited these many years at the behest of Moses," Caleb said cautiously. "It might be well to consider their petitions with some favor, lest some of the princes join together and make a rash assault on Canaan. It would be wise to invade as a unified force rather than as factions which might be easily defeated."

"That is rightly spoken, Caleb. The nations west of Jordan have watched us long. It is not likely they will fly before us like tumbleweeds before the wind. Yet, we are many and the Lord walks with us. If we enter into battle with all twelve tribes as one no nation will stand against us."

"That is true, My Lord, yet prudence has ever been with you and me. Let us gather knowledge of those of Canaan who abide closest to us before we make war. That way we will not fall into a pit cleverly dug for us."[67]

"You speak of spying, but that is a thing not easily done. Shimmur watches us from his throne in Jericho. His spies, in artless guises, walk among us by day and listen to us by night."

"Perhaps he does not watch us now, Lord Joshua. The Jordan runs high and swift with the rains of winter. They expect no one to be so foolish as to cross its raging fury."

"And they are right. A man would be swept away and drowned if he should attempt it."

"That is true if he entered the water, but what if he crossed above it?"

Joshua laughed. "And would this man have wings like a vulture that he might fly above the torrent?'

"No, but a strong man might make a light rope fast to a hook such as butchers use and cast it across, to lodge in the trees beyond. Such a rope tied high upon a breaching ladder on our shore would make an easy crossing for a nimble warrior."

"You have grown cunning, Caleb. Or perhaps it is a thing I did not notice because I was intent on my own craft. Without doubt you have already thought of a man to do this perilous chore."

"We will not send one, but rather two, My Lord. For did we not go in pairs when Moses sent us into Canaan? And these must be cunning as well as brave for they will go into the very nest of the vipers we seek to destroy. And they must be close of mouth and completely loyal to us, that word should not be noised to Shimmur before the task is finished."

"You have already decided then, who should go. And I think I know whom you have chosen. Such men are not common but stand as blades of iron among those made of bronze. Do not speak against me if I have guessed wrongly, but send me Daniel and Joha, who have often fought for the Lord's purposes, that I might give them my blessing. They will go on this perilous errand this very night."

Joha had gone first with his legs slung over the rope of flax fiber stretched tight from shore to shore. Handgrip by handgrip he hunched along, upside-down like a carcass somehow come alive and squirming on a spit. Though the river's breadth was but forty arm lengths, his muscles ached from the unaccustomed labor at half the distance. Though strong enough for the task, the rope sagged with his weight and the churning waters licked close at him.

He dragged himself on, the effort becoming greater as he began to ascend toward the anchoring tree on the far riverbank. Then, when it seemed he would he would make the shore without misadventure, the branch on which the hook and rope had tangled gave way and the hook slipped an arm length before it snagged again. It was enough! Joha splashed into the torrent and was instantly submerged by the water crashing down on him.

For the first time in his life he knew the fear of being overwhelmed by a power he could not fight. And yet, in the black of night, in a raging river, fight he did, fiercely gripping the rope and pulling himself against the terrible force that was tearing at him. For Joha, born in scrubby near-desert, had never swum a stroke and he knew that to let go of the linen strand meant death. Eventually his feet found some purchase among the slippery rocks of the river bottom and Joha dragged himself up the bank to the security of a willow thicket.

He lay there panting, wanting to call out to those on Israel's shore to assure them of his safety. But he remained silent for fear of the spies of Canaan who might even now be lurking among the trees. And so he lay there in fearful silence until his breath returned. Then he quietly drew the rope tight again and tied it to a better branch that Daniel might have a safer crossing than he. He wrung the water from his cloak and tunic and donned them again, then sat shivering in the cold as the bouncing rope heralded the progress of Daniel's approach.

"You cannot remain in such a state, Joha," Daniel said. "We must gather tinder and dry wood and make a fire to dry your cloak and warm your body."

"We might as well blow on a ram's horn to announce our presence," Joha answered. "The light of a fire against the high trees would be seen from a great distance."

"True, but you cannot remain so for fear of fever. Nor dare you enter Jericho in the morn with clothes still sopped from the river.... But what think you of this? But an hour's walk from here is the road from Heshbon to Jericho. The moon shines bright enough that we may gather large bundles of sticks and carry them there as poor wood gatherers. Then we shall not be looked upon with suspicion, for did we not dress in cloaks that are tattered and worn like those of the Amorites who labor for the princes of Canaan?"

Joha smiled. "It is true. With such a guise we can enter the gates of Jericho in the morning and none will gaze at us with suspicion. And even now we can build a fire beside the high road and warm ourselves beneath the very noses of Shimmur's patrols. Let us do it then for I swear these wretched rags I wear turn to a cloak of ice in this chill."

Shimmur stood at the top of his tower in the walled city of Jericho. He was high prince of the lands that began at the Jordan and rose into the high hills to the west, that followed the river northward from The Sea of Salt to the River Jabbok. He had not come on his high office by inheritance, but with his sword. For he was the mightiest of the princes of eastern Canaan. He was tall, strong and stout as the oaks of Bashan, terrible in combat and the sire of many sons.

But now he was at rest, for it was his habit to greet the early sun from the roof of his lofty dwelling, which raised itself nearly twenty arm lengths above the hill on which it was built. Shimmur had ordered the building of his tower home at the eastern wall of Jericho because It provided a vantage point from which the roads that crossed the Jordan might be watched. In addition, from its height he could enjoy whatever cool breezes stirred in the oppressive heat of Jordan summer.

However, Shimmur's tower was not built without some degree of sacrifice. The walls which encompassed the city and gave its inhabitants a degree of safety were in need of repair. The repairs should have been long completed and would have been were it not for the building of the tower. A severe earth tremor several years before had loosened the mortar in many places and in some, sections of rock had fallen. The populace of Jericho would be in dire danger if an assault were launched against the city and Shimmur knew it.

But on this morning, as Shimmur studied the lightening fields and roadway, he saw nothing that disturbed him. There was a small camel caravan lounging beside the road. Its drivers were heating water to make porridge as they waited for the morning opening of Jericho's gates. A little further along were a few donkeys laden with produce and beyond them two rag-tag wood gatherers were lying beside their unwieldy bundles of wood. Today at least, would be peaceful, he thought.

And yet a gnawing uneasiness was Shimmur's constant companion these days. Word had come from his spies that the old warrior-prophet of Israel had died and was succeeded by his aide, the formidable general, Joshua. The old prophet had been more concerned with spiritual things than in conquest in his last years and the region had rested in an uneasy peace. But what of this Joshua? The man was cunning and fearless, it was said and ambitious for his own glory and power. It was further said that the twelve princes of Israel were pressing him to invade Canaan and threatened rebellion if he did not.

Even so Shimmur was not terribly concerned at this moment. The winter rains to the north had been heavy and the Jordan was at flood level. It would be quite impossible to cross the raging river where the Israelites camped. In addition, Shimmur's two eldest sons commanded warriors at the fording places, should Joshua be so foolish as to attempt a crossing at one of them during high water. Still, he thought, when the rains quit it would be wise to bring all of his armies together at the city and they would begin strengthening the wall as soon as the soldiers returned.

"Get thee to the marketplace," the fat gatekeeper said to the farmer with his donkeyloads of produce. Then he turned to his companion.

"The king will have sparse toll on this morning."

"Aye, that it is already," said the thin one, as he pocketed the paltry, two geerahs he had extracted from the donkey driver.

"The way across the Jordan holds back the caravans from the east. Yet, behold what comes, ...Prince Shimmur might yet profit."

The first laughed harshly as Joha and Daniel stumbled forward beneath their great bundles of firewood.

"If there be profit to be had with those two it must be in selling them as slaves. But let us have sport with them at least. Stop them and demand toll."

"Hold and pay the toll before you enter the city!" the thin gatekeeper demanded of Joha loudly. "A geerah from each of you!"

Joha and Daniel, faces smudged with dirt and sweat, looked at him dumbly. Then Joha loosed one arm from the bundle of sticks on his back and pointed to his ear. "E-e-uh-h," he uttered in a guttural tone.

The fat gatekeeper gave another rough laugh. "Ho, what have we here, a deaf-mute? But it sounds like a donkey and it carries a donkey's load, therefore it must be a donkey. What is the toll for a donkey?"

"The prince's steward has set no toll for donkeys such as these." The thin one laughed with high glee. "Let these two pass without paying, lest they seek the king's dole to feed their worthless carcasses."

The gatekeepers were laughing so lustily that they didn't see the hardness in the eyes of the two men they had passed into the city, nor would they know until later what they had loosed on Jericho.

"If I am a donkey, then the fat one is a toad that I will trample with my hooves," Joha grumbled when they were beyond hearing. "It will give me pleasure to slit his fat throat when we take the city."

"Aye, and that pleasure you will get," Daniel smiled. "But you are a clever deceiver. They did not doubt that we were both deaf and dumb or of feeble mind."

"It was all I could think of to keep from being known. Had I spoken they would have known we are of Israel for my tongue speaks their language clumsily."

"You did well and we are safely within the walls. What say you we put down our burdens and withdraw our daggers from between the sticks? We can study Jericho more easily plodding about as beggars or errant laborers."

"That is quickly done," Joha said. "My back aches from the unaccustomed load. Did you see, as I did, that the great gates are cracked and split and the hinges are in poor repair?"

"I did," Daniel returned. "And the gate towers are so cracked and their stones so loose that a strong wind might topple them. If the rest of Shimmur's defenses are as lacking in repair there will be little need for a siege."

"Let us walk the pathways and judge the strength of Jericho then," Joha said. "I think perhaps our stay here will be short and not of great danger, since I see but a few armed men in the street."

Hours later the two spies had learned that which Joshua wished to know. They had walked the entire city for the walled portion of the city was but four hundred paces in length and only half that in breadth. The walls, though thick, were crumbling and most of Shimmur's warriors were not present. Those that remained were well armed but many were old or very young.

"I thirst and hunger," Daniel said. "Is there a place we might safely go to find bread?"

Joha grinned. "There is a place where we will be welcomed with friendly arms and indeed we will find more to please us than bread and wine."

"Of what you speak I am not certain. Nor do I know how you have gained such knowledge. Have you been to Jericho before that you would know someone who abides here?"

"I have not been here but I know someone who abides here, for often I have tarried with her on the shores of the river. Have you never met with the woman, Rahab?"[67]

"The whore who comes to the captains' tents?"

"That is the one. Though a fine whore she is indeed and has a better spirit than many women of Israel."

Daniel was unsure. "But can we trust her? Will she not give us to the guards of Shimmur?"

Joha shook his head. "She earns her silver from our men and is despised by her people because of it. Let us go to her house and refresh ourselves. She lives close by the wall in a house with mother and sisters."

"Her sisters?"

"Yes, though they are younger than she they already ply her trade. You might find them of interest to you."

At the house, they were met by a hard-faced woman who eyed them suspiciously from behind the door, which she held open a hand's breadth.

"What do beggars like you want here? I have nothing to give you!"

Joha raised a shekel before her eyes. "We would tarry a while with Rahab. We would have wine and bread."[67]

The woman opened the door a little further and snatched the coin.

"Enter quickly for I can tell by your tongue that you are of Israel! I wish that my daughters had never taken up with the captains of Joshua, it brings sorrow and dishonor on our house!"

"This woman speaks of dishonor, yet she has no protest against her daughters' harlotry," Daniel said quietly as they followed her to the house's second floor.

"She has little choice in the matter," Joha said. "For her husband is too infirm to labor and her sons are yet too young. They do as they must do to eat."

At the top of the stair they were met by a young woman who smiled at Joha with obvious pleasure.

"Do you grow impatient for my presence that you come to Jericho in a laborer's thing, Captain?" Then she became serious. "If Shimmur knew of your presence you would die horribly. You should not have come for there is word that Joshua sends spies among us."

"Then it is not safe for us to leave through the gate as we came," Joha said. "We would have bread and wine to fill our empty bellies." He smiled. "And perhaps your favor when I am filled?"

Rahab laughed. "You have the appetite of a stud donkey. Eat now, for mother brings food. Then we will see if you still have taste for other things."

While the men ate, Rahab talked. "I know what you have come for. It has long been feared that the army of Joshua would lay siege to Jericho. My people remember well when the Amorites were driven from their land and fled to us for refuge. They have seen Israel swallow up the kingdoms of Sihon and Og and destroy the tribes of Midian. It said that Israel is like a lion, which having devoured its kill, hungers for another."

"Then why do you not deliver us to Shimmur and so ensure your people's safety for a while longer?" Joha asked.

"If it were he," she pointed at Daniel, "perhaps I would because I know him not. But I would not betray you, Joha. You know that well."

Joha rose to his feet and gathered Rahab to him then carried her to her bed.

"You make me hunger for you as a starving man hungers for bread."

Rahab laughed lightly, then suddenly grew tense in his arms.

"Do not turn from me or look," she whispered. "But two young boys, children of the street, watch us from the near roof. Lay back my tunic as if in lust."

Joha parted her tunic, which was split at the front in the manner of harlots and bent his head to kiss her breasts. But Rahab pushed him away urgently.

"They are gone but they go to tell Shimmur of your presence! Come quickly to the roof! I will hide you beneath the flax sheaves that are there for drying!"

"What if they find us?" Daniel whispered to Joha as Rahab departed.

"Draw your dagger and fight to the death. You will not want to die in such a way as they will give death to you," Joha returned dryly.

"I have heard that they tear spies apart with oxen."

"Who told you so did not err," Joha returned. "Be silent, ...men run on the pathway below."

"Open to us, whore!" The words were accompanied by a loud banging on the door below.

"Open to Shimmur's guard—we know that two men of Israel are in there."[67]

"They were here indeed, the vermin!" the voice of Rahab shrilled loudly. "They took my wine and the favors of my sister and I. Then they took back their silver at dagger point and left."

"How do we know you aren't lying, whore?"

"Come in and look! Search the house! But while you do, the vermin will be escaping! Even now they have passed through the gates and run for the wooded lands!"

The voices below consulted.

"The whore bears no love for Israel, only for their silver."

"Aye, let us go and search for them. Shimmur will not be pleased if they escape."

"To the gateway then and swiftly!"

When the sun had slipped below the western horizon, Rahab returned to them.

"It is safe now. I will let you down the wall and you can escape in the darkness. But I ask you for a favor in return."

"Ask and it is granted," Joha said.

"I know that Joshua will come and Jericho will fall before him. But because I have saved your lives, grant me this—when Jericho falls let all of my family come out safely."

"So it will be," the two men agreed. "And when we come put a ribbon of red on your windows and on your door that our warriors will know to keep those within safe. But do not let anyone go out of the house until a captain comes for you for if they do they will die."

Never had there been such rains as fell that winter in the lands north of the salt sea. And never in the years since Israel had conquered Sihon and Og had Joshua seen the Jordan run so high and swift. It had been weeks now since Joha and Daniel returned from Jericho and still the gathered army of Israel camped in sodden discomfort east of the river. As if to accent their misery an earth tremor had shaken the camp momentarily, but in a moment all was still again.

"The men chafe at sitting idle with neither work nor profit," Caleb said. "They grumble that we should leave them return to their homes. Indeed, it is time to tend the vineyards and plow the damp earth for the crops of spring. And now the very earth grumbles beneath us."

Joshua nodded. "It is the nature of soldiers to complain. They will forget their boredom soon enough when we march on Jericho."

"That is true. The thought of plunder stills the whining of those who fight and Jericho should be rich from trade."

"So it may be, but there will be no plunder to be divided among the common soldiers. That which is taken from the city will go to the coffers of the Lord for it has been long since we have waged war and the Lord's treasury needs fattening."

Caleb frowned. "Is that wise, My Lord? Always the warriors have shared in the booty. It is the promise of riches that drives them forth to fight valiantly."

"They will fight valiantly for the Lord and the lands we conquer will be theirs. It is enough reward, for have not Daniel and Joha said that Jericho will fall easily?"

"So they have said and they are well tested captains. Yet this thing of withholding booty does not set easy with me."

"Yet so it will be, for I have so ordered," Joshua returned. "But enough of this. Daniel comes with a swift stride that points to news of importance."

Daniel was indeed running and hard. Now he gave a quick salute of fist to chest and spoke excitedly.

"The river, My Lords! ...The river falls swiftly within its banks! It is as though the hand of God has walled the waters that his warriors might cross through the channel!"[68]

"The river halts its flow?" Joshua looked at Daniel with amazement.

"It is so, My Lord. By now the waters that ran so swiftly are spent and the rocky bed stands dry."

"Then move the army, Caleb! Rouse them and make the crossing into Canaan! For if the Lord holds back the waters we shall not test his patience."

"It is done, Lord Joshua! ...Here runners! ...Go swiftly to the princes and tell them that their armies shall cross the Jordan within the hour!"

The sound of loud men's voices roused Shimmur from his midday rest and brought him hurrying to the tower roof. A running man had just entered the city and now the great gates were swinging shut in response to his excited shouts. In a moment the muscular form of the captain of the guard had joined the runner, then the two came at a trot toward the tower. In a few moments the captain was saluting Shimmur and the man, an errant laborer, was kneeling before him, panting with his exertion.

"This man has evil news, My Lord," the captain said. "He comes from the Jordan where he labored at cutting poplar poles beside the river."

Shimmur stroked his bristly black beard and eyed the man intently.

"What is the nature of your report, man? Speak to your king."

"Israel comes, My Lord! Joshua has crossed the Jordan and even now his warriors march toward us!" The man's eyes touched those of Shimmur and shifted uneasily away.

"They crossed the Jordan? You are either mad or take me for a fool! Not even a mighty bull could cross the river in full flood! Speak the truth, man, lest my guards take your lying tongue from you!"

"I do not lie, My Lord," the man sniveled. "The river's flow stopped before my eyes. Then Joshua's army crossed before the waters returned. It is a miracle wrought by the Israelite God!"

Shimmur glanced at the captain. "Is it indeed so, Addan? Has Joshua crossed the river?"

"It must be so, My Lord. Behold, tillers of the land and shepherds flee to hide within the walls of Jericho."

Far down the road the first of a straggling troop of people were hurrying toward Jericho. Some carried bundles and bags of possessions, others dragged children along and some drove sheep and goats before them. All were moving as fast as their burdens would allow, toward the gates of Jericho.

Shimmur looked at them grimly. "It is true. They flee Joshua's swords. You say that the river ceased to flow so that he might cross?"

The man nodded violently and looked at Shimmur with frightened eyes. Then being thus encouraged he embellished his tale.

"The waters stopped and stood as a high wall while the host of Israel crossed. It was the hand of their god, Yahweh." The last he whispered, as though speaking aloud of the miraculous power of the Israelite god might cause him to be stricken on the spot.

"I have heard of the power of this god before. There is a legend that he parted the waters of the Red Sea so that the Israelites might escape Egypt."

"And it is said he closed the waters on the army of Pharaoh," the captain added.

"It is a fable...a tale told late in the night beside a campfire, nothing more." He turned to the man who still knelt before him.

"Go on your way and do not tarry in Jericho! For if you tell these tales among the people here and so spread the fever of fear, I will have your tongue!"

The man's feeling of importance was suddenly dissolved by fear and he scurried away as Shimmur turned to the captain of his guard.

"Do you think that the Israelite god will aid Joshua if he lays siege to Jericho?"

Addan twitched his great black mustache as was his habit when perplexed.

"It is said, My Lord, that the Israelite god overcame Baal-Peor and Anath when Joshua drove the Amorites from their lands. It is also said that he overcame the gods of the Egyptians, causing a great tribulation throughout their land. It is said that the great Rameses drove the Israelites out of Egypt for fear of him and that he leads the warriors of Israel from within a whirlwind of fire, so that none can stand against them."

"These things were all before my time and their essence is made stronger with each passing generation, Addan. Are not the exploits of our heroes made greater with the passing of time? Yet, ...it is possible that the god of Israel is El, lord of all gods and therefore even Baal of Peor was subject to him. I know not and I do not fear this god. Yet, the common people will shudder with fright at the thought of him in league with Joshua. And that is what I fear, ...for if the muscles and sinews of our warriors are turned to mush by their crazed minds we will fall before Joshua like wheat before the sickle. Go Addan, send out runners to my sons, Anaz and Emmur, and to the other captains by the Jordan and bid them return their warriors quickly to Jericho. For if Joshua comes against us we shall be sorely pressed without them."

All of that day people came from the east, a straggling, disordered parade. They filled the square below with a hub-bub of human voices mingled annoyingly with the bleating of sheep and goats. At last Shimmur ordered the great gates closed and barred against them, not yet for fear of the Israelites, but because their number could not be fed if his city was beset by a long siege.[69]

As the sun slipped close to the western hills the warriors upon the wall suddenly grew silent, hushed by some mesmerizing sight to the east. Below them the rabble in the square became quiet as though infected by the silence of those on the wall. Shimmur, on his tower, stared incredulously at the sight that so affected all that beheld it.

Before him came a broad front of warriors, wide enough to fill both the road and the adjacent camping ground on which camel caravans so often lounged. They came on, rank upon rank of lancers interspersed with swordsmen, shields slung across their backs in marching manner. The column split and marched to right and left at a great enough distance to be safe from arrows but yet close enough to intimidate the men on the wall of Jericho. When at last the final ranks of lancers and swordsmen had passed the companies of archers came. They marched with bows, yet unstrung and great quivers of arrows upon their backs, to take their places behind swordsmen and lancers.

Beside the ranks of warriors the captains proudly rode. They were mounted on splendid horses bred from those left behind by the stricken warriors of Midian. Far to the rear of the armed men, where the dust raised by stamping feet had dispersed, marched the priests. They walked solemnly with the haughty pomp of their highest office, carrying the Ark of the Covenant and all of the holy things that were a mystery to Shimmur, but which filled him with a deep foreboding.

Caleb, General of the Armies of Israel, camped that night on a hillock twice an arrow's flight from the tower of the King of Jericho. Before him, encircling the high hill on which the city sat, camped the warriors of Israel. This would be Caleb's first battle as commander. Though he had marched into battle many times as Joshua's adjutant the newness of command wore at his nerves and kept him from even an uneasy, fitful sleep.

And so, he sat in the warmth of his campfire with the man who was at once his friend and his lord and watched the ebbing of the hundreds of campfires below. In the distance all was silent, the city rose above its ancient mound, stark and black against the desert moon. Neither fire nor candle burned in Jericho, save for a dim lamp that glowed feebly at the top of the king's tower. Shimmur, High Prince of Jericho, did not sleep on this night.

Long before first light the fires of Israel were rekindled to heat pots of barley porridge, which flavored with honey and sour milk would sustain the warriors. Then the encampment slowly came alive with the low grumble of thousands of male voices, as men buckled on breastplates and swords before shuffling to their places in the host that encircled Jericho.

The activity within the Israelite camp was watched intently by those on the walls of Jericho, with the anxiety that can be known only by those at the point of a sword. On the high tower Shimmur smeared a little of the soft goat cheese he favored on a chunk of wheat bread and handed it to his son, Sabin. The boy was still a stripling, long boned and beardless. But he was the only son of Shimmur's favorite wife and because of that he was favored. It was too bad he might not live to be a man, Shimmur thought as he took a piece of the bread for himself and gnawed on it without appetite. Near him Addan and several other captains watched Joshua's camp from notches in the top of the tower wall.

"Behold! A party comes from Joshua beneath a banner of truce." Addan pointed to the hillock on which Joshua made camp.

"Joshua sends a courier to make his demands," another said glumly. "He is confident of victory and would have us lay down our swords and open the gates so that he might take the city without bloodshed."

"Without bloodshed of his own," a third said. "But if we open to him our blood will flow in great rivers as did the blood of Sihon's people."

"And that of our women and the babes they suckle!" Shimmur spat the words as he raised himself from his couch and stalked to the wall.

"Moses, the old priest, was a murdering barbarian and Joshua is no better for he walks in the footsteps of the old one. Israel shall not enter Jericho while I have breath. But behold, the messenger Joshua sends is a fine bird indeed! Look how gallantly he approaches the gate with his buckler of bronze and the banner of truce held high upon his lance."

"Israel must have captains to spare that Joshua sends one as a courier," Addan said. "And a strutting cock he is. For he does not stand behind his guard but hails us with impudence, as though a Canaanite arrow could not skewer his gizzard and leave him bleeding on the path."

"He knows that he is safe. The honor of Shimmur makes him so, for never have I struck down a man who bears a flag of truce. Go to the gate tower, Addan and challenge him to come in to me. I would look into the eyes of one who comes to demand my submission."

"And if he will not enter within the walls?"

"He will enter, for one such as he longs always to prove his mettle and gain the greater admiration of his commander. He will enter—his pride will not let him refuse. Nor does he fear, for when the message he bears is heard, must he not carry the answer back to his lord? Go and bring him to me."

The captain, when he came, stood arrogantly before Shimmur, neither saluting nor bending his neck in the slightest bow. His eyes brushed over the King of Jericho with scathing contempt, as though he had already been defeated and waited now the judgement of the conqueror.

"I am Ephah, High Captain and aide to Caleb, General of the armies of Israel—I bring a letter from Joshua, High Prince and Lord of Israel."

Shimmur took the slim scroll that Ephah offered him and unrolled it. He studied it carefully, then gazed at Ephah with feigned amusement.

"Are you only a splendidly attired messenger who takes the place of a common courier before me, or do you also speak for the mighty Joshua?"

Ephah's face colored with the gibe. "I speak for Lord Joshua in that he commands you to open the gates and surrender the city to us."

"He commands me? Do I make Lord Joshua's evening fire or empty his night pot that he commands me? I am Shimmur, King of all the lands from the Salt Sea to the Sea of Chinnereth. I stand within a walled city and a great army of mighty men obeys me. Yet Joshua commands me to open unto him?"

"The walls of Jericho are as mud dried in the sun. They are cracked and brittle. And the great gates lean wearily on their hinges. These walls will not stand before the fury of General Caleb and his thousands," Ephah sneered condescendingly. "Indeed if the walls stood strong you could not defend them. I do not see the great army you boast of. There are only a few hundred warriors upon the walls, at most."

"Do not be deceived by your eyes, Captain! Even now thousands march to attack the rear of Caleb and Joshua. And you shall remain to watch while my warriors take Israel by the heel as a jackal takes a goat."

"Do you speak of your thousands camped along the fording places on the Jordan? The same thousands you sent runners to summon yesterday? Look closely at My Lord Joshua's camp.... Do you not see the stakes that stand before his tents? ...And do you not see the carcasses that hang from them, each pricked by a spear? ...Those are your runners of yesterday, Prince Shimmur! There are no mighty men marching to the aid of Jericho. Surrender the city and beg the benevolence of Joshua!"

The Captains who stood with Shimmur and Shimmur himself seemed to shrink with the awful knowledge that Ephah had divulged. They stared at the distant forms, now hanging lifeless on stakes, that had been the hope of Jericho's survival. At length Shimmur turned to his son.

"Go to your mother and comfort her Sabin, for she frets overmuch."

When the lad was gone Shimmur turned again to Ephah.

"If I gave over the city to Joshua what would his benevolence be? It is well known how mercifully he dealt with Sihon and Og. Would he let me and my sons go to a foreign land to live out our days? Speak the truth—if there be such in Israel!"

"The followers of Moses have no need to lie. Joshua's charity to you, your sons and these your officers, will be a quick and merciful death."

"And the warriors who stand upon the wall?"

Ephah shifted uneasily. "They also."

"And what of the people? What of the women and the old ones? What of the young boys and girls?"

Ephah averted his eyes. "The young girls will be saved if you give over the city now."

"You will murder all and save the young girls only? ...You wish me to give them over to be harlots for Israel while maggots eat their kinfolk? ... "Do you take us to be sheep that we will give up our lives with only a pitiful bleat? Joshua will not see the day that Shimmur bows before him, nor will you! We will fight until not a warrior stands on the walls of Jericho!!"

Ephah's features became ashen before the fury of Shimmur's anger. He had thought the king would quail before the might of Israel. He had been wrong and had overstepped.

"If that is your answer, I will carry it to My Lord Joshua," Epha said. Then he turned from Shimmur.

In an instant the mighty prince had firmly grasped Ephah by his sword belt and collar and with a furious roar raised him over his head and threw him beyond the wall of the tower. As the flailing Ephah crashed to the rocks outside the wall Shimmur screamed with a terrible voice.

"That is your answer, Lord Joshua!!"

CHAPTER 22

"Ephah's brash conceit led him into Shimmur's grasp and an evil death," Caleb said as he and Joshua turned their backs on Jericho. "It is a greater fall from Shimmur's tower than any man might survive."

"He died as he lived. Never have I known a man who was so drunk with killing," Joshua said. "And indeed, insolence was ever a part of his nature. I fear his tongue angered the prince overmuch and brought about his destruction. But with Ephah's killing, Shimmur throws contempt into the face of The Almighty God as well as me! I had thought to save the girls and perhaps a few of the young boys to be raised as eunuch slaves. But now, we will destroy all of Jericho! Not even an ass will stand alive when it is finished! Only the precious things will we save for the Lord's treasury."

"Will we attack the city now, My Lord? Shall I make a plan to storm the city walls?"

"Not yet, the will to fight is still strong in them and to attack would cost us dearly. No Caleb, march the warriors about the city with their weapons ready and with the priests making a great sound with their trumpets. We will show the warriors of Jericho our might and the might of Our God, whom they fear. And when they tremble in their terror, perhaps they will open the gates despite Shimmur's refusal."

Shimmur watched darkly as the warriors of Israel formed into a huge army before the city. When the Israelites first began forming ranks he had ordered every able bodied man in Jericho to the walls, whether warrior, shepherd or merchant. Now they stood in apprehensive silence as the awful power of the enemy was displayed before them. The battle-weathered warriors of Shimmur's palace guard raised their javelins and blades of Philistine steel high and shouted mocking insults at the Israelites, who had by now begun an encircling procession about the hill on which Shimmur's city stood. But the citizen soldiers, impressed without training or ceremony into such a dire situation, had no such bravado and stood dumbly, the misery of their fear etched deeply into their faces.

"Will they attack now?" As always Addan's voice was unperturbed in the face of danger. He was a stalwart soldier, lean and hard with years in the ranks, stoic by nature and brave in spirit.

Shimmur looked at the battle scarred face of his first captain. "Not so soon, I think Joshua seeks to weaken our defense with the cold weight of fear before he attacks us. And this he does too well, judged by the dread countenanced on those below. I think he will send us another emissary before he attacks. He has time before word of our state reaches our distant armies, so he will make his show with all the splendor he can muster. When the hearts of Canaan grow faint the hearts of Israel will swell with fervor—then Joshua will come against us."

Addan nodded his agreement. "Listen, My Lord, to the trumpets sounding and see the priests of Israel, how they march in splendor amid banners of many colors. They carry a box between them that is richly adorned and they fill the air about it with incense. What manner of thing is it that they should bestow such reverence on it?"

"It is the habitation of their god—a curiously small house for one with such great power. It is said that when they carry it with them into battle victory does not elude them."

Addan twitched his mustache thoughtfully. "It also was said by certain of the old ones, that the children of Amalek smote Israel grievously at Paran in the days before they entered Moab. And further it is said that this Joshua will not raise his hand against the Edomites because he fears them. If this god of his had such power would not the old warrior-priest, Moses, have come against us in his life?"

"Perhaps you are right, Addan, we fret too much about the presence of this god and not enough about the warriors who march this minute around our city. They far outnumber us and if our soldiers do not return soon I fear their late return will be to the ashes of Jericho and the corrupting bodies of its defenders."

"That may be true, My Lord, but we will give good account of ourselves and many of Joshua's warriors will give up their lives before Jericho bums. But yet, the conscripts have an unreasoning fear of the Israelite god and this fear may cause them to flee before the might of Israel."

"You say well, Addan. We must divert their minds from the Israelite god. Go to the priest, Alzibar, and tell him to raise a tribute to Baal the strong and to Anath, his mistress who rules over battle, that they may attend us when Joshua comes. Tonight, let the priests and priestesses lead the people in dancing and singing to the pleasure of the gods that our warriors may enter battle with a full spirit. I think that today Israel makes a great show but tomorrow they will come."

At last the day of Israel's menace ended and when the sinking sun framed Shimmur's high tower the campfires of the tribes were lit again. From the high place of the captains' encampment Joha and Daniel sat beside their fire and watched the distant figures on the walls of Jericho, until in the settling darkness they could see them no more.

"I was wondering how it would feel to be so surrounded by death as they are behind those walls," Daniel said. "For that is how it is with them, death encircles them as relentlessly as a noose."

Joha nodded assent. 'They are too few for us and now with the death of Ephah Joshua will show little mercy. They are dead—though they still walk about. Yet there are some battle tried warriors upon those walls and they will fight all the harder because they cannot flee. I think many of our own warriors will taste of the sword before Jericho falls."

"Aye, and Yahweh willing, it will not be you or I. I still remember well our first test at the hands of the Amalekites, when we climbed that evil hill and they threw rocks down or us and showered us with arrows. And when we had gained the hilltop it was only to be thrust back in defeat. This will be another such encounter, Joha, except we must climb ladders without cover of darkness to gain footing on those walls."

"Darkness would do us little good against Jericho and greater harm, Daniel. For in the dark our archers could not keep back those who would bathe us with burning oil. I would rather take my chances with the rocks hurled at us by the sons of Amalek. The death caused by hot oil is a lingering agony."

"Aye, even with the archers it will be a perilous climb to the top of the wall. It puts me in mind of our descent from Rahab's window, when the guards of Shimmur hunted us.... I wonder how the harlot fares. But for her we would have died at the hands of Shimmur's torturers."

Joha slapped his thigh. "I had forgotten her! We have an issue of trust to keep with the woman when we take Jericho. We must pass the word again to the other captains lest Rahab and her kin be killed."

Daniel stared at the campfire thoughtfully. "It seems unjust that among all the people that fight for their king and country only a harlot who is a traitor to her people will live."

"You have fought beside me for many years, Daniel. And yet you speak of what is just? War is not about what is righteous or just—it is about who is strongest. And as for me, I would rather save one beautiful woman than a hundred righteous men. But enough of this talk, Lord Caleb comes."

Caleb, General of the Armies of Israel, returned the salutes of Joha and Daniel then spoke without frivolous greeting.

"I come to give you knowledge of what will happen on the morrow. It is the day on which Jericho will fall and you, Joha and Daniel, shall lead in the assault. Joha will lead by way of the gate when the battering ram has done its work. Daniel shall take the ladders against the wall at the house of Rahab, the whore. It is opposite the gate and low and there none will defend from the window holes, but only from the roof. And those our archers will sorely afflict. When you have cleared the soldiers from the roof, Daniel, leave a guard at the door of Rahab's house that she and hers be kept safe as we have promised. Then Joha will drive Shimmur's warriors back toward you and you will take them from behind."

"And what of those of Jericho who throw down their weapons and those who are not warriors?" Daniel asked.

"Of that Joshua has not told me," Caleb lied. "It depends on what course Shimmur takes. For at first light one goes forth to demand the surrender of Jericho. If Shimmur concedes defeat something may be done to save his people. If not, Joshua will be angered and likely all within the walls will perish."

"And if he concedes...what of Shimmur himself and his captains?" Joha asked.

"The Almighty has decreed that they shall die," Caleb said. "It would be better for them that they fall on their swords or throw themselves from Shimmur's tower than to face death at the hands of the princes."

Joha nodded. "That is true indeed for there are kin of Ephah among them. They will wish to cause Shimmur much pain before he dies. But who is the one who goes before the gate to hail Shimmur?"

"He is one of Ephah's men. He is near to a giant in stature and very fierce by nature. He goes by his own petition that Shimmur might send a champion against him and so decide the fate of Jericho."

Daniel frowned. "But, Lord Caleb, if this man should lose in single combat would we retreat and leave them be?"

"This man would not lose to such as you or me or even both at once. There is no need to consider what course to take beyond that of victory."

"Listen!" Joha said. "The sound of singing and merriment come from the city. And look! The light from a great fire shines to the very top of Shimmur's tower. What folly infects Jericho? Do those within the walls celebrate the prospect of victory?"

Caleb studied the distant tumult. "No, they do not celebrate victory, nor are their songs those of merriment. They raise a supplication to their gods. They chant prayers to Baal Zebel and Anath to deliver them from us. It is in vain—the hand of Yahweh is raised against them and they shall be destroyed!"

Shimmur and Addan stood in a gate tower and watched the second forming of the army of Israel. But this time they brought the battering ram along on the roadway to the gate.

"It is as I said—they come at us today," Shimmur said. "Are the stones and hot oil ready on the battlements, Addan?"

"They are ready, My Lord. And the archers stand at their shooting places with great baskets of arrows. Joshua will pay dearly to take Jericho."

"It would be better that Jericho were not taken at all. Mind you that the warriors know the cost of falling into the hands of Israel."

"They well know that a fight against Israel is to the very death, My Lord. And the captains have pacts made between us that we shall not be taken."

"That is well. Assign some of my guard to kill me if I am sorely stricken in battle, Addan. It would go hard with me if I were taken alive."

"That is already done, My Lord, and for myself also. But look, a warrior of Israel approaches the gate. He is a giant, a fierce-looking fellow indeed."

"He is Joshua's second emissary. He will demand that the gates be opened. Or perhaps he will propose that I or my champion meet him upon the field to determine who is the victor without battle between our nations."

"And would you agree to such a thing, My Lord?"

"Neither would I open to Joshua nor make such a pact. For it is said that to make a pact with Joshua is to make a pact with a lion. He is ruled by his hunger and has no remorse for those he devours. But listen, Addan, the bull that Joshua sends bellows his greeting."

"I call to Shimmur, King of Jericho!" The voice of the warrior was harsh and angry. "I am Ehud, cousin of Ephah, who died at your hand! I speak for Joshua, Lord of Israel! Throw down your weapons and open the gates to us!"

Shimmur nodded to Addan and the captain answered. "Do you take us to be of feeble mind that we would bare our necks to you? We will never lay down our weapons while we draw breath!"

"Then choose you a champion to fight me! ...If I win you will surrender, if I lose we will leave you in peace!"

"You speak with the tongue of a serpent!" Shimmur shouted. "And if I believe your words, I am a fool! Go back to your master and tell him that Shimmur spits in his face."

"You are a coward and you are afraid to fight me!" Ehud screamed. "Come to me and I will kill you!"

Shimmur turned to Addan. "Loose some arrows—send this cur back to his master."

It was but a little while before the grey canopy that shielded the battering ram of Joshua crept forward toward the gate of Jericho. Then also the warriors that Daniel led picked up broad ladders and made their way toward the wall of Jericho where Rahab lived. But then the earth trembled, at first so slightly that it only tickled the feet of the warriors and made them pause in their labor. But then the trembling grew until the earth shook beneath their feet so that they could barely stand and there was a sound such as that made by many chariots of war! Daniel looked up to Jericho as the first stones fell from the walls. In a moment more there was a terrible rumbling as first the great tower, then huge portions of the thick wall collapsed.[67] Then all became still and the city was nearly hidden in great billows of dust.

The warriors of Israel stood transfixed, all eyes intent on the devastation that had occurred so suddenly. Before them, on the hill where Jericho stood, clouds of dust drifted slowly away to reveal great heaps of rubble that had been much of the city's walls. Inside, some buildings had fallen and some remained, though cracked and battered. Amid the wreckage figures began to rise and stumble about in a stunned, irresolute manner.

Then it was that Joshua, standing on the high place, raised his voice in a mighty shout. "It is the hand of Yahweh, God Almighty!! He has given Jericho into our hands! Go forth, Warriors of Israel, and kill the followers of Baal!! Spare none to spawn their evil anew!!"

Dazed, Shimmur raised his head, then painfully dragged himself from the wreckage of the gate tower. Beside him Addan was stirring, his face contorted with pain. Shimmur turned to look up at the great tower where his family were gathered and saw only the sun where it had stood. He staggered to his feet and reached his hand to the captain.

"Can you stand and fight, Addan?"

The warrior gained his feet, his left forearm bent at a peculiar angle. "Aye, My Lord, if you will bind this arm tight against me, I can still hold a sword."

Shimmur wrapped his sash tight about Addan so that the useless arm was bound to his chest.

"The hand of the Israelite god is strong. Have the trumpeter call to rally."

"He is dead." Addan drew his sword and flashed it in the air. "Warriors of Shimmur, rally about your king! Come, fight for Jericho!"

Out of the dust forms materialized, dirty and dazed, some bleeding and broken.

"Gather about me! Fight for your king and Jericho!" Shimmur shouted.

"But My Lord," one said, "they are too strong for us and their god is mighty. Can we not yield to them?"

"Will you die by the sword to your neck rather than to your breast, coward? Is it not a good thing to die valiantly at the hand of a god? Gather and fight, Joshua comes!"

Beyond the drifting dust there was a great shout from the warriors of Israel then the sound of hard running feet. The warriors of Jericho stood, grimly awaiting death.

Even before Joha could see the enemy the first arrows came. It was a sporadic, sparse delivery, unlike the barrages he had faced fighting the Amalekites and Midianites. Yet a few of the shafts found their marks in the dense ranks of Israel and warriors fell with screams of pain.

Then suddenly he was facing a Canaanite warrior. Joha didn't notice the lack of a shield or the bound up arm, just the flash of the iron blade as it descended. The blow fell heavily on his bronze buckler, forcing Joha back a step. He returned the blow but it was caught and deflected deftly by the other's sword. This man is a veteran, Joha thought and saw that he wore a captain's breastplate before the sword descended again. This time Joha slashed across his opponents shoulder as he caught the blow and was rewarded with a spurt of crimson. It was then he noticed the bound up arm where a shield should have been.

Addan fought methodically and cleverly—though his injured arm pained him and put him off balance. He was tremendously strong and his stoic nature made him tolerant of pain and immune to fear, allowing him to always fight with a clear mind. The scars on his body attested to many duels of this kind and the thought that he might lose never occurred to him. That the Israelite's sword had cut him was vexing but not dismaying—it merely proved that the Israelite was expert. So now he must press the attack swiftly and make the Israelite falter in some small way—it would be enough.

Though Joha himself was a powerful warrior he was somewhat awed by the incredible power of the warrior facing him. Even with one arm bound up he pressed Joha hard with a furious assault. His blows came fast and hard, his arm raising high to gain the most force on every stroke, driving Joha relentlessly back. Joha knew this warrior wanted him to trip or stumble and backing away he eventually would—he had to regain the advantage or die.

Addan was coldly calculating as he struck again and again at the Israelite. A few more hard blows to make him raise his shield—then a swift thrust under it just below the breastplate. A wound there would not kill—but it would disable—and that would end the contest. He raised his sword high then stopped as though suddenly frozen in place—the javelin of an unseen adversary had passed between his ribs just under his arm. Addan lay for only a few moments with blood gushing from his chest before his brain faded—it is a good way to die, he thought.

Joha turned from the dying captain in time to ward off the sword blow of another warrior. This one was even mightier than the first, standing taller than Joha by half a head and broader by a handbreadth. Though he wore no helmet, the warrior's breastplate of bronze carried the insignia of a golden raging bull—Joha knew at once that he faced Shimmur, King of Jericho.

From the corner of his eye, Shimmur had seen Addan fighting the Israelite. But he himself fought two others and could not aid his injured captain. Most of those who faced Shimmur were ill prepared to meet a warrior such as he and soon died because of it. Shimmur gave the one such a blow that it split his shield and cut deeply into his skull. The other he pushed backward with his buckler, then drove his iron sword to its hilt in the man's innards, ripping upward as he freed the blade. When he turned to Addan the captain was already down with blood spurting around the shaft of a javelin. Rage overcame Shimmur then and he focused its full force on Joha.

Joha staggered backward at the force of Shimmur's second blow and he saw the edge of the king's great sword bite through the top of his buckler. He pulled free and raised his own blade to return the blow but was suddenly thrust aside by a massive bullhide shield.

"Back away and give me free space, Captain, for this one belongs to me! I will avenge Ephah with the blood of Jericho's king."

Ehud placed his huge bulk squarely in front of Shimmur, his broad face twisted with a malignant sneer. He wore a scarred breastplate and skirt of layered bullhide and a cap of the same, because nowhere were there bronze ones of great enough size for him. His sword was of bronze instead of the stronger iron but was of such massive size that it could stand against blades of iron. Now he raised his shield of layered bullhide and wood and advanced on Shimmur.

The king's eyes flared wide with surprise as the huge warrior took his place before him then they grew bright and narrow with hatred as recognition came.

"Now we will see who is the greater, son of a sow!" the king roared as he struck a hard blow that bit into Ehud's shield.

"This day I will burn your carcass as an offering to Yahweh!" Ehud returned, striking a blow to the king's buckler that caused Shimmur to step back.

"You are a fat steer and make the better offering!" Shimmur thrust savagely—his blade glanced off Ehud's sword—but cut a furrow in his arm that brought a roar of pain and anger. The two swordsmen quit their insults and fought silently then except for the sound of swords clashing and the labored breathing of the combatants.

Joha stood mesmerized and though it had been only moments, it seemed as though the contest had raged much longer. Another warrior came to face Joha, a citizen soldier—he lasted through only a few awkward strokes and parries before Joha felled him. When he turned again to the two mighty men, Shimmur's shield was neatly split and the arm that bore it hung at his side—blood flowed profusely from a deep wound in the king's shoulder. Ehud grinned evilly in triumph and raised his huge sword high for a stroke that would end Shimmur. Yet in his brash confidence lay error—for in lifting his arm high he created a small but deadly opening—the sword of Shimmur found it with faultless accuracy. The tip of Shimmur's blade severed both Ehud's windpipe and a carotid artery before entering between the vertebrae of his neck. The giant fell, spewing great plumes of blood as his body gasped its last.

Shimmur stepped forward and spat contemptuously on the still-convulsing body of the giant. It was only then that he raised his eyes to Joha and in seeing him, saw his own death. For though victorious—Shimmur was spent—and he knew his next battle would be his last. Still, he raised his sword and awaited this new adversary. To him, dying by this warrior's sword would be better than dying slowly at the hands of Joshua.

In the ancient courtesy of soldiers—for those who fight bravely and well—Joha raised his swordhand to his chest in salute before raising his sword against the king. The King knew Joha could easily have joined the giant against him and that it would then be he that now lay still. For this chivalry he was grateful—he touched his own sword hand to his breastplate—an act that acknowledged Joha as an equal upon the field. Then Joha, ever a warrior—and mindful of the honor among his peers that this victory would bring—stepped around the body of Ehud to engage Shimmur, King of Jericho.

He was just eighteen with the frame of a man but with a boy's spirit, trying hard to endure this his first test in battle. Though his skill with a sword was passable at best, Jashen's supple muscles and long limbs threw javelin or spear with speed and accuracy. Because of this he carried two light javelins and a heavier spear and followed the swordsmen and those who fought by thrusting spears. It was his purpose to protect the captains and aid those beset by heavy odds.

On this day he followed Joha, the leading captain and had already struck down one of his opponents, though Joha would have denied the need for it. Then he was forced to fight a battle of his own when a spearman of Jericho engaged him. The poor fellow threw clumsily and Jashen dispatched him with his heavy spear, thrown close and quickly retrieved.

Shimmur backed away from Joha to a place less greased by blood and less strewn with rubble. Though his strength was fading his warrior spirit would not allow him to make a futile assault and so end his life quickly. Not yet, he thought, while he might yet lure this one to make a stroke where he would profit by his longer reach and finish him with a sword point to the throat as he had finished the giant. Yes—he might yet secure a victory, a last victory where defeat was sure. So thought Prince Shimmur, even as Jashen's heavy spear winged its way to pierce the golden bull upon his chest. And this it did—the point of it thrown with incredible speed by the youth, plunged through the breastplate of bronze and into the beating heart of the warrior King—so died Prince Shimmur, King of Jericho.

Most of the wall had fallen but the portion on which Rahab's house abutted still stood and through the dust Daniel saw the red banners hanging from the window shutters. He turned to the young warriors he had chosen to guard the harlot's door.[69]

"Behold, the hand of God has protected Rahab and so will you. Let no one in or out until the battle is ended. Then, God willing that I still live, I will come to lead her and her kin to sanctuary in Israel."

"And if evil befalls you Captain—what shall we do?"

"Then take her and her family to Joshua and he will give them asylum. Now it is time to take the city—may Yahweh be with us!"

Then Daniel, Captain of a Thousand, raised his sword and pointed it at the rubble of Jericho. There was a great shout from the ranks behind him and they ran forward like a huge wave, bent on destruction. Those of Jericho that remained unscathed by the collapse of the city stood and fought bravely, shoulder to shoulder, back to back. But they were caught between the warriors of Joha and those of Daniel and they died in a terrible slaughter to the very last man.

Now the warriors of Israel could go on unimpeded to kill everything that breathed in Jericho. For that was the order given by Joshua, servant of Yahweh, God Most High! The city must be destroyed—every soul within—everything that walked—down to the last lamb and donkey.

Daniel walked among his warriors as they accomplished their grisly task. He watched as mighty men entered the wretched, rubble-strewn buildings that still stood and he listened to the cries of fright and pain that followed. And when the warriors came out, blades dripping with blood, his heart was heavy. For Daniel was a true warrior—a man of battle—and to kill these pitiful, frightened creatures filled him with revulsion. And yet, he could do nothing else because he was a soldier and he must obey his commander.

So it was that Daniel turned into a narrow lane between two cracked and caving buildings. As he entered all was silent, but in the dim and dusty light he sensed a presence and brought his sword to the ready. His heart pounded hard, pushing blood to his tired arms, readying him for yet another battle on this day of many battles. Then there was a movement and Daniel's eyes focused on the new threat he faced.

She watched him—her brown eyes wide with fear as she clutched a dirty, tattered doll to her body. She was five years of age, seven at most, Daniel thought as he looked at her. A child so young should not know such carnage—one so pretty and perfect, with her long dark hair and olive skin should not be condemned to death. He stood there—face to face with an innocence long lost to him—torn between an ingrained sense of duty and the compassion that was his by nature. The little girl stood still before him, too terrified to run or even cry out.

Daniel knew he could not defy the will of his god and the girl was already as good as dead—none were to be saved. None save Rahab, the traitor whore—he spat at the thought of the great injustice. Yet how could he do such a thing and live with its knowledge? Still, if he did not another would and the child's death might be a horrid, beastly thing. Such a little one as this should depart her world with as little fear and pain as is possible. He stepped forward and gently took the little girl by her shoulders. Then he turned her about so that her frightened eyes did not peer into his—he brought his sword down hard.

When all of the women and children had joined their husbands and fathers in death, the brave warriors of Joshua killed the remains of the flocks and herds because Joshua had cursed all that lived in Jericho. When the killing was done the warriors of Joshua took all of the precious things, all of the things of iron and brass, silver and gold and put them in the treasury of the Lord. Phinehas, the priest, took the precious things under his stewardship and some soldiers grumbled privately because they took no booty. Yet none dared speak openly because they feared Joshua and the Levites.

Saved only from the city was the family of Rahab, the traitor to her people. It was the duty of Joha and Daniel, appointed by Joshua himself, to take these few to a place of safety on the fringe of the Israelite encampment, among the people of the nations.

"Your tongue is still, Daniel. Do you already have the hollowness that comes with the slaughter of battle?' Joha glanced at his friend as they picked their way through the ruins that had been Jericho.

"I am thinking of one I killed who should this night be resting on her father's shoulder. Instead she rests forever and I feel unclean. It is as though I were a murderer that should stand before God for judgement."

"You did what you must—by God's command—therefore you are innocent of wrong. It will pass, Daniel. But what think you of Rahab? Look how she already regrets her treason against her people."

The young woman's face was contorted with horror as she walked slowly past the mutilated corpses of her neighbors. Suddenly her younger sister screamed and fell to her knees beside the body of a young man. He had been perhaps seventeen and had been handsome, but now his face was gray and a pool of blood thickened about his body. The girl's cries were so anguished that the soldiers about her turned their heads away although they were accustomed to the wails of women.

Rahab gently took her sister's arm. "Come, Mitra, you can do him no good. We must go."

The girl pulled away and leaped to her feet. "He is dead and I will forever live in sorrow, Rahab! It is you who have done this thing to our people! It is you who hid the spies and led destruction to our city!"

"No-o-o! They would have come whether I protected Joha or not! What I did was to save my family from death!"

"For what did you save us? To live with those who killed our people? ...Will they be our friends? ...They will despise us, even as your Captain Joha despises you! For such a one you betrayed our people?"

Rahab stared at her sister then at Joha. "Tell me it is not so!" she cried. "Tell me you do not despise me!"

Joha looked at her and spoke with measured words. "You saved me to save your family, Rahab. Leave it so. For you are right, Joshua would have come even if I had not returned. In this you can take comfort—but for your kindness to me—you and these with you would be dead."

"But what of me, Joha? Will we not be as we were?"

"We can be what we were and nothing more—a man in lust and a harlot. If you thought otherwise, it is of your design and not of mine."

"It matters not what I thought, Captain.... Lead us to a place where we may pitch a tent. The eyes of the dead accuse me and I am weary of the stench of death within my nostrils."

CHAPTER 23

"I too feel an emptiness in my spirit, Daniel, It is as if my bowels were torn from my body and a cold hollowness was left in their place."

Joha stirred the coals of a waning fire with a piece of dry oak branch then threw it among them and watched the wood smolder and burst into flame. Daniel emptied the wine cup he held before answering.

"Aye, perhaps it is our years or simply a rebellion of our spirits against years of cruelty and death. When we fought Midian the sight of so much killing made me feel sick. But then it was different, we fought and killed to defend ourselves or to avenge the transgressions of Baal against The True God. But now we kill to empty a land so that we might inherit it."

"You forget that we have always done that—though the prophet said it was God's will. Were we not young warriors when Moses raised the sword against Sihon and Og? Did we not ruthlessly destroy the Amorite nations?"

"That is true, but it was because those kings would not grant us passage through their lands but came out with their armies against us. We defeated them and enslaved those who remained. That is the way of just war—they would have done the same to us, or worse. But this is different.... We have lived long as neighbors to Shimmur's people and they have not raised the sword against us. To kill them all—young and old, man and woman, peasant and prince—it is too much, I think."

Joha did not reply but stared at the fire. *Daniel is right,* he thought. *Yet what can we do? We are soldiers, bound to serve Lord Joshua and God—tonight we will drink too much wine to dismiss the specters that plague us. By morning's light they will be gone and our only sickness will be of the wine. Daniel takes this killing too much upon his spirit.*

"She remains with me...the little girl and I cannot cast her away!"

There was a desperate sound in Daniel's voice and his eyes were fixed as though on a person's face.

"She is before me now and all the others stand behind her! ...They accuse me with their eyes, Joha! ...They condemn me though they are dead!"

"It is the wine, Daniel. The vapors form evil mists within your mind. I see no such spirits as you describe. Let us lay ourselves down beside the fire and sleep now, for it has been an evil day—but tomorrow life will begin anew."

"It is late into the night, My Lord and still you sit awake. Drink of the wine I warmed for you. It will rest your mind and your body."

The woman's dark hands expertly kneaded the muscles of Joshua's neck and shoulders and he sighed with the pleasure of it.

"You do that well enough without wine, woman. You are a great blessing to me and I marvel that you agreed to share my tent. For I know you are a woman of wealth and need not serve any man."

"To serve a man is a need of my nature, My Lord, for it gives me comfort. But I wish that I were still young, that you would find greater pleasure in me. Does it not trouble you to take another man's leavings—and old ones at that?"

"I took The Prophet's mantle of leadership and took on my shoulders all the moaning and whining of his people, Adanah. Should I then be bothered by taking that of his which gives me solace? Your solitary counsel and consolation are a greater gift than a young woman's body. Though in truth, if such were my need, there are many willing to serve the Lord of Israel."

Adanah laughed and pulled Joshua's head against her ample breasts. She had aged well and though she was no longer slender, her body was still appealing. Further, through a combination of special oils, freedom from toil in the sun and favorable genetics, her skin had retained an unusual smoothness for her age and her neatly plaited hair was still a glossy black.

"Is it over now, My Lord?" Adanah asked. "Will we be at peace again?"

"It will not be over as long as I draw breath, Adanah."

"But why? Moses was driven for land and power and so we marched and fought until he became old and sick. Is it also that way with you?"

"I have made a promise to Yahweh and to Moses and the princes, that I would conquer the land promised to Abraham. That I will do. Nor can I do any less for the princes of the tribes have long coveted Canaan. Now that Jericho is so easily destroyed their lust for the rich lands and trade routes to the west will be greater than before."

"But will not the kings of the lands to the west join together against us?"

"No, we will take Ai next, then another city and yet another, going ever westward until we have separated the north from the south. We will rain such a devastation on those who resist us that those who remain will cower in fear. And when we are finished Israel will rule all of the lands from the great desert to the great sea. The riches of the land, the bounty of the seas and the wealth of the trade routes will belong to Israel."

"And what of you, My Lord? What will you gain for spending your last good years in warfare? Would it not be better to let others fret about future battles and instead enjoy the fruits you have so justly earned?"

Joshua laughed. "I now understand why Moses so valued your council, Adanah. Beneath your dark beauty lies the mind of a minister. And to your question, I must answer that I will gain nothing material that I do not already possess. For If I wish to eat the food of kings is served to me.... If I wish to drink, the best wines of Canaan are mine.... I am clothed in fine linen and I sleep in a soft bed beside a faithful woman. Yet all of this is for my lifetime only. But when I conquer the kings of Canaan—my name will be written beside that of Moses in the great book of our people—and the Children of Israel will sing my praise forever!"

"You are indeed like Moses! I think that is why I did not refuse you so soon after my husband's death. I like ambitious men, men of power. But listen, I hear footsteps on the pathway. Shall I tell the one who comes to return in the morning?"

"No, it may be of some importance—if not I will make this messenger rue his intrusion at such a late hour." Joshua drew a cloak over his linen tunic and went to the door of the tent. "Who comes in the hours of sleep?"

"It is Joha, Lord Joshua. I beg your forbearance for my intrusion—but a thing has happened that you must know."

"If I must indeed know of it—bring it out forthwith—my patience grows thin!"

"Then I will do so, My Lord—Daniel has killed himself!"

Adanah gasped at the words. Not Daniel, she thought, not the serious, thoughtful Daniel! He was so unlike the other captains, kind and almost gentle.

Joshua stepped outside the tent and looked hard at the face of Joha. It was drawn tight with grief the lines of anguish accented by the flame of the torch he carried.

"When? ...How?"

"We had been drinking wine—to drive away the demons of the day. I fell asleep, but arose later to piss. Daniel was gone from his bed. I thought that he had risen to walk—he did that when he was troubled. But I found him only a few steps away."

"Finish it, man—tell it all!"

"He fell on his sword but it didn't strike his heart. Daniel died slowly as his blood drained from him—but he never cried out."

"He wouldn't have—he was a true warrior. But he was a veteran of bloody battles. What could have made him so melancholy that he would do this?"

"There was a little girl in the city—Daniel killed her and couldn't escape her and the others he had killed. He said they accused him with their eyes—it drove him mad."

"There is the danger—a warrior should never look into the eyes of one he kills. They cannot curse you if you don't look into their eyes! And you, Joha, how do you fare?"

"There is something of the fever that raged within Daniel. It is the women and the little ones, My Lord. I have no regrets about the warriors I kill in battle because it is kill or be killed—but this is too much, I think. Can we not let these others live?"

Joshua laid his hand on Joha's shoulder. "Your heart is good and that is a trial for a soldier. But we will do what the Lord commands because we are warriors. Go now and bid some women to prepare Daniel's body. Tomorrow we will bury him with the honor befitting a great warrior."

Adanah went to Joshua as he entered the tent. She knew the sorrow that he felt for Daniel—but would not show. It was that way with soldiers, they were so often faced by the death of comrades that they built a hard shell around their spirits. But Adanah had no such shell and now she wept as she embraced Joshua.

"Joha speaks with his heart, My Lord. Must we kill these innocent ones and so kill our own spirits? Daniel would be alive tomorrow were it not for this brutal slaughter."

"Daniel would be alive if he remembered the commands of Yahweh. Blood must be shed to gain the promised land—though we might wish to do otherwise."

"Yes," she said quietly, "it is the price of glory and honor and a tribute made to Yahweh for the abundance of the promised land."

The easy destruction of Jericho whetted Joshua's appetite for conquest. After a fortnight of rest he once again sent Caleb to seek pledges of soldiers from the princes of Israel. His general returned angry and discouraged.

"Never have I come upon so many excuses to shirk battle," Caleb grumbled. "This prince must send his men to the fields to plant while the soil is still moist. Another must gather the flocks to shear them and tend to the lambs. Each has some pressing cause that prevents him from pledging soldiers to us. I was able to gain promise to only two thousand warriors at most."

Joshua frowned. "Why are the princes suddenly so reluctant to make war? It was but a short time past that they pressed me to enter Canaan and that we did. Jericho fell to us with little cost to our army."

“And without gain to the money chests of the princes, My Lord.”

“A-a-h, that is where the yoke chafes the bullock’s neck. The princes hold back to gain a portion of the plunder.”

“That is true, I think. There is a rumor that a certain prince would be a more generous leader than you, My Lord.”

“There are always those who would challenge my leadership—then so be it! We will take Ai in spite of the reluctance of the princes. Did not Joha’s spies see only a small force at Ai, a few hundred at most? The city is small and the people are afraid of our might. Gather a thousand warriors from those who will send them and let Joha lead them. When Ai falls the tribes will gather more solidly behind us.”[70]

“Shall I go with to fire the spirits of the men? I think perhaps the princes will send those men who have little esteem within their tribes and are not such bold or expert fighters. I think they will keep back their strongest warriors as a sign of strength, to promote their own interests.”

“All the more reason why you should stay here to lead the Levite guards and protect against those who would stir up Israel. Joha is a strong captain and a valiant warrior. He will capture Ai. Then we will be able to deal more forcefully with those princes who seek great gains for their purses.”

“How will we attack them?’ Arnan, the young captain who walked in Daniel’s place, asked Joha. They had left the camp of the Levites before the sun had risen. And now the Israelite soldiers were plodding into the highlands where Ai sat like a gatekeeper to the fertile plainsland of Canaan.

“We will go straight to the gate of their little city. We will march up this road to their very portal. I will hail their king and demand surrender.”

“Do you think they will surrender so easily? Will they not fear that they will be killed as were the people of Jericho?”

`They fear us and that is why they will surrender. I will offer them their lives in turn for their pledge to the service of Israel.”

“Slavery? Will they bow to the yoke without raising a sword?”

“Would you not bow your head to save your family from the sword?”

Arnan was doubtful. "It is said the people of Ai are great warriors, very fierce and proud."

"And we have fought against Ammalek and Midian and now Jericho. Were they not fierce and did we not defeat them? Do not doubt—your warriors will take on your fears."

"You are right in that, My Captain. Few of my men are true warriors such as you and I. Most are poor men conscripted by the princes and paid only a piece or two of silver. They will be hard pressed to stand against seasoned swordsmen."

Then it is of greater concern that the people of Ai throw down their weapons without engaging us in battle. We will make a bold approach. They will only see our soldiers—not the quaking of their hearts."

"That is well, My Captain, for I see the gate towers of Ai and the gates are already closed. Word of our coming precedes us."

Arnan stood fully a head taller than Joha, a young giant who would be numbered among the mightiest of Israel's warriors if he lived through a few more battles. In scarcely a dozen steps Joha had risen far enough up the incline on which they marched to see what was already disclosed to Arnan. He raised his hand to halt the trudging soldiers behind him and make them alert. Both men were silent now, their muscles tightened at the sight of the city before them. They were brave men—but brave men fear as greatly as cowards—and now adrenalin began racing through their veins in response to it.

"The city stands higher than I thought," Joha said. "If we are forced to assault it we will need ladders."

"And warriors who will not quail at climbing them, My Captain. I do not like the prospect of leading those behind us on such an errand. Nor do I like the slopes and rocks that rise beside this roadway. An army could lie in waiting above us."

"There is no such army, Arnan—did not our spies say there were only a few soldiers at Ai? And if they are only a few they would not place themselves outside the walls. Go and tell the other captains to bring up their men in a broad company that it might appear we are great in number. Then we will march close to the gateway with trumpets sounding and swords raised high. I will approach the gate with banner and trumpets and demand their surrender."

"Is that not overbold, My Captain? Would it not be better to send a single messenger?"

"I wish to show no sign of fear, Arnan. If they see a captain approach with such arrogance they will think us a mighty army. They will open their gates to us to save themselves. Now go and mass the warriors."

Behind Joha and his banner bearer the Israelites marched in a broad column that filled the valley to the very bases of the hillocks that bordered the roadway. Twenty men abreast, swords and lances at the ready, the warriors of Israel marched to the announcement of blaring ram's horns and clanging cymbals. Just out of the reach of feathered shafts which might come from the walls the army halted and Joha alone walked forward within hailing distance of the gate towers.

"Dezurus, King of Ai! ...I, Joha, Captain of the Armies of Israel, call upon you in the name of Joshua, Lord of all Israel! ...Surrender to us and your people shall not be harmed!"

There were long moments of silence then a huge warrior appeared at the battlement that crossed the gateway to Ai.

"I, Modan, speak for the mighty Dezurus. If we open the gates to Israel will we then be allowed to live in peace?"

"You shall do that...in the service of Israel."

"You mean as slaves? The people of Ai do not put on the yoke for any man!"

"Then we will destroy you—every man, woman and child among you!"

The warrior turned away and there was a long silence. Then Modan drew his sword and pointed it at Joha.

"To surrender without a fight would bring dishonor on Ai and that we cannot do. But we will lay the thing on the hands of a champion in combat. I will meet you alone upon the field and if I win Israel will leave us be. If I lose, the people of Ai will bend to the yoke of Israel."

Joha looked at the man upon the battlement and knew he could not best the giant in single combat.

"It shall not be so," he said. "Choose between opening the gates and certain death."

"Then we shall open the gates!" Modan said.

He leaped from the battlement to the ground below. Behind him the gates swung open and a small company of warriors flooded out of the city.

Joha drew his sword and raised it high. No other command was needed. Fifty paces behind him Arnan spoke to the trumpet bearers, who with a blaring command sent the forces of Israel forward against the city of Ai. The company of warriors of Ai formed a cluster and stood waiting for annihilation, it seemed. Their band was pitifully small though they seemed to be hardened warriors with a giant leading them. Certainly, thought Joha, the first charge of Israel would sweep through them and into the city. So he waited with sword poised for Arnan and the mass of untried soldiers that would soon taste their first victory.

So intent was Arnan on the solitary figure of his leader and the cluster of soldiers at the gateway that he did not see the archers rise from the scrubby brushwood at the side of the roadway. Nor did any other captain until the first shafts came like swift falcons stooping to drive their talons into unwary quail. There were cries of surprised pain, then a milling confusion as the untested soldiers indecisively turned to meet this unexpected assault. It was then that the warriors of Ai charged forward and a second flood of warriors emerged from the city.

Joha turned to look back at the cries behind him and saw the flurry of arrows descending on his army. Inwardly he cursed himself for falling prey to this most simple of traps. But his self-deprecation was fleeting, for now the warriors of Ai were upon him with the giant, Modan, in the lead.

If I must die now, My Lord, let it not be by this one's hands, Joha prayed. He caught the giant's first thundering blow with his bronze shield. Modan was as strong as a bull but not clever. Joha spun in under his sword and thrust his own blade into the giant's throat. The warrior's gushing arterial blood met his exhaled breath to form a scarlet plume that drenched Joha. The champion of Ai sagged to his knees then pitched forward to lie still at Joha's feet.

Joha backed up to distance himself from Modan's comrades who stood frozen in shock at their leader's quick defeat. But in a moment they regained their senses and the warriors of Ai were on him from all sides. Joha wished that Daniel was standing back to back with him for the two of them might stand even against these overwhelming numbers. But Daniel will fight with me no more, he thought. He awaits me if there is a place for warriors such as us, after we have spilled our blood and innards upon the battle field.

Out of the corner of his eye Joha saw his standard bearer running back to Arnan, an arrow bouncing from the flesh of his shoulder. Then he suddenly lost all feeling in his body as an axe bit into the back of his neck severing his spinal cord. He fell forward to the ground and settled limply with his head finding a peculiar angle so that in his last moments he stared at the captain's emblem engraved on his breastplate. He was alive and though his horrible wound bled profusely the carotid arteries were intact. His strong heart pumped blood to his brain and Joha was aware of the shouts of men and the trampling of feet as the warriors of Ai passed by him. Then the axe struck again, cleaving his skull and Joha joined his comrade for eternity.

Arnan had seen the peril his captain was in and he tried valiantly to rally his soldiers to charge the warriors of Ai. But the untested Israelites were intent on escaping the steady flight of arrows sent by the archers at the roadside and cowered behind their shields. So it was that Joha was engulfed by the warriors of Ai and Arnan with a handful of seasoned warriors rushed to his aid. The act was brave but futile for these few became the target of the archers. Arnan himself was the first struck with a shaft that entered his thigh. A second plunged into his neck severing an artery and bringing swift death. In a few moments the rest of the party was stricken or put to flight.

Beset by feathered death and demoralized by the death of Joha and Arnan the Israelites fled in panic. Behind them charged the victorious warriors of Ai giving impetus to the flight with ferocious yells and sounding trumpets. Those of Israel who were weak or wounded were overtaken and killed and their cries lent swiftness to the rest. At last the pursued reached the rocky crags of Shebarim and scattered in its broken terrain.[70] Here the pursuers would be at greater risk so the men of Ai returned to their city to feast their victory. "Sons of betrayal! You hung back in sloth and cowardice and because of it two stalwart captains and many men lie dead on the road to Ai!"

Joshua screamed his anger at the princes summoned before him.

"Already the maggots feed on Joha and Arnan who should be buried on a high place with rites of honor, while the cowards that attended them hide whimpering in their tents. Why did you so spit on the honor of Israel and hide yourselves from your duty to Yahweh?"

The princes sat in the firelight in somber silence their faces darkened more by rebellious anger than by the flickering shadows. One of the greater princes, Elizaphan, who stood high in the esteem of Joshua, stroked his gray beard and rose to speak.

"The essence of the princes' reluctance to engage in campaigns such as the one at Ai does not lie in cowardice or sloth. Rather, My Lord, it is the result of your decision to withhold the rightful rewards of these campaigns from those who risk their lives."

Joshua glared at the prince who spoke. "You speak of Jericho. Mind you that Jericho's riches should go to the Lord's treasury was not my command, but that of Yahweh. And mind you that we all shared in that deprivation and we are all equal. Therefore it is our equal duty to join together in the Lord's campaigns, though we gain nothing by it except the glory of Israel."

"If that were indeed so, we would have no argument. Yet, do not the Levites feed upon the treasury of which you speak? And do they not dwell in the cities of our lands while we dwell in tents of our making? And it is also known that some, but not all, have profited from the booty of Jericho despite your prohibition."

"That certain of the house of Levi draw their sustenance from the holy treasury is well known and is according to the law," Joshua said. "But that any other has gained by the conquest of Jericho is not known to me."

"Nevertheless it is common knowledge in the marketplace that at least one has gained greatly from the spoils of that conquest," said the prince.

"If indeed it is common knowledge speak the name of the man before this council!"

"Nay, Lord, I cannot. For those of his tribe who know of it hold his name secret."

"Then tell me in which tribe he dwells and we will make inquiry of it tomorrow!"

Before Elizaphan could speak, Caleb, who was Prince of Judah and also Joshua's general, arose.

"My Lord, I have heard rumors that perhaps one of the families of my tribe has knowledge of this thing. I said nothing because I thought it an idle rumor, loose talk of the marketplace."

"Perhaps it is, Lord Caleb, but we must put this rumor to rest before we can join the tribes as one. In the morning bring the chiefs of all the families of Judah before this council and we will search out the truth." He turned to the council. "Let no man speak of this tonight. That if one has transgressed against the will of the Lord he might not flee in the darkness."

By the early light of day the chiefs of the families of Judah stood in apprehensive silence before Joshua and the council of the elders.[71] One by one the Levite guards led them before the judges to give testimony concerning the stolen booty of Jericho. Many had no opportunity to take of the spoils and some had no one in the battle. But at last aged Zabdi, elder of the Zarhites, stood before the council trembling with fear and infirmity.

Phinehas, the priest, acting as prosecutor for the ailing high priest Eleazar, peered at the old man sharply.

"For what reason do you seem so distressed, esteemed Zabdi? Of a certainty you are not the transgressor whom we seek. For you are indeed aged and close to joining your forefathers. Do you then tremble so for another within your family?"

The old man looked up at Phinehas. A shudder ran through his frail body as his eyes met the priest's. He averted his gaze and snuffled noisily but said nothing.

"Come now, Zabdi, ...we must have testimony from you. Do you fear for your son, Carmi? Indeed I think not, for was he not a warden of the encampment and not at the battle when Jericho fell?"

The old man nodded his head rapidly, thankful for the priest's vindication of his son.

"Of a surety Carmi is innocent of this thing. He is a good son and a man of great righteousness."

"He is known to be and that must be a great comfort, for a son does not always cleave to the way of his father. Do you not have a grandson, a warrior of some repute, who fought valiantly at Jericho?"

"Yes, ...Achan, ...he is indeed a warrior of great courage and a man of honor. He fought in the forefront of those at Jericho."

"I am sure he honored his family with his bravery. Did he also take part in the sacking of Jericho?"

"He was there as were many warriors."

Phinehas frowned. "But there are those who say Achan left his duties early and alone. His captain missed him as did others. Do you know of this?"

"I know nothing of that, for his tent is distant from mine."

"Then we will ask your grandson.... Is he here?"

Zabdi shook his head "Only the elders and chiefs were summoned."

"Of course, you may remove yourself from before this council."

Phinehas turned to the captain of the guard. "Bring Achan, son of Carmi, before us. Make haste!"

CHAPTER 24

Miriam, the wife of the warrior, Achan, was depressed. Her husband had been in a foul mood since he returned from the battle of Jericho. He slept only fitfully and kept her awake with his constant tossing and turning. He seldom spoke to her or their children and when he did it was to snap at them for some minor infraction.

And then there was the thing hidden under the low table in the center of their tent. She had moved the table and lifted the rug under it to shake dust and food crumbs from it. There at its center, in a basin scooped out of the earth, lay a package wrapped in a goatskin. Miriam had replaced the rug quickly without disturbing the package. She did not want to invite the ire of her husband by meddling in his affairs.

Yet she wondered what the package contained—certainly not something taken from Jericho—the prohibition against that was absolute. And still, Achan had always wanted more than he had. He had few cattle and the stipend paid to him as a warrior under Caleb was small—the warriors traditionally enhanced their wage by plundering the lands they captured. Joshua had forbidden this at Jericho and took the valuables for the holy treasury instead. He had even ordered the destruction of the livestock—to prevent the introduction of disease into the herds of Israel, they said. There had been much grumbling in the marketplace over these severe injunctions and Miriam suspected that more than a few warriors had returned from the battle of Jericho with some small valuable hidden in their clothing.

Adding to Miriam's consternation was the sudden appearance of the Levite guards at sunrise that morning. Old Zabdi and Miriam's father-in-law Carmi had been summoned to the council quite brusquely, as were all of the elders. Rumors were soon circulated that Phinehas was directing an inquisition of sorts concerning the theft of spoils from Jericho. Achan and his brothers had gone to the meeting place to learn more. Miriam glanced nervously at the place under her table and wondered if she should remove the package hidden there. *I worry too much over trifles,* she thought. Then she woke and fed the children and went out to milk the goats.

Achan and his brothers milled about with hundreds of other men outside the curtained wall that veiled the council of elders from the people. A company of Levite guards held the people at a distance that prevented them from overhearing the proceedings. Consequently, Achan had no warning when a platoon of guards emerged from the council area and began searching the crowd. He turned his back to them and began hurrying away but was immediately halted by two of the Levites.

"No one may leave, by order of Lord Joshua," one said.

"What is your name?" the other asked.

"I am Achan, son of Carmi."

Immediately both guards laid hold of him and started leading him toward the council arena while calling to the others of the guard.

"We have him whom we seek! We have the thief who steals from God!"

Phinehas coldly regarded the warrior who was made to kneel before him. "You are Achan, son of Carmi?"

It was more a statement than a question. But even in that time it was necessary to correctly identify those who were dragged before the judges. So Phinehas waited for Achan to answer.

"I am called Achan and Carmi, son of Zabdi, is my father."

"You are a warrior under the command of Prince Caleb of Judah?"

"I have the honor to serve Prince Caleb."

"And you fought at the battle of Jericho?"

"Yes, but it was hardly a battle, it was more like a slaughter."

"Do you disapprove of destroying the unholy?"

"Not in battle, but killing women and children who cannot defend themselves is difficult. Even the brave Captain Daniel could not escape torture of his soul because of it."

"The anguish of Daniel's soul is not at question here, nor is your judgement of the rightness of the destruction of Jericho. It is known that certain of the spoils of that city were taken by a soldier of the house of Judah against the severe order of Joshua, High Lord of Israel. I put it to you quite simply, Achan. Are you that soldier?"

Achan's face blanched at the question and he glanced nervously at the judges. Finally his eyes came to rest on the stolid face of Joshua and his manner became more agitated, but he said nothing.

"Come now, Achan." Phinehas smiled now, a strange twisting of his face that displayed more malevolence than benevolence. "We must have either a confession or denial from you regarding this matter. Lacking either your silence will be regarded as certainty of your guilt."

"And would you regard as guilty all those of the warrior ranks who were also at Jericho but keep their silence?"

At this, Joshua rose from the bench of judgement and stepped past Phineas to raise Achan to his feet and search his eyes. His expression was fatherly and he spoke to Achan as one who would chastise a small boy who had taken a forbidden sweet cake from his mother's larder.

"Now, my son, you know that the accusation rests on you and not the others.[69] Answer then the question of this court with humbleness and honesty. Give glory to God with forthrightness and penitence—for with him lies your salvation.... For God knows of your guilt or innocence—and with him rests condemnation or forgiveness."

This glimmer of hope stirred Achan to the depths of his soul. Where before there stood only the implacable judgement of the law, Joshua now placed the possibility of pardon. Achan fell to his knees before his lord and judge, looking up at Joshua as a small boy might look up to his father

"Forgive me, Lord Joshua, and intercede for me with The Lord God Most High. For I have sinned grievously against God and against you. Indeed I stand guilty of the crime with which I am charged. But look at me, Lord Joshua. I am a poor soldier with but few cattle and goods and I have a wife and young children to feed. When I saw amid the ruins of Jericho a rich robe and pieces of silver and even gold I was tempted beyond my strength. For it was enough to raise me from poverty and place me in the company of greater men than I."

"And you took the rich things and hid them?"

"Yes, My Lord. I wrapped them in a goatskin and buried them beneath the rug in my tent."

Joshua turned to the captain of the guard.

"Send men to this man's tent and see that what he says is true. Bring the goods that he has stolen that they may be seen by the elders. Further, bring his family that they may bear witness of his shame."

Miriam was milling barley for bread between two heavy flat stones. She straightened and stretched to relieve the cramps in her back and smiled at her four children playing with a pair of young goats. Her two daughters, now six and four, had come first and though she had not said so to Achan she was glad because it would mean early help with the household. Though he had worried at first that he might lack an heir she had been able to present him with twin sons, now robust little boys nearing three years of age. She had suckled them longer than usual because they had to share her milk and so were smaller than the girls had been at the same age. This had delayed conception of yet another child, but now Miriam's belly was beginning to swell again and she was glad for the young legs of Hannah, her eldest.

"Hannah, bring me a gourd of water to drink, the sun is getting hot and I'm thirsty."

"Yes, Mother. Where is Father?"

"He has gone to the meeting place with his brothers."

"Will he have to go to war again?"

"Why do you ask that?"

"Because when he goes to the meeting place he has to go to war." Hannah wrinkled her nose. "I don't like it when he goes to war because he comes home all bloody."

"I don't like it either—now bring me the water."

"Yes, Mother." The little girl walked toward the water jar but then she stopped and pointed. "Those men are coming again, Mother."

Miriam squinted against the glare of the sun. Coming from the direction of the meeting place were four of the Levite guards. She raised herself to her feet and a terrible premonition of evil swept over her.

"Behold, the sin of Achan!"

Phinehas held high before the judges the precious things found in Achan's tent.

"He took of that accursed by God of which no man might take! It is because of his sin that Israel was driven out by the Amorites of Al! It is only by his punishment that God will again look on Israel with favor! You know the punishment for disobedience of God's command!"

The judges and the elders stared at Achan with dreadful solemnity, then they all shouted in righteous accord, "Stone him until he is dead!"

Achan, eyes wide and rolling, threw himself at Joshua's feet.

"My Lord Joshua! Grant me forgiveness of my sin, I beg you! For I have a wife and children who will starve without me!"

"I can forgive you, Achan, and perhaps our god will also. But I cannot pardon your sin or stay the just judgement of sentence. You must die in the manner pronounced by the judges, by stoning. Do not fear that your family will starve for they also will die, that your essence will be stricken from the face of the earth!"

"Kill me! Do what you will with me! But have pity on my woman and my little ones for they had nothing to do with my sin!"

"The word of the judges is spoken!"

On that day they dragged Achan, his wife and the little ones to a small parched valley.[71] There the righteous of Israel gathered and they threw stones until all of Achan's family were still in death. Then they made a great pile of dead wood and they put the bodies upon it. Also they killed the livestock of Achan and took all that he owned and put it in a great pile and touched torches to it. And when it burned fiercely they took that which he stole from Jericho and threw it in the fire, that he might have in death that which he lusted for in life.

All of that day and into the night the fire burned. But in the morning only smoldering ashes remained. Then the righteous of Israel gathered stones and made a great mound over the ashes that it would be a reminder to those who would transgress the Lord's commands.

"It is a bad thing to set the princes against us—and the destruction of Achan has done nothing to pacify them." Caleb's face was worried. "There may be others who stole from the plunder of Jericho but are not known by us, yet they are known to their tribes. And so the warriors will not take up their swords for us without a share in the plunder."

Joshua savored the wine brought to him and Caleb in silver cups by the faithful Adanah. "Indeed, we cannot leave Ai in peace lest the other nations of Canaan take heart from our defeat and join in an alliance to destroy us. But now they are forewarned and they will make preparations for battle so that we must set the better part of our armies against them to win. I think you are right, we must allow the princes and warriors their part of the plunder and tax only the tenth part for the treasury."

"Well said and wisely done, My Lord. With this news to spread before me I will gather you such an army as no nation can stand against. In the morning I will call the princes together and in but a few days we will be ready to march once more against Ai."

Joshua nodded. "And when we do, it shall be quietly in the dark of night. We will hide a great force beyond the city and a lesser force will approach the gates. The warriors of Ai will come out of the city again, thinking to drive us back to the hills as before. And when they have followed the lesser force far from the city the greater force will take them from behind!" Joshua slapped his hands together loudly.

"It is a good plan, My Lord. Soon we will avenge Joha and Arnan!"

And so the princes gathered once more in unity behind Joshua and it was as he had said. The city of Ai fell to the trap laid by Joshua and Caleb and there was a great victory with a terrible slaughter. When it was over the city was a smoking ruin and the princes and warriors of Israel rejoiced at the wealth they had gained. And by the deaths of the warriors and people of Ai were Joha and Arnan avenged.

In the space of days word of the destruction of Ai had spread to the most distant of the nations west, north and south of Ai. Most of these peoples, such as the Amorites and Hittites had fought against Israel in years past and bore a hatred and fear of the Hebrews. Now they counseled together, making pacts to fight Israel if need be, as a combined army.[77] However, the elders of Gibeon were not content to risk their welfare on the possibility that Israel would be defeated. The city of Gibeon stood on the roadway to the heart of Canaan, only a few hours march from Ai. This made it the next likely city marked for destruction by the fearsome Joshua. So it was that the elders gathered together to make a plan whereby they should not taste of the fate which had been the lot of Jericho and Ai.[72]

"We cannot wait for the cities beyond us to come to our aid. We must make a peace with the barbarian, Joshua, lest our great city be reduced to rubble and maggots feast on our carcasses! For Jericho, which was strong, fell to him in but a few days and none were spared the edge of the sword! And though Ai stood once against the Israelites all was lost at their second coming and now Ai is a heap of rubble." So spoke Kadesha, high priest of Zebel Baal and chief among the elders of Gibeon.

"It is true!" said Rasha, a rich and respected merchant. "It is said that this Joshua is the sword hand of his god, whom they call Yahweh and he cannot be killed. I remember yet how he went against the people of Midian and drove them from their land with a great slaughter. I was a young caravan master then and our camel caravan passed by a captive company of women and children on their way to the acacia grove where Israel camped. We stopped there for water and I even spoke to their fiery eyed, old prophet, Moses. But I did not see what happened to the captives because I feared the Hebrews and quickly left. But it is said that the old prophet had them all put to death."

A toothless and weary-eyed man named Bilel bobbed his head in agreement.

"Such was the way of Moses, exceedingly fierce and hard of heart. Did he not deal in the same fashion with our Amorite nations? In that time I carried my mother from the fair fields of Bashan to these rugged hills. My brother was not so fortunate, he died with Og, the king of Bashan. It was a foolish thing to fight the Israelites. Our people were farmers and fat merchants, while they were as snarling wolves, ravenous from their fast in the wilderness. Yet Og, in his vanity, would not bow before Moses and so we died or ran and the Israelites took our houses and fields and groves."

Annahun, the youngest of the elders and a mighty warrior, now spoke.

"We need not study the distant past to know the evil that confronts us! But there is little use in begging forbearance of Joshua, for it is in his mind to annihilate all nations that stand in his path. He will not make peace with any Amorite for he is sworn to exterminate them. Nor does he make any distinction between them and us. I will fight until my blood spreads on our soil—but be it known that their numbers are too great for us!"

Kadesha shook his head despondently. "If we cannot stand against Joshua in battle or make peace with him then we must take what goods we can and flee."

"Be not so dismayed, Your Worship, there may yet be another way," Rasha said.

"What way is there other than to fight or flee?"

"There is cunning."

Kadesha looked at Rasha suspiciously. "You are a merchant who lives by your wiliness. I am a priest who leads in praise to Baal and I know little of cunning and craft. Speak your meaning clearly. How will cunning save our necks from Joshua's sword?"

"We know that the Israelite will not make a peace with those close to him because he wants that which we possess. Is that not true?"

"It is true and the source of our dilemma," Kadesha said. "But what would lead him to do otherwise?"

"Greed."

"You speak in riddles. Is not greed the reason he seeks to attack us? How then could it be our salvation?"

"It is the driving force of the Israelites. But what if we lived far distant, out of his reach and we had something he desired?" Rasha asked.

"He would wish to make a pact with us for his nation's gain," Annahun interjected. "But we are close not far and so he will not deal with us."

"But if he thought we were from afar...he would make a pact with us."

"And he would cut our throats when he found out that we are not from afar!" Annahun exclaimed.

The withered old man started laughing, a hearty but wheezing cackle.

"It is not so, Annahun! You do not know the Israelites. Their god forbids them from swearing falsely—if the great Joshua gives his word, he will never break it—though he was deceived. It is a good plan, Rasha!"

Kadesha studied the faces of the elders. Seeing hope where before there was only despair, he nodded his head.

"Indeed it is the only chance for our survival. Rasha, Bilel and I will go to Joshua as ambassadors and Annahun will take a few warriors with us as though they were our protectors against thieves. We will disguise ourselves so that our appearance will not defeat us. Then at first light we will journey toward Gilgal where the Israelite vipers make their nest.[72]

Caleb squinted with age and the brightness of the sun. He shielded his eyes with his hand but the image he sought was still blurred. "An armed party?" he asked of the captain of the guard. There was little travel from the north since the destruction of Jericho and Ai and certainly no armed parties.

"A small party, some are armed. Three are well beyond the age of warriors—that is, they do not appear to be common soldiers—perhaps they are high officers such as you, My Lord, though they wear no weapons."

Caleb listened and wished that Joha was still at his side. This new captain was too young and he was too old to adjust to the change. He could find no fault with the man, he was brave and smart. Why then didn't his name come to him as easily as Joha's did?

He watched the blur that was the approaching party until it separated into human forms, some mounted on donkeys, some afoot. As they came closer Caleb saw that it was the unarmed men that rode and they were indeed past the age of warriors. All of the party seemed tired and were dirty and a bit ragged. The donkeys were thin as if they had travelled far without sufficient forage. The armed men were not dressed for war since they wore no armor and carried only bows and thin bladed swords. Obviously they were an escort against bandits and perhaps hunters for food. There was no threat here—Caleb strode out to meet them.

"Hail strangers!" Caleb raised his hand in greeting. "I am Caleb, Commander of the armies of Israel. Who are you, from where do you come and for what purpose do you enter the encampment of Joshua?"

Kadesha stepped forward, then he spoke slowly and carefully as though he were struggling with Caleb's dialect. "I am Kadesha and I have come from a land far beyond the wilderness, by the great sea. I and my companions come as ambassadors to seek a pact of peace with the people of Israel that both our peoples may profit. And so we would beg an audience with the great Joshua.

"But first I would ask a boon of your kindness—that we might have to eat. What little bread we have left is dry and moldy from our long trip and our wineskins are empty and sour. Nor have we lately known the taste of meat, because hunting was poor along the way." The man who spoke was tall and fully shaved, even to the top of his head it seemed, since no hair protruded from the strange head dress he wore. Caleb knew of no people such as he within nations near to Israel.

"I will seek an audience with Joshua and the princes of Israel. Until then my captain will see to your welfare. He will relieve your men of the weight of their weapons and give them food and wine. There is water for your donkeys and for bathing if you desire and a tent against the heat of the sun."

"Why would a people who live so far beyond our nation seek a pact with us?" Joshua asked Kadesha.

The sun had drifted nearly below the western hills and the air had cooled. The twelve princes of Israel sat on benches beneath a huge sycamore tree. Before them Joshua and the ambassadors rested in chairs beneath a striped cloth canopy.

"For many reasons," Kadesha said, "we have heard much of your god and my people fear him for we know of his power and the power of Israel because of him. Thus we would be his servants and also yours."

"And how would you serve us if you live far off from us?"

At this there was a humming among the princes and some asked whether the strangers might not be from near cities that were ordained by Yahweh for destruction. But old Bilel stood up and spoke to them in his quavering voice.

"Did you not see how poor our donkeys have become and how worn are their hooves? It is because of their long journey. And do you not see how worn are our cloaks? And behold, the soldiers walk on the soles of their feet for their sandals are falling off them. It is a long journey for a young man, but for one who is old like me it is torture. Look how thin my limbs have become and how the last of my teeth have fallen out for lack of decent food. It will be a miracle if I should live to return to my house. But I give up my last years gladly if it will bring peace and prosperity for my people."

At this assertion the princes became silent but Joshua frowned.

"I understand how you wish a pact with us in order to ensure peace for your people. But I do not know how such a thing would bring you prosperity."

At this, Rasha stood up and spoke while the old man settled quietly in his chair.

"My Gracious Lord, I am a merchant as are many of my people. And in my travels it has been my honor to speak with The Great Prophet himself at the Place of the Acacias.... Our city, which is called Qunrim, rests on the road to Egypt and Syria and also to your land and beyond—it would be most advantageous to us and also to your people, My Lord, to ensure peace between our peoples.

"By making a pact we will be able to send caravans to you with the riches of the east and west as well as bringing your goods for trade with Egypt. But lacking such an assurance as a pact will give, few caravans will venture to your land—for the nations beyond us fear Israel."

Again there was a humming among the princes, but now it was with a tone of approval. Joshua studied the faces of the ambassadors carefully as though to plumb the depths of their souls. Then he turned to the princes.

"Let those who would have a pact with these people stand before the Lord."

The princes rose to their feet as one and watched Joshua expectantly.

"Will you swear to The True God that neither you nor any of your people will raise your hands against these men or their people to shed their blood?"

"We swear to The True God."

Joshua turned to the ambassadors.

"Be it known to you that the children of Israel shall be at peace with your people and shall not shed their blood. For this we have sworn before the Lord God of Israel—which oath no man shall break. Also this oath is upon you, that you shall not lay a hand on a child of Israel lest this pact be broken and you shall face the righteous fury of the Lord. Go then unto your far land and live in peace."[72]

CHAPTER 25

So it was that the people of Gibeon won a peace with the invading tide of Israel. Though in fact it was a tenuous thing guaranteed only by the stern propriety of Joshua, which would not allow him to go back on his word, once sworn before his god. It was to be sorely tested, for in a few days the princes came as an ominous delegation to the tent of Joshua and Adanah, as Joshua lay dozing in the heat of midday. At their grumbling approach Adanah put down the tunic she was sewing for her husband and left the tent. She stood with her hands poised on her hips awaiting an explanation for this intrusion into her domain.

"We would speak to the Lord of Israel," Caleb said. "For there is a matter made known to us which is of a most grave nature."

"And is it indeed so grave that the princes of Israel should come upon my household like lumbering cattle with neither invitation or notice? My husband is worn with the cares of his station and he sleeps."

"We give our most humble apologies, Adanah. But it is a thing of the greatest importance. We must speak to your husband. Would you awaken him and tell him the princes humbly desire his presence?"

By now Joshua had awakened and he emerged from the tent still rumpled from sleep and with his hastily donned cloak askew on his broad shoulders. He looked at the princes with glaring assessment, like a shaggy gray bear cornered by dogs and not knowing which to strike.

"For what purpose do you come unbidden to my tent and so disturb my needed slumbers? It was but three days past that we met and I hear no war trumpets sounding. What then could be so urgent that it would not wait for an appointed council?"

Caleb looked at the other princes and when none spoke he began reluctantly.

"It is not a matter that bodes present evil for us, My Lord. But rather a matter with which we dealt unwisely, thinking to do the people great good. It is of the ambassadors whom we did peacefully receive just three days past that I speak."

"And how could they bother us so soon? Have they not returned to their distant, nation?"

"Indeed they have gone down the road on which they came. But their nation is not distant."[73]

"What say you, Caleb? I have been rudely awakened from a pleasant sleep and I have little patience to solve your riddles. Do not chew delicately on that which you have to say, but spit it out in simple terms."

"Yes, My Lord—the ambassadors who came to us to make a pledge of peace were not from the shores of the great sea. They were from the city, Gibeon, which lies but a day's march from here, just beyond the ruins that were the city of Ai."

Joshua frowned and his face darkened. "They are Amorites, whom the Lord has charged us to destroy?"

"They are Hivites, My Lord, who have long passed among us as merchants and tradesmen. They inhabit four cities in the midst of the Amorites and have long been in league with them."

"And they deceived us! They told us they came from afar! How is it that neither prince or common man knew of this, that they might so easily gain our trust?"

At this the princes shifted uneasily on their feet and one named Hanniel spoke.

"It was a clever thing they did, Lord Joshua. For well you know they made as though they had travelled exceedingly far. For in all things they were aged and worn so that we did not doubt their cause was good and honest."

"But now," another said, "the people grumble against us because we made a peace where much rich plunder would have easily been theirs if we had waged war."

"The people ever lust for riches when instead they should tend to honest endeavors!" Joshua spat. 'Yet, we cannot let this thing go without retribution lest other nations see us as fools."

"It is true," Caleb said. "Something must be done to punish these people lest others be encouraged to deal with deceit."

Joshua surveyed the sullen faces of the princes. *In their princely majesty they still wait for me to remedy their errors,* he thought, *like children seeking judgement against the transgressions of their peers.*

"Gather a thousand of your mightiest warriors," he said. "We will be ambassadors to the Hivites in our own way."

Kadesha was ill humored, he had slept little since his return to Gibeon and those slumbers were made restless by dreams of warring hordes of Israelites bearing down on his city. It was then almost a relief to him when Annahun hurried into the outer hall of the temple of Zebel Baal. Kadesha abruptly dismissed the lesser priests who stood around him receiving orders for the day's duties.

"Your face tells me you bear ill tidings, Annahun. Is it the Israelites that cause such grimness in your look?"

"It is indeed, Your Worship, a strong force approaches the city. And a messenger from Joshua demands our presence before him."

Kadesha sighed. "It is as I expected, though much sooner. Word of our deceit has travelled as on the wings of an eagle. The old lion of Israel is angry now and seeks to devour us."

Annahun spat contemptuously. "I will go to the ramparts with our warriors. They are the mightiest—greater warriors than even the Israelites. We can stand against the hordes of Israel."

"Yes, we can stand against them for a fortnight or perhaps two or even three. But in the end they will overcome us and we and our families will die and our cities will lie in ruins."

"Then what will we do?"

"We will go out to Joshua and we will talk to him as we did before. Perhaps we will yet save our necks."

"We lied to him before." Annahun said glumly. "Nothing we say will provide our salvation. Joshua is merciless with those who oppose him either by sword or by tongue."

"Our salvation is not in our word but in that of Joshua. Go and bring Rasha and Bilel. We will visit the Lord of Israel."

"You came before me and before the council of the princes and you lied!" Joshua roared. "Did you think us such fools that we would not discover your perfidy?"

Kadesha, with his peers, knelt humbly before the Lord of Israel. Around them the princes of Israel stood like so many cobras poised to strike. Fear lay in Kadesha's heart like a heavy chill and the skin of his back crawled with its coldness.

"We knew that we might go the way of Jericho and Ai because we were next in your path, My Lord. For it is said among the nations that your god has decreed that all of Canaan shall fall before you and none shall survive. We were much afraid and the thing that we did was born of our fear."

"And you sought a pact with us thinking that we would let you be, as though Yahweh had not ordered your destruction?"

"We sought a pact with you knowing that you would see a greater good in peace than in war, My Lord," Rasha interjected. "For is it not true that dead men cannot serve, nor do rotting corpses bear goods with which to trade? What we sought was the common good of our peoples."

"But you made a pact of peace in deceit. You lied to save your goods and lands and your worthless skins. Why then would we honor it if you yourselves do not honor your words?"

"You might consider that we are a people of warriors, stronger than either Jericho or Ai. Many of your women will be widows before you overcome us," Annahun said.

At these words the princes became even more hostile, with hatred darting from their eyes like lightning from threatening clouds.

Old Bilel now laboriously rose to his feet. "If I might stand, My Lord? Age gnaws at my joints and makes them infirm."

Seeing no prohibition from Joshua he continued in his wheezing voice.

"Captain Annahun is a true warrior, My Lord, and I beg your clemency for the rashness of his tongue. All nations need men such as him to guard their borders but they are ill equipped for diplomacy."

He stopped momentarily, as if the effort of speech were more than he could endure. But seeing assent in the eyes of Joshua, the warrior, he continued.

"There is no reason for you to spare the lives of Gibeon—except your sworn word. It is this which we sought—for we knew your honor is in your word before your god."

Kadesha seized the moment. "It is true! We sought safety in the honor of your word, O Lord and Princes of Israel. For we knew that your oath, sworn before your god, is a thing that is sacred to you—nevertheless, we are in your hands—do with us what you would."

Joshua frowned thoughtfully, then surveyed the princes.

"What would you have me judge? We stand before The True God, before whom we swore a pact of peace with these men. Though they lied between their teeth it does not absolve our oath."

After a brief council Caleb stood forward as spokesman for the princes.

"As men of honor before God, we cannot shed the blood of these men or any of their people lest we bring judgement upon ourselves. For we have sworn before God Most High that we shall not take up the sword against them—yet nothing prohibits their punishment in other ways. Therefore, we seek judgement that they shall be bondsmen to the Children of Israel forever! They shall be hewers of wood, diggers of wells, layers of stone, tillers of the soil and all other matter of toil that seems right before the elders and princes of the people. Thus they and their children and their children's children shall serve us."[73]

Joshua turned to the ambassadors. "You have heard the will of the princes. Do you agree to submit your people as bondsmen to serve wherever you shall be sent and to surrender all manner of weapons and armor and to give over unto Israel all things of value?"

At this, Annahun became rebellious and spoke angrily. "What you give us is not life, but death in life! I would rather die on the ramparts than to live so!"

Again old Bilel rebuked him. "You may find glory and honor in death, Captain. But what of your wife and your girl child whom you bounce upon your knee? Will they too find honor in the slash of a blade to their throats? ...No, Lord Joshua, pay no mind to Annahun for he speaks in proudness and anger. Rather, listen to the wisdom of years—I would rather choose life though it be winnowing chaff from the wheat, than to die—for in all life there is some goodness—but in the grave there are only worms."

"Well spoken, old man, with your white hair has come wisdom. Will you all then join in his wisdom? You will toil and live much as you have, though somewhat leaner? Except for one thing, ...you will destroy the temple of Zebel Baal and worship The True God."

Now Kadesha's face darkened with an angry frown for his station as chief priest of Zebel Baal was a thing that put him high among his people. But he was not careless in his words as was the warrior Annahun and so he kept his peace. Thus the Hivites appeased the wrath of Joshua and became the servants of Israel. And though their spirits smarted at the humiliation of the bloodless defeat, they lived. And that was greatly more than the people of Jericho and Ai had garnered by their resistance to the coming of Israel. Then too, the yoke of servitude brought with it a benefit. For now Joshua, as master of the Hivites, was also obliged to be their protector.

"Know you all that the cowardly Hivites have surrendered their three cities to Joshua? And know you that after the rains have passed the Israelites will once again swarm like locusts and consume everything in their path?"[74]

So spoke Adonizedec, Amorite king of Jerusalem, to King Hoham of Hebron, Piram of Jarmuth, Japhia of Lachish and Debir of Eglon. These were the five Amorite kings of the major cities spread like a fan to the south and west of Gibeon, from the rocky hills of Jerusalem through the valleys of Jarmuth to the fertile plains along the coast of the great sea.

"It is of little concern to us," said King Debir. "For we are far from Gilgal and well beyond the reach of the Israelites, while your city sits at the very paws of the lion. Why should we bring armies to protect you and so gain the displeasure of Joshua?'

"That is what we said when Shimmur of Jericho sought to allay us to him," Adonizedec replied. "But here is Joshua at our very doorstep and he will not stop with Jericho and Ai or even at Gibeon. Nor is it likely that he will turn his full forces against Jerusalem for we do not have what he seeks."

Piram, the stocky red-haired king whose city stood closer to Gibeon than the others, was listening intently.

"What then is it that the lion desires for prey?"

"The wealth of the land," the king of Jerusalem answered. "The fertile lands of your river valleys and the lowlands of Eglon. Also he greatly desires Lachish, for it is a fortress to control all of the lowlands and the trade routes to the coast, once he has subjugated them."

"I see that Joshua would want the rich lands to the west," Hoham said uncertainly. "But Hebron has little good land and it is not great in riches. Why should the Israelites come our way when there are sweeter fruits to pick?"

"Because Hebron sits astride the roads to Beersheba and to the coast of the Great Sea. By conquering Hebron, Joshua will control the caravan trade between Egypt and the lands of the east."

Adonizedec fell silent. If an alliance was to be made he had planted the seeds quite adeptly. Now the seeds needed time to germinate. The four kings studied him with narrowed eyes, calculating how much advantage he sought for himself and how much would be gained by themselves. At last King Debir of Eglon who was known to be a man of great honor and also a priest of Baal, rose from his chair and spoke.

"Are we not all Amorites—are we not descended from Ham, who in the ancient past was born of Noah—by whom the Israelites were also sired? And is it not said in the tales of our people that Ham was wrongly driven from his home because of the drunkenness of his father? Did he not settle this land to make a mighty nation—of which we are? Why then do the Israelites seek to drive us from the land as they did to Ham in times past?"

The other Kings nodded solemnly—the first glints of anger flickered in their eyes at the remembrance of their legendary shame. For these were a people of strong traditions who clung closely to the legends of their past, refusing to give up antagonisms that had festered for all of their history.

"It is so," said Japhia of Lachish. "We have built mighty cities and have planted our olive trees and vineyards these many years. And now the Israelites who have done nothing—except to spawn their kind and steal from others—seek to take them from us. Adonizedec is right, we must ally ourselves together, ...for alone our cities will fall to Joshua like ripe figs falling from a tree."

There was a murmur of assent and the kings looked at Adonizedec, waiting for him to assume leadership toward their common cause—he did not hesitate.

"Do we then stand as one against this plague?"

"We stand as one!"

"Then come together and let us seal our pledge with an oath of blood!"

Adonizedec picked up a silver cup from a table at his side. Then he drew a slim dagger from his belt with which he deftly pricked his palm. He clenched his fist so that a small trickle of blood flowed into the cup. Each of the other kings repeated the act in turn, until the blood of all five men was mingled in the cup. Then each dipped a finger into the mingled blood and touched it first to his forehead. then pressed it to the wound in his palm so that his flowing blood was intermingled with that of the others.

When this had been done, each king grasped the right wrist of another so that their clenched, still-bleeding hands formed a circle with no beginning or end.

"We stand as brothers, united by our blood! For there are no longer five, but we are one and the fate of one shall be the fate of all!" the kings swore with fervor.

After they were blood bonded the kings turned to the task of planning their resistance to Israel. It was well enough to unite against the Israelites and feel satisfied that a beginning toward salvation had been made. Yet each of them knew that waiting for Joshua to mount another offensive would be like waiting for a lion to charge before drawing bow or hurling javelin.

"Perhaps if the barbarian of the plains knows that we are joined against him he will make a peace with us. Even one as fierce as he will not reach out where he might lose a hand." So spoke king Hoham. He was well past his prime and the thought of leading his warriors against an enemy as formidable as Joshua did not appeal to him.

Japhia spat contemptuously—he was tall and hard, a warrior in his prime and he was filled with rancor toward the Israelites.

"Would we then bend our knees toward Gilgal as the Hivites did? Would you give all of Canaan to those thieves and murderers without touching a hand to the hilt of your sword? No! ...No a thousand times! We must gather our armies together and attack them while they rest warm in their tents. For when the winter rains cease, the locusts will stir from their nests and seek that which they might devour!"

"King Japhia speaks with the heart of a warrior," Piram of Jarmuth said. "And well we know his is not idle bluster—for did not his people help fend off the thrust of the Israelites when they first came forth from Paran and did they not drive them back into the wilderness? I greatly admire his bravery—and yet, my people stand closer to death than do his—I ponder whether there might be a better way to halt Joshua than to charge blindly at him with sword in hand."

"Hoham has already spoken of the way other than the sword—it is the way of old men and women!" Japhia said.

Adonizedec raised his hand. "Do not speak so arrogantly, my friend, for I think that King Piram sees a way of getting at the old lion that we have missed. He thinks to use the sword, but not against Joshua—do I think as you, King Piram?"

Piram nodded. "It may be that we can discourage the lion by killing the cub. We must capture Gibeon and make of it a stumbling block for Israel!"

"Gibeon's capture will be swift and of little risk to us, for the Hivites in making peace surrendered their weapons of war to Joshua. Yet the Old Lion left few of his warriors to guard his new conquest—for who would attack a property of Israel?' Adonizedec gloated. "The city's great walls will be our first bastion of defense against Israel. It is the gateway to Canaan and we shall close it tight."

"For this cause I will gladly pledge two thousand of my best warriors and I myself shall lead them!" Japhia said. "And I challenge you, Adonizedec, and you, Piram, and you, Debir, to do the same. And perhaps King Hoham can leave his grandchildren and summon a half of that number from poor Hebron. Then we shall have an army to take Gibeon and spit in the face of Joshua!"

"Once again King Japhia speaks bravely, as a warrior of his standing should," Piram said. "But does one yoke six oxen to the plow when only two are needed? Gibeon is nearly defenseless and it seems to me that a small army of a few thousand could quickly take it and make our cause secure, while the greater number of our warriors can remain at our cities to guard against a secret attack by Joshua."

Hoham smiled benignly at Japhia. "What King Piram says is worthy of consideration, my hot-blooded friend. For those of us whose cities lie close to the lion's paws suffer the danger of an unheralded attack by the Israelites. They are a people who are used to treading through the wilderness like skulking hyenas and simply guarding the road will not make our cities safe."

King Debir, who had been silent through the exchange, now rose and spoke in his thoughtful, priestly way.

"The plan that King Piram proposes is indeed one of great merit, for depriving the Israelites of the fortress at Gibeon will greatly hinder their ability to attack further into Canaan. Yet King Hoham makes a point that should not be ignored. The Israelites are an army of foot soldiers, supported by caravans of donkeys and camels. They do not have chariots and great lumbering supply carts and so they need not follow the roadways. It is a simple thing for them to enter the wilderness of hills and ravines in order to bypass fortresses such as Gibeon and Lachish.

"Therefore, it seems to me that it would be foolhardy to throw the greater portion of our armies against Gibeon and so risk our own cities to attack by Joshua. We should summon a smaller force and after we have taken the city we can conscript soldiers among the Hivites to defend Gibeon."

"The Hivites would not fight against Israel before. Why would they fight at our command?" Adonizedec asked.

"They chose not to fight to save their families from Joshua's swords. They will fight him to save their families from something worse."

"What would be worse than death?"

Debir smiled grimly. "Sometimes it is not death that is so greatly feared...as is the manner of it. We will take a child of every family and place them in a prison of wood and thatch. It will be a simple matter to put torches to it if the Hivites turn on us."

Adonizedec laughed. "I had thought you to be a spiritual man of compassion who would not take vengeance against the helpless—I see that I mistook your silence for weakness—but instead it is the source of ruthless cunning. Indeed, I think the Hivites will fight with such a prod at their backs.... Three thousand warriors then, brought together swiftly from our various lands and two captains from each kingdom to lead them!"

"To this I agree," Japhia said. "But I myself will go with my warriors, for an undertaking such as this is of too grave importance to leave to underlings. What say you, Kings? Will you also lead your warriors against the cowardly Hivites and having gained Gibeon, stand on its walls and spit in the face of Joshua?"

And so it was agreed. In a matter of days an army of Amorites was gathering to lay siege to Gibeon.[75]

CHAPTER 26

Kadesha's fall from power had been devastating to his ego, though not as irrevocable as it might have been. For while it was true that he had lost the prestige he had known as the high priest of Zebel Baal, the most esteemed and awesome station in Gibeon, it was also true that he still lived and that was more than he might have hoped for had the city fallen to an Israelite attack. If Joshua was unyielding in his vindictiveness toward his enemies, he was also an astute political leader who was quite capable of using deposed leaders to his own advantage.

Thus, after purification by a thorough flogging to remove the essence of Baal from him—and a fortnight spent in a prison hole outside the wall of Gibeon while the bites of the lash healed—Kadesha had been returned to his former palace. However, his return was not as the master of the city because a son of Caleb now stood in that position as a military governor. Kadesha served now as sort of an overseer and liaison to his own people, enlightening the Israelite governor in the many differences between Hivite society and that of the Israelites. The purpose of this was to ease the tensions created by the bloodless peace so grudgingly granted to the Hivites by the princes of Israel. It was in fact Israel's first experiment of the assimilation rather than the annihilation of a conquered people.

This type of ministry was a position for which the priest was well suited. He was endowed with a certain dark mysticism that immediately gained him the respect of the superstitious Hebrew. And after a few weeks, Kadesha was trusted enough to allow the Israelite governor to leave the city as he had today, on a journey to Gilgal to counsel with his father, General Caleb. Not that Kadesha could possibly foment insurrection against the Israelites, for his people no longer had the will or the weapons to do so.

So on this morning Kadesha busied himself with the task of assigning duties to his countrymen in line with their new status as servants of Israel. So absorbed was he that he scarcely noticed the hurried arrival of Annahun, once a chief captain of Gibeon's army but now a keeper of the city gate.

"Kadesha! Kadesha!" Annahun cried. "An army comes from the west![75] There are many warriors, both afoot and astride mounts of war! They have chariots and great carts carrying rams and ladders with which to breach walls!"

With a wave of his hand Kadesha sent the laborers who had not yet received tasks back to the courtyard of the palace. With Annahun close behind he hurried to the heights of the watchtower.

"From where do they come?"

Annahun pointed to the south where the caravan road meandered between the rocky hills and sparse stands of acacia and broom trees. "There, ...the first horsemen come around the hill of the sheep folds. They will be here before the sun is high."

"Of what nations do they hail? Are they from near or far?"

"They were first seen by a huntsman, a man of keen eye and sharp mind. He thought them to be of Jerusalem and Jarmuth and perhaps from Hebron. Yet there were five princes, of which two were unknown to him. And those two led the finest armies."

Kadesha frowned. "One might be Japhia of Lachish, for it is a strong fortress and he is a fierce warrior. But the other? ...There is King Debir of Eglon, who is also strong. But these last two are a great distance from us. Why would they come this far?"

"Perhaps they march against Joshua," Annahun ventured.

"How many warriors do they bring?"

"The hunter thought a few thousand, not more than five."

"It is not nearly enough to attack Joshua's host! ...They come for us! They come to take Gibeon from the hand of Joshua!"

Annahun shrugged. "Then let us open the gates to them—it would be better than being slaves to Israel."

"Are you a fool, Annahun? Do you not know the Amorites will kill us for making peace with Israel. And if we survive their anger Joshua will take Gibeon back and kill us anyway! No, we must send for help from the Israelites and bar the gates tight shut—pray to Baal, or the new god, that we can hold until Joshua comes."

Then Kadesha sent two youths mounted on swift horses to Gilgal to seek out the leader of the Israelites.[75] Each carried a scroll from Kadesha pleading for immediate help. Should misfortune befall one, thought Kadesha, the other must succeed. The dust of the horses hooves had scarcely settled when King Japhia's mounted spearmen surrounded the city. Then Kadesha praised Baal for granting him the warning of the huntsman. It would be hours more before the foot soldiers arrived, bringing with them the great clattering carts which carried the shielded battering rams and the long scaling ladders.

Kadesha looked down grimly from the watchtower at the ranks of horseman interspersed with war chariots and he felt a strong foreboding. He had men, brave, strong warriors, but little else. The princes of Israel had taken the best of the Hivites' weapons to prevent any possibility of insurrection against them. Ironically, this was now putting the small garrison of Israelite soldiers at greater risk since they could expect little help from the poorly armed Hivites against the gathering Amorite warriors.

Nevertheless, Kadesha had ordered every able-bodied man to the wall with whatever weapons they could find. Now a sort of misfit army stood upon the rampart armed with hewing axes, sickles and tent poles hastily pointed with butchering blades. A few Israelite archers stood among them, as well as burly swordsmen. As the sun passed overhead and began its descent toward the far wilderness the rumbling of great wheels drifted in on the light southerly breeze. Kadesha shivered despite the burning sun, the weapons of siege would soon test the walls of Gibeon.

"You tremble and your skin bears a chill, my wife. Are you ill with the ague of the lowlands?"

Joshua placed his aging, but still strong hands on Adanah's face and shoulder, feeling her temperature as a mother would test a child, gently stroking her as a lover would.

"It is but a chill—I fear for you, my husband. Need you go again into battle? There are strong young captains to lead the tribes. Let them earn their places in the council as you and Caleb did in years past."

"You are a good woman and wise, Adanah. Your love gives me strength like meat and strong wine—but well you know the might of the Amorites. Five kings come against Gibeon with Philistine steel in their hands. If they capture Gibeon we shall not take it so easily again and the way into the heart of Canaan will be blocked. No, my woman, Caleb and I must go again so that the tribes will fight as one instead of twelve. And when we have destroyed these kings I will return to you and let the young men lead lesser battles. But I fear for you—let the healers attend to you, that you will be well upon my return."

Adanah smiled. "I have all the herbs and ointments I need, my husband. I had a fever, but that has passed. And so will this chill with a cup of hot wine and honey and sleep beneath a robe of sheepskin."

"Sleep well then, Adanah, but call the healers if your chill remains tomorrow. I must leave now for Gibeon and a battle which will determine the destiny of Israel. We will march quietly in the night and morning will find us taking the Amorite wolves by muzzle and leg." Joshua drew on his heavy battle tunic, then motioned to a young Hivite servant to strap on his breastplate and belly shield and to bind the bullhide greaves over his battle shoes. That done, he placed his stout iron sword into its sheath and stalked into the twilight where his old companion Caleb waited.

At the edge of the Israelite campground the princes had already assembled their armies.[76] Eleven tribes were on the assembly field. Of each tribe there were a thousand experienced warriors, more or less according to the numbers of each tribe. Around Joshua and Caleb with their aides and attendants together with the company of priests the Levites, the twelfth tribe and special guards of Israel stood in grim ranks.

To the front of the armies were gathered a company of warriors unlike the rest. They were hard, unsmiling men, sinister in both appearance and manner, clothed wholly in black woolen garments. A leather girdle that held a sling with a pouch of egg-sized stones, a finely honed dagger and a slender javelin were their weapons. These were the advance guard who would clear the way for the armies, making sure that no one, warrior or merchant, shepherd or traveler, would see the advancing forces and carry a warning to the Amorites.

Caleb, General of the Armies, signed to the captain of the advance guard. They turned as one and marched into the descending darkness so soundlessly that they seemed to be a dark, drifting apparition rather than men on sturdy legs.

"I would not want to be on the road to Gibeon on this night," Joshua said as the last of the guards melted into the night.

"Nor I," Caleb answered. "I would face men with sword and spear rather than those who slip up from behind like a leopard in the night, then plunge their daggers deep between the ribs without warning."

"I too, but there are those who take pleasure in the task. And they are needed in times such as this—though we might have it otherwise."

He gave Caleb a small earthen lamp that flickered in the gentle evening breeze.

"When the wick burns dry order the march to Gibeon."

Kadesha, sleepless with worry, stood at the height of Gibeon's watchtower. He did not know the hour but he reckoned that dawn was not far distant. Scattered below the dull glow of hundreds of dying cookfires attested to the number of Amorites brought against him. Here and there a small shower of sparks burst skyward as a last resin-filled knot popped in waning embers.

Beyond the camp a horse whinnied and then another in answer. The smell of fresh ox dung drifted up to Kadesha on the light breeze. The ladder carts had arrived, he thought and with them promise of a short siege. Had his couriers reached Joshua? Or had the Amorites encircled the city with an advance company before word of marching soldiers had even come to him? If the couriers lay dead so would he by nightfall tomorrow and an Amorite officer would stand where he stood now.

One of the sentries, a young Israelite with piercing black eyes, suddenly grew tense and peered more intently into the darkness. He motioned to Kadesha to come, then pointed in the direction of what had once been the city Ai.

Kadesha stared into the darkness, but only outlines could be seen, silhouetted against the distant glow of stars and crescent moon.

"There, on that barren hilltop, Kadesha," the lad whispered.

"I see nothing, save the hilltop itself and the stars above it," Kadesha returned irritably. He was affronted by the lad's familiarity in calling him by name without using the title "Lord." Just months ago he would have had him whipped for such a lack of respect.

The lad salted the wound. "And if you had been watching more closely you would know why I called to you. Only a few moments ago three men stood there—Amorite sentries."

"Perhaps they went to relieve themselves or perhaps the guard changes."

"I can tell you are a priest and not a warrior," the lad sneered. "One may go, but never three at once. The new guard always comes before the old guard leaves."

"Then why are they gone? I heard no cries of alarm or combat."

"And you will not hear any. My kinsfolk are here—they are called 'the shadows of death,' for such they are. The Amorite sentries die, even now."

"Then Joshua comes—he received my couriers!"

"Joshua is here now. When the shadows come the armies are but steps behind."

"But how can that be? No sound has come to my ears, not the whinny of a horse except those of the Amorites, not the clink of a sword or even an ill-placed footfall or a grunted curse."

"We have learned the wiles of wilderness fighters. They walk on feet wrapped in sheepskin and tie tight their weapons and shields and they would bite off their tongues before uttering a sound. The beasts of burden come tomorrow."

"Then when will they attack, at first light?"

"I think they will fall on the Amorites when the cooking fires are rekindled before dawn. For then the warriors will rise from their beds and their wits will be dimmed by sleep. Yet they will be good targets for slings and bows in the light of the fires."

Kadesha chuckled derisively. "You Israelites set great store by your stone throwers. But these are not jackals to be driven away from the sheepfold. These are warriors with shields and helmets that can turn a hard thrown javelin. What use then is there in throwing pebbles?"

"Do the Amorites sleep in battle gear with helmets on their heads? Do they arise and eat their bread and cheese while holding fast their shield and spear? I think not, Priest—that is when those pebbles you speak of will find their mark—and men will die without touching hand to sword or shedding their blood upon the ground. For I have seen one of these men fell a great bull with just one stone placed between its eyes. And that while he stood well beyond the danger of its horns."

"Perhaps you are right. But I myself find greater trust in a bow of horn and broom wood and arrows well pointed with flint. But look, men arise in the Amorite camp. They stir the coals of the fires and place tinder on them. Take your brothers who stand watch with you and go to the captains of the guard. Tell them to put every warrior on the wall with weapons at the ready. But tell them to do so quietly and without show for we would not give the Amorites a thought that danger threatens."

Dorem, battle attendant and companion to King Japhia of Lachish, rose quickly from his bed of cedar boughs and splashed water in his mouth and across his face. Then pausing only to feed the cookfire he walked swiftly to his master's tent to awaken him. His haste was needless for Japhia was long awake and he sat on a nearby boulder already dressed for battle. The kings had chosen a high place just off the road from Gibeon to Beth Horon for their headquarters. There they were close enough to direct the attack on Gibeon but far enough to escape if the attack failed. From his vantage place Japhia was watching the walls of Gibeon. He turned and spoke as his attendant approached.

"Are the other kings awake, Dorem? There is much milling about on the walls of Gibeon."

"Adonizedec and Piram stand together beside a fire. I did not see Hoham and Debir."

Japhia laughed. "Hoham sleeps while Debir prays and makes offering to Baal. Bring me bread and meat, then I will go to counsel with our friends, for today Gibeon shall fall to us."

On the rocky hilltop a circle of tents housed the five kings and their ministers. Now the kings gathered around the central fire to make their greetings. Then they hunkered down in its warmth to confirm the previous night's plans for the coming battle. The kings sipped on hot spiced wine to warm their bellies against the chill of morning and to warm their spirits against the greater chill of the dangers of war.

It was then that the first cries erupted from the encampment below. As if stricken by the finger of God, several men fell in their tracks and others bellowed with pain. Those who were untouched milled about the fires, searching the still, heavy darkness for the source of danger while hastily pulling on helmets and body armor. There was no sound from the darkness other than the peculiar whishing sound of slings being spun in the air before delivering their missiles with deadly accuracy.

The Amorite captains were screaming commands now, attempting to rally their confused warriors into fighting units. Perhaps they would have succeeded, had it not been for the arrows which now descended on them like sheets of wind driven rain. The captains themselves were prime targets for Israelite bowmen and soon the ten that commanded the field were reduced to eight, then six. It was then that the warriors of the five kings, beset by a storm of sling stones and arrows, broke and ran.

At the top of the command hill the five kings and their ministers mounted horses and struck out at a gallop for the road to Beth Horon. They hoped that at that mountain pass they could rally their warriors and make a stand against the Israelites. But that was not to be. The heavily outnumbered Amorite army was driven before the hordes of Israel like dry leaves before the wind. Demoralized and leaderless the Amorites fought desperately in small clusters which were annihilated by the triumphant Israelites. Those who remained alive scattered and fled to their walled cities for refuge.

The five kings, separated from their warriors and stranded in a country overrun with Israelite soldiers, found sanctuary in deep limestone caves at Makkedah, well into the land of Canaan.[77] There they rested in dismal hopelessness, fearing discovery because the Israelites overran the land and the kings had nowhere to go.

"How spoke you in council, King Piram?" King Japhia asked dispiritedly.[77] "'One does not hitch six oxen to the plow when only two are needed'? I think it had been better that we hitched six to the plow and six more yet, for our army is scattered and we are undone."

"The fault is not mine," Piram retorted. "For the army that we raised was more than enough to lay siege to Gibeon. Did you not send swift horse warriors to encircle Gibeon and prevent Kadesha from summoning Joshua? They failed and so the lion sprang and now we are undone."

"Aye, that we are and much I wish that I had been struck deaf rather than listen to the pleadings of Adonizedec." King Debir made a sour face and spat vigorously. "For had I not, I would this moment be resting on my bed with a cup of wine and my youngest wife beside me."

Adonizedec scowled. "It would have been better for me by far had I not asked the help of warriors who run away from battle like partridges running from a fox. Hilly Jerusalem will stand secure when the cities of the lowlands are smoking ruins. But I will not be there. I will be remembered to my grandchildren and their children as the king whom Joshua slew."

Old King Hoham cleared his throat loudly and spat, then he looked with watery eyes at the others and spoke quietly.

"It is not a time to make accusations of fault, My Lords. But rather it is time to make peace with each other and with ourselves. I fear that Joshua will soon find us and when he does he will not be merciful. For myself, I am ready to die if it must be."

Japhia laughed bitterly. "You are but a few years from the tomb at best and so it is easy for you to speak of accepting death. But I could rule my kingdom for many years and still sire many children. I will cheat death if I can...aye, to cheat death and commit Joshua to it instead would be my wish. When night falls I will creep from this hyena den and I will run like an antelope until I am far from here and near again to Lachish."

"You will not make it alone. The Israelites patrol in small groups at night and one alone is easy prey for them. We would have a better chance together—and not to Lachish—but to Jerusalem because it will not be Joshua's first target," Adonizedec said.

"If you return toward Jerusalem I will go with you," Hoham said. "The way that is already conquered is always easier to travel because the enemy watches his front more carefully than his rear."

Piram raised his hand for silence. "What is the sound that I hear? It is like distant thunder and the stone of the cave walls shakes."

Japhia leaped to his feet and ran around the protruding wall of stone that obscured the mouth of the cave from their view. In a moment he returned his face gray as the shadow of death.

"We are found! They have rolled a boulder over the passage!"[77]

After the rout of the Amorites at Gibeon Joshua stayed two more days with the armies. They drove the enemy yet deeper into Canaan, searching out and executing those small companies that still resisted. On the third day Joshua gave Caleb a small army that would hold the conquered land and returned to Gilgal with the greater number of the princes and warriors.

When at last he returned to his tent he was met at the doorway by the wizened old healer, Bilhah. The woman averted her eyes but motioned for him to enter. He found Adanah on her bed, buried beneath blankets and skins. She was pallid, to such an extreme that she seemed not to have color, but only a sickly grayness. Joshua stopped a step or two from her, shocked by her appearance, thinking that she was already dead. But at the sound of his footfall her eyes opened and she smiled faintly.

"You are back so soon, My Husband?"

The words came faintly, in slow cadence. Adanah stopped speaking and looked calmly at Joshua. It was as though the effort of speech was too great to endure and so she must keep silence. But in a moment she summoned enough strength to beckon him to her bed with a movement of her hand. Joshua stepped forward quickly then, almost as if an evil spell had denied him movement, but now was suddenly broken. He fell to his knees beside his wife, taking her cold hands in his.

"I am back, My Wife. But you are very ill...have not the healers attended to you? If they have been negligent I will have them flogged and cast out of the congregation!"

"They have done all they could do, Joshua. My time is come. My ancestors beckon me."

"Do not speak so, Adanah. I will nurse you back to health!"

Adanah smiled. "You are a warrior not a healer, My Husband. You must go to serve your god and find fulfilment in it. I go to the place of spirits."

Adanah exhaled her breath in a gentle sigh and her spirit flew from her body. Then Joshua, mighty warrior and prince of all Israel, drew her close in his arms and wept like a small boy.

"We have found the kings! We have found the kings!"

The courier yelled between straining gasps for air. He was the last of eight relay runners that had carried word from Makkedah to Gilgal in the passing of a day's light. Now he steadied himself and knelt before a somber and weary Lord Joshua—who came at this moment with Eleazar from the interment of Adanah.

The lad spoke, his voice trembling with excitement and exhaustion.

"My Lord Joshua, the five kings of the Amorites are found. They are hidden in a cave at Makkedah, they and their ministers."[77]

A new fire entered Joshua's eyes where only grief had rested moments before.

"May Yahweh be praised, the Amorites are now undone! Their kings are ours and their armies flee! But are these kings made secure that they cannot escape?"

"They are, My Lord, by Prince Caleb's order. A boulder seals the cave mouth and guards stand before it."

"It is good! Eleazar, gather the priests of high station and the princes and warriors who remain with us. We go this day to Makkedah!"

The five kings sat in deep darkness that was diminished only by the frayed edges of light seeping between the sealing boulder and the mouth of their prison.

"Perhaps we should join in a pact of death now that we are taken," King Hoham said. "It would be easier to die by our own swords than at the hands of Israel."

"That is true," Piram agreed. "It was rumored that the Israelites impaled Amaz of Ai upon a stake. I think we will fare little better for the princes of Israel glory in adding to the misfortunes of their fallen adversaries."

"My minister has already asked permission to end his life and the others as well. I gave it to them with my blessing." Adonizedec said.

"And mine also and with a petition to Baal that they might live again to slay Israelites," Debir said. "They went far back in the cave—I think they will not return."

Hoham spoke gravely. "It is swiftest to die by a sword to the back of the neck. But one of us must honor the others by it and he himself must fall on his sword and die more painfully. Shall we then draw lots to see who shall be the executioner?"

King Japhia leaped to his feet and shouted angrily.

"And who shall place a sword so well as to kill without error in this darkness? ...But come Hoham and I will feel your neck and shave your beard with my dagger from ear to ear! Then you shall have peace and we too! ...Are we all women and beardless youths that we sit about and wring our hands for fear of dying like men? When they roll the great stone aside I will take out my sword and plunge it into Israelite hearts until I myself am done. Will you noble kings not stand with me and trade blood for blood?"

It was Debir's rich voice, the voice of a priest, resonating off the limestone walls of their dungeon, that steeled the spirits of the kings.

"King Japhia is right, My Lords. Did we not make a blood oath that all shall be as one? If we are but one body then we must stand beside King Japhia and spit in the eye of Joshua. And in doing this we will make our grandchildren proud and their children after them, though it is a bitter thing to stare into the eye of certain death."

So it was resolved among the kings that they would stand against the hordes of Israel. But for now there was nothing to be done but to ponder those ominous thoughts that visit men who are condemned to die.

"Because I did not seek counsel of Yahweh, I fell for the lies of the Gibeonites like a blundering fool. And again, I did not press the Amorites hard enough so that the kings escaped and the remnants of their armies fled to their walled cities."

Joshua reined in his horse and peered into the eyes of old Eleazar who rode awkwardly beside him on the back of a mule.

"The Lord has punished me for my arrogance. He has taken Adanah from me to chastise me for my failure."

"Perhaps," the high priest returned tentatively. "But perhaps she fell ill to the black fever because of an evil vapor and nothing more."

"You do not think Yahweh cursed me for my failure? You think she died because of a vapor from the earth? If that were so why have not others died as in times past, when the grave diggers fell prostrate with exhaustion?"

"I am unsure of the cause, My Lord, because Yahweh has never spoken to me as he spoke to Moses and now to you. But the Lord God does not punish those who are faithful to him, as indeed you are. Have you thought of those who have enmity against you? It might be a curse placed on you by one such as that."

"There are many of our people who bear me grudges for one cause or another, Eleazar. But I know of none who would have the power to place a curse on God's chosen."

"But perhaps there are those who serve other gods who have such powers. We serve the god of righteousness, but are there not gods of evil? Would they not seek to weaken the resolve of the warrior chosen by Yahweh?"

Joshua's eyes narrowed beneath his bushy gray brows.

"You think of someone, Eleazar. Name me a name that I might destroy this evil."

"Was not Kadesha of Gibeon the king of that city and was he not a priest of Baal before he fell to his low estate by your hand? And is it not said that King Debir of Eglon, who even now awaits us in the cave at Makkedah, is a seer and a slave-consort of Asherah the wife of Baal? If there is evil power in Baal, these two would surely have the might to curse a prince of Israel."

Joshua's eyes probed those of the priest and his face darkened.

"It is most surely as you say, for God speaks to me through the mouth of his priest, Eleazar. And I give my God promise that I will not be slack in my duty again!"

"The stone moves!" Japhia shouted. "Up! Up and ready your swords—glory awaits us! Now it will be sword against sword, blood for blood and death for death!"

"And may the blessings of Baal go with us!"

Debir drew his sword and flourished it at the growing light that signaled the opening of their prison.

Suddenly the great boulder lurched and rolled away and bright light flooded through the entrance. Then the opening was filled with bronze bucklers and heavy clubs wrapped with copper bands in the hands of Joshua's best warriors. Close behind them were spearmen with sharpened poles that would prick but would not quickly kill. They advanced on the kings slowly, menacing silhouettes against the blinding brightness issuing through the cave entrance. They were an unstoppable force as they engaged the kings—shields deftly catching the panicked men's sword blows as heavy clubs descended with brutal efficiency. Sharp poles jabbed at faces and bodies, pushing the five back further and further until their feet were planted amid the lifeless forms of those who had taken their own lives.

With their backs to the cave wall the kings lashed out desperately, hacking and thrusting at an overwhelming wall of warriors. The first to fall was old Hoham, felled by the blow of a club that crushed his collarbone. Then Adonizedec's sword broke and he was borne to the ground by two warriors who swiftly bound his arms behind him. Piram was knocked senseless by a hard blow to his helmet and Japhia's belly was opened by a wooden spear. Debir alone was standing at the short battle's end, pressed against the wall by bucklers, a dagger against his throat. Thus the proud kings of Canaan were overcome and dragged from the cave at Makkedah like vile and noxious vermin to be mocked and spit upon by the righteous warriors of Israel.

"These are the mighty kings who would make war on the Children of Israel, the chosen people of Yahweh, The True God!" Joshua shouted to the warriors assembled around him.

"Do you fear them now, brave men of Israel? Look how they tremble before us! They are undone and their armies are undone and now they will all die. They are struck down by the hand of God for their evil worship of Baal!"

Joshua turned to the captives who were made to kneel before him, arms bound to staves behind their backs. Hoham and Japhia groaned and sagged with pain and Piram's eyes were blank and unseeing but Adonizedec and Debir glared at Joshua defiantly. It was Adonizedec who was first favored with Joshua's attention. He grasped the king's beard and drew his face upward to meet his own.

"You thought to gather the dogs of Canaan into a pack that would defy the lion of Israel, Adonizedec. But know you now that dogs are easily scattered and cower before the jaws of the lion?"

"If we are dogs, it is true that the lion is mightier," Adonizedec answered belligerently. "But you choose the wrong emblem for your banner, it should be the hyena not the lion. For you go about with your hideous clamor, scavenging on feasts that others have hunted. You make nothing good of yourselves but you foul that which others more noble than you have built. You feast on the blood of the old and the young—but you will not stand long against the warriors of Canaan!"

Joshua gave Adonizedec a hard, open-handed slap, a punishment for women and children and an insult to men.

"You speak foolishly, dog! You will die and your spawn with you, for we will take Jerusalem and level it to the ground!"

"You will take the hills about the city—but I lay this curse on you—you shall never take Jerusalem. It shall stand as a remembrance to my people that Israel is not supreme!"

"Even facing death you speak idle threats—do you think a man such as you can curse him whom Yahweh has blessed? It would take a god, not a man, to do such a thing. But then, there is one among you who claims a god as his mentor, one who leads in the priesthood of Baal."

Joshua turned to Debir of Eglon and fiery eye met fiery eye—the one in scowling triumph, the other in angry defiance.

"What say you, Priest-king, do you too seek to defeat Israel with curses and foul incantations? Do you dream that the evil one you serve will stand against Yahweh?"

"We sought not to defeat you through incantations, but by battle upon the field, warrior against warrior, sword against sword!"

Joshua bent to the level of his captive and sneered.

"You would fight us sword against sword, but your cowardly Amorite warriors ran from us like hares before foxes and left you to hide in a hole in the ground—it would have been better to rely on incantations and spells than on such as those."

"Our warriors retreated from arrows and stones cast on them by an unseen enemy in the dark of night—an enemy too cowardly to meet as men upon the field! It is the way of you Israelites to hide in the grass like vipers and strike unseen—for if you were seen we would grind your heads into the dust like the vipers you are!" Debir spat at his tormentor.

"For that I should make you die a slow death!"

Joshua took Debir by his hair and cast him face forward in the dirt.

"Come, you brave captains who feared the kings of Canaan! Come and step on the necks of kings and never be afraid again. For we are invincible because God Almighty fights for us!"[77]

Caleb signaled the guards and the kings who still kneeled were thrown face down before the assembly. Then the captains of the tribes came forward to step roughly on the necks of the bound captives, pressing their faces into the dirt. When each had taken his turn in the coarse ceremony, Joshua spoke to the kings again.

"Because you fought as men, I give you a quick death rather than a lingering one." He turned to Caleb. "Take them and kill them quickly, then hang them upon posts until the evening. And when day is done, throw them in the cave and seal it."[77]

From that day, Joshua and the princes of Israel made war upon the nations of Canaan without fear or mercy.[78] No peace was made, save the peace of conquest and death, for it was declared that this was the ordinance of their god. Thus were the days of Joshua spent and when the promised land was fully taken he was very old. Yet he lived peacefully a few years in the infirmness of old age before he died. And his name lives as a hero in the legends and histories of his people.

*

Biblical and other references cross-referenced to book happenings. Biblical references are from The Bible-KJV.

Ref. 1 — Exodus 2:15.
Pharaoh pursues Moses

Ref. 2 — Exodus 6:20
Lineage of Moses, Aaron and Miriam

Ref. 3 — Exodus 15:20
Identifies Miriam

Ref. 4 — Exodus 2:2-10
Pharaoh's daughter raises and names Moses

Ref. 5 — Exodus 2:11-15
Flight of Moses from Egypt

Ref. 7 — Exodus 2:15-22
Moses at the well, Zipporah, Jethro

Ref. 8 — Exodus 3:1-12
The burning bush

Ref. 9 — Exodus 4:24-26
Confrontation between Moses and Zipporah

Ref. 10 — Exodus 4:29-31
Moses meets with the elders

Ref. 11 — Exodus 5:4-9
Pharaoh cracks down on the workers

Ref. 12 — Exodus 7:17-23
The plagues begin

Ref. 13 — The Oxford Companion to the Bible — p. 644
Red Sea crossing

Ref. 14 — Exodus 15:23-24
The bitter water of Marah

Ref. 15 — Exodus 4:27-28
Aaron meets Moses in the wilderness

Ref. 16 — Exodus 4:14-15
Aaron to speak for Moses

Ref. 17 — Exodus 3:14
The name of God

Ref. 18 — Exodus 7:10
Aaron's magic staff

Ref. 19 — Exodus 9: 19-26
The plague of hail

Ref. 20 — Exodus 10:3-15
The locusts

Ref. 21 — Exodus 10:28
Pharaoh warns Moses of his death

Ref. 22 — Exodus 6:23
Aaron's marriage to Elisheba

Ref. 23 – Exodus 11:2
Women to borrow gold from the Egyptians

Ref. 24 – Exodus 11:5-6
Egyptian firstborn to die

Ref. 25 — Exodus 12:31-33
Israel expelled by Pharaoh

Ref. 26 — Exodus 14:9-12
Egyptians pursue Israel

Ref. 27 — Exodus 14:5
Pharaoh changes his mind

Ref. 28 — Exodus 15:27
The oasis of Elim

Ref. 29 — Exodus 16:1-3
The wilderness of Sin

Ref. 30 — Exodus 17:1-6
The rock of Horeb

Ref. 31 — Exodus 17:8-14
Amalek attacks Israel

Ref. 32 — Exodus 18:1-7
Jethro comes to Rephidim

Ref. 33 — Exodus 18:17-23
Jethro counsels Moses

Ref. 34 — Exodus 19:12-13
Bounds set around Sinai

Ref. 35 — Exodus 32:1
Moses' late return from the mountain

Ref. 36 — Exodus 32:19
Moses throws down the tablets

Ref. 37 — Exodus 32:21-28
The killing of the idolaters

Ref. 38 — Exodus 32:21
Moses confronts Aaron

Ref. 39 — Numbers 12:1
The Ethiopian woman

Ref. 40 — Numbers 12:1-15
The sedition of Miriam

Ref. 41 — Numbers 13:1-24
Spying Canaan

Ref. 43 — Numbers 13:24-33
The report of the spies

Ref. 44 — Numbers 13:33
About the sons of Anak

Ref. 45 — Numbers 14:1-10
The people murmur

Ref. 46 — Numbers 14:36-38
Givers of ill reports are killed

Ref. 47 — Numbers 14:40-45
Failed strike into Canaan

Ref. 48 — Numbers 15:32-36
The Sabbath breaker

Ref. 49 — Numbers 16:1-35
The rebellion of Korah

Ref. 50 — Numbers 20:1
The death of Miriam

Ref. 51 — Numbers 20:2-12
Waters of Meribah

Ref. 52 — Numbers 20:14-20
Edon refuses passage

Ref. 53 — Numbers 20:28-29
The death of Aaron

Ref. 54 — Numbers 21:21-31
Destruction of Sihon

Ref. 55 — Numbers 21:33-35
Destruction of Bashan

Ref. 56 — Numbers 22:23:24
Balak and Balaam

Ref. 57 — Numbers 25:1-5
Shittim — joining with Baal Peor

Ref. 58 — Numbers 25:4
Judgement against tribal leaders

Ref. 59 — Numbers 25:5
Judgement against men joined to Baal

Ref. 60 — Numbers 25:6-8
Phinehas kills Zimri and Cozbi

Ref. 61 — Numbers 25:12-13
Phinehas receives a priesthood

Ref. 62 — Numbers 31:3-12
The destruction of Midian

Ref. 63 — Numbers 31:13-18
The atrocity at the acacias

Ref. 64 — Numbers 27:12-23
Moses' leadership to pass to Joshua

Ref. 65 — Judges 6:1-7
Future destruction of Israel by Midian

Ref. 66 — Deut. 34:1-12
Death of Moses

Ref. 67 — Joshua 2:1-24
Spying Jericho

Ref. 68 — Joshua 3:14-16
Stopping of the Jordan River

Ref. 69 — Joshua 6
Siege of Jericho

Ref. 70 — Joshua 7:3-5
Lost battle at Ai

Ref. 71 — Joshua 7:18-26
Sin of Achan

Ref. 72 — Joshua 9:3-15
Gibeon's trick

Ref. 73 — Joshua 9:16-27
Gibeon's trick discovered

Ref. 74 — Joshua 9:2–10:3
The five kings gather

Ref. 75 — Joshua 10:1-6
The five kings attack Gibeon

Ref. 76 — Joshua 10
Battle at Gibeon

Ref. 77 — Joshua 10:16-27
The death of the kings

Ref. 78 — Joshua 10:28-43
Campaign of destruction